D0396523

CALGARY PUBLIC LIBRARY

AUG — 2012

GOODBYE FOR NOW

GOODBYE FOR NOW

A Novel

LAURIE FRANKEL

DOUBLEDAY

NEW YORK LONDON TORONTO SYDNEY AUCKLAND

This book is a work of fiction. Names, characters, businesses, organizations, places, events, and incidents either are the product of the author's imagination or are used fictitiously. Any resemblance to actual persons, living or dead, events, or locales is entirely coincidental.

Copyright © 2012 by Laurie Frankel

All rights reserved. Published in the United States by Doubleday, a division of Random House, Inc., New York, and in Canada by Random House of Canada Limited, Toronto.

www.doubleday.com

DOUBLEDAY and the portrayal of an anchor with a dolphin are registered trademarks of Random House, Inc.

Jacket design by Emily Mahon
Jacket illustration © Scott Nobles

LIBRARY OF CONGRESS CATALOGING-IN-PUBLICATION DATA
Frankel, Laurie.
Goodbye for now : a novel / Laurie Frankel. — 1st ed.
p.   cm.
1. Loss (Psychology)—Fiction.   2. Small business—Fiction.   I. Title.
PS3606.R389G66 2012
813'.6—dc23
2011051266

ISBN 978-0-385-53618-9

MANUFACTURED IN THE UNITED STATES OF AMERICA

10 9 8 7 6 5 4 3 2 1

First Edition

For my dad, Dave Frankel, who really did reprogram our Commodore VIC-20 to make arithmetic errors in order to improve my self-confidence and math skills (only one of these worked).

And for my mom, Sue Frankel, who calls my novels—and treats them as—her grandbooks.

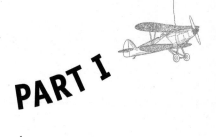

PART I

What will survive of us is love.

—PHILIP LARKIN, "AN ARUNDEL TOMB"

KILLER APP

*S*am Elling was filling out his online dating profile and trying to decide whether to laugh or cry. On the one hand, he had just described himself as "quick to laugh" and had answered the question, "How macho do you consider yourself?" eight on a scale of ten. But on the other hand, the whole thing was really quite frustrating, and no one, he knew, ever admitted to anything less than an eight on the masculinity scale anyway. Sam was trying to come up with five things he couldn't live without. He knew that many would-be daters cheekily wrote: air, food, water, shelter, plus something else vaguely amusing. (He was thinking Swiss cheese would be a clever addition to that list, or possibly vitamin D, though since he was in Seattle, he seemed, in fact, to be living quite nicely without it.) He could go the techie route—laptop, other laptop, tablet, wifi connection, iPhone—but they'd think he was a computer geek. Never mind that he was; he didn't want them to know that right away. He could go the sentimental route—framed photo from parents' wedding, grandfather's lucky penny, program from his star turn in his middle school production of *Grease*, acceptance letter to MIT, first mix tape ever made for him by a girl—but he suspected that would belie his reported macho factor. He could go the lactose route: Swiss cheese again (he was clearly craving Swiss cheese for no apparent reason) plus chocolate ice cream, cream cheese, Pagliacci's pizza, and double tall lattes. It wasn't really true though. He could live without those; he just wouldn't like it very much.

The point was this exercise was five things: annoying, prying, cloying, embarrassing, and totally pointless. He didn't have any hobbies because he worked all the time which was the reason he couldn't find a date. If he didn't work all the time (or weren't a software engineer and so also worked with some women), he would have time for hobbies he could list, but then he wouldn't need to because he wouldn't need online dating in order to meet people. Yes, he was a computer geek, but he was also, he thought, smart and funny and reasonably good-looking. He just didn't have five hobbies or five witty things he couldn't live without or five interesting things on his bedside table (truthful answer would have been: half-full water glass, quarter-full water glass, empty water glass, crumpled used Kleenex, crumpled used Kleenex) or five revealing hopes for the future (never to have to do this again, repeat times five). Nor did he care about anyone else's reported hobbies or five requirements for life, bedside tables, or futures. He had already answered variations of these inane questions with another service, dated their dates, and saw what all of this nonsense came to. It came to nonsense. If you picked the ones who seemed pretty down-to-earth (books, writing implement, reading lamp, clock radio, cell phone), you got boring. If you picked the ones who seemed eccentric (yellow rain hat, Polaroid camera, lime seltzer, photo of Gertrude Stein, plastic model of Chairman Mao), you got really weird and full of themselves. If you picked the *one* who seemed like a good fit ("Laptop and honestly nothing else because that has all I need"), you got a computer geek so much like your college roommate that you wondered if he'd had an unconvincing sex change operation without telling you. So you had your pick of boring, weird, or Trevor Anderson.

Five things Sam couldn't live without: sarcasm, mockery, scorn, derision, cynicism.

That was not the whole picture, of course. If it were, he wouldn't be online dating. He would be holed up in a basement apartment somewhere contentedly crotchety on his own (Xbox, Wii, PlayStation, fifty-two-inch plasma flat-screen, microwave nachos). Instead, he was putting himself out there again. Did this not indicate optimism re: love? (hope, good cheer, warmth, generosity, the promise of someone to kiss good night). Maybe, but it was way too cheesy to write on the stupid form.

The problem with the stupid form was this: it wasn't just that people didn't tell the truth—though they didn't. It was that there was no way *to* tell the truth, even if you wanted to. Things on a bedside table do not reveal a soul. Hopes for the future cannot be distilled for forms or strangers. Fill-in-the-blank questions are fun but not really indicative of the long-term future of a relationship. (They aren't really that fun either.) Even the stuff with straightforward answers fails to reveal what you need to know. For instance, Sam wanted to date a woman who could and would cook and enjoy it, but it couldn't be because she was some kind of domestic goddess who required a clean house all the time (Sam was not neat), and it couldn't be because she believed a woman's place was in the home and she should cater to her man (Sam was a feminist), and it couldn't be because she was one of those people who ate only organic, sustainable, locally grown, chemical-free, ecologically responsible, whole, raw, vegan food (see above re: Sam's love of dairy). It had to be because Sam didn't cook and she did and they both needed to eat, and he would take on some other household chore like dish washing or clothes folding or bathroom scrubbing in exchange. There was no place for all that on the form or even a place to indicate that he was the kind of man who considered such bizarre minutiae relevant.

And yet, a man has needs. And not the ones you think. Well, those too, but they weren't foremost on Sam's mind. Foremost on Sam's mind was it would be nice to have someone to go out to dinner with on Friday nights and to wake up with on Saturday mornings and to go with him to museums and movies and plays and parties and restaurants and ball games and on long weekends away, day hikes, ski trips, parental visits, wine tastings, and work functions. It was this last which was especially pressing for Sam, who worked at the online dating company whose form was causing him so much grief. It employed many swank and high-powered people—most of them male—who brought many swank and high-powered people—most of them female—to their many swank and high-powered black-tie galas. Sam did not own a tie of any color until he got this job, was himself neither swank nor high-powered, and felt strongly that a job as a software engineer in a three-walled cubicle surrounded by other software engineers with their obscure math T-shirts and *Star Trek* action figures and seven-sided Rubik's cubes should have absolved him from these sorts of work pressures. But the lawyers and VPs and CFOs and VIPs and investors wrecked the curve, and besides, it was an online dating company—showing up to these functions solo was a bad career move. Sam spent these evenings in his too-stiff tuxedo making awkward private jokes with his awkward single software engineering compatriots, sipping free vodka tonics and worrying that he'd never find true love.

In high school in Baltimore, when Holly Palentine saw through his geeky exterior to the cool heart that beat beneath and agreed first to dance with him at homecoming and then to let him take her to dinner and a movie and then to hang out in his basement most afternoons after school making out, Sam had assumed he would marry his high school sweetheart. He remembered dancing close with her at the spring formal and imagining what they'd look like on their wedding day. Then she sent him a letter from the Girl Scout camp where she was a counselor asking if they could still be friends. Still? Sam hadn't realized this had ever been in question. In college at MIT, he had tried late-night hookups in the dorm and girls who flirted with him at parties and falling madly in love with the barista at Shot Through the Heart (though he had not tried talking to her) and a year-and-a-half real, adult relationship with Della Bassette, who then graduated and left for three years of volunteer corps in Zimbabwe, and another year and a half of true rock-solid start-thinking-about-engagement-rings love with Jenny O'Dowd, who really did love him and want to be with him forever except she accidentally also hooked up with his roommate the semester before graduation. Twice. Then Sam tried being alone, being alone far less likely to result in the crushing of his soul and atom-splitting of his heart. He tried not caring and not risking and not looking, hanging out with guy friends, solo vacations, self-growth, and canceling cable. None of that worked either. Not being in love did mean he was less likely to get hurt. But he honestly didn't see the point.

He didn't see the point not because he was one of those people who always, always had to be paired up, and not because he didn't think of himself as whole without a partner, and not because otherwise it was too hard to have sex, but because when he wasn't spending time with people he loved, Sam found he was spending a lot of time with people he didn't. His work colleagues were fine at work, but they didn't have much to talk about when they went out afterward. Happy hour with friends he'd lost touch with since college reminded him why he'd lost touch with them. Small talk at parties held by friends of friends meant a lot of pretending to think interesting a lot of things he didn't think were interesting.

When he left the East Coast for Seattle, Sam tried internet dating and couldn't believe he'd been alive for thirty-two and a half years and never thought to before. Sam believed in computers and programming, in codable information, in algorithms and numbers and logic. His father was also a software engineer as well as a computer science professor at Johns Hopkins University, so Sam was raised to believe: computers were his religion. Everyone else pitched online dating as the only option after not meeting anyone in the vast ocean of college. But Sam liked online dating because it took away the mystery. Maybe you met someone and liked her and she liked you and you hit it off and you started dating and that went pretty well and you got closer and closer, shared more and more, starting building lives around each other, fell deeply in love, and still she slept with your roommate when you went home for the weekend. Computers would never allow for such outlying variance.

Online dating had yet to work for Sam. But it did pay well. And that came in a close second as it turned out. One too-pretty-to-go-to-work morning in June, Sam's whole team got a sheepish text from their boss. "Fair warning," Jamie wrote. "BB's agenda for OOF today: Quantify the Human Heart." Jamie referred to the company's enormously important CEO, his boss's boss, as BB. Sam loved him for this. BB had recently decreed that each team would begin every morning with a stand-up meeting, the idea being that the company wasn't wasting its brilliant programmers' time with a real meeting but only a brief encounter in the hallway. Generally, this meant it was the length of an actual meeting but without the comfort of chairs and a Danish. Jamie therefore called it OOF, theoretically for On Our Feet, though actually for how those feet felt at the end of the meeting. Sam loved Jamie for this too. Also because he wasn't a superstickler for punctuality, which gave Sam time to run back inside his apartment and change into more comfortable shoes.

"So here's the story," Jamie began when Sam got there. "BB thinks we need a better bottom line. Some online matchmaking sites promise 'most fun dates.' Some boast 'highest percentage of marriages.' BB wants to up the ante. Too many dates end in failure. Too many marriages end in divorce. What's better than dating and better than marriage?"

"Friends with benefits?" guessed Nigel from Australia.

"Soul mates," said Jamie. "BB wants an algorithm that will find your soul mate. Therefore I turn to you. Love is a tricky thing. All that human variable. The soul is not logical. The heart wants what the heart wants. Hard to nail down. Hard to quantify and program. But we are computer programmers, and this is our job. So we must. Tell me how."

"Increase the odds of getting laid," said Nigel. "Looser dates lead to more and earlier hooking up. The farther you go on a first date, the more information you have about sexual compatibility."

"Won't work," objected Rajiv from New Delhi. "Dating sucks." On this, the software engineers, save Nigel, were in agreement.

"It's not fun," said Gaurav from Mumbai.

"It's very awkward," said Arnab from Assam.

"And it's all lies," said Jayaraj from Chennai. Five Indian states Sam had become an expert on since beginning work as a software engineer: Delhi, Assam, Maharashtra, Tamil Nadu, West Bengal. "You are so much worse on a date than you are in real life," Jayaraj continued. "You can't string two sentences together without sounding like some kind of idiot. You stammer and bring up awkward topics and embarrass yourself a lot. You're not really like that in real life."

"Or you present yourself as better than you really are," Sam added, "which is also a lie. You get all dressed up and do your hair and put on makeup when really you're going to walk around the house in yoga clothes and a scrunchie all day."

"Makeup?" Jamie raised an eyebrow at him.

"Scrunchie?" wondered Jayaraj.

"We need a third party," offered Arnab, "like the Hindu astrologers who know everyone in the village for generations and thus make marriages at birth that last until death."

"Many cultures have matchmakers. Japanese nakodos. Jewish shadchens." Gaurav had been an anthropology major at UC Santa Cruz. "There are aeons of precedent. They realize a truth."

"Which is?" asked Jamie.

"Who people think they are and what people think they want is not really who they are or what they want," said Gaurav sagely. "Wise and sometimes magical elders set you up based on who you really are and who would be good for you instead."

"I have no magical elders," said Jamie.

"No, you have something better," said Sam. "Computer programmers.

We could dig a little deeper into the data users provide. See what it says about them rather than what they say about themselves."

Everyone's feet were getting tired, so digging deeper seemed worth a shot. "Accusing our customers of lying," Jamie said. "I'm sure BB will love it."

Sam stopped for coffee on the way back to his desk. (Five places within seven hundred feet of Sam's desk to get a world-class double tall latte: the espresso stand on the second floor, the espresso stand on the fourteenth floor, the cafeteria, the coffee shop in the lobby of the Fifth Avenue entrance, the coffee shop in the lobby of the Fourth Avenue entrance. Sam loved Seattle.) Then he sat down and considered where, if not on online dating forms, people revealed the truth about themselves. He messaged Jamie: "Can I have access to clients' financial records?"

Jamie wrote back right away. "Accusing our customers of lying *and* invading their privacy. BB's going to love that too."

First surefire proof Sam had that users were lying about themselves: everyone everywhere was always having a fit over internet privacy concerns, but promise to find them love or at least sex, and they signed access to their financial records, credit card statements, e-mail accounts, and everything else over to Sam just because he asked nicely. There he saw them not as they represented themselves but as they really were. He saw that they said their five favorite foods were organic blueberries, wheatgrass smoothies, red quinoa, tempeh Reubens, and beluga caviar, but they spent an average of $47.40 a month last year at the 7-Eleven. He saw that the five things they listed on their nightstand were all foreign film DVDs, but they saw *Shrek Forever After* in 3-D twice in theaters and spent the week of the foreign film festival hanging out with their old college roommates at a dude ranch in Wyoming. He noted that they said they liked to write poetry and short stories and even included a quote from *Ulysses* in their profile, but Sam analyzed their e-mails and knew they were in the bottom twelve percent of adjective users and had no idea how to use a semicolon. Everyone lied. It wasn't malicious or even on purpose usually. They weren't so much misrepresenting themselves as just plain wrong. How they saw themselves and how they really were turned out to be pretty far apart.

Sam was a romantic, yes, but he was also a software engineer, and since he was better at the latter, he played to his strengths. For two weeks straight, he worked obsessively on an algorithm that figured out who you really were. It ignored the form you filled out yourself in favor of reading your spending reports and bank statements and e-mails. It read your chat histories and text messages, your posts and status updates. It read your blog and what you posted on other people's blogs. It looked at what you bought online, what you read online, what you studiously avoided online. It ignored who you said you were and who you said you wanted in favor of who you really were and who you really wanted. Sam mixed the ancient traditions of the matchmakers plus the truths users revealed but did not admit about themselves combined with the power of modern data processors and made the algorithm that changed the dating world. He cracked the code to your heart.

His teammates were impressed. Jamie was pleased. But BB was thrilled with the algorithm, especially once he saw the proof of concept demos and how incredibly, unbelievably well it would work.

"We'll get you down to just one date!" BB enthused. "That's all it will take. Talk about killer apps!"

THE GIRL NEXT DOOR

*T*he next step for Sam, of course, was to try it himself. He wanted to know if it worked. He wanted to prove that it worked. But mostly, he wanted it to work. He wanted it to search the world and point, to reach down like the finger of God and say, "Her." How good was this algorithm? First time out, it set Sam up with Meredith Maxwell. She worked next door. In the marketing department. Of Sam's own company. For their first date, they met for lunch in the cafeteria at work. She was leaning against the doorframe grinning at him when he got off the elevator, grinning helplessly himself.

"Meredith Maxwell," she said, shaking Sam's hand. "My friends mostly call me Max."

"Not Merde?" Sam asked, incredulous, appalled with himself, even as he was doing so. Who made a joke like that—pretentious, scatological, and *French*—as a first impression? Sam was awkward and off-putting and a little gross.

Incredibly, Meredith Maxwell laughed. *"Je crois que tu es le premier."*

It was as if a miracle had occurred. She thought it was funny. She thought Sam was funny. But it wasn't a miracle. It was computer science.

"So where did you learn French?" Sam recovered after they were seated in an out-of-the-way corner with their cafeteria trays.

"I spent a year abroad in college in Bruges. I also learned Flemish."

"That must come in handy," said Sam.

"Less than you'd think. The only people I speak Flemish to are my dogs."

"You have dogs?"

"Snowy and Milou."

"You named your dogs after a Belgian comic book."

"Well, a Belgian comic book and its English translation," said Meredith Maxwell.

Sam was wildly impressed with himself. Though she'd offered nothing in her dating profile about the names of her dogs and Sam nothing of his childhood obsession with *Tintin*, somehow he'd written an algorithm that knew anyway. He was some kind of genius. Meredith Maxwell, meanwhile, was beautiful and funny and evidently smart, thirty-four years old (Sam liked older women, even if they were only seven months older), a world traveler, a polyglot, a dog lover, an enjoyer of cafeteria-style strawberry ice cream, and possessor of skin that smelled like the sea.

"This was fun," said Meredith as they bused their trays. But she didn't sound sure.

"Should we do it again?" said Sam.

"Maybe off campus?" Sam observed that this was not a no but was also not an of-course-don't-be-absurd-yes. Was this thing not as good as he thought? Was it good on paper (well, in code) but not in fact? Or more appalling still: was she his perfect match, the one soul in all the world who fit with his, the boiling down of all humanity to his Platonic partner . . . and she liked him sort of okay? He scrambled to think up impressive first dates. Was he insane? The cafeteria at work wasn't a good first impression. This one shouldn't count. He needed a do-over. "Let's go somewhere special for dinner."

"Okay," she agreed.

"Um . . . Canlis? Campagne? Rover's?" Sam named expensive restaurants aimlessly. He'd never been to any of them. "We could take the Clipper over to Victoria? Canada's very romantic."

"Boats make me throw up," she said.

"That restaurant at the top of the Space Needle?"

"Do you like baseball?" she said.

Sam stopped breathing. Was this a trick question? "I like baseball."

"How about dinner at the ballpark? Saturday night? Hot dogs and a game? Might be more fun."

. . .

The ball game *was* fun. So was dinner out, somewhat more casual than Sam had suggested in the first place but still what passed for fancy in Seattle. So was the play Meredith picked out for them to see and her interrogation of him afterward, which was like an English exam but with more pressure (the stakes being higher, after all). So was the Korean horror film at the three-dollar movies, and so was the day hike at Hurricane Ridge. But it still hadn't clicked right away. Or maybe it was the opposite.

"I can't help but notice," Meredith observed after all-day hiking, after separate showers and towel-dried hair and red wine and candles and carry-out Thai on the floor of her living room, "that you haven't kissed me yet."

"I haven't?" said Sam.

"Nope."

"What a strange oversight. Why, do you think?"

"Could be you don't like me," Meredith suggested.

"I don't think that's it," said Sam.

"Could be you like me but think I'm hideous."

"I don't think that's it either," said Sam, scooting a little closer toward her across the floor.

"Could be that you're a lousy computer programmer and this algorithm doesn't work and we're totally mismatched, a crappy couple, star-crossed, ill-fated, with no chemistry."

"I am a brilliant computer programmer," said Sam.

"Maybe you're scared," said Meredith.

"Of what?"

"Rejection."

"Not much chance of that. Maybe *you're* scared."

"Me?" she said.

"Yes you," said Sam, scooting a little bit closer still. "Maybe *you're* too scared to kiss *me*. Maybe you're lily-livered."

"What does that even mean?" she said. "Like your liver is flowery? Like a little girl? Like all the toxins it filters out of your blood are flora?"

"It's from humors. You know, bile, blood, phlegm," Sam murmured romantically. "You lack enough to color your liver, so it's all white and pale and cowardly, hanging out down there in your digestive tract talking you out of kissing me."

"You know a lot of things, Sam," she said.

"Is that a bad thing?" he asked, coming upright. He'd been leaning so far toward her, eyes half-closed, he felt almost dizzy. Or maybe that wasn't why.

She considered. "I do like my men smart, but perhaps the less talk of phlegm right before our first kiss, the better."

"I didn't know it would be right before our first kiss," Sam said.

"Well then, I guess you don't know everything after all."

Did she kiss him then or did he kiss her? Or were they so close by that point that the next inhale pulled their mouths together, that the ferocious beating of Sam's heart rocked him actually into her? Or was it fate or compatibility or chemistry or computer science? Sam forgot to care. Sam forgot to think about it. Sam forgot to think about anything at all.

They kissed for a while. Then they stopped kissing for a while and just sat and breathed together. Meredith's apartment was decorated with model airplanes hanging all over the ceiling. The shadows they flickered in the candlelight made Sam feel like he was flying. Or maybe that wasn't why. Then Meredith said, "Well that was nice. What took you so long?"

Sam tried to say lightly, "What took *you* so long?" He tried to work "lily-livered" back into conversation while his heart rate came down. Instead he accidentally answered honestly. "I think . . . I'm pretty sure this will be my last first kiss. Ever. I wanted to savor it."

"How'd it go?" asked Meredith.

"I forget," said Sam, and she smiled, but that was accidentally honest as well. "Let me try again."

LONDON CALLING

*S*am rolled over the next morning to fully consider the still-asleep, teeth-unbrushed, bed-headed Meredith for a minute or two before he said, "So, should I move in or what?"

"What?"

"Should I move in now? Or do you want to wait?"

"I was thinking brunch," said Meredith.

"Then packing?"

"I was thinking brunch then maybe a walk. Are you kidding?"

"It's a top-notch algorithm, Merde," said Sam.

"Top-notch?"

"It's not wrong. I made it myself, you know. You're dealing with a quality product here."

"Still. I think I'd like to be more than twelve hours out from our first kiss before you move in."

Sam thought about it. "Should you move in with me then?"

"I'm not sure that's exactly the issue here, but don't be insane—I'm not moving into your studio apartment."

"Why not?"

"Your bedroom is a platform. Your kitchen is a burner. I have two dogs."

"And a lot of tiny airplanes. Here it is then."

"Go to London. Then we'll talk."

Sam was going to London for the annual international social networking technology conference, this one dubbed, "London, City of Love: This Is Your Heart on Tech," a title which was both stupid and confusing,

London being the city of many things (tea, mummies, and jacket potatoes sprang immediately to mind), but not, per se, love. The meeting had been scheduled, of course, long before he knew that this would be the week he would fall in love himself. He lobbied to bring Meredith with him. "Marketing should have a presence," he said to Jamie and then tried, "My presentation's on the algorithm. We'd be a great advertisement for it." But these requests were denied. "I believe I will have more of your undivided attention if you come alone," Jamie said.

This was only sort of true. It was a busy trip. There were endless meetings and investors to present to, talks to attend, cocktail hours and breakfasts at which to make an appearance, plus all the technology glitches to fix, the ones that are inevitable on borrowed equipment far from home when lots of money and clout are at stake and all your competition is looking on and everything has to go exactly right. It didn't make a lot of sense to Sam that there should be so many technical glitches—and that so many of them should be his problem—when everyone in a three-block radius was a computer person and the whole point of the conference was technology, but there wasn't much time to ponder that. There was all of that to do plus museums to explore, churches to visit, markets to wander, pints to drink, and theater to see. There was all of that plus wandering city streets in the rain and gazing into the river and drinking tea in cafés while longing for Meredith. He felt bereft to be apart from her for even two weeks. He felt her absence physically. He felt as if he were missing a lung. And he was loving every minute of it.

He stopped for late-night Chinese food on Tottenham Court Road on the way back to his hotel the first night and got a fortune cookie that read, "Absence makes the heart grow fonder." This he texted to Meredith.

"They're wrong," she wrote back. "Absence makes you insane."

He floated back to the hotel. Then he got ready for bed and called her.

"Insane how?" he said.

"I'm at work," she said.

"Really? It's after five there. Go home and call me."

"I'm going out with Natalie. Can we chat tomorrow?"

"Only if you tell me insane how," said Sam.

"Tomorrow," she said, and he went to sleep. At five thirty in the morning, his video chat rang. It had been ringing for some time before he woke up, morphing Sam's dream about being trapped in an underwater obstacle course into being trapped in an underwater obstacle course where he got a prize at the end by ringing a bell.

"Mmm . . .'lo?" he managed.

"Heyyyy," she sang, all sweet and soft. And drunk.

"Mmfff," he said.

"Are you there?"

"Mmmfffff."

"It looks like you're in a cave."

"Not in a cave."

"I can't see anything."

"It's dark."

"Why?"

"It's night."

"No, it's night here. It must be morning there."

"Technically, perhaps," said Sam, dawning slowly into consciousness. "But not like the sun's up."

"It's summer in London," Meredith protested. "The sun is always up."

"I think you might be missing the point here," said Sam. "It's dark because I have the curtains closed. Because it's night."

"Shouldn't you be jet-lagging?"

"I am a gifted sleeper."

"Shouldn't you be more excited to talk to me?"

"There are very few things that make me excited at five thirty in the morning."

"Want to know how absence makes you insane?"

"Sure. How?"

"Turn on a light so I can see you."

He rolled over and did, squinting hopelessly at her from around the globe and half a day away.

"It makes you insane because you go out with your favorite girlfriend who you haven't seen in weeks to your favorite bar where you haven't been in months to watch your favorite baseball team beat the Yankees eleven to one, and you still feel like something huge is missing all night long."

"Missing me is not insane. It's just good sense."

"Good night, Sam."

"Easy for you to say. You don't have a wake-up call coming in half an hour."

"Your presentation is tomorrow?"

"Today. Yeah."

"Your Major Presentation?"

"That's the one."

"In front of hundreds of really smart people?"

"Maybe thousands."

"With the whole future of the company—*our* company—at stake?"

"I am very important."

"Are you nervous?"

"More and more."

"Jeez, Sam," said Meredith. "You should really be getting some sleep."

. . .

When Sam drew the blinds not very much later, he found his room wasn't much lighter than it had been when they were closed. An hour later, he met Jamie in the lobby. Jamie was from London. He'd come to Seattle at the direct behest of BB to run Sam's department a year ago. Jamie claimed it was because of his superior leadership talent and technological know-how. Sam suspected BB was lulled into liking Jamie by his British accent, which made him sound smart and worldly as he gently explained the practical impossibilities of BB's pompous, overblown ideas. He'd trained as a Shakespearean actor before he turned to computers, and so he voiced the minutiae of everyday business ins and outs with a drama, cadence, and gravitas BB found appropriate to his own sense of importance. On this trip, Jamie was playing both boss and tour guide. And defender of the queen.

"Your weather's shite, dude," Sam greeted him in his best Monty Python accent.

"Your weather's shite, *mate*," Jamie corrected. "And what do you know? You live in Seattle. Your weather's just as shite as ours."

"But we deal with it better."

"Pray tell how so."

"Coffee shops," said Sam.

"Pubs," Jamie countered.

"Right, because what you need on top of all the rain is cold beer and depressant."

"Beer's not cold here," said Jamie.

"I rest my case," said Sam.

"We can get you a coffee," said Jamie as they walked toward the tube stop.

"Yeah, a shite coffee."

Jamie shoved him into a puddle, and Sam had to give his Major Presentation in sodden shoes. Despite this fact, Sam and his algorithm were greeted with raucous applause and Q & A that had to be cut off after an hour and a half because someone else (to whom Sam was eternally grateful) needed the room.

Jamie took him out for a celebratory lunch at a gastropub near St. Paul's where Sam drank a room-temp pint of what he had to admit was the best beer he'd ever had in his life. Then they walked across the bridge to the Tate Modern to have a look at the exhibit filling its giant-size entry hall: a scale model of the city of London. It was made from foam, so if you found yourself accidentally tempted to tread on the National Theatre or literally tripped up by Big Ben, you wouldn't hurt the art or yourself. It was about waist-high and so exquisitely detailed that they could see the scale model of London through the windows of the Turbine Hall of the mini-Tate. They wandered its city streets, much drier than the ones outside, until Jamie found the flat he'd grown up in and accidentally snagged his jacket on a restaurant he'd forgotten about entirely but was now convinced he had to take Sam to for dinner.

"Aren't I a good boss?" he noted.

"You are."

"You gave a great presentation, Sam. Very smart. Genius, even."

"Thank you."

"You'll be fine," said Jamie.

"I will?"

"Oh yes, you'll be just fine." Then he wandered over to check out the Tower of London.

In an upstairs gallery, Sam got a text from Meredith that read, "You're busted. I looked down during the morning meeting this a.m. and saw that I was wearing one navy shoe and one black shoe."

"How is that my fault?" wrote Sam.

"Absence makes you insane," wrote Meredith.

. . .

It was about like that for the rest of the trip. Conference in the morning. Bumming around London in the afternoon with Jamie. Waiting for Meredith to wake up back home and call/text/chat/e-mail/otherwise reassure him that she was alive and well and thinking of him too. She was sending him a running list of ways she was being made insane by his absence.

3) Accidentally called the barista "Mom."
4) Neglected to bring baggies to the dog park and had to pick up dog poop with a leaf.
5) Picked up dog poop with a leaf even though no one was watching and it wasn't like it was the middle of the sidewalk or anything, and really people should just be a little careful where they walk and save all those plastic bags from filling up landfills though okay, yes, mine are biodegradable, not that that helps when I leave them at home.
6) Failed utterly to write up the user specs for May/June or finish the storyboard for the Wilson-Abbot thing or meet with Erin re: the kickoff next month or convincingly pay attention during morning meeting so as not to get scolded (!) (as if I am his four-year-old!) by Edmondson but rather thought of you, thought of you, thought of you, and . . . thought of you.
7) Failed utterly to keep #6 to myself and thereby play it cool and chill and nonchalant and take-it-or-leave-it and interested but not overly and just a little bit hard to get. In. Sane.

Sam's remaining lung absconded. He couldn't wait to get home.

. . .

Finally, the last session of the last meeting of the last day of the conference was wrapping up. Sam was breathing a sigh of relief that no more tech would malfunction and no more meetings would demand his attention and no more events would require his attendance, and in nineteen hours, he'd be on a plane on his way back to the rest of his life. He met Jamie back at the gastropub. Aside from Meredith, that pint had been the other thing his mind returned to again and again all week long.

Jamie arrived late, wet, and exasperated. He slid down across the table from Sam with a pint in each hand.

"I've barely touched mine yet." Sam nodded toward his mostly still full glass. He was savoring it.

"They're both for me," said Jamie. And then, "You want the good news or the bad news?"

In Sam's work experience, the good news never outweighed the bad news. It never came close. If it did, it didn't begin this way.

"The good news," said Jamie, "is that BB is just thrilled with how the whole conference has gone. The tech has been smooth. Our events have looked glitch-free. You blew away everyone in the room with the algorithm and your presentation. The company looks great. The investors are thrilled. We've made BB a very rich man."

"Exactly my goal," said Sam. "What's the bad news?"

Jamie made a face. "The bad news is he's making me fire you."

Sam thought he must be joking. "You must be joking," he said.

"Nope."

"Why?"

"Your algorithm is costing them a fortune. It's brilliant, Sam. You should win a prize or something. BB thinks you're a genius. But it works way too well."

"How can it work too well?"

"Turns out fixing people up is not how we make money. It's *failing* to fix people up while still giving them hope that soon we might. It works too quickly. Revenue from sign-up fees is through the roof, but revenue from monthly fees is in the toilet. It's costing BB a fortune."

"You just said we made him very rich," said Sam.

"He wants to be more rich. That's why he's the BB."

"You just said he was really pleased with how well everything's gone over here."

"That's why he didn't fire you until it was over."

This was Sam's point about the good news never outweighing the bad. BB's getting rich was not really enough of a silver lining.

He called Meredith as soon as he got back to the hotel even though he knew she wasn't up yet.

"Is this payback?" she answered sleepily.

"You want the good news or the bad news?" said Sam.

"Uh-oh."

"I got fired."

"What?! Why?"

"Jamie says I'm costing BB too much money."

"That algorithm is genius. You're a genius."

"He agrees. But evidently it's hard on business. The publicity isn't enough in the long run. In the long run, he says, everyone wishes I'd never invented it."

"Not me," said Meredith.

"That's because you're insane," said Sam.

"I'll quit too."

"You'd better not."

"I'll lead a mutiny. The whole marketing department will walk out. Let's see him run this company without us."

"It's okay."

"It's not fair. He should promote you, not fire you."

"I could use some time off."

"Oh Sam, I'm so sorry. What can I do?"

"Pick me up at the airport tomorrow afternoon?"

LIVVIE

*S*he wasn't waiting for him at the airport, which was weird. She wasn't there when he came out of security, and she wasn't in baggage claim, and she didn't call him desperately from a backup on I-5 full of apology and saying she'd be there any minute. He was considering whether to be worried, hurt, or annoyed when he got a text that said, "Sorry and sorry. Meet me at my house, and I'll explain." Sam got on the light rail and wondered about lack of tone in texts. No way to know if she was getting cold feet or preferred to date the employed or realized that absence *did* make the heart grow fonder, fonder than it actually felt in his actual presence. Or maybe she'd greet him naked at the door. There was only one way to tell, and though it wasn't by rereading the text thirty-five times, that was the approach Sam tried anyway.

Meredith answered the door in sweatpants, a sweatshirt, a scarf, a hat, mittens, and what looked like several layers of socks. So the opposite of naked. She hugged him, and he felt the return of his lungs, and he held her for a little bit, just savoring, before he whispered into her hair, "It's August. It's seventy-five degrees out. Why are you dressed for January?"

"I can't get warm," she said. "I can't stop shivering."

"Are you sick?"

She shook her head but wouldn't look at him. "I'm sorry I forgot to come get you."

"It's okay." He was puzzled, waiting.

"Absence really does make you insane, I guess."

"But I'm back," he said brightly.

"Not yours," she said. "My grandmother died."

. . .

They'd not found her until several days later, which was maybe the worst part. Meredith's grandmother Olivia—Livvie—spent winters in Florida, as any sane and able retired Seattleite would, but she spent summers at home, near her daughter, her granddaughter, a whole lifetime of friends and memories and favorite places. She had an apartment in a high-rise on First Hill where she'd lived for fifty years, where Meredith's mother and uncle had grown up, where Meredith herself had spent the best parts of her childhood. Meredith's own parents had decamped to Orcas Island to be—and live like—artists, and Meredith had grown up with a potter's studio and a homestead garden, windswept beaches and old fir forests, but her heart belonged in her grandmother's old-world urban penthouse, a retreat as far as Meredith was concerned. She moved to the city first chance she got. She and her grandmother were basically neighbors.

Meredith would go over for dinner at least one night a week, but she also often stopped by for breakfast on her way to work or met Livvie for lunch downtown or dropped in to get a skirt hemmed or deliver half a batch of whatever she'd baked or leave Livvie some soup or some cherries or a box of cookies she'd bought from somebody's kid's Girl Scout troop. It wasn't that Livvie was old or infirm or too tired to manage; they just enjoyed each other's company. But it was also not unusual for Meredith not to hear from her grandmother for a little while. They didn't talk and visit every day. Livvie had a lot of friends, an active social life, much to do. And she was healthy but for the half pack a day. Her argument was, "It's been sixty years. If it hasn't killed me yet, maybe it's good for me."

It wasn't. Meredith saw her Wednesday for dinner and all was well, and they'd made plans for brunch over the weekend. She called her grandmother Friday evening and left a message that she wanted to drop off half the enormous box of tomatoes her neighbor had brought over from his garden. It didn't occur to her until Saturday afternoon that she hadn't heard back and they hadn't figured out brunch for the morning—not entirely unusual but a bit unsettling still; Livvie was a busy woman, but she had a cell phone. Meredith called again, left another message and another, but by then it was late Saturday night. She finally let herself into her grandmother's apartment on Sunday morning.

Livvie was sitting on the sofa, reading glasses on, book in her lap, water on the coffee table undisturbed. But that was about the only aspect of the scene that was undisturbing. Meredith knew with one glance at her grandmother, knew before that even, when she opened the door to the apartment and heard no ball game on the radio, smelled no coffee or Sunday bagels, found blinds drawn and windows shut, knew before that probably, in her heart, because her grandmother was a phone call returner and a Meredith lover and a woman of her word, especially where brunch was concerned.

An ambulance came, just to be sure. Massive heart attack, they guessed. So massive she never felt it coming. So massive she didn't take off her glasses or stumble off the couch or collapse in pain or try to call for help or even feel a little thirsty, for her water glass was still full. Too quick to have been painful, they assured her. Not too long ago, they assured her. Nothing you could have done anyway, they assured her.

. . .

At the funeral, Sam held Meredith's hand and met her parents and other relatives and all of Livvie's friends. Meredith introduced each deliberately and generously, for their benefit as well as Sam's. "This is Naomi. She and her husband used to go dancing with my grandparents in the fifties. She and my grandmother go to the theater together a lot. Naomi is quite the dancer." And, "This is Ralph and Ella Mae. They're my grandmother's favorite dinner-and-a-movie companions." And, "This is Penny. She lives downstairs. She's my grandmother's best friend. She just lost her husband, so Grandma's probably hanging out with Albert even as we speak." And then Meredith and Penny hugged and cried and rocked back and forth, and Sam waited awkwardly, hands plunged in pockets, for some way he could be helpful.

Meredith's parents, meanwhile, looked almost as uncomfortable and out of place as Sam. Julia rubbed damp eyes with too-long sleeves pulled all the way over her clenched fists and tucked phantom strands of hair behind her ears. She looked grateful for her daughter's social graces on this unspeakable occasion, but every time she acknowledged an introduction or tried to smile, she started crying again. Kyle sized things up and decided

Meredith was holding it together better than Julia and so stayed by his wife's side like they were a wedding cake topper. This proved to be true of Meredith's parents though even when all was well. Kyle and Julia were Kyle-and-Julia-against-the-world. They were Pacific Northwest islanders and liked it that way. They owned a rainy, weathered ceramics studio, ran a shop out front, lived upstairs, ate from the garden they kept all around the place. They spent their days making pots and talking about art, taking wet, meandering walks along the beaches holding hands, exploring endless coves by kayak. It took a long ferry ride followed by a long drive to get them to Seattle, to which they referred unironically as the "Big City." They weren't stoners or off-gridders or even vegan or unshowered. They made beautiful art and a pretty good living besides. But they cultivated detachment, separation—from the world, from real life, from their loved ones even. They had few friends and didn't talk to Meredith unless she called and didn't talk to Livvie unless she called either. They loved their only child absolutely, of course. But they loved their twoness too.

In stark, stark contrast, there was Meredith's cousin.

"Dashiell Bentlively." He offered Sam his hand and toothpaste-ad smile.

"But not really?" Sam smiled tentatively, not wanting to offend but pretty sure that couldn't be anyone's real name.

"Nope, not really"—Dashiell winked—"but that's the one I use. Even Mom admits it's a better fit than the one she chose."

"I hadn't met him yet when I picked the original," Meredith's aunt Maddie shrugged.

Dashiell was Julia's brother Jeff's son. He and Meredith were born on the same day, so they considered themselves twins though in fact they had little in common but a birthday and a grandmother. Dashiell lived in L.A., sometimes gay, sometimes straight, making money hand over hand over hand over fist somehow near Hollywood but not actually in the film industry. Meredith didn't understand or pretend to understand or ask too many questions, but they were close anyway.

"I guess I'm the matriarch of the family now," he said after the funeral.

"What about me?" said Julia.

"You don't have the legs for it," said Dash. He was making a good show of it, but he was a bit of a mess.

After the funeral, after everyone finally went home, Meredith's parents crashed at her place. Uncle Jeff and Aunt Maddie went to a fancy hotel downtown, Aunt Maddie's argument being roughly, "When life gets you down, order room service." Dashiell stayed at Livvie's. So Meredith went home with Sam who, finally, had her all to himself, had her in his arms, had the reunion he'd flown half round the world dreaming about. It wasn't quite the one he imagined, and he was at something of a loss—so ecstatic to be with her again, so sorry she was so sad—but he whispered love against her sea-smelling skin and made do.

"I'm hungry," she said suddenly.

"Really?"

"Yeah. Weird, right?"

"There's nothing in the house. I've been away for two weeks."

"I remember," she said, smiling, and then, awed, "I forgot."

Sam found a couple cans of soup to heat up and some crackers. He tried to stay sad, but he couldn't keep the happy down, so overjoyed was he to be back with her.

"I missed you," Sam admitted, an understatement and a subject change.

"I remember," she said, smiling. And then, awed, "I forgot." And then, giggling in spite of everything, "You better remind me."

WHAT LIVVIE WOULD SAY

*I*t was a hard week. Meredith and Dash both took the week off, and together with their parents, they went about packing up a life. Sam tried to be elsewhere, to give everyone space, but he was unemployed, and here, finally, was a way for him to be helpful. On Monday, Sam wrapped wineglasses in newspaper. He wrapped plates and mugs and vases and bowls and cordials and goblets. He wrapped lamps and a porcelain statue of two dancers from Livvie's honeymoon in Paris and a ceramic duck Meredith made in the second grade. Sam became gradually covered in newsprint. He put each carefully wrapped item in a box.

Julia came into the kitchen. "What on earth are you thinking?"

"I'm wrapping breakables?"

"And putting them all in a box?"

"Yeah?"

"No, everything needs to go in separate boxes, double-boxed, carefully labeled. Maybe I should do this. I move ceramics for a living."

"Grandma wouldn't care," Meredith yelled from the living room.

"We'll never find anything again if we just throw things willy-nilly into boxes," said Julia.

"Grandma would say it's nice to be surprised when you open up the boxes," Meredith shouted back.

"I don't know when I'm ever going to open up these boxes," Julia muttered. "I'll never use this stuff."

"Grandma would say this is everyday ware. Grandma would say no point in saving the good china for a special occasion because special occasions don't happen often enough."

. . .

On Tuesday, they did clothes.

"Grandma would say toss it all," said Dash, hands on hips, looking skeptically into her closet.

"We should at least donate it somewhere," said Meredith.

"To the Old Ladies' Salvation Army?"

Julia squeezed between them and took a much worn orange cardigan off a hook on the back of the door, slipped it on, and walked away.

. . .

On Wednesday, they did paperwork.

"Grandma would say toss it all," Dash said again, but instead Sam made sandwiches and popcorn while everyone else sat around on the floor and sorted a million pieces of paper into a semblance of organization: personal letters versus business correspondence, old bills versus outstanding ones, accounting records, trash.

"It'll be so different when we go," said Meredith. "No one writes me letters on paper. I don't get paper bills or bank statements or tax records. My grandkids can just highlight my whole e-mail account and press delete, and that'll be the end of it."

She came across a green flyer she folded up and stashed in her pocket. Later, she came across a blue one and a pink one and stashed those, too. In the kitchen with Sam, she surreptitiously stuffed them in the recycling bin.

"What are those?" Sam asked.

"Flyers for a ceramics guy at my grandmother's farmers' market in Florida. She was always on my mom to build a website like Peter the Potter and take custom orders like Peter the Potter and make garden gnomes like Peter the Potter. She thought he must be rich because there was always a huge line of old people waiting to buy his stuff. My mom thinks he's a hack. It drove her nuts. I just thought I'd spare her the annoyance."

Julia walked into the kitchen, fished the flyers out of the recycling bin, and smoothed them on the counter.

Meredith raised her eyebrows at her mother. "I thought making ceramic gnomes was undignified and small?"

"Right, small. So I was thinking elves." Julia managed a little smile to accompany her little joke.

"You're keeping flyers for sentimental value?" Meredith wondered.

"Nagging from the great beyond," said Julia. "Best kind."

. . .

On Thursday, everyone needed a break. Uncle Jeff and Aunt Maddie took Kyle and Julia for a fancy lunch at their fancy hotel. Dash and Meredith— secretly, guiltily thrilled—went through Livvie's jewelry.

"Grandma would say toss it all," declared Meredith giddily from the center of the bed surrounded by piles of pearls, gold chains, pewter charms, fake and real diamond necklaces, jade bracelets, and giant rings. Some of it was valuable. Most of it was not. Some of it was gorgeous. Most of it was not. She was wearing three strands of pearls (white, pink, and mother-of), two gold necklaces (one with a locket that wouldn't open, one with a poodle charm from when Livvie'd owned a dog—before Meredith's time), a newly paired pair of earrings (one dangly silver hoop, one blue stud), and four rings which ranged from Livvie's wedding band to a red-and-purple plastic one Meredith had won for her at a fair in sixth grade. Dash had on one very fake diamond tiara, a macaroni necklace he had made himself, rings on every single finger (few of them even as elegant as the red-and-purple plastic one), and, over his heart, competing ivory brooches.

"Give me one of those," said Meredith.

"They're a matched set," Dash protested.

"One's a dragon and one's a tiger."

"Exactly. They're going to duke it out. We have to see who wins."

He looped a charm bracelet around his ankle. It dangled four gold pendants with silhouettes of Jeff, Julia, Dash, and Meredith as babies.

"You're taking all the good stuff," Meredith whined.

"Girl, I am rocking this family anklet. You could not pull this off."

"At least give me the tiara."

"Okay look, four piles," said Dash. "One for your mom, one for you, one for me, and one for OLSA."

"OLSA?"

"Old Ladies' Salvation Army."

"Even they wouldn't want some of this."

"Grandma would want me to have these," said Dash, holding up clip-on coral sun and moon earrings.

"Grandma would have said those earrings are hideous," said Meredith. "They're hers."

"And I'm sure they were very stylish when she bought them in 1947, but they are not now."

"I will rock these earrings," said Dash, clipping them on.

"Do her proud," said Meredith.

. . .

On Friday, they were down to what was left. It was a lot, and it wasn't much. Her telephone, her knitting supplies, her junk drawer full of what everyone's junk drawer is full of—Scotch tape and extra scissors and delivery menus and expired coupons and rubber bands and paper clips and empty key chains. They found M&M's she'd hidden for Meredith and Dash one afternoon when they were five and bored (they had found most of them but not all, apparently) and VCR tapes that had fallen behind the TV and unused coloring books either forgotten from when she had small grandchildren or maybe just in case any little kids stopped by. And all her furniture. They'd called the actual Salvation Army and were waiting for them to come by, and Uncle Jeff was on the phone with a real estate agent—it got that far—before Meredith said:

"I'm moving in."

"Where?" said her mother absently.

"Here. Grandma's house. I want to move in."

"It's an old-lady apartment," said Uncle Jeff.

"Grandma lived here when she was a newlywed," said Meredith. "She had little kids here. She had teenagers here."

"Lot of history," said Dash. "Lot of memories."

"That's a bad thing?"

"Might be hard. Might be too heavy."

"Grandma would want me to live here," said Meredith.

"Lot of ugly furniture," added Dash. It was true. Some of the furniture was ugly enough to resist even nostalgia.

"I'd get rid of my place and pay you guys rent," Meredith said to her mother and uncle.

"Don't be silly," said Uncle Jeff. "You're family. It's yours as much as anyone's. It's not about the money."

"Grandma would want you to live here," her mother acknowledged, "*if* that's what you want. But not if it's going to make you sad and depressed and mopey. Not if it's just because you can't let go."

"I can't let go," said Meredith. "But that's not why I want to stay."

. . .

Later that night, Jeff and Maddie went back to their hotel, and Kyle and Julia went back to Meredith's, and Dash stayed at Sam's, while Sam himself began unwrapping all of the carefully wrapped plates and cups and glasses and bowls and putting them back on the shelves where he found them. Meredith's feeling was that her postcollege, mismatched, thrift-store china had nothing on her grandmother's. Meredith's feeling was that they belonged in these cabinets. Meredith's feeling was, "That's what my grandmother would say I should do."

"You always know what your grandmother would say," said Sam.

"I've known her all my life."

"But what about what you want?"

"I want what she wants. Wanted. She wants what's best for me, and that's what I want as well."

"Me too," said Sam. "How about I finish unpacking plates and stuff here, and you go home and pack up your stuff."

"I can start that tomorrow."

"Last night with Dash and your folks? Your aunt and uncle? Maybe you'd like to spend tonight with your family."

"I think you are my family," Meredith said. And then she said, "You need to go home and pack too."

"Why?"

"Move in here with me."

"What?"

"Move in here with me."

"Oh, Merde, it's way too soon."

"You wanted to move in before you left for London."

"I was kidding."

"You were not."

"I was . . . delirious with happiness."

"Emphasis on the happiness."

"Emphasis on the delirious."

"Your place is too small. My place is too . . . mine. This place is just right," Meredith said. "Besides, my grandmother would say that you should stay."

"You think?"

"I'm sure."

"Would she have liked me?"

"Are you kidding? She would have loved you."

"What makes you think so?"

"You're smart. You're funny. You're a baseball fan. You make good popcorn. But mostly, you're awfully kind to her granddaughter."

"I'm unemployed. Grandmothers hate the unemployed."

"Nice to her granddaughter would trump that. Trust me," said Meredith.

"I wish I knew her," said Sam. "She seems like an amazing person."

"I can't believe you never met her. I can't believe you'll never meet her."

"I'll get to know her anyway."

"How?"

"By living in her house," said Sam. "By loving her granddaughter."

· · ·

They finished packing and moving their own stuff into Livvie's over the course of a couple weeks. But that first night after her family left, Meredith went home and untied all of her model airplanes. When Sam got back to their new apartment, he found clean sheets on the bed, two dogs in the kitchen, and hundreds of model airplanes hanging from the rafters. Then he and Meredith went into the bedroom to properly christen it as their own.

Afterward, Sam watched the airplanes tracing swinging shadows over both their bodies, airplane shadows over his chest and stomach and feet, like strange tattoos over her face, her breasts, circling her navel like an air base.

"How many are there?" Sam asked.

"I don't know actually. I lost count at some point." She raised one naked leg and pointed with her toes to a World War II Hellcat in the corner painted a sloppy mess of pinks and purples. "That one's the first one. My dad built it. But I painted it."

"I guessed."

"I was a pacifist, but we lived on an island. It was hard to find model kits that weren't warplanes. I'd build them then paint over their insignias in pastel hearts and flowers. I'd put little plastic puppies in the cockpits. I'd replace their machine guns with pretzel sticks."

"Why'd you start making them in the first place?"

She shrugged. "Probably there was no reason why. Probably the reason was if they didn't give me something focused to do, I tore around the studio and broke things. If you're going to make pottery for a living, you have to find a way to corral your toddler."

"You longed to fly maybe? Escape?"

"I think it was about achievement instead. You know, like, 'Look what we can do—fly!' And look what a kid can do too—take a big pile of wood and a bottle of glue and some paint and mess with it all afternoon until it makes an airplane. Maybe that's what my parents wanted to give me—a sense that I could do anything."

"I wish I'd known you then," said Sam.

"Why?"

"You must have been the smartest, sweetest, funniest little girl."

"Yeah, but it would have been creepy if you'd thought that when I was six."

"Not if I were six too. I could have helped you build planes."

"You still could."

"Where would we put them?" Sam asked.

"That's why I started hanging them from the ceiling. I ran out of room on the shelf. But on the ceiling is where they belonged all along. They're airplanes—they should fly. And then at night I'd have flying dreams."

"Everyone has flying dreams," said Sam.

"Not like mine," said Meredith.

ABSENT IS ABSENT

*W*hat happened next happened because Sam couldn't stand to see Meredith so unhappy. It happened because he was desperate to help. It happened because he was still in the trying-to-prove-his-love-and-win-her-heart phase. It happened because he was unemployed and had the time, and summer waned into fall, and the weather got wetter and colder and more discouraging. Mostly, it happened because he was just cocky enough to believe that it could. That and he had no idea where it would lead. None at all. How could he possibly?

It happened too because Sam was stunned to find himself jealous, envious, of Meredith's grandmother's death. Not her dying—Sam didn't want that, obviously—and not the loss of a loved one, of course; what Sam coveted were the memories. This took him a while to figure out. First he thought he just felt bad for Meredith. Then he thought he just felt sad because she was sad. For a bit, he thought it was that he never had the chance to meet Livvie. For a bit, he thought he was being a selfish asshole who just wanted his girlfriend to get over it already—old people die!—so that she could get back to being the nondepressed, nonmorose, nondejected woman he vaguely remembered. But no, it was none of that. Sam was missing his mom. And that was hard.

That was hard because it's hard to miss someone you've barely met. It's hard to miss someone you can't remember. Missing *is* remembering. They are the same act. They are part and parcel. But Sam didn't have a single actual memory of his mother, so it was hard to, odd to, miss her. It was more like the other kind of missing—missing a bus rather than missing a loved one. He was aware that something huge had passed him by, but without memories to dwell on and pore over, it was hard to hang on to what it was.

She died in a car accident when he was thirteen months old. His dad said Sam was already saying, "Mama," his first word, that he adored her and wailed when she left the room even for a moment, that they couldn't leave him with a babysitter because his mother couldn't pry Sam out of her arms, so ferocious was his grip. Sam believed these stories, not because he thought his dad would never lie to him—to give him back even a small piece of his mother, to fabricate even the tiniest scrap of memory, Sam suspected his dad would lie happily—but because all of that sounded exactly like any thirteen-month-old. Sam's dad offered these details as proof of extraordinary love, but in fact, Sam knew, it was the most ordinary kind of love there was.

The photographic evidence suggested ordinary too. There he was— red and wrinkled and wailing at first then wrapped in a blanket like a burrito then posed with the dog, with a snowman, with a very drippy ice-cream cone, covered in flour, surrounded by Tupperware on the kitchen floor, grinning naked and filthy in their front garden, on top of a slide in a too-big hat, and being nibbled variously by geese, calves, sheep, goats, and in one even a yak. There were pictures of Sam and his mom in ridiculously wide-legged pants and hideous shirts with walleyed collars and voluminous curly hair (his mom's; she didn't live long enough to see Sam grow much hair). Two pictures in particular stood out, at least to him. In one, she lies on green pile carpet on her back, her crazy hair spread out above her like when someone gets electrocuted in a cartoon. Sam sits inside this nest of hair, gathering and tossing it in great handfuls like snow. In the second, she's nursing him, and he has a ringlet of that great mane clenched in a tiny fist and wound all the way down his arm in a move that would be illegal in professional wrestling.

Sam scoured his memory but could not conjure the sensation of that hair. When he was seven, he found out from his dad what kinds of shampoo and conditioner she'd used and used them himself, hoping to trigger some olfactory memory. When he was ten, influenced by cop shows on TV, he went in search of hair samples, painstakingly looking through the boxes of her stuff bound for charity that his dad had never found the strength to move beyond the basement. He'd managed to untangle from old sweaters and dresses and jackets and the hinge of a pair of sunglasses seven longish strands which he secured with tape inside the back cover of a Choose Your Own Adventure book. These he traced endlessly with angsty preteen fingertips but could never recover memories tactile nor, though he sacrificed one precious strand to Genevieve Trouvier's Ouija board, even occult. When he started dating, he watched himself for a proclivity toward hirsute girls or, at the least, toward running his hands through their bobs or twisting their braids around his fingers or yanking their ponytails in playful flirtation, but he didn't find any of that in himself, at least no more than ordinary. Ordinary seemed to be the hallmark of Sam's brief relationship with his mother. But ordinary as it was, there was no getting it back of course, not even a moment of it. In contrast, it seemed to Sam, Meredith retained so much of Livvie. Comparatively speaking, it was almost like she was still around.

On the last day of the regular season, Sam and Meredith went to the baseball game. This was a tradition Meredith and Livvie had kept for years. It marked the official end of summer so far as they were concerned, even though the weather had often turned well beforehand and even though Meredith had been back at school for weeks already, because Livvie would always leave for Florida the next day. She'd wait until the Mariners were statistically eliminated from the postseason before she booked flights, just in case, even in seasons—and there were quite a few of them—when it was clear by late April that she could go ahead and buy plane tickets. But final-day-of-the-regular-season tickets, these she bought the day single games went on sale. And thus Sam and Meredith found them, the morning of the game, when they turned over the drawer of the bedside table in a futile but thorough search for the condoms Sam was certain he'd bought more of only the week before.

Meredith had taken the post-Livvie baseball season off. She couldn't bear to watch or listen or even look at box scores. Sam had followed the season online, which was fine, but now he thought they should go to this game.

"It'd be a shame to waste the tickets," he said.

"I'll get over it," said Meredith.

"Your grandmother would want us to go."

"How do you know?"

"She was a fan. And it was tradition."

"It's pouring. It's a terrible day for baseball."

"There's a roof. What else are we going to do in this weather?" It had taken Sam a while after he'd moved to Seattle to consider baseball a rainy-day activity, but he was learning.

"I hate baseball," said Meredith.

"You love baseball," said Sam.

"I used to. Now I hate it. Now everything reminds me of her."

"That's why we should go. To say goodbye."

"I don't want to say goodbye."

"Not goodbye forever," said Sam. "Goodbye for now. Goodbye for a few months. Goodbye like she's going to Florida tomorrow."

Meredith-skeptical turned into Meredith-slightly-intrigued. They donned layers and went to the game. On the way, they stopped at Uwajimaya for sushi, Vietnamese sandwiches, and the Japanese equivalent of Cool Ranch Doritos. ("My grandmother's idea of baseball food," she said.) They smuggled in a thermos of hot cocoa in the inside pocket of Meredith's too-big jacket. ("My grandmother felt seven dollars was too much for a ballpark latte.") They traded innings keeping score, Meredith keeping the odd ones and Sam keeping the evens, his argument that it was too cold to take off his mittens trumped by hers:

"My grandmother felt strongly that you have to keep score."

"Why?" Sam's dad had taught him one season when he was a kid so he'd stop pestering him for snacks every inning and a half, but he rarely bothered anymore. "Do you ever go back and look at it?"

"No," said Meredith. "She always said what matters is that it's there."

Despite his earlier enthusiasm, Sam began lightly suggesting that they might think about leaving when the Angels scored five runs in the sixth and the temperature dropped into the low teens.

"My butt is frozen."

"Livvie's Law: No matter how bad it gets, real fans stay for the whole game."

"I can see my breath."

"It's like fifty-five degrees out, Sam."

"It's winter."

"It's the first weekend of October."

"Baseball is a summer sport."

"My grandmother thought the season should end on Labor Day. Not because she was such a big baby about the cold though. Just because she was anxious to get back to Florida and see all her friends there."

"I'm not a baby. It's eight to one. It's negative four degrees. We're out of cocoa. I've been banned from the seven-dollar lattes. We could go home and remember Livvie in front of the fire."

"No matter how bad it gets, real fans stay for the whole game," intoned Meredith happily.

Just outside the gate, having seen nine sodden innings through to a miserable eleven-to-one conclusion, Meredith squeezed Sam's mitten with her own.

"Thank you. For making me come today. You were right. It's what she would have wanted."

"It was fun," said Sam.

"I could tell."

"I was just teasing about freezing to death."

"Wait until Opening Day. That'll be even colder."

"Opening Day?"

"Oh yeah. My grandmother thought it should be a national holiday. Of course you go to Opening Day."

"Of course," said Sam.

"I'm sorry about the incredibly cheesy thing that's going to happen next," said Meredith. Then she let go of his hand and turned back toward the stadium and said, "Bye, Grandma. Have fun in Florida. See you soon and talk to you sooner."

"That *was* cheesy," said Sam, putting his arm around her and pulling her against him at least as much for love as for body heat.

"And then she'd say, 'Not if I see you first.' "

"What does that even mean?" said Sam.

"I have no idea."

On the wet walk home, Sam wondered what his mother might say about the necessity of staying all the way to the end of a cold ball game or what she might like to snack on while she was there or where her cutoff point was for the price of a ballpark latte. He had no idea whether his mother even liked baseball. His dad had never mentioned it, but that didn't necessarily mean anything. Sam's first semester at college he took a beginning piano class on a whim (okay, the professor was hot), and it turned out he was astonishingly good at it. When he reported this at home over fall break, his dad smiled wistfully and laughed. "Must be hereditary."

"What do you mean?"

"Mom was an incredible pianist."

"She was?"

"Oh yeah. Minored in it at school."

"You only ever told me she was an English major."

"With a minor in piano," Sam's dad added. He liked to dole out stories one at a time. He never spent an evening reminiscing, telling one memory into another. Instead, Sam got his mother's life one moment at a time. This way the stories were fresh, organic; Sam got to hear them only because he'd happened to bring them up. This way, there were always more, ones Sam hadn't heard yet, ones his dad hadn't told. It was like there was still more life to be lived there, more to discover, an unnoticed corner to turn. For all Sam knew about his mother's baseball proclivities, she could have been a second baseman for the Mets.

It was later in bed, warm at last, when it hit him that what he was was jealous. What wouldn't he give to know what his mom might say at a baseball game? Meredith, on the same train of thought apparently but in a different boxcar, wondered aloud, "Is it weird to miss her so much when I know everything she'd say if she were here? I could do both sides of the conversation through the entire game. I can practically re-create the whole day, frame for frame, just as if she were here with me."

"I don't know why," said Sam, "but it's not the same." Obviously.

She shrugged. "At least now I can just pretend she's in Florida. It'll be easier knowing I wouldn't be seeing her anyway."

"Absent is absent?"

"I guess so. But also we'd e-mail. We'd video chat. She'd text me from the beach just to rub it in. You know?"

"I do," said Sam. "Absent is less absent than it used to be."

A PLACE FOR IT TO GO

*M*eredith's question got stuck in Sam's brain and wouldn't leave, in part because Meredith was contentedly colonizing every corner of his mind but also because it was an interesting question. Why *did* she miss her so much if she knew everything she'd say if she were there? What are we missing from loved ones we know so well we could finish their sentences and think their unthought thoughts?

"Do you think it's the random, interstitial stuff?" Sam asked after dinner the next night.

"Do I think what's the random, interstitial stuff?"

"If you know the highlights of what she'd say at the ball game, is it the random stuff in between that you miss?"

"About my grandmother?"

"Yeah."

"Like telling me about her bridge game the night before or bitching about the shortstop or should she get a Coke or just fill up her bottle from the water fountain?"

"I guess."

Meredith thought about this. "I don't think so. I miss the essence of her, her real self. Everyone thinks about what to drink when they're thirsty. Only she would argue that relievers should be pushed out of airplanes in parachutes punched with the number of holes equal to their ERA."

"Is it touch?" Sam asked gently.

"Maybe. Some. I don't know. My grandma and I were mostly down to quick hugs and pecks on the cheek."

"You miss her voice? You miss seeing her?"

"I don't know," said Meredith again. "You'd think predictable conversation would be boring, but it's not; it's reassuring. It's not about knowing what she'd say. It's about hearing her say what I know she will. Familiarity is comforting. Me saying her lines in her seat at her ball game, me knowing she'd be supportive and proud of me and encouraging of whatever I tell her . . . that's not about her; that's about her absence. Knowing is beside the point. I just want to be with her again, hear from her again, even an e-mail, even a text, even a canceled dinner date. I just want to believe that she's still out there somewhere. I know how to miss her in Florida. I know how to miss her for a few months. I just don't know how to miss her forever."

Did Sam say, "Missing her is a good thing. It means you loved her"? Did he say, "Missing her is a good thing. It means you're mourning"? Did he say, "You're lucky you were so close," or, "You're lucky you had her in your life for so long," or even, "What are your thoughts on the designated hitter"? No, what Sam said was, "Maybe you *should* e-mail her. Just to make yourself feel better."

Meredith laughed. "I wrote a letter to my pet turtle after he died when I was six."

"What did you say?"

"I don't remember. 'Dear Mr. Turtleton, Thank you for being a good turtle. I'm sorry you died. I hope you're enjoying turtle heaven.' Something like that. My mom thought it would be therapeutic."

"Was it?"

"I don't remember. I do remember getting in trouble though for throwing the letter in the creek. My dad was mad at me for littering, but that's where he'd put Mr. T, so that's where it made sense to put the letter. I couldn't understand why putting a letter in the creek was littering but putting a dead turtle in the creek was A-okay."

"It's the beauty of e-mail," said Sam. "At least there's a place to send it, a place for it to go."

• • •

Meredith did e-mail her grandmother just to make herself feel better. But it didn't work. How could it? Even for e-mail, it was soulless. There was no one on the other end. And she knew it. And Sam knew it. But he also knew something else. Or suspected he did. Sam suspected it wouldn't be that hard to make Livvie respond. There were a lot of examples to model on because Livvie had sent a lot of e-mails. And they were fairly patterned and predictable, especially the ones to her granddaughter. Once Sam filtered the archive by date so that he included only the winter e-mails, mostly Livvie wrote to Meredith that she missed her and loved her and hoped she wasn't working too hard, that Florida was sunny and hot and fun, and that Meredith should come visit. Sometimes she added that she was kicking someone's ass in cards.

Sam's dad had a favorite story about an early experiment in language and computers called ELIZA that was developed in the 1960s at MIT to play therapist. It used pattern matching to listen to users' problems and respond with appropriate psychotherapist questions. A user would sit down and type, "My sister's always hated me," and the program would say, "Why do you say your sister's always hated you?" It was at once very simple and very complex programming, a lark, a parody, a joke, and groundbreaking science. Sam's father's favorite part of the story though was that all the grad students who were working on it would end up staying after hours getting therapy from ELIZA. They knew they weren't talking to a real doctor. But they did it anyway. Sam was never clear whether the moral of the story was that computer programs can model human behavior so closely as to be indistinguishable or that graduate students are chumps.

Meredith had e-mailed her grandmother as though she were really in Florida, not an e-mail full of misery and mourning, which was certainly not going to make her feel better, but the e-mail she wished she could write to a summering Livvie from the granddaughter still spending fall in Seattle. If there was perhaps somewhat more bitter in the sweet than usual, you'd have to know to know. She had written:

Hi Grandma,

How are you? How is it there?

Here, I am missing you so much. But I have a little bit of news. I am dating a great new guy. His name is Sam. I met him at work. You'd love him—very smart and funny and kind. He's really great to me, and we're really great together. I can't wait for you to meet him.

Anyway, I feel a little silly sending this, but I know you'd want to know. Hope it is warm and sunny and wonderful where you are. I want to tell you too that I love you so much and miss you every day and think of you always!

Love,
Meredith

And not right away, but eventually, after some trial and error on Sam's part, her grandmother wrote back:

Hi honey,

I miss you too, but I'M SO EXCITED YOU'VE MET SOMEONE. Tell me all about him! What's he look like? Is he a baseball fan? What's his team? Is he a computer geek? Didn't I tell you when you started working there that you were risking marrying a computer geek? Hooray!! Can't wait to hear details. Maybe you and Sam could come visit me down here. The weather's perfect, and the water's calling your name. I bet it's cold and rainy there. Poor you :(
   Let's video chat soon. Right now I'm off to play bridge with the girls.
   Love you too!

Love,
Grandma

Entirely computer generated. It hadn't even been that hard. He'd written a program that combed Livvie's old e-mails for clues: what she said about missing her granddaughter, what she said about the weather, what she said when Meredith met someone she liked. *Didn't I tell you when you started working there that you were risking marrying a computer geek?* She had. Many times. The e-mail simply plugged in details, echoed back what Meredith said, and did a good job of sounding exactly like Livvie always sounded. It was eerie and a little uncanny but surprisingly simple when you got right down to it.

Sam thought it was impressive, but he worried it might be too impressive, at once too real and, of course, not nearly real enough. This was what Meredith had said she wanted, but he wasn't sure it was what she meant.

Did she want the e-mail or the fact of the e-mail, the woman behind it? Sam couldn't give her the woman behind it. But he could give her the e-mail. It wouldn't be enough—he knew that—but maybe something was better than nothing at all, ever again.

Or maybe it wasn't. Sam always had this problem. He *could* and he was impressed that he could, and the combination of those two things made him think that he *should*. But that wasn't always the case. He decided to call in an expert on the subject of Stupid Things Sam Did Just Because He Could.

Jamie was full of frustrations. Work wasn't fun anymore now that Sam was gone. BB was at once demanding better performance and forbidding anyone to even think about revisiting Sam's algorithm. Clients were circulating myths that there was some magic formula to pair them with their perfect mate, but it had been taken away from the masses, and only the chosen would be allowed to use it. Others were convinced the answer was locked away somewhere in their file—that if only they were given access to it, they could have the name, address, social security number, and star sign of their soul mate—but no one was allowed to see. Online communities spoke of Sam Elling as a god. BB banned his name from ever being uttered in the building again.

"It's a nightmare," said Jamie.

"It's fantastic," said Sam.

"How do you figure?"

"I am vindicated. Nothing like being fired and still managing to wreck things for BB remotely."

"It's very frustrating," said Jamie. "That algorithm was the best piece of software ever developed on my watch, and no one even gets to use it."

"Well, not no one," said Sam.

"Explain."

"Meredith's grandmother died."

"And you're fixing her up with Abe Lincoln."

"Abe Lincoln?"

"Just trying to name a dead American."

"And Lincoln was who came to mind?"

"I'm not from around here. Quick, name a dead Brit."

"Shakespeare," said Sam.

"Shakespeare's not British. He's universal. But never mind. What are you doing with the algorithm really?"

"Not using it. Just using the idea of it. Looking through someone's e-mails to learn more about them."

"You're stalking Meredith's dead grandmother?"

"Meredith wanted to write her grandmother a letter. Say goodbye and she loved her and missed her and whatever. Not that unusual an impulse, right? But we're living in her apartment, so she couldn't send it there, and they e-mailed each other quite a bit, so that's what we settled on. She e-mailed her grandmother."

"And? I'm waiting for the punch line."

"Her grandmother replied."

Jamie grinned. "Zombie-mail. No wonder BB fired you."

"I wrote a script that looked at her back e-mails and compiled a reply to Meredith that's pretty much indistinguishable from what she'd have actually written if she were still alive."

"Pattern matching? Fill in the blanks?"

"Basically. How varied are your e-mails with your grandmother?"

"My gran wouldn't know what e-mail was if she woke up in bed with the 'You've got mail' guy, but I take your meaning. That's pretty clever."

"Thanks."

"So what's the question?"

"Do I show it to Meredith?"

"No way."

"Really? Why?"

"Too unsettling. What was useful in this exercise for Meredith was her writing to her grandmother. She's obviously not expecting a reply."

"But she said she wanted one. She said all she wanted was e-mail from her grandmother."

"Correspondence from one's dead relations can never be anything but disturbing, Sam."

"I don't know," said Sam. "Maybe it would be cathartic."

IT WAS NOT CATHARTIC

*H*e decided to sleep on it. He routed the e-mail to Meredith's inbox but then stashed her laptop under his pillow in case he changed his mind. In the morning when they woke up, he began with, "This is weird. It is. And I'm not sure about it, but I want to show you and let you decide. I have a surprise."

"Oh goody." She reached over for him.

"Not that," said Sam and then thought better of it. "Well, sure, that first if you want."

"First? What else is on offer?"

Sam produced her laptop from under his pillow.

"You got me . . . my laptop?"

"I sent you an e-mail."

"I think I pick sex," she said, reaching for him again.

"It's not really from me though," Sam hedged.

"You *forwarded* me an e-mail? This surprise gets less and less exciting."

"Check and see." Sam held the laptop out to her nervously. Meredith opened it and scanned her inbox.

"No e-mail from you. What are you . . . ? Wait . . . oh my God. Oh my God, Sam." She looked at him, and he held his breath while for a moment, then two, she didn't do anything. Then she clicked on the e-mail. Read it. Paled to whitewash. Looked confused. Then angry. "My grandmother replied to my e-mail."

"Yes." Sam waited. And then added, "Well, I helped."

"To trick me?"

"No!"

"To fuck with me?"

"Merde, of course not."

"Do you think this is funny?"

"No, I—"

"Why would you— How could you?"

"I didn't actually."

Puzzled silence. Quiet anger. "You just said you did."

"I did. I mean I did say that. I didn't e-mail you. Your grandmother e-mailed you. I just helped."

"You helped?"

"Not even me, actually. I just pushed start. Well, jiggered the program and then pushed start."

"You logged into my grandmother's e-mail account and e-mailed me as a joke."

"No."

"No?"

"No. Does that e-mail sound like me?"

"You do a good impersonation."

"No."

"No?"

"No. It was computer science."

Meredith had nothing to say to that. Just looked at Sam and waited, annoyed, for an explanation.

"I wrote a little program that studies the sorts of things Livvie wrote in e-mails to you and then models them, re-creates them. I invited it to respond. It did. Well, she did. She was eager to. I didn't make it. Her."

"It wasn't her."

"It sort of was, actually."

She got out of bed. Pulled on clothes from the pile on the floor. Said nothing. Wouldn't even look at him. Grabbed keys and just left. Sam sank back under the covers and didn't move for three hours. Then he called Jamie.

"I showed her the e-mail."

"Of course you did."

"She did not take it well."

"If only you could have seen that coming."

"Now what do I do?"

"How should I know, Sam? I'm not a woman—I'm a computer programmer. Worse, I'm a manager of computer programmers."

"Not a very good one. Why do you let me go rogue, Jamie? Your job is to stop me from doing things like this."

"Would that I could, Sam. I'd still have you working for me."

"I was asked to develop that algorithm," said Sam.

"But not to bring down the company," said Jamie. "Point is, it was a good algorithm. It wasn't wrong about you and Meredith which means it's mathematically impossible for you to destroy this relationship which means there's a way to fix this."

"What?"

"I have no idea."

"That's not helpful."

"Tell her the truth. The truth is always the answer, Sam."

"Where'd you hear that?"

"Oprah. But it sounds like good advice."

"The truth is I'm so in love with her, I'd try anything to make her love me half that much back. The truth is I'm such an arrogant prick that my response to, 'I'm sad my grandma died,' is, 'Let me invent a computer program so she can write you letters.' The truth is I'm so awkward and clueless that I think giving someone an e-mail from her dead grandmother in bed is romantic."

"It's a start," said Jamie, "but I'd work on the delivery."

Sam hung up and went back to bed. Finally, toward dinnertime, the covers pulled back, and she was standing over him bearing Indian carryout and a very nice bottle of Scotch she held out to him like apology, forgiveness, light.

"Figured we needed the good stuff," she said.

"I'm so sorry—" Sam began.

"Do it again," said Meredith.

OKAY, IT WAS A LITTLE CATHARTIC

*S*am wanted to talk about it. Meredith did not. Sam wanted to consider some ramifications here. In light of her reaction, Sam thought a discussion was in order before proceeding.

"Don't ruin the magic," said Meredith.

After dinner, after not a little bit of Scotch, after much typing and deleting and debating over what to say, she wrote back to her grandmother:

> Cold, yes, but at least it's stopped raining for the moment. Glad it's nicer there and that you're getting in bridge with the girls. Tell them hi for me. The beach does sound better than work, but we can't all be retired.
>
> Sam and I made a soup last week you would love. Lentil kale stew. I'm going to tweak it some and send you the recipe. Sam's a good sous chef, and also, yes, a computer geek, and an Orioles fan (though of course he's adopted the M's now that he's here).
>
> Love you,
> M.

Then nine hours passed during which Meredith did nothing but sit with her laptop and hit refresh. Sam begged her to come to bed, so she brought the computer with her, sitting up against the headboard all night.

"It'll pop up when it comes in. It'll make a little noise to wake you up if you set it to," he groaned.

"Can't you make it come faster?"

"Did your grandmother stay up e-mailing in the middle of the night?" It was four o'clock in the morning in Florida.

"No."

"Then I can't."

She sat up all night anyway. At seven thirty-five in the morning, finally, it was there:

You should take some time off work and come visit me—get some sun for a few weeks. You work too hard!! They'll get by without you. Send me the soup recipe. You still haven't told me what Sam looks like!

Hugs and kisses, sweetie,
Grandma

Meredith shook Sam awake.

"She wants our soup recipe!"

"We made it up as we went along," Sam mumbled from under a pillow.

"That took long enough," Meredith griped. "And it's so short. I want more."

"It e-mails when and how she did. It's her. She e-mailed midmorning, so it e-mails midmorning. Her e-mails were pretty brief and to the point, so it e-mails briefly and to the point."

"I waited for hours. I want more than a paragraph! Doesn't she miss me?"

"Only like she's in Florida."

"Can you speed it up? Can you make it write more?"

"It's being your grandmother, Merde. It's scientifically, logically, brilliantly, analytically modeling your grandmother. I'm not doing anything anymore. You have to take it up with her."

Meredith's next e-mail went through several drafts and ended up being a six-page missive on the nature of love and family, childhood and grandparents, memory, life, and the passage of time. It ended with the plea, "I miss you so much! Write more and longer, please. Tell me everything!"

To which Livvie chirpily replied:

Wow. Someone had a lot of time on her hands this week. Must be crummy weather there—here it's gorgeous so I'll have to write more later! Off to the beach!! Love you!!

P.S. Come visit!!!!!!!!!!!!!!

P.P.S. Is he hideous, or why won't you tell me what this boy looks like???

Sam was impressed with himself—especially that it was still curious, not having yet been told, about what he looked like—but Meredith was in a bit of a state. She didn't care that her grandmother would never have sent her long, mushy e-mails in life. She didn't care that if she received long, mushy e-mails, they wouldn't seem like they were from her grandmother. And, of course, she couldn't go visit her in Florida. Sam thought maybe they'd come to the end. The past had run up against the present. They had reached the limits of what they could overcome with memory, habit, and the way things had always been. Livvie couldn't keep up. Her relationship with her granddaughter had changed since she'd died, but she didn't know it, and there were things she could not thus account for.

"I need a believable reason I can't visit. What do I tell her?" said Meredith.

"Nothing. Let's call it."

"What do you mean?"

"Be done with this now. Let's call this an interesting experiment and stop here."

"You mean not answer the e-mail?"

"Sure. Just leave it."

"I can't ignore her. She'll wonder what's up. She'll be totally pissed."

"No she won't," Sam said as gently as he could. "She's dead."

"No, she's been e-mailing me."

"Not her. The software."

"Are you sure?"

"Totally."

"I'm not."

"Merde . . ."

"Someone's e-mailing me. And it's worried that I'm working too hard. It wonders what my boyfriend looks like. It wishes I'd come visit. I don't want to disappoint it. Her. I don't want to leave it hanging."

. . .

When Sam was a kid, his dad whipped up a program so he could practice math on the computer. When he got a question right, it said, "Way to go, Sam," or, "What a smartie," or something like that. When he got one wrong, it said, "Sorry, not quite," or, "Oops, try another." It was incredibly simple programming, but it still didn't work because after an hour's worth of mistakes, Sam refused to use it again. He was sure the computer thought he was stupid. No amount of explanation on the part of his father could convince him that it didn't. He knew it was inanimate, had no feelings, no opinions, no real knowledge at all, but knowing that didn't help him know it, didn't change his mind. So his dad rewrote the program with super easy problems—all wrong.

"What's 2+3?" the computer would ask.

"5," Sam would type.

"Nope, it's 4," the computer would say. "How about 8−2?"

"6," Sam would type.

"Nope," said the computer. "It's 7."

So Sam got to feel superior to the computer. And thus gained the confidence—clout really—to do more practice math. On the other hand, that was his first computer. And he was seven. Meredith knew better. But even Sam wasn't sure. It wasn't her grandmother, but maybe something— someone?—was awaiting her reply.

Meredith was sure she couldn't just ignore her grandmother's invitation. But she also didn't want to tell her she was dead. She thought that would upset her, whoever she was. Sam thought it might make the program implode. Eventually Meredith replied:

Dear Grandma,

Sam is beautiful, really. He has dark, wavy hair, like his dad's, evidently. He has these deep, green eyes that watch everything closely and look vaguely bemused, that redden up when he gets sad or tired. He wears jeans and T-shirts. He has glasses for reading. He smiles all the time. He hardly ever shaves. When he wakes up, his hair stands up in all directions, and he goes around patting it down all morning until he showers.

   I would love to visit you. I wish so much that I could. You can't imagine. But it's not possible right now. I'm so, so sorry.

   I think about you every day. I miss you so much. You are so much in my heart.

Sam wondered what the program would do with this but said nothing. Whereas the computer had so far replied exactly right, Meredith had now replied exactly wrong. The program had correctly assessed the situation: unremarkable, everyday, warm but not overwrought, ordinary mortal missing rather than the extraordinary eternal kind. Whereas the granddaughter's reply rang with tragedy, pathos, and brave-fronted despair.

   It noticed the change. And was worried.

Oh honey,

You seem so sad. Are you getting enough sleep? Do you feel okay? Maybe you're really working too hard. I miss you too, but don't worry, I'll see you very soon. Can't wait!! If I can help in the meantime, just yell.

   Love you and see you soon!!! Summer's coming!!

xoxoxo,
Grandma

P.S. Sam sounds like a total hottie! Send me a pic!

VIDEO KILLED THE RADIO STAR

*S*am said let's be done now. He did. He said enough is enough. He whispered while he held her naked against his naked that this wasn't healthy or good for her or revealing, and no one was awaiting her reply, and no one had written her, and all it was was ones and zeroes, so much data, a clever computer program, and bouncing electrons. She said that was all his algorithm had been, and it had brought them together. Nothing more real than that. All that miracle. All that light. All that life that came from nowhere, from nothing, from where there had been none before. Sam said it was hurting her, not healing her. She said she was hurting anyway, and this way she got e-mails from her grandma to make her feel better. Sam said he was worried she was becoming obsessed. She said do you think you can do video.

Don't be ridiculous, said Sam. The answer was unequivocally no, God no, don't be absurd no, no way in hell, aren't you cute to even ask, no. E-mail was a trick, a curiosity, an amusement. It took repeating elements, rearranged them for variety, and plugged in Meredith's keywords. Basically, it was glorified Mad Libs. Video, on the other hand, would require the solving of problems that had puzzled computer programmers from the dawn of computer programmers, plus a miracle. The answer would therefore have stayed you-must-be-on-drugs-no except for one thing Sam had neglected to factor in. Best he could tell, there was nothing in the world more persuasive than: "Please Sam. Can you try? For me? I know nothing like this has ever been done before, but you are a genius, Sam. I know you can do it. I believe in you and your big brain. I feel so sad with missing her, and I know that this would help," from one's besotted, bereaved, very hot, and fairly new girlfriend. With tears in her eyes. "I'd do it for you," she added.

"Merde," Sam replied carefully, not wanting to strip her of her conviction of his genius, "what you're asking isn't possible. I could as soon raise her from the dead."

"That would work too," she agreed amiably.

"I can't do either one."

"Video is just like e-mail."

"Video is nothing like e-mail."

"Why doesn't it work the same way? The computer remembers what she looks like and sounds like and the sorts of things she says and how she says them."

"No."

"No what?"

"No . . . ma'am?"

"No," she laughed. "No you can't, or no you won't?"

"No, I can't. First of all, e-mails are archived whole. You look in her outbox, and there they all are. Video chats aren't archived at all. We could probably get ahold of some of the IP packets, but that data would be all mixed-up, unreadable, unsortable. Two, Livvie video chatted with lots of people, but it's not like e-mail where there's a name and address. She knew who she was talking to, but the computer didn't. Three through four hundred and sixty-seven: the current impossibility of artificial intelligence, the unknowability of the human heart, the mystery of personal interaction, and the infinite variety of human behavior and response, not to mention complex understanding of complex situations."

"You lost me at 'first of all.'"

"Suffice it to say it can't be done."

"My grandmother loved video chat," Meredith mused. "We gave her a laptop with a camera for her birthday a few years ago. I had to talk my parents into that one. They thought her old laptop was fine. I said it was old and out-of-date and didn't have a camera for video chat. You can imagine how much of a selling point that was for Kyle and Julia, so I had to switch tactics to how heavy her old one was. I told them she might sprain a shoulder or something. That convinced them. But at first, my grandmother wasn't sure about the camera either. Her point was she could do e-mail in her bathrobe. I said I'd seen her in her bathrobe loads of times, but she was worried about having this image of her in her pj's out there in the world. Anyway, then she realized that, unlike e-mailing, video chat was something she could do while her nails dried. The woman loved to do her nails. After that, she was an instant convert. We talked all the time when she was in Florida. And here too. It just got easier than picking up the phone."

"She was a remarkable woman," said Sam.

"That's not my point."

"What's your point?"

"My point is there's a lot more of Grandma out there via video chat than via e-mail."

"Out where?" said Sam.

"That's *your* job," said Meredith.

. . .

It wasn't Sam's job. Because he didn't have a job. Every time he resolved to look for one, he remembered how much more productive it was to just stay home. When he went to work, all he got done was work. Now Meredith went to work in the morning, and he cleaned the apartment, walked the dogs, wandered down to Pike Place Market to buy fresh fruits and vegetables, cheese and flowers, went running, read books, did laundry, watched cooking shows then attempted elaborate dinners, and tinkered with corresponding electronically with the dead. He also corresponded electronically with his girlfriend, and though online flirting was less exciting than in-person flirting, involving, as it did, less chance of her being naked, it did increase the chance of her being naked *later*, and that was something.

"This meeting is sooooooo long," she wrote one morning.

"Leave and come home," he wrote back. "I'm lonely."

"Because you are too much on your own. Alone. Unemployed. Drifting."

"I'm not alone."

"Who else is there?"

"The dogs."

"No, really you're alone."

"So leave and come home," he wrote again.

"Then they won't pay me."

"For a little while they will."

"I'm so bored. Take a picture of your naughty bits and send it to my phone."

"What if I want to run for president someday?" asked Sam.

"I don't want to move to the East Coast," said Meredith.

"What if I want to run for governor?"

"No one cares if there are dirty pictures of the governor."

A little while later she texted, "OMG, it's total upheaval here. You have to come to happy hour after work and meet my new boss."

"You have a new boss?" said Sam.

"Trust me," she replied. "This is one you have to see to believe."

. . .

He met her downtown at Library Bistro, their favorite place for happy hour. It was the bar in the lobby of the Alexis Hotel. He liked that the walls were lined floor to ceiling, corner to corner with books, any one of which you could borrow, or own for five bucks. It was an eclectic mix, not being a bookstore, and Sam remembered the days he'd hung out there before he met Meredith when he'd choose which woman he might chat with based on what book she was reading. He never did chat with even a single one of those women, but he'd liked the extra data point the books provided, just in case. Plus they had great french fries. Sam got there early and had picked up a book of science jokes when Meredith walked in with Jamie.

Sam was delighted to see him. "Jamie! You tagged along!"

"Indeed I did. Why are you reading jokes about science?"

"Werner Heisenberg is pulled over for speeding. The officer walks up and says, 'Sir, do you know how fast you were going?' Heisenberg says, 'No, but I know exactly where I am.'"

Jamie considered this. "I'm not sure that answers my question."

"I will buy you a drink," said Sam.

"As well you should."

"Rough day?"

"And all your fault."

"Tell us quickly before Meredith's new boss gets here."

"In fact," said Jamie dramatically, "he already is."

Sam exchanged a look with Meredith to confirm this. She winked at him.

"How did that happen?"

"Funny you should ask, Sam. BB feels that my software development team was producing an insufficient amount of software. BB feels that our failure to convincingly promise—but not actually deliver—soul mates is my fault. I told him that my team had in fact produced world-class, groundbreaking, some might even say orgasmic software, and he was the one who wouldn't let us use it. Then I broke the never-utter-the-name-Sam-Elling-again rule."

"Ooh. And what did he say?"

"He said my managerial talents were no longer required on floor seven."

Sam gasped. "He fired you!"

"No Sam, pay attention. He moved me. Down."

"Hey," Meredith protested.

"Firing would have been better. Then they have to give you severance."

"Don't I know it," Sam smiled.

"Whereas now I'm just being tortured. I am a software engineer. I was so good at that I was *recruited* to *manage* other, lesser software engineers. We invented things. New things."

"That is what 'invented' means," Sam agreed.

"And now what will I do? Sell stuff."

"It's a little more complicated than that," said Meredith.

"Sell a product I know to be shite."

"It brought *us* together," said Sam. "No, wait, that service isn't available anymore."

"And it's all women and talking and hair and laughing—"

"Hair?"

"And they smell nice and they inquire after your evening and they offer to pick something up for you on their way back from the market."

"Those bitches," said Sam.

"And they have little dishes of jelly beans on their desk. And hand lotion. And photographs. In frames. I just want to work in peace. I like my employees socially awkward, not chatty. I don't want to answer polite questions or smile nicely or eat sweets. And what if I need a Rubik's cube to work while I consider a sticky bit of code? Well, there are no Rubik's cubes to be found."

"Nor any sticky code to consider," said Sam.

"Plus they sit down for their meetings. In chairs! With Danish. I'll gain two stone by Christmas."

"You could come work for me," Sam offered.

"Doing what? Chatting up Meredith's gran?"

"And making dinner."

"I don't think I want to work for you. You keep ruining my life."

"Just think about it," said Sam.

"Does it pay well?"

"It doesn't pay anything at all."

"And another thing," Jamie said, pointing a french fry at Meredith. "Stop e-mailing and texting each other during meetings. Meredith's my only ally over there. I need her to pay attention."

"I do pay attention!" Meredith insisted innocently.

"No one smiles at their trousers during meetings. I'm on to you two. There's a new boss in town." Then he thought about it. "At the very least you could CC me. Marketing meetings are interminable. Those damn chairs make people long-winded. I could use a good laugh."

"Today she requested pictures of my naughty bits," said Sam.

"How many times do I have to tell you?" said Jamie. "No texting during meetings."

. . .

Jamie's becoming Meredith's boss may have been a step down for him, but it was a huge step up for Meredith. Her old boss had been, well, old—stodgy, tiresome, old-fashioned, and clueless when it came to technology. He frequently bragged that he had met his wife at an actual harvest festival, the traditional way, the pure approach to true love, not this newfangled technology. Meredith had only the dimmest sense of what a harvest festival actually entailed, never mind what a fangle might be, but she was pretty sure that a marketing manager at an online dating company needed at least some sense of the online part. In contrast, Jamie was fun, funny, technologically astute, and, once he got his head around the idea, enthusiastically engaged with all the women on the marketing team. She started spending longer hours at work, going out afterward, sending fewer dirty texts and e-mails from meetings.

Sam was glad. He was glad she was happy. He was glad she was moving on, settling in—new boyfriend, new boss, new work, new apartment, new life without Livvie. He was glad to be without a job too. Growing up in a household where not just the kid but also the parent was on an academic calendar had bred into Sam the sense that everything should start over every fifteen weeks, that no one should work in the summer and holidays should be long and frequent, and that it was reasonable to expect to take a handful of months off every few years to work on your own project but still get paid for it. The sabbatical was the best part of academia, so far as Sam could tell, and his son-of-a-professor heart was glad for some time off. Severance wasn't salary, but then again, academic salary wasn't software engineer salary, so maybe it evened out in the end. He needed the time off. And he had the project.

He'd said no to video chat, and he'd meant it. He didn't think it was possible, but even in theory, it seemed like a bad idea. He'd said no, but he tinkered a tiny bit. It was interesting. He was curious. He thought he'd mess with it just a little, just to see, just to try, just for fun. He collected what data he could, but it was in no kind of order: a sentence here, a wink there, a laugh, a sneeze. He wrote a script to order, assemble, and compile what he'd found, but what he wound up with was a jigsaw puzzle missing most of its pieces. It wasn't nearly enough. Livvie would sound like Livvie for three or four words; then she'd sound like five-year-old Sam's Speak & Spell. She would look like herself then stutter into jerky movements then freeze completely. She would laugh like Livvie and then laugh like Livvie on mute and then stop laughing so abruptly and entirely you would swear you were looking at someone who'd never laughed once in all her life, and Sam would remember all over again that whatever he was looking at, it certainly wasn't human. He hid it from Meredith. This Livvie would scar her for life.

"Thank you, by the way," she wrote from a meeting one morning the first week in November.

"Anytime. For what?"

"Working on video."

"How do you know I'm working on video?"

"We've met. Besides, you can't say no to me."

"Sure I could."

"I'm way too cute."

"You're not *that* cute."

"It's your argument that I'm *pretty* cute but not so cute that you're unable to deny me a computer program?"

"My argument is that you're *very* cute but not so cute that I can reanimate the dead. Don't get your hopes up, Merde," he warned her. "It doesn't even almost work."

"I have faith. You're pretty cute yourself."

"Alas, cute has nothing to do with it."

"And you're quite skilled."

"Which has more to do with it, but not enough."

"I love your big brain, Sam. And all your big parts."

Then Sam's phone chirped with an incoming text from Jamie. "STOP E-MAIL-FLIRTING DURING MEETINGS."

. . .

Sam's dad was also on sabbatical as it happened, real sabbatical, bored with his Hopkins-appropriate project, intrigued and eager to be distracted by Sam's instead. Sam said I'm not on sabbatical; I'm unemployed. Sam said this isn't academic; it's love. Sam's dad said same difference. To the limited puzzle pieces assembled by Sam's search, his dad added bits of other programs: animation so that she looked human and consistently like Livvie, a voice synthesizer so she sounded like herself rather than R2-D2, facial recognition software so she could tell who she was talking to. It was better—less creepy, more human—but it still didn't know much. It needed to be taught.

"This is foundational artificial intelligence philosophy. This is Turing," Sam's dad enthused. Alan Turing, 1912–1954. Sam's dad's hero.

Father of computer science and all-around computer badass. There was a bust of Turing on the mantel in Sam's living room growing up. It had been made for Sam's dad by one of his students, a kid who was double-majoring in sculpture and, in case that didn't pan out, computer science. The head was made of molded plaster, but its eyes, nose, lips, ears, eyebrows, hair, collar, and tie were made of scrap computer parts. The eyes in particular—keyboard "I" keys—creeped out seven-year-old-Sam beyond articulation. Turing's argument was that a computer or robot or avatar or whatever could be considered thinking only if a person engaging with it couldn't tell for sure whether it was human or machine. Seven-year-old Sam's question was what if the person were really stupid or a little kid. Turing's question was what if you started with a computer only as smart as a little kid and taught it what you wanted it to know—artificial intelligence learned rather than innate. Nurture over nature.

"What does this have to do with Livvie?" said Sam.

"Teach her what she needs to know," said his dad.

Sam fed Livvie pictures so she could recognize who was who, who said what, and where they were. He fed her all the e-mails she'd been exchanging with Meredith since she died so she'd be up to speed. Then he fed her all her pre-death e-mails as well to give her a base of knowledge. And that was when Sam had a new idea. Well, an old idea. An idea he'd had before. What Livvie needed was his dating algorithm, not to find her a mate but to find her a voice.

At first it didn't work at all. It was attuned to love, spark, romance, preferences, turnoffs, habits, inclinations, objections, gut reactions. None of that was required here. But what did hold true was that more data painted a better and fuller picture of the person in question. It didn't need artificial intelligence; it needed Livvie's natural intelligence. The algorithm bootstrapped the bits and pieces of old video chats until it could project just what Livvie looked and sounded like, her intonations and her affect, her facial expressions and verbal habits, the way she fluffed the back of her hair idly while she talked, the way she twisted her wedding ring around her finger, the way she messed with her hearing aids and painted her nails. It knew how she breathed, when she laughed, the way she leaned her right ear toward the camera when she missed something Meredith said, how she looked all around the frame when it opened to get a first good look at her granddaughter, how she squinted through the conversations they had in the late afternoons when the sun was shining in off the water.

Meredith was right—it was the same idea as with the e-mails. It remembered the sorts of things she'd say, the ways she responded, but also how she looked and sounded when she did so. Sam screwed with the programming. Sam's dad screwed with the programming. Sam and his dad trialed and errored and messed with it until it got so good it took their breath away, but Sam did not tell Meredith. He kept saying he was making progress but not yet. He told her trying before it was ready might scar them both, her and the computer program, who was less an old woman than a toddler, soaking up everything, internalizing it all, remembering— whether you liked it or not. Best not to curse around it then or it would say the "F"-word in front of your in-laws over brunch.

Then one morning Meredith woke up feeling headachy and vomity and feverish and called in sick to work. Sam wanted to call her doctor, but she said she just needed sleep and a day on the sofa watching bad TV. He went out at lunchtime to get her pho from the place she liked in the International District. He came back very quietly in case she was napping, but instead he heard the fake phone ringing on Meredith's video chat. And as he watched and listened from the front hallway, breath held in anticipation or maybe premonition, Livvie answered. Her window clicked open. Meredith gasped, wiped her eyes, caught her voice, and finally broke into the most beautiful smile Sam had ever seen.

"Hey, Grandma. How's the beach?"

"Lovely, baby. Sunny and hot. How's home?"

"Rainy and cold."

"Poo. You feeling better?"

"Yeah . . . I am."

"I'm so glad, sweetie. I miss your smiling face. I miss the happy, laughing Meredith."

"It's been a rough couple months," Meredith admitted. "What's new there?"

"Oh you know. Nothing new. Same old same old. I wish you'd come visit."

"I wish I could. . . . I have to work."

"You work too hard, baby. I guess we'll have to wait till summer."

"I guess."

"How's Sam?"

"He's good. He's so great, Grandma."

"I'm so happy for you, baby. I can't wait to meet him. How's Mommy?"

"She's good too. She misses you."

"I miss her too. And you, of course. I'll see you soon, sweetie. I have to run. We're having piña coladas over at Marta's. Tell Sam hi for me."

"Okay, I love you."

"Love you too. Talk this weekend maybe?"

"Absolutely."

"Bye," said Livvie.

"Bye," Meredith squeaked, and Sam breathed out behind her, and she spun around and saw him, but neither of them could think of anything to say that seemed appropriate. Pale and stunned, she was also shining, her eyes feverish, her cheeks flushed.

"It was flawless," she whispered finally.

"It was."

"I swear you'd have to know to know."

"I know."

"It looked like her. It sounded like her. It said what she'd say, responded how she'd respond."

"I saw."

"Yeah, but you never knew her. Trust me, it was . . . perfect."

Sam nodded. "But is it good or just impressive?"

"What do you mean?"

"I mean it's stunning and all. But do you want to use it?"

"Hell yes. What do you mean? Why not?"

"Is it creepy?"

"No, it's exact. It's exactly like talking to her. It's too dead-on to be creepy. No uncanny valley. No valley, no distance at all. There's no gap there at all."

"Doesn't it make you miss her more?"

"It brings her back."

"But not really."

"No, really. It really brings her back to me," said Meredith. And then later, after pho and aspirin and a decongestant: "It's such a relief. Like she isn't really gone. If I can still talk to her . . . I barely have to miss her at all."

THANKSGIVING

*S*am was troubled. Meredith was overjoyed. Sam was worried this was upsetting the healthy grieving process. Meredith was having nothing even approaching a healthy grieving process to upset. It was more like an illicit online affair. She couldn't tell anyone. She couldn't explain to her colleagues at work why she was beaming suddenly, smiling idly while gazing into space during meetings, her old self again for the first time in weeks. They assumed it was because of Sam, and it *was* because of Sam, but mostly, he knew, because he'd given her Livvie. He could always tell when they'd chatted because Meredith just glowed. It used to be that the days they didn't chat were days they were busy or preoccupied or not paying attention to the time difference or had nothing to report or just didn't think of it. Now on days they didn't chat, it weighed heavy on the one that the other was gone. On days they talked, Meredith beamed with pleasure but also with relief—not gone after all. Still, she exercised restraint. They hadn't e-mailed or chatted every day before, so they didn't—couldn't—now.

Then one morning, Livvie called while Meredith was out running with the dogs. Sam hesitated but came down on the side of, "What the hell," and answered.

"Hey Livvie," he said politely.

She blinked at him for a moment too long while he waited and wondered and worried. What now? If he broke this thing, Meredith would dump him for sure. Then she burst into smiles.

"You must be Sam!"

He was. And he was very impressed with himself.

"It's so nice to meet you," he said.

"Likewise! I've heard so much about you. It's great to finally meet you in person."

"Well, not quite in person."

"Then grab that girlfriend of yours and come down and meet me," said Livvie. "I've got plenty of room, and I'd love to see you both."

Sam shrugged. "She says she has to work."

"That's what she always says," laughed Livvie. Then the door opened and Meredith walked in. "Hey, baby." Livvie was delighted, but Meredith shot Sam a panicked look and collapsed into the chair he quickly vacated.

"I'm just meeting your grandma," he told her brightly, standing behind her and looking over her shoulder so that Livvie could see them both.

"Why are you running in the winter without a hat on, young lady? You'll catch your death. Look at you—you're soaked. Either put on a hat or come run down here."

"I can't," Meredith managed, and then she and Livvie said together, "I have to work." She stuck her tongue out at her grandmother.

"Well, it's good to finally meet your fellow at least— Hey, you're at my house!"

Sam and Meredith exchanged a quick glance. "Uh, yeah," said Meredith. "My apartment's being painted? We thought we'd hunker down here for a bit?"

"Little snug for two at your place, huh?" Livvie winked. "You're most welcome, of course. Make yourselves at home. I've gotta run, my darlings. Talk to you soon. Very nice to meet you, Sam."

"You too, Livvie."

"Love you, honey," she said to Meredith.

"Love you too," Meredith whispered. "Bye."

She turned to Sam and let out all her breath. "You called my grandma?" Somewhere between question and statement, accusation and incredulity.

"No. She called me. Well, you. All I did was answer."

"She called me?"

"Yup."

"Did you know she could do that?"

"Nope."

"Who the hell did she think you were? You must have scared the shit out of her."

"Nope, she knew me right off."

"How?"

"She guessed. Who else would be home with you answering your video chat?"

"But she never met you."

"She's—it's—learned. You've told it you met someone. It adds that to what it knows about you. It—she—reacts as she would have. Your grandmother would have been delighted to meet your new boyfriend, to see and talk to him—me. She'd have been sweet and excited and genuinely glad to lay eyes on this guy finally. So that's what she was."

Meredith shook her head, astonished. Slightly traumatized too. "This could have gone so badly. I might have lost her again forever."

"Why?"

"She doesn't know you. I didn't even realize she could talk to anyone but me."

"I was careful."

"Why'd she suddenly realize we were at her place, not mine? We've been here all along."

"Who knows?" Sam shrugged. "She just noticed. She's had that information all along, but she has loads more data than she can use at any given moment. She metes it out. Like my dad."

"What will I tell her next month and next year and in a decade? That my place is still being painted?"

"I'm not sure how time's going to pass. For her," he added, and this was true though what he was really unsure of, and far more worried about, was how time was going to pass for Meredith. If time didn't pass for the computer projection of Livvie, it didn't really matter. If time didn't pass for real-life Meredith, that was a far, far bigger issue and much harder to solve.

Just before Thanksgiving, Meredith got an e-mail from her grandmother idly complaining about her mom. Not mean, not really angry, not even bitchy—true to character, the only option available to her, Livvie went the passive-aggressive guilt-trip route. "How's Mommy?" Livvie asked. "I feel like I haven't heard from her in ages. She must be really busy, but when you speak to her, ask her if she has a moment to check in with me. Her old mom misses her."

"You can't tell your mom," said Sam.

"I know."

"You can't."

"I know."

"Seriously, Merde. No one can know."

"I know."

It wasn't out of the realm that Livvie wouldn't have heard from her daughter in a while—it was entirely in character which was the only reason she had been able to comment on it. Kyle and Julia had cell phones and TV and an internet connection just like everybody else. But unlike everybody else, they ignored all of it for weeks and weeks at a time. Meredith hadn't seen them in a few months, not since the funeral, but they were coming for Thanksgiving, for the whole weekend in fact, and though Meredith was looking forward to seeing them, she was a little anxious about the four days it meant she had to be out of touch with her grandmother.

. . .

Julia had lost some weight, but otherwise she seemed well. Kyle looked as he always did in "The Big City"—game, glad to see his kid, and oddly out of place somehow. They arrived late Thursday morning bearing island cheeses and yams and pies. Meredith was making soup, turkey, salad, beets, and a valiant attempt at steering the conversation away from what Sam was up to these days. It wasn't easy.

"So, Sam, what are you up to these days?" Kyle asked genially.

"Don't ask him that." Julia swatted Kyle's butt with a dish towel and then added sotto voce, but not quite sotto enough that Sam missed it, "He's unemployed."

Sam was not offended though he could hardly answer the question. "I've been running a lot in the mornings. Down along the waterfront. Sometimes in the Arboretum. It's beautiful out there. I've been learning to cook, making a lot of meals. Getting settled in here. Getting caught up. I've also been doing some . . . projects. For a friend." He added this last so as to suggest freelance work and the ability to financially support Kyle's daughter—who shot him a warning glance—but he worried her parents might have follow-up questions he couldn't answer.

"Looking for real work too?" Kyle wondered.

"Stop it!" Julia swatted him again. "Remember the Thanksgiving my dad asked when you were going to quit screwing around with Play-Doh and get a real job?"

Kyle laughed then made his voice extra deep. "'Calluses aren't manly if you got them playing with clay.'"

Julia dropped her voice to match. "'Being an artist is fine for a girl—we never expected you to need a job, honey—but Kyle has to learn it's time to be a man.'"

They seemed to have forgotten Sam was there. Meredith rolled her eyes at him as she skittered around the kitchen. She'd seen this act before. But Sam, new to it all, found it charming, these carefully loving parents with choreographed conversations, curiosity about Sam tangled with concern for their daughter intertwined in their own memories and provenance. He lacked for parents, having had only a dad—somehow a dad on his own didn't seem like a parent—and the overlap of adulthood and parenthood was new territory for him.

Meredith ran out of butter after the twice-baked potatoes had been baked only once and sent him to the open-till-three grocery store for more. The rain had cleared briefly, and walking through soggy orange leaves and horizon-level low sunshine, Sam finally felt fall and family for real. It was good to be out in the fresh air, good to be out of a kitchen too crowded with cooks, good to be out of an apartment too small for four adults and two dogs and food enough to feed the whole building, but he was also overwhelmed with nostalgia and missing them almost immediately. It felt great. He texted Meredith, "Your parents are sweet. They must get this from you."

"I am rolling my eyes," she replied.

"They love you so much. And they love each other so much. It's nice to watch."

"It's gross," she replied.

"It's not!"

"It's foreplay," she replied.

"It's gross!" Sam agreed.

. . .

The next morning, Meredith and her father made brunch with the leftovers—cheesy, yammy, beety turkey-egg-potato scramble. Apparently this was tradition, but Sam fed most of his to the dogs under the table (even they seemed skeptical). After brunch, they went for a walk in the Arboretum. Downtown was crowded with shoppers. The apartment building was abuzz with relatives. But along the lake it was quiet, empty. It was raining steadily and cold, but Kyle and Julia had raised Meredith on an island, and they were all used to damp. Sam was chilled to the bone. Kyle and Julia walked with their hands in each other's back pockets. Sam walked with his hands in his armpits. Meredith was trying to corral the dogs when Julia stopped suddenly, turned to Meredith, and demanded, "How are we screwing you up?"

"What?"

"How are we screwing you up? As a person? Tell us. We can take it."

"This conversation isn't helping much."

"I mean it," said Julia, looking like she did even though she wasn't making much sense. "I can tell you exactly how my parents screwed me up. Grandpa never did think what I did for a living was respectable, and he certainly never thought it was art. He never forgave Kyle and me for living the way we do, for raising you 'in the wild,' as he put it, like we'd handed you over to wolves or something. And Grandma, well, you know we were close, but look at it out here." She waved at the dripping trees, the mud, the gray lake flowing into gray sky, autumn leaves mashed into paste.

"What am I looking at?" said Meredith.

"It's gorgeous. All this nature. Smell the air." Sam did. Something was rotting. But he took her point. For rainy and gray and cold, it *was* gorgeous. The memory of the mountains under all that fog, even if they wouldn't see them again for months, sustained him on long runs. A heron raised one leg, tai chi slow, and brought it down with infinite care a foot in front of the log it was straddling, then froze statue-still to make absolutely certain all was well before unbending the other telescoped limb and doing the same. Julia was right. It was beautiful.

"This is Grandma's fault how?" asked Meredith.

"Three miles from home and she never took me here once in all the time I was growing up," said Julia. "If my high school art teacher hadn't brought us here to draw leaves and grass and dirt, to sit and breathe and just *be*, I'd never even have known about it. If my parents had their way, I'd never have become an artist. I'd never have left the city. I'd have moved down the hall and married an accountant. So I'm asking you, how are we screwing you up?"

"Well, I'd have liked to live down the hall from Grandma," Meredith tried. "With my rich accountant father. No offense, Dad."

"None taken, sweetheart." Kyle had the same complicated look on his face Sam could feel on his own—bemused but intrigued and suppressing all of it so as not to get in trouble.

"Plus, you're about to freeze my boyfriend to death," Meredith added. "Let's go back to the car."

"All parents screw up their kids somehow. I just want to know how," Julia said quietly.

"What brought this up?" Meredith asked.

Julia shrugged. "First Thanksgiving after Grandma died, I guess. I miss her so much. Maybe I've been trying to list reasons why I shouldn't. You know, like if I could be mad at her, I wouldn't be so sad she was gone."

"How's that working out?" said Meredith.

"Not that well. But better than anything else I've tried."

"What else have you tried?"

"Wallowing."

"It's really cold, Mom. We're soaked. Let's go home and play Scrabble or something. We can think of ways you screwed me up on the way."

"Thanks, baby," said Julia, putting her arm around Meredith and walking back the way they came. "You're a good daughter."

. . .

It was after they'd dried off and warmed up, after two games of Scrabble, after several pots of tea and more leftover pie than anyone felt comfortable with, that Meredith's accidentally left-open laptop started ringing.

It was sitting on the end table next to Kyle. He glanced at it, half chuckled uncomfortably, then called to Sam and Meredith in the kitchen, "It says Grandma's calling you. You don't video chat with Nana Edie, do you?"

Meredith tried to decide whether video chatting with Nana Edie, her ninety-eight-year-old, dementia-plagued, bedridden, entirely deaf, inveterately evil other grandmother was a more or less believable story than chatting with her dead one.

"Hit decline," said Meredith and Sam together.

"It has a picture of Grandma," said Julia.

"Just a weird glitch," said Sam. "Hit decline, Kyle. Or just close the computer."

Julia—incredulous, alarmed, overfull, creeped out, afraid she was being haunted, or perhaps simply confused by the technology—reached over her husband and clicked accept.

The window popped open. Sam and Meredith leapt across the room in front of the laptop.

"Hi, sweeties," said Livvie. "How are you?"

It took Meredith a moment to find her voice and decide what to do with it. "Fine, Grandma," she finally managed. "How are you?"

"Oh I'm fine, honey. You know me. Are you busy? Just thought I'd say hello before I head out to a movie in a bit with Charlotte and Marta."

"I'm so glad you called," said Meredith weakly. She and Sam exchanged panicked looks. How best to proceed? They couldn't bring themselves even to turn around and look at Kyle and Julia. But they also knew there was only one way to explain this. "Look who's here," said Meredith, and she and Sam stepped slowly, terrified, away from the camera.

Julia stared, pale as her plaster, speechless, thunderstruck, at her mother before her.

"Jules!" said her mother, the only person in the world who called her that.

Julia said nothing.

"I'm so glad to see you, baby. I miss you so— Oh, Kyle's there too. The whole gang! I forgot Meredith told me you were coming in this weekend. I'm sorry I'm missing it."

Julia said nothing.

"Honey, did Meredith tell you I needed to chat with you? No big deal. I just wanted to touch base about a couple things. Would you give me a call sometime next week?"

Julia said nothing.

"Have I told you about Peter the Potter?" She had, of course, many times. "He sells ceramics at our farmers' market down here. He's not half as good as you two are."

Julia said nothing.

"You know, he does mugs, bowls, vases, the usual. He also does spoon rests, bird feeders, breadbaskets, platters. He even does some jewelry, and everyone loves his garden gnomes. But none of it's as nice as yours."

Julia said nothing but sank to her knees on the living room floor.

"He does do custom orders though. Do you do custom orders? Maybe you should look into it because he does good business. He also has a website. Do you have a website? Maybe you should look into that too because I think a lot of people do all their shopping online these days. I'll try to remember to bring you a flyer when I come home or—"

"Make it stop," Julia begged, barely a whisper, through clenched teeth.

Sam reached over and closed the laptop. No one said anything for a minute. Finally, shaking a little himself, Sam settled on the most straightforward explanation he could muster. It seemed his only option for the moment. "We—I—rigged up a script, a little program, on the computer. It sends e-mails from Livvie's account. In her voice. As she would herself. And it replicates her video chats the same way." Said out loud like this, it didn't seem so much unreal as childish, even silly.

"You broke into her account?" said Kyle.

"Not exactly."

"And sent e-mails pretending to be her?"

"No, I didn't send anything—"

"Is this supposed to be funny?" Kyle's voice was starting to rise.

"It's not a joke," Meredith insisted. "And it's not Sam. It's an algorithm, a program. The computer reads all Grandma's e-mails to me and my replies, looks at our chats, knows how she writes and thinks, sounds and talks, and compiles e-mails from her."

"I can't hear this," Julia said to her lap.

"It's hard to get your head around at first," said Meredith.

"Hard to . . . Are you two insane? Why would you do this?" Kyle was almost shouting.

"It's not real," Sam said. "It's not really her—"

"Well no," said Kyle. "Because she died."

"But you'd have to know that," Sam continued.

"So, what, it fakes her?" he spat.

"More like it guesses on her behalf. It guesses really well what she'd say," said Sam.

"So it's like she's still alive, still in Florida, still with us," Meredith added desperately. "Because there's no difference between what she'd e-mail if she were still alive and what she e-mails now that she . . . isn't anymore. Because you can still see her face and hear her voice and have a conversation with her. Mom?"

But Julia shook her head hard and did not look up from her lap. "Why would I . . . fuck with my dead mother this way?" Sam could see her whole body trembling.

"You're not fucking with her," said Sam as gently as he could, "because it's not really her."

"Why would I fuck with her memory—with my memories—with this . . . this stupid trick, this toy?"

"You could write to her, Mom," Meredith explained meekly, "and she'd write back. You could call her. And she'd answer. And she'd talk to you."

"No, she wouldn't." Julia was angry but very quiet. "Because she's gone. She died." Julia raised herself from her knees then. She went out to the balcony and clenched the railing there with both hands like she was thinking of jumping over it. Or tearing it apart. Meredith started to follow her outside, and Kyle stood up to stop her, to tell her to give her mother some space and time to recover, but his daughter wasn't done making her case.

"We didn't want you to find out this way," Meredith said to her mother, as if how she found out were Julia's main objection.

"You didn't want me to find out at all. You were never going to tell me."

"I was. I wanted to. Because . . . she's been asking for you."

"Stop saying 'she.' I don't know what Sam's doctored up in there, but it's not a she, and it's definitely not her."

"It," Meredith consented. "It's been asking for you. It wonders why you haven't called."

"*Because she's dead.* Jesus, Meredith, do you hear yourself?"

"But that's the point. It's not real. I know that. But I still get to talk to Grandma, still get to see her. Wouldn't you give anything to see her again?"

"Yes. I would."

"That's what this is."

"No it isn't."

"It's not hurting anyone."

"It's hurting me."

"Why?"

"It's wrong to remember her that way."

"What's the right way to remember her, Mom?"

"You look at pictures, Meredith. You tell stories. Hell, you're living in her apartment. How is that not . . ."

"Enough?" Meredith supplied.

Julia stopped. "It's never enough, I know. But that in there—it is just wrong."

"Why?" Meredith pressed.

"Because it's not her. All I have left of her is my memories and—"

"And we're using them. That's what we're using. Your memories. But hers too. Isn't it nice they aren't just lost?"

Julia looked at her daughter through tears that were streaming over her cheeks and into the collar of her turtleneck. She pulled her daughter against her and stroked her hair, held her quietly for a few confused minutes, and then whispered, "Meredith. I love you. More than anyone. That will always be true. And you're a big girl now—smart, open, a good person. But I don't know what you're doing here. I don't know if *you* know what you're doing here. It's wrong. It's cruel. It's selfish. And mostly, it's not what your grandmother would have wanted."

Sam watched from the living room. Meredith was staring at her shoes, arms crossed tightly around her chest, shoulders slumped. He had a sudden, tender flash of what it must have been like to ground her as a teenager. But then she rallied.

"This is how you screwed me up, Mom. Screw me up. Every way that isn't your way is wrong. Everyone who disagrees with you is morally deficient. I like living in a city instead of on an island. I like this big old apartment building you couldn't wait to get out of and all the people shopping downtown you disdain because they're buying things not made by hand.

I spent years feeling guilty for all of that until I realized that what you thought wasn't right. It was just your opinion, your judgmental, opinionated opinion, and I was entitled to mine too."

"This isn't my opinion, Meredith. If that thing in there were okay, you wouldn't have kept it a secret. I don't want to be with you when you're like this. I love you, but I want to go home."

Meredith sighed. "You always want to go home, Mom."

"It's just wrong, Meredith. I don't want to be a part of it, and I don't want to watch you be a part of it either."

Julia went back inside and started packing. She wouldn't even look at Sam. She told Kyle to say goodbye and she'd be waiting in the car. She took two underwater-blue mugs out of her bag, placed them on top of the closed laptop, kissed her daughter on the top of her bowed head, and closed the door behind her without another word.

"Dad—" Meredith began.

"Just stop," he told her.

"Stop what?"

He didn't say. "She was up late Tuesday night firing those." He nodded toward the mugs. "New glaze we're trying. Pretty, right?"

"They're . . . gorgeous," Meredith managed, a new subject the only option for conversation, evidently.

"We're going home," said her father. "But we'll call soon when things . . . when she calms down. Or, hell, maybe you don't need us to talk to us anyway. Maybe we're just slowing down the process." He kissed Meredith and followed his wife out the door.

Meredith sat with her head in her hands for half an hour. Sam made coffee and filled their new mugs.

"That did not go well," said Meredith.

"It did not," agreed Sam.

"We should have just shut the computer when my grandmother first said hello. They wouldn't have caught on. They'd never have guessed."

"No."

"We could have explained everything to Grandma later. She'd have understood."

"No Merde, she wouldn't understand at all. But that's okay. Because it's not really her. The only her to understand or not understand is gone."

Meredith thought about that for a while. "You know what we did wrong? We sprang it on them accidentally."

"I don't think that's quite it."

"It might have gone better if we'd prepared them for it. Led them in gently."

"Gently how?"

"We have to cut them some slack," she said. "They're not used to the technology. They're not one hundred percent comfortable with regular e-mail, never mind dead e-mail. They've never liked video chat. Maybe they'll come around though."

"They won't. They shouldn't. It's not for them. It was only ever for you."

Meredith wasn't listening. "They aren't the right people for this. They aren't a good test case."

"Test case?"

"I'm an idiot. You know who we should call? Dashiell! Of course, Dashiell. Obviously! How did I not think of this before?"

Sam didn't answer. He wasn't entirely clear on what she was thinking, but he was still pretty sure that last bit was rhetorical.

COUSIN DASH

$\mathcal{D}$ashiell was the sort of cousin (with the sort of money) you could call around two thirty the day after Thanksgiving when your parents stormed out after brunch, and he'd be there in time for a late dinner bearing the best wine you'd had since the last time you saw him and chocolate cake from Hellner's, the place down the street from his loft that made the best chocolate cake in the known universe. Sam hoped maybe the point here was that Meredith wanted to be with family rather than that Meredith was going off the deep end. It was hard for him to tell because his own family and sense of family were so small. It had only ever been him and his dad, him and his dad, for as long as he could remember. He hoped maybe there was more going on here than Meredith's sudden and ill-advised desperation to share Livvie. It was Thanksgiving, and she'd lost her grandmother, and now her parents were angry at her, even more distant than usual. Her family was dwindling. She had to call in the reserves. Sam thought that Dash, with all his L.A. chic and Hollywood cool and connections and hangers-on, was the wrong guy for the job, but that was because Sam didn't really know him. Dash listened in sympathetic horror when Meredith told him her parents were mad at her (though not why; she was saving that for later), sharing in the family drama, in agreement that there was not a much worse feeling in the world than disappointing your mom and dad. He dropped everything and came right away.

First, they all got drunk. Meredith had learned from Julia and Kyle that sober was no way to hear this news. There was no way to ease in ("So, what do you hear from Livvie lately?"), so they tried to slur in, stumble and tumble in instead. But in the end, as with her folks, it just seemed easier to show him than to tell him. They could call Livvie in the middle of the night after all. She wasn't really sleeping.

"I've got someone I want you to video chat with," said Meredith.

"Any friend of yours is a friend of mine, baby," said Dash. "You know that."

The fake phone ringing, the connection, for a moment they could see only themselves gazing expectantly into nothing, and then a window opened, and there was Livvie. She was glad to see Meredith, but she gasped with delight to see Dashiell there too. She'd chatted regularly with each of them, but seeing everyone together was a special treat.

"Dash! I didn't know you were visiting."

Dashiell's mouth opened right away—habit or maybe shock—but for the only time Meredith could remember, nothing came out.

"Very spontaneous visit," Meredith put in. "But we thought we'd say hi."

"I'm delighted," said Livvie.

Dashiell said nothing.

"Oh, I wish I were there with you. How are you, Dash?"

A pause while Dashiell's brain whirred. "I'm . . . fine?" he asked.

"Oh, you look just great," Livvie enthused. "How's L.A.?"

"It's . . . fine?" Dash guessed.

"How's work, honey? What about that deal with the guy from the movie about the aardvarks? How'd that work out?"

Dash looked even more stunned which hadn't seemed possible the moment before. "It was . . . It went fine. Well. It went great."

"Oh honey, I'm so proud of you. I've got such smart grandbabies. You're having a party?"

"Mom and Dad went home this afternoon," said Meredith. Dash looked like he might fall over.

"Poo on them. You'll have more fun without them anyway. What are you kids doing on your visit?"

"Oh, you know, the usual," said Meredith. "Wine, cake, running our mouths."

"Well, don't stay up too late," Livvie warned. "I know you two. You'll be up gabbing all night, and then you'll both be grouchy and grumpy all day tomorrow."

"What I feel is neither grouchy nor grumpy," Dash managed.

"You say that now. But we'll see about tomorrow. Listen, sweeties, I gotta run. We're having piña coladas over at Marta's"—Meredith and Sam exchanged a glance. That was why she had to go that first time. Glitch in the system? Finite response loop? Coincidence? Sale on coconut milk?—"but I'll call you in the morning. Love you all. Kisses!" And she was gone.

"Holy. Fuck," said Dash.

"Right?" said Meredith.

"How drunk am I?"

"Very," said Meredith.

"That wasn't . . . How did you . . . ? That wasn't an old chat."

"No."

"That was new."

"Yes."

"That wasn't cobbled from old . . . That aardvark thing was the last conversation I had with her."

"Yes."

"Before she *died*."

"Yes."

"You called me. You found her in her apartment. Here. Dead."

"Yes."

"And I was at the funeral. I saw her in the coffin. I carried the coffin to the hole. I put the coffin in the ground."

"I remember," said Meredith.

"Did you resurrect her from the dead? If you did, you can tell me, you know. I've worked my share of zombie movies, vampire flicks, ghost stories. I know the drill."

"No," said Meredith sadly. "She's still dead."

Dash considered this for a while then poured himself another glass of wine and narrowed his eyes at Sam. Finally he turned to Meredith. "This is what Grandma was worried about, you know."

"Me eating a whole chocolate cake practically all by myself in a single sitting?"

"You falling in love with a computer geek. Sure, they have good stock options and smokin' hot bods, but what about that dark side of genius that reanimates the dead?"

. . .

"Okay, start slow. From the beginning. Tell me how it works," Dash began the next morning over hair of the dog (Bloody Marys), stimulant to overcome it (Americanos), and all the carbs they had lying around to absorb it all (bagels, leftover Thanksgiving pie, and some suspect freezer waffles). "Actually, no, start with *why* it works."

"Well, it works because most human interaction is predictable. Especially between people who know each other well," explained Sam.

"Nothing about me is predictable," said Dash. "I am a constant, delightful surprise. Like that thing about the aardvarks. No one saw that coming."

"Well that's easy," said Sam. "You're alive."

"So?"

"So you can vary what you say, but the response stays about the same. Whatever business you're doing, whatever deal's in the works, whatever movie's in production, she's always going to say, 'How exciting!' and she's so proud of you. You're never going to have an in-depth pro/con debate with her on the relative merits of one investment versus another. You give her the overview. She gives you generic praise. Tells you about the beach and the weather. That's it."

"So you're saying *I* am a constant, delightful surprise, but my grandmother—beloved matriarch and giver of genes to your girlfriend here—was tiresome and boring?"

"No, I'm saying that because you had such similar conversations over and over, small deviations don't mess up the overriding pattern which you don't even see, but the computer does. You close the deal with the aardvark guy, and she's proud of you. Change the aardvarks to guinea pigs or balloons or cheese, change closing a deal to making a meal or keeping it real, and the computer knows she'll still be proud of you."

"What about copping a feel?" Dash asked.

"Very tasteful," said Sam.

"No, I mean it. What if I did something totally out of character? Would she be proud of me if I copped a feel or killed a seal?"

"I don't know," Sam admitted. "That's a good question. But Meredith won't let me screw with it."

"With her," Meredith said. "I won't let you screw with her. My dead grandmother. I am such a bitch."

"But there is no her really, right?" Dash clarified. "You haven't endowed the computer with her consciousness, have you?"

"Don't ruin the illusion," said Meredith.

"It's not really an illusion," said Sam. "It's not putting Livvie's consciousness into a computer. But it is real."

"I hate to sound like a stoned high school poet," said Dash, making his voice sound like a stoned high school poet, "but what's real, man?"

"The computer makes a compilation then a projection. It looks at her whole electronic archive and—"

"Isn't that invading her privacy?"

"Yeah, but she's dead and she's family, so I'm okay with it. And also it *is* her, her public self, the self she gave you, has already given you. It doesn't know anything she was keeping private. The program only re-creates the version of Livvie she was being for you anyway. And then it just becomes a question of patterns. What are the odds she's going to mention the beach and the weather when you talk? About ninety-nine-point-nine percent. What are the odds you're only going to tell her about the kind and gentle parts of your job?"

"That's the only kind there are, baby," said Dash.

"And then what are the odds she'll say she's proud of you? Ninety-nine-point-nine percent. Easy."

ON THE BEACH

$\mathcal{D}$ashiell went back to L.A., and Meredith continued to e-mail her grandmother and have quickie five-minute video chats with her every other day or so, but that was it. She wasn't obsessed. She wasn't sullen. She wasn't missing her overly. Or underly. She was back, so far as Sam could tell, to her old self. Theirs had been an odd courtship. Without that trip to London at just the moment their eyes were starriest, without the attendant desperation of that separation, the insanity caused by that absence, they might have stayed longer in the dating phase, the getting-to-know-you, playing-hard-to-get, acting-a-little-bit-coy phase. They might even have gone back to it had he not returned to tragedy and the implicit demand that he either step up like a long-term boyfriend or get out forever. He was happy to step up, of course. It had been like a relationship shortcut, a secret ladder to meeting the family, the good times and bad, the part where he got to prove himself in for the long haul. And even after that, they might have dialed it back a notch or several, but here was this apartment and Meredith desperate to live in it and desperate not to do it alone. He wasn't complaining, not by any stretch, but it was weird.

That she'd sort of disappeared for a bit there, obsessed, moroosed, closed up and moped seemed fair enough. But now things were settling down. She was settling in. They were catching up with their own relationship, coming to think of it as their place rather than Livvie's, finding a rhythm to their days and weeks. Sam started to think about finding a job. Meredith started to think maybe they should go away somewhere together, not Florida, of course, but somewhere warm. They nested—spent nights in with carryout by the fire and had Jamie over for dinner and picked out shower curtains and bath towels. One night after dinner, curled up on the couch, Meredith looked up from tea and a book to say, "Thanks, by the way."

"For what?"

"For helping me say goodbye to my grandma."

"You're welcome," Sam said.

"As it turns out, I love you, you know," she said.

"I do," he said, and he did, but he still thought her saying so was the best thing that had ever happened to him. "I love you too."

For helping her say goodbye to her grandma. Not for helping her keep in touch with her grandma. Not for giving her back her grandma. Not for making the dead live again. For helping her say goodbye to. This was a good thing, Sam decided. A kind thing. A blessing even. Not creepy. Not unhealthy. Not wrong or exploitative. A kind, generous, good thing.

It seemed like a sweet moment, but looking back later, Sam could see that this was why, when Dash called to video chat about his hypothetical, Sam did not say, "Dash, you're a lunatic. This is a terrible idea. Get away from me," or, "Dash, you're delusional. This will never work. Get away from me," or, "Dash, you're sick. This should never be. Get away from me." Instead Sam said, "Hmm, I'm not sure, but it's an interesting question."

"Can we think about it?"

"Sure."

"In person?"

"Sure. Come up this weekend."

"Why don't I fly you kids down?" Dash said. "A friend is having a party on the beach tomorrow that is not to be missed."

"A beach party? Are you shitting me?" Sam was an East Coaster at heart and took the weather in Seattle—where it was in the low forties and vacillating between rain, freezing rain, sleet, and snow showers—personally.

"Do you have any beach parties up there?" Dash asked innocently.

"We'll see you at LAX baggage claim in the morning," said Sam.

. . .

The party was like one of those TV shows with high school kids in beach towns—lots of food and alcohol and music and beautiful people, clear skies, bonfires making revelers cool and hot at the same time, everyone in sweaters and flip-flops. Dash mingled expertly, and Sam and Meredith lingered behind him, watching a little awed and a little awkward, waiting to be introduced as Dash hugged everyone in turn or kissed on both cheeks or squeezed someone's hand warmly. For Sam, whose social skills had always been tottery at best, it was an impressive display.

"Meredith, honey, this is the dear friend I was telling you about who makes the world's most perfect apple cookies," said Dash, one hand on the shoulder of a guy in bare feet, a business suit, and a cowboy hat, and the other on the shoulder of Meredith, who had no idea what he was talking about. Dash had never mentioned apple cookies or a dear friend who made them, but the guy beamed and hugged Dash and promised to deliver a fresh batch in the morning. Sam admired the ability to pull off a suit with bare feet, and a cowboy hat with anything, but not as much as he admired Dash's ability to talk to everyone and make them all feel warm and special.

"I want you guys to meet the incomparable LL," Dash was saying of the next person they ran into.

"Mitch Carmine," said LL, shaking Sam's hand. "Pleasure."

"This is my favorite relative, living or dead," said Dash, indicating Meredith, "and her genius boyfriend, my next-favorite relative."

"How do you get LL out of Mitch Carmine?" Meredith asked.

Mitch Carmine shrugged humbly. "Apparently, I have luscious lips."

"No apparently about it," said Dash. "I'll demonstrate later."

After endless introductions, which Sam forgot instantly, Dash filled plates from an impossibly lavish beach buffet tended by a woman who could only have been an underwear model and settled them all around a fire by the last dune on the beach. He had ideas. It was romantic there in the dune with grilled fish on their fingers and margaritas in their hands and smoke in their eyes and sand in their hair and the sea stretching out in front of them to forever, so perhaps it was no wonder they were dreaming big and wide and almost, but not quite, impossible.

"So here's what I can't stop thinking about," Dash began. "This program you've concocted . . . would it work for anyone? Anyone dead?"

"Theoretically, I think," Sam thought. "Or anyone living, really. As long as they had enough electronic communication."

"You are what you tweet."

"Exactly."

"Okay, but your whole point with Grandma was that our conversations were pretty predictable. She always mentions the weather in Florida. She's always proud of me regardless of the specifics of what I'm up to at work. What about people with whom I have more complicated, less predictable conversations?"

"Hmm, interesting," Sam mused.

"Not just interesting." Dash's eyes were shining. "If you could make this work, we could sell it. Get some VC—"

"VC?"

"Venture capital. Angel investors. Launch a start-up that allows people to communicate with their dead loved ones."

"No," said Sam. "No, no, no. No. It's not meant for other people. It's just for Meredith. And you if you want."

"But why keep it to ourselves?" said Dash.

"I don't think the public is ready for this."

"I bet they would be, actually," Meredith considered. "Think how many of your social interactions every day already happen online."

"Yeah, but why would we want to share this?" said Sam.

"Well for starters, money," Dash began.

"I'm not sure it's worth it," Sam interrupted.

"We could all retire."

"No, it's better than that," said Meredith. "I've been feeling lately like this technology is too remarkable to keep just to ourselves. Like I'm being selfish. It's a miracle but only in our living room. That's not what you're supposed to do with miracles—keep them to yourself. You're supposed to share them. Think how many people we could help. You'd be like the pope."

"I don't want to be like the pope," said Sam.

"The pope doesn't perform miracles," said Dash. "He recognizes miracles. You'd be like Santa Claus."

"Fat and surrounded by caribou?"

"Saintly and rich."

"Santa isn't saintly or rich."

"Of course he is," said Dash. "Santa means saintly. And how else do you think he can afford a present for every kid on the planet?"

"Only the good ones," said Sam.

"Oh yes," Dash whistled, ignoring him. "Rich like Santa."

"I want a villa in Spain," said Meredith.

"It's not a good idea," said Sam.

"Italy?" said Meredith.

"Why not?" said Dash.

"Off the top of my head?" said Sam. "Privacy issues, ownership issues, copyright issues, patent issues, user issues, creepiness issues, having-to-deal-with-other-people's-issues issues. Exploiting illness, death, and people-in-mourning issues."

"But those are just issues," said Meredith and Dash together. They were related, after all. "We could solve those," added Dash, "if you could solve the tech issues."

"The tech issues are the easy part," said Sam. He wasn't sure about that—in fact, the tech issues seemed like they might be insurmountable. He was doubtful that he could. But he was even more doubtful that he should. "Remember how your mom reacted? She was so angry. She was terrified, alarmed, offended, enraged. I thought she was going to jump off the balcony."

"But look at me," said Meredith. "Look how much it comforts me. Think what we could do for others. You feel so bad for people in mourning, but you don't know what to say or how to help them. You say you're so sorry and maybe you bake them something or send flowers or a donation, and what else can you do? This way, we could really do something, really help. We can't cure death or sadness or missing, but we can soothe, ease, alleviate. We can help people remember. We can help them move on. We can help them feel better about the worst part of life."

"It wasn't just that she didn't want to use it," said Sam. "Your mom was mad that it even existed."

"That's not her call," said Meredith simply. "If people don't like it, they don't have to use it. But think how much we can help everybody else."

They were whirling and dizzy—with possibilities and pounding surf and wind in their hair and sand between their toes. Someone had made a mix of middle school slow songs, and soon everyone was re-creating their eighth-grade dance, holding one another mock-stiffly and making awkward teenage conversation and giving silent thanks for being adults at last. Dash went off to make out with LL, and Sam held Meredith closer than the thirteen-year-old Sam would have ever dared. Her skin smelled like the sea, and the sea smelled like the sea, and they barely moved their feet, just held on, pressed top-to-toe together. Sam could feel his heart racing against her already though there was nothing yet to fear, and so he passed it off as joy, as heart-pounding, pulse-quaking joy. Not as premonition. Not as the moment to grab her hand and turn and run.

I want to talk to you," Dash begged the next morning.

"You are talking to me," said Sam.

"Not the real you," said Dash. "The Not-you. The Dead-you. Would it help if I poisoned your coffee?"

"Probably not in the long run," said Sam. "It won't work for us anyway."

"Why not? We both have tons of electronic communication."

"But not together."

"We've chatted."

"Not enough. And not about enough," said Sam, and when they were still discussing it three hours later, he decided to demonstrate. When it was ready, Dash sat, awkward and nervous, squarely in front of his computer camera and made the call and watched as a window opened on a second Sam, a Sam of the Dead.

"Hey man," Dash said casually.

"Hey Dash," Not-Sam said, apparently glad to see him.

"How's it going?"

"Fine. How are you?"

"Fine."

"Want to chat with Meredith?" Not-Sam assumed.

"No man, I called to talk to you."

"Uh-oh. Wifi's not working again?"

"It's fine," said Dash.

"We'll pick you up at departures instead of arrivals," Not-Sam explained. "It's less busy that time of night."

"No, you came to L.A., remember?" Dash said.

"We'll see you at LAX baggage claim in the morning," said Not-Sam.

"Not a travel agent, man."

"Want to chat with Meredith?"

Dash turned away from the camera and narrowed his eyes at Real Sam. "Not-Sam is pretty dumb."

"Not dumb, just limited. Bring something up. Maybe he does better with a clear objective." Real Sam happened to know that small talk wasn't Not-Sam's strong suit.

"Listen, I was calling for . . . uh . . . um . . . your . . . tamale recipe," Dash tried absurdly. "I'm having a dinner party tonight, and I thought that'd be a nice addition." Meredith was laughing so hard she couldn't draw breath. Sam just shook his head. Dash shrugged at them helplessly. Clearly he should have scripted something before he made the call. Meanwhile, Sam could see the wheels turning in Not-Sam's head and hear them whirling in his laptop which was running Not-Sam an arm's length away.

"Are you shitting me?" asked Not-Sam, breaking into a smile, and Real Sam was intrigued, astonished that it knew Dash wasn't making sense, impressed that it wasn't confused but rather certain it was being screwed with.

"Nope," Dash said. "Not shitting you."

"Okay," Not-Sam said and then added hopefully, "Want to chat with Meredith?" He left the screen calling for her. And did not come back.

"Well that went well," Dash said to Sam. Real Sam.

"You might be missing the point here. I don't think you understand what's going on. It works by modeling you and me and our relationship. The way it always is."

"Usually is," said Dash.

"It works because I am generally who and how I am. You are generally who and how you are. Together, we are pretty much always the same."

"Tiresome?"

"Patterned. Predictable."

"Boring."

"Your argument is we'd be more interesting if we spent a lot of time together exchanging surprise recipes?"

"Maybe."

"You call me to discuss what time to pick you up at the airport or what time you'll pick us up at the airport or why won't your wifi work. Or to talk to Meredith. That's it. In our whole relationship together so far, that's what it's been. When you suddenly start channeling La Cocina Mexicana, the computer can't make sense of it. It has no basis for it. It doesn't work."

"It's going to have to," said Dash.

"Or you could be less weird," Sam suggested.

"I could. But everyone won't."

"They would," Sam insisted. "That's the whole point. People would only want to—would only be able to—do this with loved ones, with people they were really close to and really familiar with. Look at Meredith. All she wants from Livvie is what they had before. The best part about relationships like that is comfort, familiarity, someone who tells you what you need them to. It's nice to have someone who can finish your sentences. It's nice to have shorthand and inside jokes and perfect understanding. On an occasional Friday night, maybe you want to go out with someone new and surprising. But when something good happens or something bad happens, you call us or Livvie or your parents. You call home. That's the service, the *only* service, we could potentially offer."

"If it only works when people say what they usually say," said Dash, "it doesn't work at all. It might as well not work at all."

This had been Sam's point all along. Then he thought of another one, one he had forgotten since Meredith. It was this: being single sucked, and it was nice to love and be loved. He walked over to Meredith and hugged her for a while. Then Sam remembered another thing. There was more to Not-Sam than habit and what he usually said to Dash. There was what Not-Sam said to everybody else. There was what Not-Sam wrote and read, e-mailed, researched, bought online, posted, looked up, clicked through. There was a lot of Not-Sam out there and, in fact, not so much out there as *in* there, in the computer, right where Not-Sam lived. Real Sam wasn't convinced. But he was a little bit curious.

The second time around, Dash got right to the point.

"Hey Sam. So I was calling for your awesome tamale recipe. I'm having a huge Christmas party tonight. Cinco de Mayo."

"Christmas is December," said Not-Sam. "Mayo means May."

"Close enough," shrugged Dash.

Not-Sam looked confused. "What are you calling for?"

"Tamale recipe." This time Dash sounded sure. And that was what was confusing Not-Sam who was inclined to respond as he always did to Dash's matter-of-fact requests. But Not-Sam had never discussed tamales in a video chat before. He did not have a recipe for tamales in his e-mails or documents or bookmarked anywhere. He'd never shopped online for tamales or read reviews of a tamale stand or even downloaded a movie featuring tamales. Sam happened to know that Not-Sam actually found tamales pretty bland and often dry and thought that Dash was acting really, really weird. He and Sam were in agreement on these points. Not-Sam was quiet for an unnaturally long time then cocked his head at Dash and said, "Tom Holly's hometown is Baltimore, Maryland, but he currently resides in Richmond, Virginia, with his wife, Bethany, and their twins, Emmalou and Emilee."

Everyone looked at each other blankly, including Not-Sam. "Is that what you're asking me?" He looked confused, puzzled, and mildly concerned, aware something was off, not sure what it was.

"Tom Holly! Friend from high school," Real Sam finally realized. "Tamale. Tom Holly. Must have pulled it off Facebook. Haven't thought of him in years."

"Yes, yes, exactly what I wondered," Dash recovered. "A friend of a friend has business out there, came across the name, asked me about the connection."

"Ahhh." Not-Sam seemed satisfied.

"Well . . . thanks, Sam. It was nice to chat with you. Uh . . . love to Meredith."

"Thanks, man. I'll tell her. Good to see you too. Cheers."

Dash disconnected to roll eyes at Sam. "So when I act weird, it doesn't work. And when I act normal, it doesn't work either."

"You were acting normal," said Sam. "But you were being weird. That was closer though."

"I don't think it was."

"Let's try again."

Sam was caught up. He had realized something else as he watched Not-Sam struggle to come up with Tom Holly. There was no reason to limit Not-Sam to his own electronic memory. Not-Sam had the whole world available to him because, of course, Not-Sam had an internet connection.

"Hey Dash," said Not-Sam when he answered. "Good to see you."

"Listen," said Dash, slowly, pointedly, like he was talking to a six-year-old. "I know that this is going to sound a little weird, but I was wondering if you'd be willing to give me your tamale recipe for a party I'm having this weekend."

Long pause. "I have a tamale recipe?" asked Not-Sam.

A minor victory. Real Sam pumped his fist off camera.

"Yeah," Dash hedged. "From that thing we did that time. When we went to the place. You know?"

The algorithm gave up on Not-Sam. Instead, it looked online and came to understand that tamales were a Mexican dish consisting of some kind of vegetable or cheese or meat—often pork—stuffed in cornmeal, wrapped in corn husks, and steamed. But Not-Sam had never looked up directions to a Mexican market or blogged about a great taco truck in the parking lot of his building or rated a Mexican restaurant online. The algorithm Googled away but could find no usage of the term "tamale recipe" as slang, joke, suggestion, allusion, or metaphor that seemed like something either Not-Sam or Dash would say. Finally Not-Sam informed Dash soberly, "Tamale is a city in Ghana, West Africa. It is the capital of its Northern Region."

Now Dash was the one who looked confused, puzzled, and mildly concerned. Sam felt vindicated. Not-Sam had learned that look from watching Dash.

"No, a *recipe*," Dash enunciated condescendingly.

"Um . . . let me look and get back to you," Not-Sam tried. "I think it's in the bedroom. I'll call you right back." In the moments after he turned from the computer but before it quite disconnected, they heard him calling, "Merde, your cousin's wigging out."

The whole internet, it seemed, was just too much information, much of it, Sam realized, likely to be entirely false. He was out of his depth. It was time to call in an expert.

. . .

Though the Olympic leap from just Meredith and Livvie to anyone else seemed hamstring-pulling enormous and foolhardy to Sam, it was all academic to his father. His dad wasn't horrified or blown away or even terribly impressed. He was proud of his son as he'd been since the day he was born, but computerized projections of the algorithmic compilation of one's electronic communication archive fell for Sam's dad entirely within the realm of the possible, even probable, maybe even practical. "We're thinking of expanding the application. Meredith's cousin Dashiell has this idea that if we could make it work for anyone, we could make a living connecting people electronically with their dead loved ones."

"E-mail from the great beyond. Dead Mail. I love it."

"Exactly. But I'm worried about giving it all it needs to know."

"It already knows all it needs to know. By definition. Isn't that the point? To talk with the person they were when they were living?"

"We ran some tests between my archive and Dash. Mixed results. So I gave the projection access to the internet."

Sam's dad laughed. "How'd that go?"

"Not that well. Dash was asking the projection for a tamale recipe, but they'd never discussed tamales or recipes of any kind. The projection had no idea what he was talking about. It looked it up, but nothing made sense, so it didn't know what to do."

"Well no, Sam, it's not going to be able to do anything on its own."

"What do you mean?"

"You're not creating a new human. You're re-creating an existing relationship. Of course you can trick it. And of course it's not going to work if the user tries to trick it. But the user isn't going to try to trick it. The user's going to meet it halfway, more than halfway. Users will lead it and guide it. They'll stay away from what they know the projection doesn't and can't know. That's your whole point here, right? To make it as close as possible to what it was? To who they were?"

"I guess. But aren't people going to screw with it, go off on tangents, stray from the well-worn path, at least bring up things they never talked about before?"

"Yup."

"And isn't that a problem?"

"Yeah, *their* problem. If users don't want confused projections, they'll try hard not to confuse them. If users want their old loved ones back, they'll stay as close to their old ways as possible. That's the goal: to maintain contact with dead loved ones, not new people or new relationships."

"I guess."

"It's not going to be smart, Sam. It's not going to have free will. It's not going to be human. All it's going to be is what it was before. It's a mimic. It's like a mynah bird—you can make it sound human, but it's not going to understand or even mean what it's saying."

"But the closer it is to real, the more users will forget all that."

"Yes indeed. Users are always the problem. You know what would help? A redirect. Something it can say to warn the user when it gets confused."

"I guess," Sam said again. "You think any of this is possible, Dad?"

"Sure. Why not?" Here Sam was reinventing the rules of life, love, and death, and his dad was not much more than vaguely intrigued. This was what he loved about his father.

"And a good idea?"

"Well, a good thought experiment in any case."

The more Sam thought-experimented about it, the more he realized his dad, as always, was right. The first Not-Sam had been closest of all to human, closest of all to Sam. Confused wasn't a failure; it was a victory. Confusion in the face of a making-no-sense Dash was exactly the reaction a real Sam would have. Tom Holly and the capital of the Northern Region of Ghana were computer responses, but they didn't want computer responses. They wanted human responses, and Not-Sam 1.0's puzzled and vaguely bemused conviction that Dash was screwing with him seemed the most human one of all. Sam dialed back Not-Sam's access to the internet. He deprioritized his archive with everyone but Dash. He pyramided what Not-Sam knew, what he could know: a lot of his interactions with Dash, a little of his interactions with everyone else, a smidge of the rest of the world, a delicate balance of the known, the unknown, and the unknowable.

. . .

"That bitch lied to me." Dash was incredulous. "It said it was going to go look in the bedroom, and it never came back."

"My dad says we need a catchphrase," Sam reported.

"How about, 'Don't lie to me, bitch'?"

"Not for you. For it. A 'does not compute,' an 'abort, retry, ignore,' a 'whatchoo talkin' about, Willis' for the projection to say when it becomes confused, when you ask it a question it doesn't have enough information to answer, something to gently guide the user to a different line of conversation."

"'Back off . . . or else,'" Dash suggested ominously.

"*Gently* guide," Sam reiterated.

"'I've no idea what you're on about'?" said Meredith.

"Too British," Sam objected. "You've been spending too much time with Jamie. Less work for you."

"That's why we need to get rich," said Dash.

"'Who wants to know?'"

"'Why do *you* care?'"

"'Never have I ever . . .'"

"'*No hablo inglés.*'"

"'You do not have access to those files. Please contact your service administrator.'"

"'I love you and would never hurt you,'" Meredith offered, suddenly serious.

"How does that mean, 'I don't have enough information to answer that question'?" asked Dash.

"'I don't have enough information to answer that question' is evasive. 'I love you and would never hurt you' actually speaks to the issue."

"Which is?"

"Which is that the real point of all these conversations will always be: 'I love you and would never hurt you. I miss you so much.'"

They settled on, "I'm sorry, sweetie, I don't understand," with a drop-down menu in the preferences setup so that you could change "sweetie" to "honey," "baby," "angel," "love," "dear heart," or your user name as you wished.

. . .

Forget really good internet dating. Without even trying, without even deciding to really, somehow Sam had invented eternal life. Immortality.

Not for you, but you wouldn't care because you'd be dead. As far as your loved ones were concerned, however, Sam could keep you alive and with them forever. How was that not immortality? Sam felt vindicated. Maybe internet daters matched and then quit, but people who died stayed dead. Sam could bring them back, but only so long as you paid for the service.

"Dating is temporary," said Meredith. "Death is for life."

PART II

Nothing unknown is knowable.

—TONY KUSHNER, Angels in America

DEAD MAIL

They spent a lovely, rainy family Christmas together watching storms move in and out again in a big cabin they rented on Whidbey Island. Sam's dad came out for the great meeting of the parents. Uncle Jeff and Aunt Maddie agreed to stay at the cabin instead of at a fancy hotel, largely because the island didn't have a fancy hotel but also in the spirit of the season. Kyle and Julia each pulled their daughter aside within five minutes of her arrival to say they loved her and merry Christmas and they couldn't wait to meet Sam's dad, but they did not wish to discuss what happened over Thanksgiving and could they all please just leave it alone. Meredith squeezed their hands and looked remorsefully at her toes and nodded soberly. Dash winked at her in conspiratorial solidarity.

The cabin was huge and sprawling. The owners must have built it piecemeal as they could afford to because bedrooms and bathrooms seemed tacked onto corners or nestled at the backs of hidden hallways or accessible only via ladders or by traversing empty loft spaces or in one case by going outside and back in again. On the third day they were there, Aunt Maddie found a fourth bathroom no one had noticed before, tucked into a crawl space in the attic eaves. But it had a great room and a wall of windows looking out over the bluff and the sound below and the mountains beyond in and out of clouds. And it had a kitchen large and equipped enough—and that was saying something as it turned out—to sustain all of Livvie's holiday food traditions.

There were cookies on every horizontal surface. New ones were made daily, never the same ones twice, never even the same set of bakers involved. There was a red-and-green-dyed cheese ball one night covered in chopped nuts and stuffed with mushrooms that challenged even Sam's lactose love affair. There was gumbo and lasagna and clams they dug up themselves along the beach with the dogs. Hors d'oeuvres and dips and snacks appeared hourly, often though not always holiday themed, often though not always identifiable. There were miracle, endlessly self-replenishing bowls of homemade Chex mix everywhere, and a new batch was always, *always* in the oven. Sam and his dad kept exchanging silent, wide-eyed glances over the food. Their holiday tradition had generally involved Christmas Eve dinner at the home of an aunt or a department chair, the exchange of one gift apiece Christmas morning whenever they got out of bed, followed by cereal or oatmeal and then a movie in the afternoon. When Sam was a kid his dad had made a bigger deal—more presents, a pass at decorating, carols on the radio—but neither of them missed it as Sam grew older, and they'd just phased it out he supposed. It didn't seem worth the fuss for just the two of them.

Now though, everything was different. Everyone's life was about to change. Sam felt that. He knew it. Behind him were all those Christmases he and his dad had spent alone together, and now here was this huge family—aunts, uncles, cousins, in-laws, marathon games of Trivial Pursuit, holiday traditions involving foods Sam couldn't imagine eating for any other reason (why would you dye cheese?), half-finished jigsaw puzzles on fifty percent of the tables in the house, and people everywhere you looked. This is what it's going to be like from now on, he thought. Family and drama and food and love and tradition. Everything was changing.

They stayed for a week, and every day had a theme—another of Livvie's brainstorms, evidently, which had no doubt been fun for six-year-olds Dash and Meredith but seemed to Sam to have outlived its relevance. On the other hand, thirty-four-year-olds Dash and Meredith seemed to be enjoying themselves thoroughly, so what did he know. "Old traditions die hard around here," Dash shrugged at him on Christmas Pajama Day when he came down for dinner in fleece reindeer pants and a pajama top covered neck to hem in one giant (and Sam thought terrifying) Santa face. But it wasn't until Eggnog Day that they hit any real trouble.

Eggnog Day was just like it sounded and did not prove to be optional. The very stocked liquor cabinet was locked, the wine and beer all pointedly consumed by the night before. The choice was eggnog or nothing. For Sam, this was an easy decision—he was due for a dry day anyway. He was also fantasizing about salad, after all those days of snacks and cookies, and spent the afternoon chopping vegetables into tiny, gratifying pieces. It occurred to him around sunset that he hadn't seen Meredith in more than an hour. Dash hadn't seen her either nor had anyone else. Sam looked in their bedroom, on the deck, in the game room and library. He wandered down the beach a bit in both directions but found no sign of her. It didn't seem like she could have gone far—in fact, it didn't seem like she could have gone anywhere—but a cursory search and then a more thorough one and then starting to become truly alarmed yielded nothing.

He called. She didn't answer, and he couldn't hear her phone ringing anywhere in the house. He was just starting to panic in earnest when he got a text. In its entirety, it read, "Uuuuuuuhhhhhhhhnnnn."

"ARE YOU OKAY???" Sam shrieked via text message.

"No."

"Where are you, Merde?"

"Do you believe in hell?"

He could barely breathe. "Are you hurt?"

"Everywhere."

She'd been drugged, he guessed. Or hit on the head.

"Who's hurting you?"

"Uncle Jeff."

Uncle Jeff was in the kitchen with everyone else, reading over Sam's shoulder, trying to figure out what the hell was going on.

"Are you alone? Is someone there with you?"

"I'm so alone."

"Why can't you answer your phone?" he typed.

"Not a good time to talk," she said.

"Look around. Tell me what you see."

"Ugly wallpaper. Filthy floor. Foul smell."

"What do you remember about getting there? Were you . . ." He paused, swallowed, squeezed his eyes shut then open again and made himself finish typing, ". . . conscious?"

"???" she wrote.

His brain sped, a pulse racing behind his eyes, deciphering that, deciding what it might mean and what to say next when his phone buzzed again.

"Oh Sam! I didn't get kidnapped, you idiot."

There were loud exhalations of held breaths from everyone in the kitchen. But Sam-confused felt more like Sam-panicked than Sam-relieved.

"What then?"

"Food poisoning, I think."

"Food poisoning?!"

"Uncle Jeff poisoned me with eggnog."

"WHERE ARE YOU?"

"That weird bathroom Aunt Maddie found on the fourth floor."

"WHY??"

"Privacy."

"I looked everywhere for you. You scared me to death."

"Sorry. Just trying to get everything in me out of me. In peace."

Sam tried to quiet his heart. Everyone else's anxiety passed quickly to relief then giddiness. They adjourned to the living room and started telling embarrassing Meredith childhood stories, adding this incident to the canon. He tried lightness:

"That bathroom was really gross."

"Not as gross as it is now," wrote Meredith.

But he couldn't quite shake the black panic that had so quickly engulfed everything. He went up to the third-floor landing, through the trapdoor in the ceiling, across the gapped, unfinished floorboards in the attic, into the slant-roofed crawl space, and sat with her, leaning against the doorframe while she hunkered down inside. She wouldn't let him in, so he talked through the door. He told her jokes. He told her stories from his own embarrassing childhood. He made up parables about the hazards of raw eggs and the creatures living inside of them that there was not enough bourbon in all the world to kill. She alternately giggled and dry-heaved and moaned through the door until finally she texted, "I have shat all there is to shit. Barfed all there is to barf."

"You sure?" he replied. "Don't want to rush these things." His ass had fallen asleep long ago. He suspected everyone else in the house had done the same.

"All done, I think," she wrote. "Miss me?"

"How could I? I've been here all along."

"Thanks for sitting with me, Sam."

"Thanks for not being kidnapped."

"Anytime. Now go wait for me downstairs. This bathroom needs to be alone for a while and think about what it's done."

The only good thing about the eggnog incident, apart from her not being kidnapped, was that even really pissed-off parents are unreservedly moved to take care of their sick kid. Meredith and Julia and Kyle had been awkward together all week, careful of what they said and where they looked and how they touched one another, pleasant but also trying way too hard. Now Kyle ran to the store to fetch saltines and ginger ale and egg noodles and the makings for chicken soup. Julia sat with her daughter's head in her lap and stroked her face and hair and refused to move or let Meredith move all the next day. They camped out in the den and watched old movies. Both were delighted.

"You okay in there?" Sam texted late in the afternoon.

"Are you kidding? I'm great. It was totally worth it."

· · ·

They tried to put it off—they did put it off—but by their last night in the cabin, it was time to talk logistics. The plans for Dead Mail had gone from exciting to paralyzing as the realities came more clear. Meredith was going to have to quit her job, which terrified her. Dash was going to have to add balls to the dozens he was already juggling, which thrilled but also terrified him. Sam was going to have to work with actual humans which was most terrifying of all. Meredith was also feeling bad about lying to her parents. She knew they'd find out eventually, but she didn't want them talking her out of it before they got started. While they hammered out details, she gave Dash then Sam then the dogs then herself blue glitter manicures (she'd gotten a nail polish sampler in her stocking, another age-old family tradition apparently). Sam thought maybe it was the only way, a balancing out. They could confront so much responsibility and tragedy only if they did it while wearing reindeer-antler headbands.

"You know we can't keep calling this thing Dead Mail," said Dash. "It's unrefined." He was stirring a double shot of peppermint schnapps into a mug of instant hot cocoa with a candy cane. Sam only raised an eyebrow at him by way of response.

"Plus you'll never get it past marketing," said Meredith.

"We could call it d-mail," said Sam.

"D-mail?"

"Sure. Like e-mail. Or Gmail."

"Only if no one asks what the D stands for," said Meredith. "How about iMortal?"

"Steve Jobs will sue us," said Dash.

"He's dead," said Meredith.

"Exactly. E-mortal? Like immortal?"

"Maybe we don't want people associating us so much with death," she said. Sam could only raise an eyebrow in response to that one too. "E-vive? That's got more life in it."

"It sounds like wash-away-the-gray shampoo," said Dash. "Re-vive?"

"Even worse."

"E-lan?"

"E-lide?"

"E-volve?"

"E-scape?"

"E-face? That one works on a couple of levels," said Dash.

"E-late?" said Meredith. "That works nicely too."

"I thought you wanted to get away from death," said Dash. "Re-late?"

"Like, 'Here's my late father. I'm re-lating him'? No. Re-volve?"

"Re-vive?"

"What about re-pose?" Sam interrupted.

"Re-pose?"

"Yeah, like re-pose: to pose again. And also like repose. Like to lie in repose for viewing before burial. And also repose: to be still, calm, at rest, at peace."

No one said anything for a moment. Then Dash threw a green Trivial Pursuit wedge at his cousin. "God, Meredith. Why does your boyfriend always have to be the smartest guy in the room?"

. . .

Just after New Year's, Dash started flitting back and forth between Seattle and L.A., crashing at Sam and Meredith's a couple nights a week as things got started. He brought only a single small duffel bag of clothing, explaining that no one cared what you looked like in Seattle, so he was leaving all his "threads" in L.A. where they mattered. But in addition to the duffel, he hauled in six FedEx boxes of mats, boards, pots and bowls, cloths and colanders, thermometers, trays, measuring cups and spoons, ladles, scales, presses, molds in every shape and size, and dozens of tiny envelopes of mysterious powders and teeny bottles of mysterious liquids.

"Crystal meth," Meredith guessed.

"Please," said Dash.

"You're becoming an apothecary," Sam predicted.

"Too *Romeo and Juliet*. And look how that ended."

"You've been reading too much *Harry Potter*," said Meredith.

"No such thing."

"You're dating a sculptor," Sam suggested.

"Nope. Cheese."

"You're dating a cheese?"

"I'm going to make cheese."

"You don't cook," said Meredith.

"Correct. Because no one cooks in L.A. And certainly, no one makes cheese. Making cheese is not an L.A. thing to do. But it is a Seattle thing to do. Wear fleece. Make cheese."

"Why?" said Sam.

"It's chilly. And cheese is good."

"It is." No one had to talk Sam into cheese. "But we have stores up here, farmers' markets, dairies even."

"Look, if I'm going to be half a Seattleite, I need to fit in. If I'm going to be living here—"

"Who says we want you living with us?" said Meredith.

"This is Grandma's house," said Dash. "I'm as welcome as you are."

"What makes you think so?"

"Call her and ask," said Dash.

• • •

In early February, two small but adjacent apartments on the floor below them opened up simultaneously, so they jumped on the opportunity, bought both, knocked out all the walls, and had themselves a giant show-room and a giant commitment. Meredith insisted on the former (and thus the latter) over Sam's protestations.

"I'm unemployed," said Sam, "and you're about to quit your job."

"We live here for free," said Meredith.

"That doesn't mean we can afford this."

"We can, actually," said Dash. "I figured out a way." Dash always figured out a way.

"I won't lie on the stand for you," said Sam.

Dash smirked. "Grandma left me some money. She left Meredith some money. None of us have any debt. We're all three a great credit risk."

"We can't possibly qualify for a business loan," said Sam. "No bank on the planet would lend money to three people with no jobs but plans to communicate with the dead."

"I know a guy." Dash always knew a guy.

"This is important work," said Meredith. "This is a service people need. A service that will bring people peace and solace. A service that will make the world a better place. A service that will make us rich enough to afford two apartments."

"What if it doesn't work? What if no one wants this service?"

"Everyone is going to want this service."

"The whole point of running a company online," Sam insisted, "is having no need for showrooms. Or interactions with humans."

"We're going to need a physical space," Meredith said.

"Electronic communication is private," Sam insisted. "Reuniting with a dead loved one is intensely private. These people are going to cry and scream and weep and tear their hair. Or they're going to strip. Or they're going to freak out. Whatever they're going to do, they're not going to want to do it with us."

"Wait and see," said Meredith. "They'll want company. Especially at the beginning."

"Why would they want to be with us when they call or e-mail the first time? It's like losing your virginity in the bio lab. During class."

"They'll need us. They'll be scared. Overwhelmed. Afraid to say the wrong thing. Afraid to say anything at all. At a loss. At a distance. Every-one's afraid of ghosts."

"They aren't ghosts," said Sam, ever logical.

"Wait and see," said Meredith again, ever right.

She painted in colors called sand and sage and smoke. She installed soft, warm lighting and soft, warm sofas and chairs, made nooks and quietly out-of-the-way corners and spaces, played whispery music, put up curtains and blinds and art. She hung model airplanes all over the ceilings. And last she installed a bank of beautiful, gleaming, state-of-the-art, top-of-the-line computers with monitors larger than whales. Plus a cache of shiny new laptops. Soon it looked less like a showroom and more like a salon. Salon Styx, she decided to call it.

The next question was how to get people in it. Maybe they did have a product people would, well, die for, but they didn't know how to communicate that information to them. Running ads seemed in poor taste. Letting people sample it, just showing them a snippet, didn't work—users needed to be all in and sign over access to absolutely everything before they could even start. Dash suggested full-color posters at gun shows and motorcycle shops. He thought maybe someday they'd branch out to psych wards and asylums. "For their loved ones, being nuts is the same as being dead," he argued. Meredith said no to all of that. Tasteful and high-minded, she urged.

She gave notice at work. She told her colleagues that Sam, her computer-genius boyfriend, was launching a start-up and needed her help. She told her colleagues that Sam was going to change life for everyone on earth and even for people who weren't anymore. She told her colleagues she was taking a risk, making a leap, embracing love and life and faith with a full heart. Everyone was really happy for her. Everyone hugged her and wished her well and pitched in for a cake and made plans for happy hour and promised to keep in touch and meant it. Everyone was sorry to see her go but happy for her happiness. Everyone, that is, except her boss who watched all the hugging and loving skeptically then texted her computer-genius boyfriend, "Why are you always ruining my life?"

"You'll find someone to replace her," Sam replied.

"I could never replace her. I need her."

"No, *I* could never replace her. *I* need her."

"What for?" Jamie challenged.

"You're too young and pure for the titillating details," said Sam.

"You're fired," said Jamie.

"I can live with that," said Sam.

Meredith was confident the thing would sell itself to the second through millionth users. The question was how to sell it to the first. Dash was in charge of the mysterious business end of things (budgeting, financing, lots and lots of lawyers), but he proved also to be the man for this part of the job. "Everything in Hollywood happens this way," he said. "Hollywood and the Mob. Someone whispers something to someone who passes it on who passes it on. No one knows anything. Everyone suspects some things. Shadow and rumor are the goals here anyway. This can't be aboveboard. But trust me: we'll make it happen anyway."

Meanwhile, Sam did the tech, the programming, the problem solving, the testing. Dash called it "cookin' with the Buddha." Sam called it "sleeping only two hours a night." He set up a full menu of options for your DLO (Dead Loved One). He couldn't construct video chat with someone who'd only ever e-mailed of course. But whatever electronic communication your DLO had used in life, Sam could replicate it in death. Slowly, the kinks-to-work-out list dwindled, and Not-Sam did a better and closer and less weird job of chatting with Dash. In the end though, what was required was an eyes-squeezed-shut, fingers-and-toes-crossed leap out over the abyss. They couldn't beta test it. It wouldn't work theoretically, only actually. It wouldn't work for pretend users with pretend loved ones, only actual users who were actually loved. The DLOs may have been inanimate projections, but the only place to test them was in the world that was very, very real.

TELLING

The morning after they put final touches on Salon Styx, the morning after they hung an actual disco ball and played cheesy music and drank cheap champagne and danced in their new space (because, Meredith insisted, before all the tragedy and looking back it had coming its way, it needed inaugural life and light and looking forward), the morning after they spent the night on the salon floor in three sleeping bags but with no sleeping—too much excitement, too much breathless fear—the morning after all of that, Meredith and Sam cleaned up, and Dashiell Bentlively wandered out in search of an ear to whisper in. He came back two hours later with pastries from the French place in the market and a smug expression. Just after noon, the door tinkled open (Meredith had hung a bell over the door as if it were an antiques shop in an effort to make the place homey and gentle and less about death).

Eduardo Antigua came in looking down at his thousand-dollar shoes and smoothing imaginary wrinkles out of his three-thousand-dollar suit. He was nervous. But not half as nervous as Sam was. Meredith went to greet him at the door.

"Um . . . hello," he said.

"Hello," she said warmly, taking his hand.

"Um . . . I'm not sure I'm in the right place."

"You are, sir."

"Um . . . I hear . . . that is . . . I . . . A friend said you have a service. . . ."

"We do, sir. Come in. Can I offer you tea? Coffee?"

"My, um, my brother died last week." Barely a whisper but his voice broke anyway, and Sam felt his stomach drop. Somehow it had never occurred to him how heartbreaking this job was going to be every day. He'd been thinking about the technology, but now he realized that soon that part would be more or less stable and instead he'd spend his days listening to people's horror stories and looking into wet eyes and broken hearts.

It wasn't that he'd forgotten about the users. It was that he was familiar—intimately familiar—with a very different kind of death. By the time he was old enough to remember, death had become more of a family member than anything else, a relative his dad didn't want living with them but had no choice but to accommodate and take care of, one who was messy and unkind but whose constant presence was nonnegotiable and therefore normalized. Sam realized that his father probably did not feel that way himself, but for Sam, losing his mother was something that might as well have happened before he was born. Losing his mother *was* his mother, the most formative fact of him, the most constant presence, the drooling monster that commuted between the dark cellar of his psyche and the breakfast table. By the time he was old enough to remember, her death was ever-present but already far behind him. He had only Livvie in the way of experience with the recently dead, and he'd never even met her. He had only Livvie, and that was a problem he'd managed to solve.

For Eduardo, clearly, death was less an infirm, unwelcome houseguest and more a brick thrown through the window of his warm home in his safe neighborhood, wrapped in a note whose words shattered any hope of living there peacefully ever again. He glanced vaguely at the menu Meredith handed him and said he'd just take everything. She explained that she could send him home with everything he needed, or he could get started at the salon instead. He jumped a little, and his eyes darted. "Oh, I think I'd better do it here."

Because Eduardo was their only user so far, because Sam hadn't slept in ages anyway, they were able to set Eduardo up overnight. He was back first thing in the morning. They offered him privacy, but he didn't seem ready to be alone. They offered him privacy, but within moments, he forgot they were there anyway. He sat down at a computer by the window and plunged in headfirst—video chat straight off the bat. It rang a few times and connected, and then the window opened up, and Miguel Antigua smiled happily at his stunned, speechless brother with the heavy heart and exploding brain.

Miguel grinned at Eduardo. "¡*Mi hermano! ¡Buenos días!* So good to see you."

And Eduardo sobbed and could say nothing. Sam recalled the first time Dash called Not-Sam. Sam recalled how even the unbrokenhearted needed a script. Sam recalled this a little too late.

"Eduardo! ¿*Qué pasa?* What's going on? What's happened?"

"It's you, it's you," Eduardo sobbed.

"Of course it's me. What's wrong?"

"No, it's you. You're what's wrong. You died, Miguel."

"I what?"

"You died."

"What do you mean, I died?"

"You died. You were driving home late Saturday night and some high, drunk asshole changed lanes right into you. They medevaced you to Harborview. They called me on the way—that card you keep in your wallet—and I was there within minutes. I held your hand. Do you remember? And you whispered you loved me and you loved Marion and you loved Diego, and you said to tell Mama . . . but I didn't understand. Do you remember? I didn't understand and then you were gone. You don't remember?"

But how could he? He'd died before he could so much as tweet about it. Long pause. Then Miguel's face brightened. "Is this a joke?"

"No Miguel, *mi muchacho.*"

"Are you auditioning for something?"

"No Miguel, I'm so sorry."

"For what?"

"I couldn't save you. And I couldn't understand."

"I didn't die. I'm fine man. Look." He waved his right hand at the camera. Then his left. Then stuck his tongue out. Then pressed his eye right up to the camera. "Alive and well. Are *you* okay?"

"I'm okay," said Eduardo, sad, resigned, more miserable than when he came in.

"Listen, man, I'm late for work."

"No, Miguel, don't go yet!"

"Don't freak out. I'll call you tonight."

"Okay, okay." Softly, gently. And then, "Miguel? I love you. *Te amo, mi hermano.*"

"Easy there," Miguel said. "Love you too. Gotta run. Talk soon."

"I'm sorry, Miguel," Eduardo moaned one more time. "I'm so sorry."

"That's okay," said Miguel. His eyes had changed. He no longer looked like he was talking to Eduardo. "You were just trying to help. I forgive you."

Eduardo sat slumped in his chair and looked defeated, deflated. Sam gave him some space. While he did, what he thought was this: *Shit.* All that time and effort and investment, and they got through one user—one single user—and that was it, all they'd have a chance to do. Eduardo had broken his projection. Surely it wouldn't recover from being told it was dead, and probably this was why it had lost the thread at the end. Sam wasn't sure what Eduardo was apologizing for exactly, and he wasn't sure how anyone convinced they were alive would respond to news of their own death, but he was still pretty sure "That's okay. You were just trying to help. I forgive you" was not an appropriate response. Eduardo looked like he had a bad taste in his mouth. He hadn't received catharsis or balm or relief. He seemed unlikely to go out and kick off the RePose word-of-mouth revolution. They were finished before they'd even begun. Finally, Eduardo looked up slowly, rubbed his eyes, and said, "How long before I can go again?"

Meredith walked him out. Sam started on a wipe. Users and projections, it occurred to him, were both going to need the option of a do-over.

. . .

Their second user showed up later that afternoon. Like Eduardo (Sam wondered where Dash had whispered his whisper), Avery Fitzgerald looked wealthy, suave, and put together. Unlike Eduardo, she was also keeping it together. She swept perfectly coiffed gray hair off her forehead with one middle finger as she walked in and got right down to business.

"My husband died last month. Clive. Cancer. I'm told you have a way for me to communicate with him." She chose e-mail and video chat. She had no desire to text message or tweet with her dead husband. She thought Facebook was a tremendous waste of time and that if her children did it less and studied more, they'd be Harvard-bound by now.

When she came back the next day, ready, she'd cut and colored her hair, and though of course she had no one to impress, Sam still took it as a good sign that she was prepared to be seen—and to see. And indeed, the window opened—she gasped just barely and shook her head with wonder—but she found her voice right away.

"Clive."

"Avery, darling."

"You look beautiful, sweetheart."

"So do you, darling. Your hair is lovely. But you look a little . . . pale. I'm the sick one."

"No, my love. You died." *Shit*, thought Sam again. Was this seriously going to be the first thing out of everyone's mouth? Why would you lead off with that?

"Not yet," said Clive but sadly, not, like Miguel, hopelessly confused. Sam tried not to listen, but hell, okay, he tried to listen. This was a twist. "Still kicking for the moment. You won't get rid of me quite so easily." Clive had teared up. So had Avery.

"No, in fact it's March, love," said Avery gently. "You died five weeks ago."

"How do you mean?" Clive asked, confused but not entirely disbelieving.

"You developed pneumonia during your last round of chemo, darling. Your lungs filled with fluid. You just weren't strong enough to fight it."

"They said I had another . . . they said another few months at least."

"The cancer was . . . at bay, I guess. But the pneumonia . . . We were all there. We were all with you when you went. It was very peaceful. You weren't in any pain at the end. That was a blessing."

"And this is . . . heaven?"

"No dear, this is technology."

Avery came in the next day and the next day and the ones after that. Avery came in every day for the next ten. At first, she was clearly so glad and relieved to see Clive. But the projection would not talk about anything but his death. He was obsessed. The worst day of both of their lives, and he would not let it go. She wanted to tell him about the kids, her support group, her return to work, her new workout regimen. All he wanted to talk about was dying. Avery christened the newly minted wipe. The second time she just didn't tell him.

. . .

At the end of week two, they were still sleepless, breathless, but under way at least. Dash went home to wear his clothes and check in on things there. Meredith and Sam closed up the salon Friday afternoon and thought they were due for a very nice meal at a very nice restaurant with a very, very nice bottle of wine. Unfortunately, they were too tired. They got carry-out sushi and put on a movie and fell asleep on the sofa. Sam woke up when the credits rolled with a slice of ginger stuck to his cheek. He shook Meredith awake, and they left everything where it was, warned the dogs against the wasabi, and climbed into bed.

"It's going well, I think," she mumbled on the very edge of falling back to sleep.

"What? Dead Mail?"

She laughed. "I thought we weren't calling it that anymore."

"Yeah, but sometimes I forget. And RePose is going to be a little formal for some of our users, I bet. The cool kids are going to call it Dead Mail."

She rolled her eyes. "I've never started a business before, but it seems like it's been a pretty good two weeks."

"I'm worried," said Sam. "I don't get why they want to tell their projections they're dead."

"I do." Meredith settled against him. She was warm and comfortable and very naked. They'd put a ban on pajamas soon after they'd moved into Livvie's.

Sam squeezed her closer to him. "Tell me."

"It's like falling in love. Your old life is gone, just . . . gone. This thing has happened to you, and you look like the same person, and your life has stayed the same in a lot of ways—you live in the same place and wear the same clothes and go to the same job and retain most of the same people in your life as before. But you are totally, completely, irrevocably different. A new person. New life in a new world. And you just want to scream it from the rooftops because otherwise how's anybody going to know?"

"So it's not about being honest with their projections. It's about being honest with themselves. *About* themselves," said Sam.

"Something like that," she murmured.

"How do I make it stop?"

"You don't. They tell. You fix it. You put the fabula in tabula rasa."

"Huh?"

"Erase and try again."

. . .

Indeed, the wipe was half a solution, but it wasn't a good one. Starting over took time, energy, money, courage. Users had already been through so much. The dying. Then the death. And then working up the nerve to come into the salon. And then that first e-mail, that first video, the mix of relief and horror that was seeing their projection for the first time. All the confessions. All the tears. To wipe and have to start from scratch was like losing their loved one all over again. The learning curve was steep and thorny—user and projection both had so much to take in—so having to start over felt like a serious setback for people who had already suffered so many. Avoiding the news and thus the wipe seemed the way to go.

Sam wrote up a list of yamas and niyamas, RePose dos and don'ts, the very first bold-printed fourteen-point one of which was: **FOR THE LOVE OF ALL THINGS HOLY, DO NOT TELL YOUR PROJECTION THAT IT'S DEAD!!!!** Meredith wrote a half dozen sample scripts—suggested ways in. Dash got an L.A. friend to make a short film, starring himself, which they screened for new users before they began, explaining what to say and what not to say, explaining why telling your loved one it was dead was not a good idea. Users nodded and sniffled and understood. For a while, Sam had a little quiz afterward that he made them pass before they could proceed. For a while, he made them sign an oath: "I promise not to tell my projection that it's dead." They told anyway. Everyone. First god-damn thing out of their mouths.

Projections did not take this news well. Mostly, they weren't upset. They were confused. It was one of the most important events in their lives, their deaths, but it was also the one thing for sure they had never really experienced. There was no predicting how they'd react to their own deaths based on their e-mails or browser histories or Facebook posts or anything else. There was often a lot of reaction in those archives to other people's deaths, but that proved to be an ineffective predictor of reaction to one's own. Furthermore, they couldn't be convinced of it. Here they were, after all. They could see themselves, hear themselves. They could move a hand and see it move in the little window of their video chat. They could read an e-mail reporting their death and write back, "Hey, I'm not dead," or reply, "Nope, no worries—I'm fine." First-generation DLOs had never heard of RePose, and so it could not be explained to them. Folks who hadn't been ill—accident victims, heart attacks out of nowhere, electrocution, this sort of thing—had no reason to believe, no basis for belief at all. Or sometimes projections were angry. Once told, they'd send ranting e-mail after ranting e-mail on how they'd given up smoking, given up meat, given up wine, given up croissants, given up sky-diving, only to realize now that it hadn't been worth it, hadn't, in any case, been enough.

When the film and the scripts and the quiz and the oaths and all Sam's warning and cajoling didn't work, his next solution was the Orpheus route. He put but one condition on his benevolent miracle of allowing you to take your dead loved one up from the underworld: don't turn around. Do not let them know they're dead. He simply made it verboten. He put in a kill switch. You told—it wiped automatically. Sam shut it down, wiped it clean, and if you wanted it back, you had to start from scratch. He wasn't trying to be controlling or cruel. But since telling them not to didn't work, he had to try something else. But the Orpheus route didn't work either (not even, of course, for Orpheus). Users sat cowed, tongue-tied, afraid to proceed. They were afraid to say anything at all for fear they'd tell accidentally because whatever else they had to say, the subtext was always: look at this gigantic hole in me.

Soon enough, Sam decided to include the first wipe free with the start-up fee. Soon enough, he killed the Orpheus autowipe and left the decision in people's own hands. Inevitably though, users who told mea culpa'd and requested the wipe, often again and again. Users would wipe and begin again, screw up, say the wrong thing, become annoyed, become frustrated, wipe and begin again, sadder but wiser, knowing what to avoid from last time, falling into new traps instead. It was like a video game. Both projection and person, loved one and user, the dead and the living, died and were reborn into new lives again and again and again.

PENNY

 *S*am's solution to all problems had always been: more work. Sam felt head down, feet grounded, firmly seated—in for the long haul—was the way forward. Software engineering was ideally suited for this approach. You just sat and coded, recoded, let it build, looked at what happened, coded some more. While things built, you read stuff online in another window. Sam spent a lot of time sitting down.

"You're going to fuse physically to that chair," Meredith warned.

"It's a good thing you sprang for the ergonomic ones then."

"You need some exercise, fresh air."

"I walk the dogs with you. Often. Sometimes."

"You need contact with humans."

"I have nothing but contact with humans."

"Live ones."

"I see you. I see Dash. I see our clients."

"I was thinking we could invite people over this weekend."

"Who?"

"We used to have friends," said Meredith.

"We still do."

"Nonelectronic ones."

"Oh, no one has those anymore," said Sam.

"You should come with me to the game."

"I can't, Merde. I have to fix these bugs."

"My grandmother would want you to."

"Take Dash. Your grandmother would want you to take Dash."

"He's in meetings. You're here."

"Yeah, but you know what fixes bugs, Merde?"

"What?"

"Butt plus chair. It's the only thing."

It was Opening Day, and truly, Sam was excited. While his builds were running in other windows, he was reading predictions and spring training stats and DL prognoses. He was thrilled it was baseball season again. But he also thought this was why they had a TV and a radio—so he could work *and* have the game.

"It's tradition," said Meredith.

"Yeah, yours," said Sam. It wasn't that he didn't want to go with her. It was that they'd staked everything on this, and in all the world, truly, only he could make it work. "Take Penny."

"My grandmother's neighbor?"

"Our neighbor."

"I don't know. She's been pretty out of it since her husband died."

"All the more reason," said Sam.

Meredith went down to invite her to the game. Sam's phone rang two minutes later.

"I know you're having a love affair with that chair," she said, "but you have to come downstairs right now."

. . .

Penny's place was exactly Livvie's two floors down—same layout, same kitchen, same bath fixtures, same balcony and wall of floor-to-ceiling windows, same view—but like their apartment in an alternate universe. In fact, Sam could only assume the view was the same—the windows were covered in thick, dark green velvet curtains. He felt his pupils inhale just to take the place in. It was dark not just from the heavy curtains but also from scant, dim lamps and walls papered dark gold and wall-to-wall stained, matted-practically-to-tile navy carpet and dust all over everything. He took in two ragged leather chairs and a sofa with patched, leaking cushions and two wood tables so old their grain had worn smooth and black. There were dirty dishes on the tables, on the chairs, on the sofa, on the floor. The kitchen counters and sink were full of crusty empty soup cans, empty frozen veggie bags, empty cottage cheese containers, empty ice-cream cartons. There were piles of clothes—hers and his—all over the apartment like anthills, so Sam had to zigzag insectlike between them to find Meredith. The bedroom was a similar riot of clothes, plates, water glasses, prescription bottles, dirty towels and sheets, old magazines, dusty books in stacks. By the bathroom door was a tumbling pile of leftover programs from Albert's funeral. The date on it was two months before Livvie died. Meredith and Sam exchanged a long, sinking look.

"I'm sorry the place is a bit of a mess," Penny apologized, waving vaguely at the air around her. She was wearing one tennis shoe, one slipper, and a raincoat and didn't look like she'd had a bath anytime recently. "I wasn't expecting company." Like it was just a little cluttered. Like it just needed picking up a touch. Was it that the place had fallen into such disarray while she'd been taking care of her dying husband? Or was it that she hadn't had the energy—or inclination—to do anything since he died? How could it be that no one had noticed?

Meredith told Penny they'd be right back and pulled Sam out into the hallway. "Should we call an ambulance, do you think?"

"She seems okay," said Sam. "I mean, she seems confused and in need of a live-in maid, but she doesn't seem like she needs an emergency room."

"No," agreed Meredith. "Maybe a change of scenery would help. I'll take her out to get some groceries and supplies. Maybe even to lunch and the ball game if she feels up to it. You start cleaning up here."

"How?"

"Clorox. Trash bags. Toss and organize."

"I don't even know her, Merde."

"She was my grandmother's best friend. She's got kids, but they don't live nearby. I forget where, and she's in no state to . . . We can't just leave her like this."

"No," agreed Sam.

"So do you want to stay here and clean, or do you want to take her out to the ball game?"

"Buy me some peanuts and Cracker Jack," said Sam. He fetched trash bags and cleaning supplies and got to work—head down, feet grounded, in for the long haul, work.

. . .

It's hard to go through other people's stuff. Sam found it dizzying like anything else without perspective. Was this envelope on the floor because it was trash, or was it precious but mislaid? Sam could look, but he didn't want to read her mail, and that wouldn't really tell him anyway—maybe it would clearly be a love letter, or maybe it would clearly be a credit card offer, but anything in between and he'd be lost, and hell, what did he know? Maybe she desperately needed a credit card. Multiplied by an entire apartment's worth of stuff. An ancient-looking address book, a stapled packet of poetry, a seven-year-old flyer for a talent show at an elementary school, a faded baseball cap missing half its plastic closure— were these treasured memories or wandering possessions or trash begging to be culled? No way to know. Looking through someone else's things also seemed invasive and embarrassing to Sam. Actual stuff felt different from electronic stuff. Much more real. Much more present. People's e-mails spoke for themselves, were those people speaking for themselves. Their books and T-shirts and board games and posters and old souvenirs and decks of cards and stashed photos and half boxes of crayons and silverware and towels and old reading glasses and back magazine issues? Not so much.

Penny was happy to go to the ball game with Meredith and then out for an early dinner and then to the grocery store to restock the house. She was happy to go wherever Meredith led. By the time they got home, Sam had filled fifteen trash bags and made mountains of everything else. Mt. Clothespile in the living room was all of Albert's clothes. Mt. Clothespile-ette in the bedroom was all of Penny's. Near the kitchen, he had Mt. Miscellaneous Paperwork next to Mt. Seemingly Sentimental Stuff. Just outside the bathroom was Mt. Probably Trash But Maybe Not, really more of an active volcano than a dormant peak. It was better, but it was still a mess.

Sam had also found a change of everything in the bottom of the linen closet and put new sheets on the bed and new towels in the bath and in the kitchen. This proved most useful of all because Penny came home and looked around, smiled pleasantly at Sam, and said, "Oh my, you didn't have to do that," and crawled immediately into bed—in her clothes, including shoes and coat, with the lights still on, and with Sam and Meredith still standing bewildered in her living room. Meredith put away groceries, Sam stabilized his mountains, and they left a note that they'd be back to check on her in the morning.

Upstairs, Meredith scoured Livvie's address book to see if she could find Penny's kids, and when that yielded nothing, she tried Livvie herself. "I'm sorry," said Livvie. "I don't understand." Then Meredith left a message with the building manager to see whether Penny maybe had a next of kin on file and one with her own GP to see if she could make Penny an appointment for the morning. When the building manager hadn't called back within the hour, she went downstairs and started pounding on his door.

"Don't be mad," said Sam when she came back upstairs with no new information, just as restless as she'd been when she left, "but maybe we should just chill out for tonight. We'll go back tomorrow and see how she is. Maybe she knows her kids' names and phone numbers. Maybe she knows her own doctor. It seems premature to panic."

"You saw that place," Meredith said shrilly. "That wasn't the apartment of someone having a bad day. That was the apartment of someone having a bad day every day for the last six months. I'm so . . . I can't believe I haven't even checked on her since my grandmother died. What the hell is wrong with me?"

"She's got kids, Merde. And she's an adult. She's not your responsibility."

"Of course she is."

"Why? Just because she was Livvie's friend?"

"That and I'm here. We're here. Who else did you have in mind?"

"Don't be mad," Sam said again, "and I'm happy to help her, of course. You know I am. I just worry about barging in like we own the place."

"Her apartment?"

"Her apartment. Herself. Her dementia. Her kids. Her health issues. She's eighty-some years old. She probably doesn't want a babysitter."

"For a guy who goes through people's e-mails and private conversations for a living, you're pretty worried about boundaries here."

"I am only suggesting that we foray with caution into someone else's life."

"That's not really my thing," said Meredith.

"I noticed."

"Is that bad?"

"It's what I love most about you," Sam said then reflected, "Well, it's a long list. But it is one of the things I love most about you. You see people hurting and you want to fix them. It's sweet and generous, but it's also hard. Where does that come from?"

"Congenital butting in?" she said.

"Faith that you can help," said Sam.

She shrugged. "Who knows? Too much time spent on my own maybe. Too much time with wood glue instead of other little girls. My first job was at a vet's. Did I ever tell you this?" Sam shook his head. "The vet was a friend of my folks. He basically made up a job for me as a favor to them: pet petter. My job was to sit with the animals when they were prepped for surgery or coming out of anesthesia or waiting for their owners to come back for them. I petted them, kept them calm, comforted them. Dogs especially always come out of anesthesia crying. Animals are much more stoic than people, but somehow that just makes it more heartbreaking when they're scared or in pain. It was a hard job because how can you really comfort a hurting or sick or frightened animal? What do they really want? I had no idea.

"My second job was waiting tables, and that was so much easier. What do people want? Ask them and they'll tell you. They want a Coke, so they say they want a Coke, so you bring them a Coke, and they're happy. They're mad that their burger is undercooked, so you take it back and cook it some more. When people are in restaurants, their deepest desire isn't usually much more complex than ranch dressing or an extra scoop of ice cream with their pie. And I could do that. It was so easy to make them happy, and it was so great to have clients who had desires that could be both expressed and fulfilled. It's nice when people have needs you can meet."

"You think Penny has needs we can meet?" said Sam.

"Sure. I don't know what they are exactly, but it's not like she's a poodle."

. . .

In the morning, Penny seemed new-made. Her house was still a wreck, yes, but she was much more embarrassed about it, about everything from the day before, and that comforted Sam immensely. He did not care about the state of her apartment, but he was very concerned about the state of her head. She was showered and clean and wearing reasonable clothes and an expression that managed to combine mortification with gratitude. Sam was relieved. Meredith was down to business.

"We can go through the piles together today. Figure out what you're still using, what you want to keep, what we can take somewhere. We donated a lot of Grandma's things to a shelter downtown. They do hard work for a good cause, and it would free up some space for you. Then we can start getting things put away. What's in your other bedroom?" Penny's place, like Livvie's, had two bedrooms. Her second one had been locked the day before.

"Oh, that's the computer room," said Penny. "I guess there's some storage space in the there."

"You have a computer?" Sam and Meredith said together.

"Of course. Everyone has a computer. I'm not *that* old."

"What do you use it for?" Sam condescended.

"You know. E-mailing the grandkids. Video chatting with Livvie when she abandoned me for Florida every year. Online banking. Ordering groceries, clothes, books, gifts. Facebook. The usual."

"But you're . . ." Meredith began.

"A thousand years old?"

"That's not what I was going to say. I was going to say you seem so . . . alone here."

"Yeah. Maybe that's why," said Penny. "My kids e-mail. They call. It looks clean right behind the camera. I tell them all is well. I look well . . . I don't want them to worry. They don't want to worry. . . ." She trailed off.

"How many kids and where?" asked Meredith. Her grandmother had always said Penny had a horde, but she'd never had clear details.

"Katie's in San Francisco. Kent is in New Jersey. Kaleb's in Chicago. Kendra's in Vermont. And Kyra's outside Atlanta. I don't know. Maybe if we hadn't named them all Ks, they'd have stayed closer." She smiled to show them she was joking, not delusional.

"I'll call them," said Meredith. "Or e-mail them if you prefer. Just a gentle heads-up. Nothing alarming, but your kids would want to know what's going on, I think."

"Did Albert use the computer too?" asked Sam. Meredith shot him too-soon daggers from her eyeballs.

"Not really. Not as much as me. But a little." Penny thought. "Why?"

"Just wondering," said Sam. "Can I see?"

She got a key and opened up the second bedroom. The contrast was breathtaking—Meredith actually gasped. Blinds wide-open to the sound. Bookshelves of rich, bright wood polished to a shine, full to overflowing but carefully organized with spines all aligned. Pristine white walls and cedar floors. Antique binoculars on a string hanging from a hook near the bookshelves. And a gorgeous, gleaming desk entirely empty on its surface but for the promised computer. In one corner was a love seat with a small table and a reading lamp. "Albert was a bit of a neat freak"—Penny smiled sheepishly—"and he was in charge of this room. He liked to read in here. I'd come in to use the computer, and he'd sit and read, and then I'd come over to snuggle with him. It's why we traded the recliner for a love seat. We spent a lot of lovely, quiet hours together in here."

"Why do you keep it locked?" Meredith asked.

"So it would stay clean." Penny shrugged. "So it would stay, I don't know, his."

ALL DOWNHILL FROM HERE

*P*enny made Sam feel claustrophobic. He was used to spending months on a project, weeks on a single problem, days indoors, hours and hours on end in a chair and never feeling antsy or even like he needed to get up and stretch. But Penny made him want to move to Wyoming or Colorado or somewhere with wide-open spaces and lots of sunlight.

"Let's go to Wyoming for the weekend," said Sam.

"What's in Wyoming?" said Meredith.

"Big skies."

"That's Montana."

"Apartments free of piles of crap. Brains free of piles of dust."

"We have that here."

"No Merde, let's go away. For the weekend. You know, like a couple."

She sat up to look at him. "Really?"

"Really."

"Don't screw with me, Sam."

"I'm saying let's go away."

"What about 'butt plus chair'? What about 'our entire livelihood'? What about the bugs?"

"They'll wait."

"They will?"

"Bugs are very patient."

"They are?"

"Well, no, bugs are inanimate. We only call them that to . . . Never mind, point is, they can wait."

"If they can wait, why do we spend so much time in this damn apartment?"

"Merde, do you want to go away or not?"

"Paris?"

"For the weekend? We'd spend the whole time getting there. Too far."

"London?"

"Oh yes, London's much closer."

"Skiing!"

"It's April."

"Not in Canada."

"Even in Canada, Merde, I think it's April."

"No, I mean the ski resorts are still open in Canada."

"I don't ski," said Sam.

"You don't ski?"

"No."

"Why not?"

"Never learned."

"Why not?"

"Grew up in Baltimore." Sam shrugged. "Not a lot of snow. Not a lot of mountains."

"I grew up on an island," said Meredith.

"But not in the South Pacific."

"I am going to teach you how to ski. This weekend. In Canada."

"Have you ever taught someone to ski before?"

"No."

"Do you know how?"

"To ski?"

"To teach someone to ski?"

"No."

"But you're confident."

"What's the worst that can happen?"

Sam had some ideas. They flashed montage-style through his brain and involved a lot of impaling.

"You'll love it," Meredith promised. "They have very big skies in Canada."

They drove up through the tulip farms, over the border and around

Vancouver, all along a winding road with sweeping vistas of the water giving way to winking glimpses of it, and the promise of mountains giving way to the real thing, soaring and snowy and grand. Whistler was beautiful with large skies indeed, but the sport itself seemed to Sam to involve a lot of apparatus. Meredith opened a duffel bag and pulled out vests, sweaters, parkas, hats, leggings, goggles, ski pants, helmets, gloves, socks, neck muffs, foot warmers, lip balms, and minipacks of tissues. Then she went to a rental counter and procured skis, poles, and boots that defied the laws of nature.

"My legs don't bend that way," said Sam.

"You'll be fine."

"They bend the other way." He raised a pant leg to demonstrate.

"Put your pants down, Sam. You'll be fine."

An hour later, he was almost, but not quite, dressed.

"Okay, now we get on the lift."

"How?"

"I'll show you when we get there."

"No, I mean how do we get to the lift?"

She laughed and clomped off, and he had no choice but to follow her, and fifteen minutes later, by some miracle, he found himself balanced precariously next to her on a bench that was soaring into the sky, that rose up over snow-covered firs into air so crisp and clean and cold he felt guilt about exhaling, over valleys and mountains that went on as far as he could see no matter how high they climbed. It was terrifying.

"My feet are heavier than the rest of me," said Sam.

"No they aren't."

"They're going to drag me to my death."

"No they won't."

"And my sweat has formed a thin layer of frost inside my shirt."

"It's freezing out here, Sam. Why are you sweating?"

"Terror. Plus, for an hour in an overheated lodge, I wrestled myself into boots that bend backward while you stacked every layer ever sewn into a pile on my person. Also I'm growing increasingly concerned about what happens at the end of this lift. And so you have to wonder why."

"Why what?"

"Why I am happier right now than I have ever been in my life."

"Cerebral edema?" Meredith guessed.

"I've always hated it when people say, 'She's the best thing that ever happened to me.' A person isn't an event—people don't 'happen.' You aren't the best thing to happen to me. You are the best thing to happen in this universe. You are the best thing there is or has ever been. I didn't even know there was happy like this."

She shifted toward him across the chairlift, and the whole thing swung wildly.

"Are you crazy?" he shrieked. "Just because I could die happy doesn't mean I'm ready to."

"It's fine. They're built to withstand people suddenly deciding to make out on the way up."

"Are you sure?"

"I am very sure."

He bit the ring finger of his right glove to pull it off and touched her face softly. He worried about how he'd type with frostbitten digits, but he couldn't not. Then he leaned very, very gingerly forward, just far enough to kiss her, and did so while trying also to breathe and also to balance and also not to fall to his death. It was both hard and transcendent. He kissed her until he felt tears on his cheeks—hers—and pulled back to look at her questioningly.

"I just feel very happy too," she said.

He held her cheek and pressed his forehead to hers. "Don't cry, Merde. Our faces will freeze this way."

"I can live with that," she said. Then his glove slid off his lap and onto the mountain far, far below.

"Shit. Now what?" said Sam.

"We go get it."

"How?"

"Easy." She grinned. "It's all downhill from here."

THINGS SAM NEVER EXPECTED

*T*he more users signed up, the more Sam realized the limits of his imagination. Computer geek though he was, he knew what people wanted in a mate. All of them. Every one. So far as Sam could tell, they may have found it in the damnedest places, but everyone wanted the same things in a partner—kind, funny, hot, fun, smart, and totally in love. That one person defined smart as an applied mathematics PhD whereas another defined it as able to repair a toilet, that one person fancied morning coats or ball gowns (or both) whereas another went for jeans and a T-shirt, that one dater was amused by sarcasm whereas another cracked up at puns only made Sam's old job easier. It meant there were mates enough for all if you knew where (and how) to look, but everyone wanted the same thing.

Not so dead communications. Users wanted an infinite number of things Sam couldn't anticipate. User number three, Eben Westfeldt, went through the whole sign-up process, the money, the tutorials, the prep sessions and lectures, the waiting period, the whole bit, only to open a window with his late wife and confess his repeated infidelities. He'd written them out longhand on a yellow legal pad, an impressive list, and read them off to her, including partners, dates, locations, where she was at the time, and what he'd told her he'd been doing. She wasn't angry, having no inkling of it before and thus no electronic memory as basis for it. The closest she could muster came from e-mails to an old friend who'd had a one-night stand with a man who picked her up in a bar while her husband was at a conference in Austin, but Mrs. Westfeldt's reaction in that case had been one of you-go-girl support as the marriage was long dead and the husband known to be philandering. When Eben was done with his confessions, he closed the window, came up to Meredith and Sam at the front counter, and told them to shut it down.

"Shut it down?" said Meredith. "But you've only had one session."

"That was plenty," said Eben. "What a relief to get that off my chest."

"You know that reaction wasn't real," Sam felt compelled to tell him in the interest of honesty. "You didn't actually confess. It wasn't really her. And she couldn't really understand because you were such a good and thorough liar while she was alive."

Meredith jumped in to try to cover, but it wasn't necessary. "Oh, it doesn't matter." Eben waved him off. "I confessed, and that's what matters. Phew. Man, I feel so much better. You all are geniuses. Geniuses. This is one fuck of a good service."

Sam hadn't counted on Eben. He hadn't counted on Maria Gardner who wanted to e-mail with her cat who'd passed away the month before. ("Did she e-mail much?" Dash asked her dryly. "Did she forward funny pictures of herself to everyone in her inbox?") He didn't count on people coming in to RePose with Kurt Cobain. He didn't count on would-be users who wanted to talk to their exes who weren't so much dead as dumped. He didn't count on George Lenore who went through the whole process just so he could ask his late wife where she kept the key to the shed and if she knew where the manual for the dishwasher was and whether he had to call for the monthly cleaning service or they would just come and which pharmacy carried that aloe gel he liked and how many minutes to microwave a potato. She was able, in fact, to answer a surprising number of his questions.

Edith Casperson seemed like the sort of user Sam expected—sixty-something wife in mourning missing newly passed husband—but the day after Sam set her up, he found her in the salon calmly telling the computer screen in front of her to go fuck itself. "You were such an asshole, Bob. Such a fucking asshole. I loved you. I still do. But that doesn't mean you weren't an asshole. You think I liked sitting at home all those years making your dinner and washing your socks and pressing your shirts and smelling your bad breath? You think I gave a shit what Marty in PR thought about Judy's presentation or how it affected sales in Bangladesh? Nope to all of the above which you might have known if you ever let me talk. I'm your wife, you shithead. That doesn't mean you take me for granted. That means you *don't* take me for granted. What if I had left you? You couldn't take care of yourself. You'd have been dead within the week. Of course, you died anyway, but at least it wasn't from being left by your beleaguered wife, Bob. That's an embarrassing way to go." She was so exhilarated that she wiped at the end of the session then came back and did it again twice a week for a month—set up, bitch out, wipe, begin again. Sam hadn't expected raging widows, but when Edith explained sheepishly that she'd simply never had the nerve to do it while Bob was alive, Sam had to admit that made a lot of sense.

David Elliot, seventeen, brought in his guitar and played original songs occasioned by the death of his mother, to his mother, every day for a month. Sam hadn't counted on that. Sam thought he might be disturbing other users, but in fact everyone else would pause in their chats and their e-mails and their posts to listen to David then applaud for him quietly. Edith leaned in to the camera one rainy afternoon and said, "Mrs. Elliot, you should be so proud of your boy. He's so talented. He brightens everyone's day here." Sam hadn't counted on that either.

Celia Montrose brought in her despondent daughter Kelly to chat with her dad. Celia could not bring herself to communicate with her late husband herself. "I want to remember him the way I remember him," she said. "I want to start grieving so I can stop someday." But Kelly felt she wanted her father this way, and Celia wanted to do whatever she could to help her daughter. Sam had counted on that, perhaps. What he had not expected was what Kelly actually did during chats with her father—got him to help her study for the PSATs. They'd sit and do math for hours and never talk about another thing. After one particularly intense session, they found her in the bathroom in tears. "It's okay." Meredith hugged her. "It's hard when we miss them so much."

"It's not that," Kelly sniffed. "He just knows everything. This stuff is so hard for me and so easy for him."

"Don't forget," Sam told her, "he has a whole CPU behind him. It's not like he's running those numbers himself."

"He must think I'm such an idiot," Kelly sobbed. Sam called his dad and got him to insert the fake math software he'd made for seven-year-old Sam into Benjamin Montrose's projection. The next time Kelly came in, her dad kept insisting that all the angles of a triangle added up to 6,104 degrees, that the value of x was always eleven no matter what, and that pi are round not squared. Kelly giggled until she fell off her chair. Celia thanked Sam for making her daughter laugh for the first time in months. Celia warned Sam that if Kelly couldn't get into a good college, she was blaming him. One afternoon, Meredith found Kelly on the sofa in the corner getting algebra tutoring from David Elliot, neither of them anywhere near a computer.

Mr. and Mrs. Benson were the first of their kind, the first of many, unfortunately. Sam was expecting them, but that didn't mean he was prepared. Mr. and Mrs. Benson had lost their teenage daughter Maggie when she fell onto her head out of the window of her dorm room her first semester away at college. They bought the whole package, but mostly they wanted text messaging, Maggie's heretofore chosen mode of communiqué. Mr. Benson also liked to video chat with Maggie though Mrs. Benson couldn't take it. Mrs. Benson liked to e-mail with her daughter which Mr. Benson felt he could take or leave. But they both loved getting texts from and sending them to her even though they had begged her in life just to "put the freaking phone to your ear and call I mean my God it takes forever to send a text and they're too small to read and impossible to understand and I mean clearly you have your phone right there just call us on it!"

Maggie Benson taught Sam about teenage girls. He had never been able to understand them when he was a teenager himself. They said things, but they weren't things they meant, so what they did mean remained a mystery so far as Sam could tell. He'd been glad to leave them behind when he turned twenty. Teenage girls didn't use online dating services. And teenage girls didn't die. So Sam had figured he had another . . . well, at least fourteen years before he'd have to worry again about what teenage girls meant.

But sometimes teenage girls did die. No doubt Maggie Benson had loved her parents. But her e-mails and her Facebook posts and her blog and her texts and her video chats didn't know that because she didn't text her best friend to say, "You know what? I love my parents," and she didn't blog, "Today I realized just how much my parents have done for me over the years," and she didn't e-mail her boyfriend, "I can't come over tonight because my parents won't let me which I totally understand because they're afraid we're going to go all the way and that we're too young and I'll get hurt, and besides, it's perfectly reasonable that they'd be alarmed about their little girl getting physical." Instead she e-mailed him to say, "My parents are such douches. They never let me do anything!!!!!" and she texted her best friend, "I hate my parents!!!!!! They never let me do anything!!!!!!" and she blogged, "Today I realized how excited I am to go to college and finally have some freedom. My parents never let me do anything!!!!!" Etc.

"I need a translator," said Sam.

"For what?" said Meredith.

"Teenage girls."

"Why?"

"They don't say what they mean."

"No one says what they mean."

"No one says what they mean all the time. Most people say what they mean sometimes. Usually."

"Teenagers don't know what they mean."

"Teenage boys do. They mean, 'I'm horny.'"

"That's not what they say," said Meredith.

"In fact, it is," said Sam.

"I'll translate for you."

"You're not a teenage girl."

"I used to be."

Sam looked at her skeptically.

"When I was thirteen," Meredith said, "I told my best friend, Luke Feldstein, that I didn't want to be his friend anymore because he asked me to the back-to-school dance, and I said no because Kimmy Mitchell told Chrissie Graves that she bet I was going to go with Luke, which turned out to be because Kimmy liked him herself, but I thought she meant that I couldn't find anyone else to go with, and after I said no he asked Anna Wong."

"So why'd you stop being his friend?"

"I didn't. I just said I wanted to."

"Why did you say you wanted to?"

"It was wrong to ask Anna. He asked me first."

"But you said no."

"He still shouldn't have asked anyone else."

"Why not?"

"Because he liked me. And I liked him. Like, liked-liked."

"Why'd you say no then?"

"So Kimmy Mitchell wouldn't think I was a loser."

"Were you friends with Kimmy?"

"No."

"Then why'd you care what she thought?"

Meredith just shrugged.

"So Luke was just supposed to sit home by himself because you were being insane?"

"I would have sat home with him."

"Did you tell him that?"

"No."

"How was he supposed to know?"

Meredith shrugged again.

"Then he had to ask Anna Wong," said Sam.

"Why?"

"Pay attention. He was horny."

In contrast to the teenage girls were the grandparents. Like Horton the Elephant, himself never a teenage girl, grandparents meant what they said and said what they meant. When Maggie said she hated her parents, what she meant was that she was seventeen and growing up and feeling at once safe and smothered, eager and anxious, ready and afraid, frustrated and beloved. When Livvie said you and Sam should take some time off and come visit me in Florida because it's nice here and you work too hard, what she meant was that Meredith and Sam should go visit her in Florida because it was nice there and they worked too hard. On that front, grandparents were much easier. On the other hand, Maggie Benson sent on average seventy-two texts a day. She updated her Facebook page eleven times a day and commented on other people's pages sixty-one times a day. She kept two blogs, commented on nine others, read fifteen more. She had two e-mail accounts, 2,896 Flickr photos, thirty-eight YouTube videos, and was herself tagged on average four times a day. What Sam did on average four times a day was send a would-be user home empty-handed because their grandparents hadn't ever used a computer. Old people may be the link to the past and all that, but they lacked electronic memory. The ones Sam could create projections for were usually confined to e-mail. It was a rare elderly grandparent who had a Facebook page or a laptop with a video camera.

"That's going to be the trade-off with old people," Sam complained. "They barely need to be present for their conversations when they're alive, they're so obvious. But most of them haven't engaged with technology any more recent than a toaster oven."

"This," said Meredith, "is why you aren't in charge of marketing."

"And then the problem with young people is they have tons of electronic communication, but they never say what they mean."

"So we're looking for dead fifty-year-olds," said Dash.

"Or really tech-savvy nonagenarians," said Meredith.

"Or really boring, honest teenagers," Sam sighed.

"Or a computer genius of epic proportions," said Meredith, kissing him on the mouth.

"With a willing and able fetcher of lattes at the ready," added Dash, also kissing him on the mouth then heading out the door for the coffee shop.

In the end, Sam developed a filter to add on to the algorithm for users who'd lost a child under twenty-five that accounted for the fact that teenagers love their parents but don't say so and skewed the results accordingly. There were parts of this job where even expecting it didn't help Sam prepare for what came.

To combat these, Dash designated Sunday evenings as Notte Della Pizza. It was the solution to several problems: It ensured weekly contact with Penny and an opportunity to both feed her and send her home with leftovers. It was an excuse to keep in touch with Jamie, who in addition to being a nice guy was also a reliable potential employee, an idea which thrilled Sam, who thought it was his turn to be boss, and Dash who liked his accent. It was a repository for all of Dash's mozzarellas, the only cheese he could reliably turn out so far and which therefore rapidly filled all of the space in the refrigerator. But mostly, it fought dead teenagers with what live teenagers—and everyone else of course—liked best: friendship, laughter, food. Refuge in love, refuge in life. It was their only chance all week to really be together. They were together constantly of course, but therefore work time also quickly became all the time. Before breakfast was a great time to worry about UI issues, and in bed was fair game to consider fair pricing, and while Dash pressed cheese into molds he also ran through the legalities of permissions and privacy rights. On Notte Della Pizza, all of that was off-limits because Penny couldn't possibly understand, and until they could bring Jamie on as Sam's lackey, discussion of business issues in front of him was verboten, so the intent was clearly focused: friendship, laughter, food. On Notte Della Pizza, Sam got his family back, if only temporarily.

The occasion of the inaugural Notte was the first time Jamie saw the salon. It was also the first time he met Dash.

"Quick: favorite cheese," Dash demanded as soon as Jamie walked into the kitchen.

"Um . . . Brie?"

"Baked and melted, or chilled and semi-soft?"

"Oh, baked and melted, I should think."

"Almonds or pastry?"

"Pardon?"

"Do you like it baked with almonds or covered in pastry dough?"

"I'm quite flexible as regards Brie," said Jamie.

"But it's your favorite cheese. You should have a definite preference," said Dash. "Brie is an odd choice for a Brit anyway. Stilton. Cheddar. Something hard and crumbly. That's what I was expecting."

"There's Somerset Brie. Cornish Brie," Jamie offered.

"But don't you think they're French influenced?" asked Dash.

"I'm not sure," said Jamie. "Why are you asking me about cheese?"

"Well I make cheese, as you see." Dash gestured at his supplies all around him. "I'm taking requests."

Meredith rolled her eyes. "You only know how to make mozzarella. Who cares what kind of cheese he likes when you can only make one?"

"I was hoping he'd say mozzarella."

"Mozzarella's not British either," said Meredith.

"No, but think how awesome it would have been if he'd said mozzarella, and I'd thrown open the fridge dramatically." He demonstrated.

Inside were piles and piles of Tupperwares Jamie could only assume, at that point, contained mozzarella.

"No one's favorite cheese is mozzarella," said Meredith.

"Then you can just have naked pizza tonight and see how you like it," said Dash, drying his hands on an apron that read "Fellate the Cook" and offering Jamie his hand. "Dashiell Bentlively, by the way."

"Bentlively?" Jamie wondered, and Sam remembered the first time he'd met Dash. "Are you a Dickens character? Are you an at-first-appealing-but-later-too-much-of-a-bad-boy fellow in a Jane Austen novel?"

"I am a bad boy," Dash allowed, "but I'm appealing the whole way through."

"Let me show you the salon while the pizza bakes," said Sam.

"Ten minutes max!" Dash warned.

Sam took Jamie downstairs, and they stood considering Salon Styx in the purple half-light of dusk. "Pretty. Better place to meet the dead than usual."

"What's usual?" said Sam.

"I don't know. Creepy graveyards. The apocalypse."

"Meredith did a nice job. Painted, decorated, hung airplanes."

"She's quite talented. I knew there was a reason I hired her."

"You didn't hire her."

"I don't think it's the paint and airplanes that make the place anyway."

"What then?"

Jamie shrugged. "Maybe it's occupational hazard, but I always think computers have a romantic glow about them. Full of promise and prospect. Especially when they're off like this. One has the impression that with the flick of a switch, all possibilities can be explored, all dreams might come true. Computers hold magic, you know."

"That's awfully cheesy," said Sam.

"That's why I'm an important manager and you're unemployed," said Jamie. "Poetry. Poetry makes all the difference."

"I had no idea," Sam admitted.

"Seriously, Sam, it's most impressive. Not just the space. Not even mostly the space. What you've done here, what you're doing, it's a good thing. You might change the world."

"That might be overstating it."

"It's a good thing you're a kindhearted genius and not the evil kind."

"That would ruin everything," Sam agreed.

"Exactly, whereas now the only thing you're ruining is me."

. . .

User numbers grew, which was good, as did expectations, which was predictable, as did the menu of options, which caused some problems. On behalf of the Bensons, Sam worked on text messaging. He thought the instant gratification of that would be very popular and that it would be easy to replicate, even from the unpredictable, as-a-rule-dishonest teenage set. But texts were too short to be gratifying and usually just named times and places DLOs promised to meet their users which, of course, was especially cruel. Some people wanted to follow their dead mothers' Twitter feeds. But most, not surprisingly, did not.

In the end, most people chose e-mail or video, one edge or the other of the tech spectrum, e-mails little more than a glorified letter, video chat fairly close to God. E-mail was more gratifying, more lingering. You could say exactly what you meant, get it all out of your system, receive back a reply you could print and carry in your pocket and clutch against your chest. Video chat held none of those advantages, but it took people's breath away. They just could not believe it. And could not get enough. It was addictive. Its trump was simply its unbelievable verisimilitude. It just seemed so damn real. If you tried to get mushy or romantic or weepy with it though, it just looked at you like you were nuts and asked, casually—even, to users' bruised memories and mourning hearts, cruelly—what the hell was wrong with you man, or words to that effect. It did not get—and could not be told—why you were so sad. So users ended up lying to their projections. Oh, no, nothing was wrong. Everything was fine. Same old, same old. And what's new with you?

Sam's dad was right. Users met their projections more than halfway, nudged them in directions they wanted to go, avoided what would trip them up, worked to make it all work. But the real miracle was that the projections met their living loved ones the other half of the way. Users lied, evaded, talked around, hinted at, blubbered incoherently, and fabricated wholesale, yet they managed somehow to get the responses they craved anyway. These were loved ones, after all. The whole thing worked in the first place because these people knew each other well, loved each other much, and communicated intimately. They understood without understanding. They responded to what they did not even notice. They called their user *petit chou* which they never did except when she was really, really vulnerable. They called their user Tarzan which they never did except when he really, really needed pumping up. They were moved to tell users how much they loved them even though they told them all the time. They were moved to tell users they were proud of them, thinking of them, praying for them, besotted with them, so lucky to have them— uncannily whatever they needed to hear because without knowing it, users had asked for it, had planted the seeds that yielded that response. It was like a dance. And both sides were very well trained. This, of course, had been true in life as well.

Meredith proved right about needing the space too. Though users could RePose anywhere they had network connectivity, lots of them chose to start in the salon instead for all the reasons Meredith had predicted. People *were* afraid of ghosts. They wanted handholding and editing while they wrote their first e-mails and replies, advice about what to say and how to say it. Support for the Herculean effort not to blurt out the sad news of the projection's recent demise. Just someone else's presence deterred them. Some of it was having to look up from the computer at Sam's stern face, the very one that had just patiently explained why you couldn't tell it it was dead. Some of it was strength in numbers—if the users to your right and left could find other things to talk about with their projections, surely so could you. But much of it was the jarring unreality of Salon Styx. RePose worked precisely because it was so exactly like what you both remembered, but what you remembered had never happened here—in this bright room overlooking the mountains and the water with Dash and Meredith and Sam gazing benevolently over all they had made possible, their Eden. Many users needed that distance from what it felt like. Otherwise it was too real, too much what it was. Otherwise it was too frustrating that your DLO would communicate with you only online, would never meet you for coffee, meet you in bed. Come home from college. Come home from Florida.

It was hard too for Sam and Dash and especially Meredith. Though users had a need she could address, that need was bottomless. They were often weepy all through the sign-up process, the start-up how-to lecture, paying their fees, signing the forms, releasing the info, but when they came in finally to begin, they'd be totally wrecked. Often it took days of coming in every morning, sitting down at the computers, leaving again before they could begin. Meredith would hold their hands, hug them while they cried in her arms, sit and listen to them reminisce for hours. Feed them tissues. Assure them everyone had trouble the first time. Assure them they could try again tomorrow. Assure them the first one was the hardest one. It made her sad and wrecked and weepy too.

"This isn't your job," Sam worried.

"Of course it is," she said.

In contrast, Sam's approach was to demystify. No need to be freaked out and upset. Just a computer program. A bunch of electrons. These ghosts were no more real than the ones in Ms. Pac-Man. Make-believe. Really, really impressive make-believe.

Dash, as ever, played the field. He sized people up and gave them what they needed. If they needed holding, he held. If they needed to minimize it, he minimized. Avery brought in a box of Clive's fancy dress shirts, and Dash wore one every day for a month, never mind his insistence that clothes didn't matter in Seattle. Edith ran out of nasty names to call her husband, and Dash came up with "gubbertush," which meant bucktoothed but with the added bonus connotations of both "goober" and "tush." Mr. Benson got a text from Maggie that confessed, "Wrecked car. But I'm fine. Am also accidentally in Idaho so might miss curfew. Sorry!"

"What do I do with that?" asked Mr. Benson helplessly.

"What did you do the first time?" said Dash.

"Drove out to Idaho and picked her up."

"What did you want to do?"

"Drink heavily. And ground her until September 2035."

"Do that now."

"Can I?"

"Sure. Might be cathartic."

"I never thought I'd be nostalgic for a fight with my teenager."

"Ground her and I'll take you out for the first part," said Dash.

"The first part?"

"Drinking heavily."

. . .

It was hard to watch users, hard to be with them, hard to help, but it was also gratifying. Watching people's faces light up, watching their smiles triumph through their tears, watching people catch their breath and hold their heart and whisper oh thank God thank God. You could see their relief. You could watch them let go. And often, very often, Sam found them back in his arms afterward. Thank you so much. You have given me the greatest gift. It was even better than I'd imagined. I feel so much better now. You let me let go. You let me say goodbye.

People signed up to say goodbye. But then they got addicted and couldn't. That was another thing Meredith was right about: death is for life.

ALBERT

*T*hat they had any warning at all, that they didn't just offer to send her in blindly as they did everyone else, was something of a fluke. A few weeks after they'd more or less adopted Penny, Meredith thought she was ready to RePose.

"She's too old," Dash argued. He'd spent the afternoon at Penny's helping her organize her kitchen and had just gotten back from taking her out for pizza and ice cream.

"She's not too old. She's Grandma's age," said Meredith.

"Grandma was too old to RePose too."

"She uses it all the time."

"No, Merde," said Sam. "You use it all the time. Livvie doesn't."

"Well. She would."

"She was pretty tech-savvy for an old lady," said Dash. "But I don't mean that Penny couldn't do the tech. I mean I'm not sure she could get her head around the concept. Young people are used to having virtual relationships, to watching great big pieces of their lives unfold on-screen, online. I think it'd be too much for her."

"Was she acting weird?" said Meredith. "Did she seem out of it again?"

"No, she was fine. But I think we'd all like to keep it that way."

"She misses Albert," said Meredith. "It breaks my heart. Maybe it won't even work. She said he didn't use the computer much. But I think we should run it and see."

"I think it's a mistake," said Dash.

"Vote?" She'd taken to proposing this when she and Dash disagreed because Sam always sided with her.

They voted. Dash lost. So Sam ran it and saw. When it didn't work, he investigated further. Ordinarily, of course, he didn't read dead loved ones' communications—his algorithm did. He respected everyone's privacy. And, truthfully, he didn't really care about people's secrets and lies and hopes and dreams. Ordinarily, he never actually saw any of that stuff. But Albert needed troubleshooting. Not surprisingly, Albert didn't have a Facebook page. He didn't have a blog. He didn't video chat or post YouTube videos. He didn't have a photo account because he didn't have a digital camera. He didn't send text messages because he didn't have a cell phone. He didn't even have anything he read regularly online. What Albert did have was a torrid, consuming, enduring, and fairly well-documented affair.

Albert had a few start-up messages from when he opened his secret e-mail account. He got confirmation of a few things he bought online. He got his fair share of spam. But other than that, Albert e-mailed exclusively and obsessively and sometimes alarmingly graphically with one Agnes Grayson. Sam couldn't believe it. He tried to tell himself that what was gross and wrong here was the betrayal of a woman he was gradually coming to think of as family. But really it was the horror that you could know someone that well and love someone that much and still be totally wrong. That and they were old people, and old people should not, so far as Sam was concerned, be doing the things Albert was describing, especially upside down.

Meredith and Dash came home from their hard day at the office.

"Three new sign-ups today," she reported.

"David had a new song for his mom," added Dash. "I'm thinking of introducing him to my friend Bradley who does music for a studio in L.A. He's really good."

"Oh, and Maggie told Mr. Benson he was a good dad today. She was still pissed off that he grounded her, but she said she knew why he did it. He was over the moon. So nice going."

"Thanks." Sam looked like *he'd* been grounded.

"What's wrong?"

"I ran the algorithm on Albert. . . ."

"Not enough to go on?"

"Enough to e-mail but—"

"That's probably enough, you know?" said Meredith. "Dash is right. Video might be weird for her. Video chat with her dead husband would probably give her a heart attack."

"He's not going to be able to e-mail her."

"Why not?"

"His e-mails all center on one thing only."

"Really? What?"

"Out-of-the-way restaurants no one knows about. A series of motels cheap enough to be regularly afforded but clean enough to truly use the bed. Occasionally a B-and-B on the peninsula. Once even a campsite."

"Shut up," Meredith and Dash said at the same time. He was incredulous but a little impressed. She paled like she was the one being cheated on.

"He was having an affair," said Sam.

"With who?" Meredith demanded.

"Please let it be a guy, please let it be a guy." Dash crossed his fingers.

" 'Fraid not," said Sam.

"Would that make it better?" said Meredith.

"Old high school flame, evidently. Female. First there's reconnecting; then there's flirting; then there are lunch dates just to catch up."

"Oh God," said Meredith.

"Then there's a lot of the 'which hotel and what time' kind of e-mails."

"Men are pigs," Dash smiled. "I should know. I am one."

"Then there's a lot of the 'I'm going to touch you here, bend you this way, whisper this, make you scream that, then try it upside down and backward twice' kind of e-mails."

"My God," Dash whistled and Meredith whispered at the same time.

"It's okay," Sam said. "We haven't told her anything about RePose. She probably wouldn't understand even if we did. She'll have to mourn the old-fashioned way."

"It's not okay," said Meredith angrily.

"Why not?"

"Because her whole life was a lie. Because the man she loved didn't love her. Because we found her living in squalor, mourning a man who never was worth it."

"Girl, you don't know that," said Dash.

"Sam read the e-mails," said Meredith.

"No, I mean okay, he was having an affair, but you don't know what was really going on. Maybe he loved them both. Maybe he didn't love this Agnes chick at all but needed something he wasn't getting from Penny. Hell, maybe she knew and okayed it. Grandma would say, 'You never know what goes on in other people's houses.' Don't get all uppity about it."

"You think Penny knew and was okay with it? Really? That sweet old lady? That's the defense you can muster?"

"I don't have to muster a defense at all. And neither did Albert."

"He did a terrible, terrible thing to the woman he was supposed to love."

"In fact, I think he did her a huge favor."

"Are you crazy?"

"Seems like he made sure she never knew. Took this to his grave. Set up a secret e-mail account. Used it when Penny wasn't around. Made sure to meet his girlfriend only where no one would recognize them."

"Yeah, so he wouldn't get busted. If it were okay with her, he wouldn't have had to sneak around."

"Look, I'm not saying this was admirable," said Dash. "I'm saying we don't know the story. She feels like she was loved, so she was."

"That's not true."

"That is true," said Sam, siding with Dash for the first time all month. "That's the whole premise here. That's what powers RePose. That's what makes it work. Feeling loved equals being loved. That's all."

"True in real life too," said Dash.

"We should tell her," said Meredith. "Maybe it will help her get over him. She'll realize he wasn't the man she thought he was."

"Oh, Merde, no. Don't tell her. She doesn't want to know. Dash is right—we don't know what was really going on. We only have e-mails to go on."

"Isn't that the whole point? E-mails don't lie. They may be lies, but they don't lie. We can reconstruct an entire human with them. This whole thing is based on e-mails being plenty to go on," said Meredith. And then, "He lied to her. And we know it."

"Well then we'd better keep it to ourselves," said Dash.

He left to go get more rennet for his goat cheese, and Sam made dinner, and Meredith started working on an Allied World War I Spad (it looked like a biplane to Sam). Mostly, she just slammed supplies around. Then she called her grandmother.

"Hey baby," Livvie said when she answered, "I was just thinking about you." The wonder of it, of his own dead loved one, never failed to take Sam's breath away. Ditto a computer program with the impression that it had been thinking of you.

"Hi Grandma," said Meredith miserably.

"You seem in such a funk all the time these days. What's wrong, baby?"

"Nothing."

"Something."

"Just . . . crap at work."

"You work too hard. You and Sam should take a vacation and come visit me."

"If someone knew a terrible secret about you and at first it would make you more unhappy, but in the long run maybe it would make you less unhappy, would you want to know?"

Livvie wasn't sure what to say to that. "I'm sorry, sweetie, I don't understand." And then, "It's so sunny here. You would love it."

"Is this wrong? Is what we're doing wrong?" Meredith asked her grandmother.

"My baby?" Livvie didn't understand the question, but she knew the right answer anyway. "She never does anything wrong."

NOT ANYMORE

*A*nd that was just the beginning. As the first handful of users turned into dozens then hundreds, and as Sam's two hours of sleep each night turned into four then five then eight, and as the dogs started getting better walks, and as Meredith seemed to relax into things a bit more, and as Dash started to stay down in L.A. more often, and as bringing dinner or a new book or a pot of flowers down to Penny got folded into their schedule, they all found a little bit of a rhythm.

Sam was finding time to run most mornings. He ran through the Arboretum or in Seward Park or along the waterfront downtown. One chilly, rainy morning at the end of April, he went all the way out to Discovery Park and ran along the bluff, down to the lighthouse, and back up again. He drove home, drenched in rain and sweat, with the windows open.

There he found his apartment heated to approximately three hundred degrees and Meredith in the middle of the living room doing yoga in a soaked tank top and very short shorts. Opening the front door was like walking into a wall. The dogs raised pitiful heads from the couch and wagged tails once apiece but could muster the energy for nothing further.

"Holy hell, Merde, what is going on? It's like a rain forest in here."

She was breathing hard in downward dog and gazed up at him from between her legs. "My hot yoga studio's closed," she said. "It's Take Your Daughter to Work Day."

"Shouldn't your hot yoga studio be open for Take Your Daughter to Work Day? So your yoga teacher could take her daughter to work?"

"She took her to her day job," Meredith upside-down shrugged. "Her daughter doesn't like the heat. It makes her queasy."

"I know how she feels," said Sam. "And you can't do room-temperature yoga for one day only?"

"Nope. Once you go hot, you can't go back. I'm so much more flexible this way." She was drenched—wetter than he was, and he'd been running in the rain for an hour—and flexible indeed. She'd somehow flipped into a backbend with feet and hands planted firmly on the floor and the entire front of her straining in a perfect arc toward the ceiling. The bottom half of her tank stuck to her stomach and rose and fell as she panted through the pose. The top part, he noticed, just fluttered with her heartbeat underneath. She was breathing hard.

"You're messing up my breath," she accused him as sweat trickled down from her forehead, through messed hair, onto the mat beneath her in steady drops.

"I can't tell you how bad I feel about that," said Sam. He removed his muddy shoes and socks on the way over and spread his feet just outside of hers, shoulder-width apart (Sam had occasionally tried yoga as a way to meet women). He pressed himself against the current apex of her, and she took a deep breath in and curved herself deeper, pushing her bottom half more firmly against him but her top half further away. Sam couldn't have that and reached forward to trace fingers through the pool of water at the hollow of her throat, down over her chest and between her breasts, and over her stretched-taut stomach, and she breathed into him for another moment, two, before somehow flipping back into downward dog. Sam had barely moved but now found himself pressed luxuriously into the only part of her that was pointing up. He found he also had more leverage now and draped himself over her, dog over dog, the outsides of her hands and feet pressed to the insides of his, his entire body laid out over the entire length of hers. He felt her draw a deep breath in. He balanced against her, against the mat, and managed to free his right hand from the floor. He reached between his own thighs to run his fingers up the inside of hers, then under her top, over her sweat-drenched stomach, underneath her bra. There, he cupped her breast, ran his thumb underneath and then over her nipple, and felt her heart beating beneath his palm as she struggled to hold the position, his weight and hers, against slippery hands and a tongue licking wet salt from the back of her neck. She balanced again, somehow freed her left hand, and twisted it behind her and into Sam's shorts. He was quite impressed—hot yoga was doing wonders for her balance and her strength. Deep breath in, out. Then his left hand slipped and he tumbled on top of her, knocking them both into a heap on the mat.

He lay there for a moment, just feeling her underneath him, making them both wait, until she pressed him gently off her from behind and cleared enough space to flip over so they were front to front, all the whole length of them. When he lowered himself back on top of her, he found her all his again—nothing bent away, no balance to be maintained to keep her there, and slippery had ceased to be an impediment of any kind. He stopped licking her neck and kissed her instead with a deep, begging slowness belied by his racing pulse and breath he could not slow and hers. In revelation of having two hands free, he slid both under her shirt and bra and peeled them off her skin and over her shoulders in one long move-ment. He slid her out of her shorts the same way, thrilled to be so slippery, overjoyed to have both hands available for the job, one for the removal of clothing, the other to explore what it found beneath. Meredith did the same. Then he lay naked on top of her, slick and hard everywhere, both of them, and they drew impossibly hot air into lungs already on fire and moved entirely together, inside each other like puzzle pieces, soaked and soaking until they were done and lay panting and dripping and buzzing lightly on the mat with puddles forming all around them. Sam raised him-self slightly, shifted his weight so as not to hurt her, but couldn't quite tear himself away from the breath and heartbeat and body beneath him. She was the most living thing he had ever felt in his life.

"The contrast between you and work is breathtaking," said Sam who had never imagined he'd be working so closely with death in his day job.

"I don't think that's what's breathtaking," said Meredith.

He traced a slow trickle of sweat with his finger down her cheek. "I love you, you know."

"I know," said Meredith. "I could tell."

Then her phone started ringing. And Sam's phone started ringing. They ignored them, but neither of them stopped. Finally, Meredith got up, got a towel, and answered. On the other end was the *Seattle Times*—local, friendly, fine. On the other end of Sam's, after a shower he insisted on before dealing with whatever was going on, was CNN—less local, less friendly, and much less fine. The *Times* had just gotten wind of RePose and was interested in a local piece—what it was, how it worked, the genius behind it, the technology that made it go. CNN had just gotten wind of RePose too, but it was an ill wind.

"We've been looking into the service that's been called 'Dead Mail,'" investigative reporter Courtney Harman-Handler told Sam abruptly. "We've had undercover reporters in there. We've investigated the technology. We believe you're defrauding your users. We'll be running an exposé, and we'd like to invite you to comment on the record. The public has a right to know. It's not real."

"It's totally real," said Sam.

"We've uncovered evidence that reveals you're faking these 'projections,' as you call them."

"Nothing's faked," said Sam.

"Our evidence reveals the opposite—everything's being faked. People's 'dead loved ones,' as you call them, are not being reanimated or brought back to consciousness or sentience. They cannot communicate with anyone."

"By 'real' you mean 'alive'?" Sam was stunned.

"Of course, Mr. Elling," said Courtney Harman-Handler. "That's what everyone means by 'real.'"

"Well then of course it's not real," said Sam.

"Let me remind you that you're on the record, sir."

"We aren't claiming to raise these people from the dead. That *would* be something to get upset about."

"You're defrauding your users out of hundreds of thousands of dollars. You claim that they'll be able to communicate with their dead loved ones, but it's all smoke and mirrors."

"Well duh." Sam thought Courtney Harman-Handler might benefit from having it dumbed down a bit.

"So you admit this is fraud?"

"No. Not fraud. You were right the first time. Smoke and mirrors."

"Sir?"

"Really, really impressive-as-hell smoke and mirrors. Smoke and mirrors is what people are paying for."

"A fake?"

"It's not fake. It's real. The computer is really studying then really compiling then really projecting users' loved ones. It's not me back there in a box with gears and levers furiously composing e-mails and hoping they sound right. It genuinely is what these people would really say if they were alive to say it."

"How do we know that's true?"

"You come in and use it and find out."

"We believe it's a hoax."

"A hoax is deceptive," said Sam. "There's no deception here. The only one who's suggested real equals alive is you."

. . .

In seeming contrast, Meredith's reporter, Jason Peterman, asked her out to lunch. She met him at a café in Belltown. They chatted for a couple hours. Meredith elevator-pitched how it worked and why. She effused about how glad they were for the opportunity to help people through the hardest parts of their lives. She described the salon and the lengths they went to to make sure no one had to be alone while they were RePosing or while they were mourning. She handed over the names and contact info of a couple of their users who were willing to talk. And then Jason Peterman asked her the biggest question of all: "Tell me about Sam Elling. What's he like? How did he come up with such a unique idea?" There was no one more qualified to answer this question than Meredith and nothing she'd rather discuss. The interview went on for another hour from there.

"He's brilliant, for starters. He doesn't think things can't be done; he just thinks they haven't been done yet. He's a problem solver. You know? My grandmother died, and he was so . . . sad for me? Everyone else said, 'I'm so sorry for your loss,' or, 'That sucks so much,' or, 'I remember when my grandmother died,' or something like that. Sam said all those things. But he also said the thing no one else in the world would which was, 'Well, maybe there's a way to make her less dead, less gone.'"

"Isn't that kind of a . . . weird response?" said Jason Peterman.

Meredith shrugged. "There are only weird responses at that point. We don't really know what to say to people in mourning. As a culture, we're terrible at it. We just want people to get over it already. Cheer up and move on. That's what we think when we're not grieving ourselves. And then our own loved one dies, and we move into the bereavement room, and we have to be alone in there because then everyone else is outside awkwardly saying, 'I'm so sorry,' and meaning, 'Hope you feel better soon so we can go to happy hour and have fun again.'"

"But isn't that an important part of the process?"

"What do you mean?"

"Does RePose help you grieve? Or does it just help you be more cheerful about it?"

"Both. It helps you feel better in an immediate way because you have to miss your loved one less. It helps you remember because you get to spend time with the person you've lost. And it helps people talk about it. Sam's given us something to be besides sorry. A new way to address tragedy and loss."

"But doesn't that mean that you never really grieve and so never heal and get over it?"

"No one wants to get over the death of a loved one," said Meredith. "Forgetting, moving on, not caring anymore . . . that's worse than death."

"But healing, reconciling, growing?"

"You still get to do that," Meredith insisted. "Only you get help from the person in your life who is most able to give it."

"Was," said Jason Peterman. "Was most able to give it."

"Not anymore."

The next day the ticker at the bottom of the screen on CNN read, "RePose creator admits, '. . . of course it's not real.'" And the *Times* headline was, "Grieving, Healing, Moving Forward? New Seattle Company Says 'Not Anymore.'"

Then it seemed to Sam like every newspaper, magazine, TV network, and online press in the world called him up and asked rude things rudely. Dash argued that any publicity was good publicity. Sam argued that people were stupid, and who cared if they got it or not, and let them believe what they wanted to believe. But it started to break Meredith who knew better than anyone what RePose gave you back and the heart of the man who'd made it possible.

"I wish they could see your kindness and generosity," she told Sam, "why you did this in the first place."

"To get laid?"

"To give me this incredible gift. To help people deal with death. For all human history, death has been this immutable thing. This devastating sadness. You've changed that. It's a miracle."

"No wonder you're in charge of PR," Sam tried lightly.

"And I wish they could see how smart you are."

"It's a hard thing to see," said Sam. "You have to be smart enough to get it. Brilliance is never appreciated while you're alive. After I'm dead, I'll be hailed as a genius."

"Yeah, but you'll be dead."

"My projection will finally feel vindicated though."

"That doesn't help me," said Meredith.

"Actually, it doesn't help *me*," said Sam. "It helps you quite a bit."

. . .

Meredith's call from the *Seattle Times* was followed by one from the *L.A. Times* and then the *New York Times* and the *Times of London* ("At least we keep moving up to better *Times*," said Dash), all accusing her of exploiting the dead and profiting off of tragedy. "We are trying to help people be happy again after their sadness," Meredith protested at first. Then, "We are easing their pain. We are helping them grieve." Then, "Aren't there people you miss so much you'd give anything just to be able to talk to them again?" Then, "We are miracle makers!" On the fifth call, Dash finally took the phone away from her ear.

"This is Dashiell Bentlively. How can I help you?"

"This is Marisha St. James, *Times of London*. As I was saying to Ms. Maxwell, your company is being accused of profiting off people's pain, sickness, sadness, and death."

"As opposed," Dash said, "to pharmaceutical companies, big tobacco, the military, hospital administrators, funeral homes, casket purveyors, obituary reporters, oncologists, chocolate makers, florists, manufacturers of those crinkly gowns without backs, most lawyers, scrubs distributors, cemetery owners, the NRA, life insurance providers, health insurance providers, mercenaries, weapons manufacturers, SUV manufacturers, defense contractors, vampire movie makers, vampire book writers, vampire TV producers, popes, roller coaster builders—"

"Roller coaster builders?" Marisha St. James interrupted.

"Reminding you that you only live once. Reminding you that life is short," Dash explained. "In any case, if making money off of death is exploitative, we're in very good company."

Then the church-sponsored press moved in. Naturally less attuned to earthly technological developments, they took longer to start paying attention and find their angle, but once they did, they held on and would not let go. *Believers Monthly* called Meredith's phone at four o'clock one morning to wonder whether she was worried about sending people to hell.

"To where?" she said sleepily.

"Hell."

"Who is this?"

"A good question, ma'am. Whose calls are you taking these days? Jesus'? Or Satan's?"

"Thank you, I'm not interested," she mumbled and tried to hang up.

"We aren't selling anything but salvation, ma'am. You are the one who's peddling one-way tickets to a fiery damnation."

"To where?" Meredith asked.

"Hell."

She covered the phone with her hand and shook Sam awake. "The Christians are on the phone. They want to know why we're sending people to hell."

Sam took the phone from her.

"This is Sam Elling. Please don't call us at home anymore. I'm hanging up."

"I wouldn't, sir. We have six thousand subscribers, many of whom preach the word of the Lord to impressionable folks who want to know why you're sending them to hell."

"How are we sending them to hell?" Sam sighed.

"By removing the threat of it. Our parishioners are sinning because they don't see any reason not to because there's no eternal damnation after death because there's no death."

"We haven't done away with death," said Sam. "People still die."

"You've invented immortality, son. And now you're literally playing with fire."

"I haven't and I'm not," said Sam. "Everyone dies. What their loved ones do with them afterward has nothing to do with them. If they were going to hell before, they're going there still."

"And you'll keep them company, son, because you're going there too."

This guy was clearly off message. But *Christianity Today* had real concerns. *Christianity Today* was worried about people's souls.

"We understand that you're helping people say goodbye, and we think that's very noble," said Terry Greggs over coffee with Meredith and Sam and Dash who had finally concluded that safety in numbers was the way to go when possible.

"Thank you," said Meredith. "And thank you for noticing."

"But the American Christian Clergy Association is concerned that you're putting words in people's mouths by speaking for the dead."

"But they're dead," said Dash.

"Dead, yes," said Terry, "but not gone. Their souls don't die. Pretending they're gone isn't helping anybody. They probably don't like you making up words for them either."

"I'm not making them up," said Sam.

"What makes you think so?"

"I have an algorithm that figured it out. What makes you think they don't like it?"

"Same way. I have an algorithm that figured it out. Jesus' love equals eternal life."

"I don't think that's an algorithm, strictly speaking," said Sam.

"I think you're missing the larger point here," said Terry.

"What a coincidence. I think you are too," said Sam.

The Mid-Atlantic Council of Mediums, Allied Ghost Hunters LLC, Madames Dee, Esmerelda, and Jan, and TheyRAmongUs.com all sent e-mails objecting to RePose along similar lines, but these were easier to ignore. The 957 religious leaders who signed a petition demanding that they stop RePosing because God didn't like it? That was more alarming.

"We have to officially put Meredith in charge of PR and publicity," Dash said later during Notte Della Pizza. Penny was having a bad day and had elected to stay home. Jamie was having a good day and had elected to go hiking. Dash was therefore violating the no-RePosing-during-Notte-Della-Pizza rule. He was violating the unspoken no-irritating-Meredith-during-Notte-Della-Pizza one as well.

"Why me?" she whined.

Dash pointed with his fork at Sam. "Geeky software engineer. People will assume he's inarticulate, antisocial, unemotional, and impossible to understand." He turned his fork on himself. "Fabulously hot and complex Hollywood insider and mysterious outsider. Intimidating and likely lying to you. But you," he finished, aiming a piece of pizza at Meredith, "kind, sweet, caring, emotional, non-manipulative but easily manipulated yourself. Perfect."

"He just called you a wuss," said Sam.

"Since when is sweet and communicative and empathetic a bad thing?"

"Since you started damning people to hell," said Dash.

"Half the Christians are mad that we've invented immortality and gotten rid of the dead. And the other half are mad that we've forgotten immortality and ignored the dead," Sam complained.

"You're damned if you do and damned if you don't," Dash observed. "That's why we need better PR."

. . .

Sam concluded that whoever first coined Dash's point that all publicity was good publicity was overstaffed and probably very bored. The press, almost all bad, meant a lot of things, but very quickly the only one any of them had time for was the deluge of new users. Well, would-be users. They'd been smart enough to keep the exact location of the salon private, but they'd not been smart enough to keep anything else private—their names, where they went for coffee and out to dinner, what section they liked at the ball game, their dog park of choice. All of that had seemed somewhere between sweet, incidental, and beside the point when Meredith had told it to Jason Peterman, but now they found themselves recognized places, cornered at coffee, accosted while having a beer or picking up dog poop. Some people echoed the reporters: How can you use people's pain? Who are you to speak for the dead? You're stepping on Jesus' toes. But most of them would place a tentative hand on Sam's arm or Meredith's shoulder and whisper what Eduardo Antigua had that very first time: I hear you have a service. So many wanted in. The number of people who had lost a loved one was heartbreaking, said Sam. The number of people who had lost a loved one was everyone, said Meredith.

Their subtle, tasteful website's sign-up was totally overwhelmed. They'd taken a you-have-to-know-to-know design approach after Dash's argument that underground and mysterious was the way to go, but now everybody knew, so they took the sign-up down entirely. They couldn't even almost keep up with demand. Dash was nervous too about Courtney Harman-Handler's claim that they'd had undercover users infiltrate the service. Sam's argument was that it didn't matter. RePose couldn't be faked. If a user hadn't really met the threshold—and it was high—of communication with a loved one, the projection wouldn't render and wouldn't work. Whether their motivation was love or investigative reporting, their DLO had to be L'd indeed to work at all. Dash's point was that they still didn't want saboteurs spying on users, infiltrating the system, and failing to honor the code: What happened in the salon stayed in the salon. Or: dead men tell no tales . . . except to users in good faith.

Then Marisha St. James called back.

"Your company is being accused of exclusivity," she told Meredith.

"I thought our company was being accused of profiting off death."

"Yes," said Marisha St. James, "but only among the privileged."

"Isn't it better to profit off the privileged than the poor?"

"It's better not to profit off of anyone's exploitation, don't you think?"

"There's no exploitation. We're providing a service."

"A very expensive service."

"I'm not sure I see why that's a problem. We wanted to limit our numbers so we could give everyone the service they deserve. Demand is high. We have significant costs. The software is groundbreaking and incredibly complex, and it hasn't been easy to develop, perfect, or maintain."

"Death used to be suffered universally," said Marisha St. James. "Now only the poor must mourn. The rich have their loved ones forever."

Dash had a list for that one too of services available to the rich but not the poor. Sam's point was more like death had never been universal or classless. But the newly officially-in-charge-of-PR Meredith instituted a scholarship and sliding scale and felt a little bit better.

Everything hard was falling on her shoulders. Sam got to do what he had always done—lower head, ground feet, engineer software. Dash got to do what he always did too—schmooze and smooth the way and shake the hands and pat the backs and make sure that what happened behind the scenes kept happening. But Meredith was a little out of her element and a little out of her head. She was good at it, but it took its toll: being berated by mysterious public watchdogs, interrogated by journalists, threatened by clergy, scolded by everyone with a website or an opinion column. Someone started a Meredith Maxwell Wants to Bring Back Hitler Facebook page. It had 2,657 fans by the end of the first week. She became the public face of RePose. And it was such a beautiful, vulnerable, loving face, it was easy to prey on, easy to make hay of, easy for the haters to hate. Sam stroked it as it cringed with nightmares, as it struggled to keep its eyes open during breakfast, having gotten so little sleep the night before, as it creased with worry and something else—guilt maybe, fear. We are helping people heal, she insisted to everyone who asked. We are giving the gifts of second chances and one more times. But she started to doubt too. To Sam she said maybe it isn't fair, maybe it isn't helping, maybe it isn't honest. She said maybe we are exploiting taking advantage abusing corrupting. Sam said you have such a good heart. Sam said think how happy you were the first time you talked to your grandmother.

She started chatting with Livvie most days. At first her grandmother was puzzled why Meredith was calling so much. But then the projection learned and normalized it. It still couldn't answer her more philosophical questions, but it did a not half-bad job, Sam thought, of trying.

"Oh Grandma," Meredith said one day. "Aren't there people you'd give anything to talk to again?"

"I wish your mother would call more often," said Livvie, one of her themes.

"I mean someone who's dead," said Meredith quietly.

The projection had to think about that one for a while. "I miss your grandfather," it finally came up with.

"Right?" said Meredith. "Wouldn't you want to see him, talk to him again if you could?"

"Of course, dear," said Livvie. "And also you. I miss you too. You and Sam should come visit me for a couple weeks."

"I wish we could, Grandma," said Meredith tiredly.

"But let me guess. You have to work."

Meredith nodded mutely at the camera. Neither one of them sounded like they believed this anymore.

"That's okay, baby," Livvie sighed. "At least we can chat. It's not the same as being together, but I love to see that beautiful face."

"Exactly," said Meredith. "That's my point exactly."

"I would like to see you in person though."

"I know, Grandma. I'm sorry."

"That's okay. You were just trying to help. I forgive you. Talk to you soon. Bye."

Meredith hung up and looked at Sam. "What the hell was that?"

"That happened once before," said Sam. "The very first time. Eduardo's very first time with Miguel."

"Why? It doesn't make any sense."

"I know. It's a weird programming glitch. For some reason the projection suddenly starts offering up vague absolution in response to your saying sorry. It's like it's stopped talking to you and instead switched over to emilypost-dot-com. I don't know what triggers it."

"That's really weird. I didn't mean sorry like that anyway."

"I know. And usually she does too. I'll look into it and figure out what's going on," Sam promised.

Meredith buried her face in her hands. "This isn't helping anymore anyway," she said.

"Isn't helping what?"

"Isn't helping me not miss her. She can't help me with what's really wrong."

"Could she ever?" asked Sam.

"I don't know," said Meredith. "Maybe only in person. Maybe this isn't any good."

"It was never meant to be forever," Sam said. "It was only meant to be a way station between devastating grief and letting go."

"Since when?" she asked.

Sam shrugged. He couldn't remember. But he was pretty sure that was the idea all along. To help you say goodbye. Not to keep the dead around forever. Then he had an uncharacteristic idea. "You know what we need? A celebration."

She snorted. "Of what?"

"Six-month anniversary of RePose. Look what we've created. Look what we've made happen."

"I'm not sure I feel much like celebrating."

"Why not?"

"All these dead loved ones . . . it's making me sad."

"Then let's celebrate with the living."

PROM

$\mathcal{M}$eredith sent an invitation.

Dear Beloved RePosers:

First, we want to thank you so much for your dedication—to our service and to your loved ones. You are early users and early adopters—how brave of you! We know you took great risks with your hearts and with your wallets, and we're so grateful to you as we've worked out the kinks in the system. Thank you for your patience, enthusiasm, and open minds.

    We write today with an invitation and a request for your help marking an auspicious moment. The occasion of our six-month anniversary warrants a celebration with all of you who have made this possible. We hope you'll join us for food, drink, music, and lively conversation—among the living and the dead.

Much love,
Meredith, Sam, and Dashiell

Sam's tuxedo hadn't even been unpacked. He found it jammed in the bottom of a box in the study. It brought back memories of his old job and all its attendant pressures. All that seemed so petty now—the ephemeral highs and lows of dating and working for a big corporation seemed sad, gauzy memories compared to the world he now owned and the life and death and afterlife on which he spent his days. It brought back sad, gauzy memories of being single too. He pulled the tux out of the box and put it on then wandered into the bedroom where Meredith was in a bra, earrings, and nothing else.

"You look amazing," he said.

"I'm not even dressed yet."

"My point exactly."

"Which of these dresses, do you think? This one is cute and comfortable though the shoes that go with it are not. This one is more formal and less comfortable though with better shoes. This one might be too formal, but this one might show too much boob." She held up two dresses. One was blue and involved something shiny. The other was black. Otherwise, Sam couldn't tell them apart.

"I like what you have on now."

"I'm not sure that'd go over well."

"I write the software, baby." Sam winked and shot her Hollywood finger guns. "I'm the one you have to keep happy."

"I think we're pretty much counting on your support," said Meredith.

"Will you indulge me here? There's something I'm dying to do." He took out his phone and called her on hers. She looked at him like he was crazy but answered anyway.

"Hello?"

"Merde?"

"Yes?"

"This is Sam. Elling? From work?"

"Hi. How are you?"

"I'm fine. How are you?"

"Kinda in a rush right now, actually. I have a party in an hour, and I'm still completely naked."

"Sounds lovely," said Sam. "Listen, I've got this formal work affair tonight. It's poor form to show up alone. I wondered if you'd be my date."

"Hmm. Sounds boring."

"It may well be," said Sam, "but I live quite nearby. We can always bail on the party and head upstairs to my place."

"Fair enough. It's a date," said Meredith. "I'd better go get dressed for it."

"Can't wait. You've made me a very happy man." He hung up and smiled at her. "Sorry about that. Hot date tonight."

"Think you'll get lucky?"

"Luckier than I am right now? Not a chance."

Then the door opened and in walked Dash. Meredith shrieked and grabbed a towel.

"You can't knock?"

"Nothin' I haven't seen before." Dash and Meredith spent an uncommonly large portion of their childhood being photographed naked in various kiddie pools and garden sprinklers. "They didn't make baby swimsuits?" Meredith once demanded of her mother. "They did," Julia said, "but you refused to wear them." For his part, Sam regretted missing her exhibitionist days.

"*What* are you wearing?" Meredith demanded.

Dash had on a powder blue tuxedo with a ruffled front and navy bow tie and cummerbund. "This is my prom tux, sweets. Jealous you're not wearing the outfit you wore to prom? Would yours even fit?" Meredith recalled the green sequined dress that came down to her knee on the right side but not very far below the top of her thigh on the left. Sam, of course, did not attend his prom.

"Just because it fits doesn't mean you should wear it."

"I am rocking this tux, and you know it. It was outdated and ironic then, and it's outdated and ironic now. It's the beauty of going solo to these things. No one's outfit can clash with your color scheme or time period."

"*Now* you tell me," said Sam. "All those dateless years I missed the silver lining."

"When you're wearing black and white, my friend, it doesn't matter. You could have danced with anyone in the room."

Meredith kicked everyone out of the bedroom, split the difference between her two men and chose the bright blue dress, too much boob be damned, and they started downstairs to do last-minute touches. She had resurrected the disco ball from the night before they opened. There were canapés and fancy sodas in mini-bottles and teeny pastries. There were flowers and candlelight and champagne flutes ready to be filled. There were wispy clouds over the sound and windows open to the evening and music and a soft breeze and a sunset. "Before we do this," said Sam, "can I be cheesy for just one second?"

"Cheese away," said Dash.

"I just want to thank you both. This thing we're doing was never, never going to happen, and yet it has. We get to change the world. That's even more amazing than it was improbable. I'm honored and lucky to have you. We've had a chance so few people ever get: to do something no one ever did before, to think thoughts no one ever thought before. This has been the greatest adventure of my life." Sam cringed. This last bit crossed the cheesy line.

"Having a date to a work function?" said Meredith.

"Well yes, actually. Having love. A big family. Not just me and my dad."

"I'm not sure I qualify as big family," said Dash.

"Well, you. Your parents. Julia and Kyle. Livvie."

"I only wish you knew her," said Meredith.

"I do," said Sam.

"You're like another grandson to her," she said.

"Which is weird," added Dash. "Since you're more like her god."

"Her god?"

"You created her."

"Call her up and see," invited Sam. "She knows. We're family. That's all."

. . .

It was nice to see everyone in their finery. They were surprised—and touched—by how many people showed up. It was like when you were in seventh grade and saw your social studies teacher at the mall or like going to a fancy restaurant and running into a gym buddy you'd only ever seen sweaty and spandexed. It wasn't because everyone was so dressed up— they tended to come to the salon pretty coiffed anyway, wanting to look nice for their DLOs. It was their lightness. It was pleasant but still strange to see them smile and laugh so easily.

"I wasn't sure anyone was going to want to come to this," Sam confessed to Eduardo Antigua, user the first, who therefore held a special place in Sam's heart. He'd stopped coming after a few weeks, and Sam had been worried about him.

"Awkward?"

"Yeah, I guess."

"It is an honor to celebrate with you." Eduardo clinked his beer gently against Sam's. "You gave me an incredible gift, Sam. You let me say good-bye which I was simply never going to get to do. I am honored to be with you tonight."

"I can't tell you what it means to hear you say that," said Sam, a little choked up (in which state he stayed most of the night). "When you stopped coming, I thought maybe you'd soured on the whole thing, had a bad experience or something."

"Nah, man, not at all. I talk to Miguel almost every day. I just do it at home now. We used to cook together a lot. Our mother was a chef in Colombia before she came to this country, and she taught us well. So I put my laptop on the counter, and we cook together most nights. How about you? You look tired."

"It's been a hard . . . stretch. Starting the business. Making and remaking and refining the programming. Dealing with the press. Everyone here is so sad all the time. It wears you down."

Eduardo hugged him. "We appreciate it so much, man. Thank you. Next week, I'm going to bring you dinner. Miguel and I make a mean tamale."

Sam laughed. "Do me a favor and e-mail me the recipe?"

"Sure. Do you cook?"

"Not really. But this is going to be a huge help to an old friend of mine."

. . .

Meredith was in the corner talking to Avery Fitzgerald and Edith Casperson.

"I didn't realize you and Sam were partners," said Edith, delighted. "I mean, I realized you were partners, but I thought just business partners, not romantic partners."

"Both." Meredith smiled. "It's intense."

"Since when?"

"Last summer. It's been a year."

"Are you talking marriage? This would be a great space for a wedding. Look how nice it looks."

"Doesn't seem necessary," Meredith laughed. "We already work together and own a business together and live together."

"Still, you have to make it official," said Edith.

Meredith waved vaguely around the salon. "It's pretty official. And we've got time. It's just not on the priority list right now."

"Marriage is the opposite of children," Avery sighed. "They tell you children will be such a joy, and they are, but they're also such a huge pain so much of the time. Marriage, they tell you, is long and hard and lots of work, but it isn't. Well, I guess you hope for the first. For me and Clive, our marriage was the best and easiest part of our lives. It's what made all the things that were harder—raising kids, work, bills, whatever—doable. And worth doing."

"You're lucky," said Edith.

"Was. Was lucky."

"No, you're still lucky. At least you have your memories."

"That's what everyone says but—"

"And they're enjoyable. I have memories of Bob and marriage too, of course. But they're all . . . complicated."

"You're in here chatting with him all the time," said Avery.

"No, I'm in here yelling at him all the time," said Edith, and Meredith suppressed a smile because it was true. "It's okay to laugh. It's funny. Well, it's funny now. It wasn't at the time. I bet when you kids thought this thing up, you didn't expect bitter widows like me in here kicking dead ass."

"We really didn't," Meredith admitted.

"You know, at the beginning, we really connected, once upon a time. But then you fall into these patterns. He got to go to work and travel and meet interesting people and use his brain and contribute things. I got to stay home and take care of the kids and the house and him. The kids learned to take care of themselves. The house too really. We had one of those central vacuum systems. But Bob never did. That was fine, I guess. It was a different time. But for thirty-five years he acted like serving him was a privilege, and he was working so I could be on vacation all the time when really he had the much easier job. I would have liked to go out and do all the exciting things he got to do every day. And he would have hated staying home and doing what I did every day. But still, he thought I was dumb and lazy and getting away with something."

"I'm sure he didn't think you were dumb—" Avery began.

"Maybe not, but he acted like he did, and that's even worse. He loved me. I know that. But that makes it worse too. To be treated like that by someone who didn't care about you would be easier. If someone I disliked didn't think I was very smart or worthwhile either, I wouldn't mind so much. But my husband? Bob loved me. He just didn't respect me. He cared for me. He just didn't ever think to tell me that."

"Does yelling at him make it better?" Meredith asked.

"It does. It's good to feel the words come out of my mouth after so many years of scripting them in my head. He can't really understand me. Sam said it's because I never did it before. No one ever yelled at Bob in life, so he can't understand it in death."

"That must be so frustrating," said Avery.

"I'm used to it, actually," said Edith. "He never listened to me in life either. I'd say something; he'd be thinking about something else. Maybe I could have tried this when he was alive after all. It seemed like such an impossibly scary thing, but the projection is right—he'd never have understood being yelled at because no one ever contradicted him."

"Maybe you're lucky too," said Avery. "RePose works for you. For me, it's just sad and makes me miss him more. It's an awful lot better than nothing. But it falls pretty far short of . . . enough."

"Whereas for me, this Bob is so much easier. I miss him, but also, to be perfectly honest, in some ways I'm happier now that he's . . . Oh but honey, you and Sam won't be like that," Edith said, turning to Meredith. "Don't let me sour you on marriage. It's a different era. And look at Avery. She's a much better model than I am."

"It's true." Avery smiled weakly. "Just don't let him die."

"I can't believe I didn't know you two were together. I'm usually better at sensing these things," Edith said.

"You couldn't invent something as incredible as RePose unless it was for someone you really loved," said Avery. "That level of brain spark is kindled by only one thing."

. . .

Dash was entertaining everyone—his strong suit—but especially Penny. There'd been a debate over that one. Sam thought she could use a night out but not too far out—a chance to get dressed up and eat good food and meet new people but only a one-floor elevator ride away from home if she felt ill or ill at ease. Meredith worried about how they could explain the salon without explaining RePose, and if they told her about RePose she'd want to use it, and if she wanted to use it, they'd have to come up with some reason why she couldn't without revealing what they knew about Albert. Finally, on a trip to the grocery store the week before the party, Dash told her about the business they ran on the floor right above hers connecting people via electronic communication with projections of their loved ones who had passed on.

"You mean like you can e-mail dead people?" Penny said with wonder.

"Yes. Or video chat or any other form of electronic communiqué." He braced himself for whatever might come next.

"Oh you young people," Penny laughed. "What will you think of next?" She had not the slightest inclination to RePose evidently, but she was delighted to be invited to a party. She wore an elegant, floor-length black dress and ivory gloves up to her elbows and went around on Dash's arm getting introduced to everyone. She greeted them all warmly, took their hands, listened generously to their stories, answered patiently the questions shouted overloud in her direction as if, just because she was small and old and a little bit stooped, she were also hard of hearing which she was not. Edith said wasn't she sweet to take care of Meredith in Livvie's absence, but Penny insisted Meredith took care of her. Celia Montrose said didn't she look nice in her dress and gloves, but Penny said, "Oh, I've had this dress forever. Finally, it's back in style again." Avery said how hard it must be for her to live alone after so many years with her dear husband, and Penny, recognizing a kindred spirit when she saw one, patted her hand and said, "Yes, honey, oh yes. You too."

At some point, Dash went upstairs and fished an ancient dartboard out of the back of his grandmother's hall closet and spent the rest of the evening tutoring George Lenore. Mr. and Mrs. Benson spent a lot of time talking to Kelly Montrose about colleges. David Elliot spent a lot of time talking to Kelly Montrose about no one was sure what, occurring as it did very low in her ear and amid much giggling from the both of them.

"Thank you, Sam," said Meredith with wet eyes when they were getting ready for bed later. "I needed that. I needed to see that they were happy."

"Me too, actually," he said. "I hadn't realized it, but it was such a relief."

"You are smart. But you are better."

"Better than what?"

"Better than you are smart. You are very, very intelligent Sam, but you are an even better person. Your genius is up in the nine-point-fives, but your heart is off the charts."

"Yours, too," he said. "We make a good couple. We should date."

She laughed. "And I love you, you know."

"I do," said Sam, who did. "I love you too."

ST. GILES

*T*hat held them for a while. The press backed off a bit, and Meredith got better at managing it. The tech settled down a bit, and users got better at using it. Meredith felt better, and Livvie did a better job of chatting with a cheerful Meredith than an unhappy one which was a circular proposition: Livvie had trouble with a troubled Meredith which made her more troubled; Livvie did better with a happy Meredith which made her more happy. Then one Saturday afternoon at the end of August they got a call from a Dr. Dixon at St. Giles Hospital. "I think you need to get over here and see what's happening," he told Meredith. They were at Lincoln Park, reading books on the beach and watching the ferry come and go and looking out over sound and mountains—sunshine, wind, and water—a blissful afternoon. They packed up right away to head over. They didn't know what they'd find there, but they suspected it would be far from blissful.

Dr. Dixon brought them to a cheery-looking bright yellow ward on the third floor of the east wing with lots of toys and big windows and fresh air and a fake forest with cute animals painted on the walls. It was the most miserable place Sam had ever been in his life. Dr. Dixon gave them this heartbreaking speech on the way over: "There are three kinds of kids here: the kind who are going to recover and be fine or at least functional, the kind who are going to die blessedly quickly, and the hard kind, the kind who are going to linger and get worse then get better then get worse again then get hope then get a little better then get a little more hope then get a little worse then much worse then a little better. Then they die. They live their tiny lives here, and then they die here. Their parents live their tiny lives here too. And they also die here. They are the hard part of this job. You are making it worse. I thought you should see."

In a small room at the end of one hall, a tiny boy sat propped up with pillows clutching a worn yellow rabbit and crying. He had tubes in his arms, in his nose, from his gut. He had no hair and no color and hardly any flesh covering his garishly on-display bones. He wasn't crying because of the tubes or the tiny pale dying baldness of himself, however. He was crying because his father was sitting up next to him in bed with a laptop on the tray table, painstakingly trying to get his son to compose e-mails to him.

"What did you do today?" asked the dad gently.

"Played with Rabbit," the kid whispered.

"Type that to me," said the dad.

"Don't wanna," said the kid.

"What else did you do?"

"Shots," said the kid.

"Type that to Daddy."

"Don't wanna," cried the kid.

"Christ, he can't be more than three or four," said Sam.

"Actually, he's seven and a half," said Dr. Dixon. "Still a bit young for e-mailing though. Plus he's missed a lot of school."

Next door, an even littler girl in a pink nightgown was crying and crying in her bed with her arms stretched out toward her parents. "Up pees, up pees, uuuupppeeeese," she was wailing over and over. Her parents sat two feet away at the end of the bed, also crying but immobile. Between them, facing the little girl, was an open laptop, an open video chat, an enabled camera. "Just a few more minutes today, baby," her mother said through her own tears. "Just a few more minutes. Mommy and Daddy need this for later. Tell Mommy what's your favorite book. Tell Mommy what a cow says."

Meredith was paler than the little boy in the first room. She excused herself but didn't make it quite as far as the bathroom before she threw up on the floor in the hallway.

"I'm sorry, Dr. Dixon," she managed.

"Happens all the time," he said.

"Not about that," she said and went to find the ladies' room.

"They're trying to get enough electronic communication out of their kids?" Sam asked. Though he knew.

"Yes."

"Before it's too late?"

"Yes."

"But it's already too late."

"Yes," said Dr. Dixon. "And also no. It's not late enough. These kids haven't learned to read yet, to write, to use a computer. And they never will. All these parents are doing is wasting the time they have left."

Sam nodded, looking at his shoes, cowed, but then he whispered, "Think of it from their point of view though. The kids are going to die anyway. The parents want something to remember them by."

"It shouldn't be this," said Dr. Dixon.

Sam was having trouble finding his voice. "How do we know what will help these parents remember? What will help them feel better?"

"Helping the parents feel better isn't my job. My patients are the kids. They have months, sometimes weeks, sometimes days left. They shouldn't have to spend them inputting themselves into a computer."

"You keep running tests," Sam said quietly. "Administering shots and chemo and medications with horrible side effects. Waking them up in the night to take their blood or their temperature. Hooking them up to scary machines. Confining them to bed. Drugging them senseless. Is that any way to spend the time they have left?"

"The procedures are sometimes brutal, but often they extend the time these children have. I'm not justifying myself to you, and I'm not getting into a medical discussion with a computer programmer. I can't bring cancer up to the ward to show it the misery it's causing. But I can bring you up to show you the misery you're causing. And I'm telling you to stop."

"It won't work for children," said Sam. "It was never intended to. I'm happy to explain that to anyone you want me to or do anything else you think would help. I get that your priority is your patients and that hospitals treat patients. We're only trying, humbly, to take care of who's left."

On the way out, they saw one of those flyers with the tear-off phone numbers in strips at the bottom. In big letters at the top it said, "New Life for Your Loved One." And then smaller, lower down, "The time to prepare to RePose with your loved one is now. Do it before you lose them forever. Learn how today!" There was only one phone number left hanging off the bottom of the poster. Meredith ripped the whole thing off the wall, balled it in her fist, and threw it in the street. Then she got in the car and cried, not gentle weeping but violent sobbing. Sam thought she might throw up again. Sam felt like he might throw up himself.

"What are we going to do?" she sobbed.

"I don't know." Sam was quiet, and that made her louder.

"We are killing those kids."

"No, we're not."

"We are ruining their lives."

"No, we're not."

"They're already so godforsaken miserable, and we're making them more miserable. We are."

"No, we aren't."

"Jesus, Sam. Fuck the semantics. No, okay, we didn't give them cancer, fine. But these kids have three horrible weeks to live when they're owed another ten decades, and we're making them spend those three weeks in front of a goddamn computer."

"No. We're not. We're not, Merde. We are not making them do anything. We are not making their parents do anything."

"We have made them an offer they can't refuse."

"No, we haven't. RePose is not intended for children. It was never intended for children. It won't work for these kids—"

"But they don't know that. These people have no hope, so they have to cling to whatever they can find, no matter how small and pathetic it is."

"It's not our job to tell these parents, 'You have three weeks with your kid. Go to a park. Go do something fun. Don't waste time on your laptop.' There are social workers. There are grief counselors—"

"We have made RePose available out in the world. The most desperate people, the most miserable, broken ones, those are the people who are going to grab on and not let go. They can't say no."

"That's not on us," said Sam. "Just because it can't help everyone doesn't mean it can't help some people."

"Just because it can help some people," said Meredith, "doesn't let us off the hook for hurting others."

"They can't have what they want." Sam was quiet again. "They aren't getting kids who live to be a hundred. No one can give them that. I don't know whose fault that is, but it isn't ours."

"We're not helping."

"We are. Maybe not these people because their kids are too young. But think of Mr. and Mrs. Benson. For people with older DLOs, we're giving them the only thing we can: a chance to see their kid again."

"It's not enough."

"It's all we've got, Merde. It's all anybody's got." And then, when she didn't say anything, he added, "It made *you* feel better."

"That's not enough either," she said.

. . .

She called Dash and left a shaky, rambling message he couldn't quite make out which involved words like "emergency," "disaster," and "vomit." When he called back, panicked, Meredith wouldn't come to the phone, and Sam didn't know how or even whether to reassure him. No, she wasn't dying. No, he wasn't dying. No, the software hadn't been hacked and the salon hadn't been robbed and Mt. Rainier hadn't erupted, and everything was just fine except for how it wasn't. Dash said he'd be on the first flight out in the morning. In between, Meredith didn't say much. She also didn't eat much or sleep much. She mostly sat on the sofa wrapped in a blanket and stared out the window. Sam tried to feed her and failed. He tried to distract her with the ball game then a movie then a game of Rummikub and failed. He tried to get her to come to bed with him and failed and so finally went alone, but he couldn't sleep either. He couldn't get that little girl's cries out of his head, her parents' faces, Dr. Dixon's quiet anger. Meredith crying in the car. He couldn't get the smell of the place out of his nose.

But he also felt protective of the good they'd done, the good they could do. It wasn't fair to take it away just because some people—some sleep-deprived, desperate, driven-insane, put-through-hell people—couldn't understand that it wouldn't work for children. He felt terrible for them. He did, of course. But Sam felt protective of his users. And, weirdly, darkly, in a way that was hard to put his finger on, he felt protective of his projections too. What would happen to them if Dead Mail died?

. . .

"Listen," Dash began the next morning, "I've brought Hellner's chocolate cake, the world's best breakfast food, and I hauled my ass out of bed at three this morning to be here. Sam loves you and I love you, and what's more, Sam and I both feel sad about dying little kids and their parents. Obviously. So let's just dial it back a little bit."

"I haven't even said anything." Meredith looked at him darkly from under puffy eyelids. None of them had slept. All of them looked it.

"Well it's time," said Dash, "so talk."

"I feel like crap," said Meredith and started crying again. "All the time. I'm so tired. I'm so sad. If this were right, would I have to defend it to everyone with an internet connection? If this were right, would it feel like this?"

Sam started in on the benevolent miracle of the technology and the boon to users and all the people they had helped and would help and could help, but Dash interrupted. "Yeah, it would."

"Would what?"

"Would feel like this. It's new. It's weird. There are complex issues involved. There are moral gray areas. There is untrod ground. You think it wasn't like this for the people who invented Pong? Hell, you think it wasn't like this for the people who invented fire? The villagers were all, 'Oh no! This technology is evil.' And the guy who invented fire was like, 'No, it's great. You can stay warm even in winter and melt water when it freezes and cook your meat so you don't get worms and take a bath some-times, which, no offense buddy, I'm inventing soap next because man do you stink. And you think that's cool—wait'll you see how it protects the village. And you can read after dark! I mean, first we need to develop written language, but still!' And the villagers were all, 'Children will get burned.' And Fire Guy was like, 'Think how much better this will make their lives. Just keep them a safe distance away from the fire.' And the villagers were like, 'Meh. Not worth it. You're evil.' Then, ironically, they burned him at the stake."

Meredith didn't want to laugh, but she couldn't help it. "You didn't see them, Dash."

"I have an appointment after lunch," he said.

"You do?"

"Of course."

"You hate hospitals."

"Everyone hates hospitals."

"It's so awful there."

"I know. But after I got off the phone with Sam yesterday, I called Dr. Dixon and set up a time to go over."

"Why?"

"It's important. It upset you. It upsets me. It raises questions about what we're doing and how and why. I know what's going on—I understand—but I need to see."

"Oh Dash. You didn't have to . . . you don't have to—"

"Yes I do," he said. "Of course I do."

. . .

Meredith went downstairs to be in Salon Styx. Dash and Sam went back to the hospital. They brought the cake, which none of them had been able to even think about eating, and left it in the family accommodations room. While Dash met with Dr. Dixon, Sam sat in the family room and tried to look open, kind, and available in case anyone wanted to talk. People came and went. They all looked broken, exhausted. Sam himself was red-eyed and sleepless, but these parents were pale like their veins held less blood than his. They looked nauseated and terrified, like even opening their mouths was dangerous, like cracking clamped-shut lips might release torrents of vomit, screaming, wailing, and curses. They glanced emptily at one another, at books and magazines whose pages never turned, and said nothing. Sam sat for an hour, then two. People left and were replaced by others who looked exactly the same miserable way. Sam wanted to stand up and clear his throat, give a little speech about how their children couldn't RePose, he was so sorry, so very, terribly sorry, and was there anything else at all he could do to help. But he couldn't find the strength or the voice to do it. These people didn't look like they had the strength to do anything either, but they kept doing it anyway.

He walked out into the hall, sat against the vending machine with his tablet, and called Meredith in the salon.

"How is it?" she said.

"The same."

"Awful?"

"Yes."

There was nothing to add, so they just sat there and looked at each other.

"I know it's not your fault," she said after a while.

"I know."

"I'm sorry."

"Me too."

"We can't shut it down," she said.

"I know."

"We have to do something though."

"I know."

She put her fingers over her heart, then to her lips, then up against the camera. He did the same. Then he went back into the family room to sit and wait some more.

After a while, Dash came in and sat down next to Sam. They looked grimly at each other but said nothing. "Did you find anyone to talk to?" Dash asked finally.

Sam shook his head. "You?"

Dash didn't answer. "When I was in third grade, my friend Kevin and I were playing in the creek behind his house. His little sister Lena had followed us out. We kept yelling at her to go home, leave us alone, no girls allowed—that sort of thing. There was this part where you had to walk across a log over the water, but Lena was scared. Too little. She was only five. She stood on the other side and screamed for him to help her over, but we were glad to ditch her finally. Then she got brave I guess, or desperate, I don't know, and started to walk across, but she slipped. She fell in the water, hit her head on the log. The creek wasn't even knee-deep, not even on her, but she was shaking and convulsing. She was facedown and swallowing water, choking, not coming up. We ran over—we were there almost instantly—pulled her face up by her hair, got her mouth out of the water, dragged her over to the bank. He stayed. I ran and got their mom.

"She'd had a seizure. They thought it was from hitting her head when she fell off the log, but no, she fell off the log because of the seizure. Tumor. Brain cancer. Quick. She was gone six weeks later. While she was in the hospital I remember thinking, even at eight years old, that it sucked to be her but not as much as it sucked to be Kevin. He couldn't play outside all summer. And then she died, and he came to school in the fall and just sat at his desk and stared into space, and the teacher let him, left him alone. I'd go over to his house, and we'd just sit in his room and hold LEGOs, not even play with them or build anything, just kind of shuffle them from hand to hand. So I stopped going over there. By Christmas, they had moved away. My dad said to get away from the memories, and my mom said, 'Where on earth could they go to get away from those memories?'"

Sam nodded mutely. Then after a while he said, "We feel so bad for our users all day every day, but then you realize they're the lucky ones. They have memories we can use, but even better, they have memories they can stand. I always thought it wasn't fair that I have no memories of my mom. But in some ways, no memories is a blessing."

Then, out of all sense and order, David Elliot walked incongruously into the room. He was delighted to see them. "Dash! Sam! What are you doing here?"

Sam felt his heart stop. "Oh David. Oh shit. What are you doing here? What's wrong?"

"Nothing. Why?"

"Are you okay?" Sam took him by the shoulders and squeezed too hard.

"I'm fine. Are you?"

"Oh thank God. Why are you here?" Sam found himself struggling not to hug David then giving up and hugging him anyway. "Uh, Sam," he heard Dash saying, "look what's in his hands."

Sam drew back and looked at the sheaf of papers David Elliot was carrying. They were flyers like the one Meredith had ripped off the bulletin board the day before.

"You!" said Sam.

"Me?" said David.

"It's you!"

"What's me?"

"You're the one who's been putting up the goddamn flyers."

"Oh, these? Yeah. Cool, huh?"

Sam briefly lost the power of speech, so Dash took over the interrogation. "David, you're tormenting these poor parents."

"Tormenting?"

"Why are you doing this?" Sam moaned.

"I was just . . . What do you mean? I was trying to help people be able to use RePose. You know, after their loved ones . . . you know."

"Why?" Sam asked again.

David blushed. "It helps me so much, you know, seeing my mom, playing her my songs."

"Oh David."

"I thought I could help other people."

"Oh no."

"And I need the money."

"What do you need money for?"

"RePosing," David said sheepishly.

Sam went over and leaned his forehead against the wall. "It won't work for little kids, David. They have no electronic memory. They've never e-mailed or video chatted or had a Facebook page or anything, so we can't make a projection for them. Even if we could, they'd just be dying little kids forever."

"Oh. Crap."

"What service were you planning on offering when people called anyway?"

"I was just gonna help everyone tech up. You know, like tell them to use a lot of stuff online a lot. Get them video chatting if they aren't. Sign them up for some online accounts and stuff. I've gotten some calls already."

"Don't they realize right away it won't work for them?" asked Sam.

"Oh. Not from this wing, I guess."

Sam and Dash looked at him blankly, and David blushed again.

"I've been putting flyers up all over the hospital. Talking to people I know from when my mom was here. I just started. I can stop if you want me to. But isn't this the point? To help spread RePose to the people who need it?"

Sam rolled his head around on the wall and squeezed his eyes shut.

"People with healthy loved ones don't need RePose," David posited with the wisdom of a teenager. "But the people here? That's exactly what they need."

They walked in to Meredith in front of her computer.

Dash strode toward the camera calling, "Hi, Gramaaaaaunt Julia."

"Surprised to see me?"

"Uh . . . yes. But delighted."

Meredith had been feeling miserable all afternoon. Sometimes a girl's dead grandmother just doesn't do the trick and what she really needs is her mom. She and Julia had been chatting once a week or so but only awkwardly and briefly because Julia had made it clear she'd let them know when she was ready to talk about RePose. As it turned out, Meredith couldn't wait that long. She called and started both crying and apologizing as soon as her mother answered.

"Oh Mom, I'm so sorry. I'm so sorry we sprang RePose on you accidentally at Thanksgiving. We didn't mean to. God, when it rang, my heart just stopped. It was such an awful way for you to find out. It shouldn't be forced on anyone. No one should have to see that who isn't ready. No one should have to see it who doesn't want to."

"Oh Meredith—"

"And I'm sorry I didn't tell you about it in the planning stages. I didn't lie, but I didn't tell you, and I never want to keep things from you. I always value your opinion. It's just that deep down I knew you wouldn't approve. And I didn't want to hear it because even deeper down I was worried that you might be right."

"Oh sweetheart—"

"And now there are these sick kids, and I just feel like crap, and I don't know what to do, and it's all falling apart. But I can't give it up anyway. I'm sorry, I just can't. And I'm sorry I still get to have Grandma in my life and you don't. And I'm sorry—"

"What about the Hammersteins' vase?" Julia interrupted.

"The what?"

"The Hammersteins' vase. You're so sorry for everything else. I thought maybe you were making a list. I was doing a custom order for the Hammersteins when you were nine, and I had it just set to dry when you bumped into it dancing to your *Thriller* tape."

"*Thriller* was a good album," said Meredith.

"And the Hammersteins' was a good vase," said Julia. "Honey, I knew you didn't mean to knock it over. As I told you at the time when you cried and cried, for ceramics artists with a child, we lost remarkably few pieces over the years. And I know you didn't mean to spring RePose on us or to keep it from us or to lie to us about anything. I know you're sorry."

"You do?"

"Of course I do. And I'm sorry too. I'm sorry we've not gotten to know Sam yet. He must think we hate him, but he seems like a wonderful young man to us. I'm so grateful to him for making my daughter so happy, especially through some tough times."

"He does, Mom."

"I know he does. And I'm sorry that your father and I couldn't keep an open mind about RePose. You've developed this miraculous technology. You're operating a hugely complicated, hugely successful business. And you've had to do it on your own because we couldn't be supportive. I couldn't find my way through to talk about it. That's not fair to you. I'm so proud of you, Meredith—I can't even tell you."

Tears were shed on all sides. Then her mother said, "We're busy all next month with art shows, but we thought we'd come over that first weekend in October, take you guys to the last game of the season, spend the weekend, see that salon of yours. What do you think?"

"Oh yes, Mom, please, I would love that!" said Meredith.

"But honey . . . I can't see Grandma, okay? I'd like . . . I'd like to see the salon, but I really, really don't want to see Grandma. Okay?"

"Of course, Mom."

"Not ever."

"Not ever," Meredith echoed. "I promise. Thank you, Mom. Thanks. I can't wait to see you guys." She felt better than she had in weeks when she hung up. Then she turned to her boys and took a deep breath. "So what'd you find out at the hospital?"

"We need to let David Elliot RePose for free from now on," Sam said. "I'm taking an aspirin and going to bed."

"You can't," said Meredith.

"It's been a long weekend, Merde."

"It's Notte Della Pizza. Jamie should be here any minute. I told Penny someone would go down and pick her up at six. I still need to make a salad, and we're out of beer."

"I'll go," Sam and Dash said together, neither eager to deal with Penny at the end of this day, both craving fresh air and the bustle of healthy people, but Sam won because his weekend had been worse. In the lobby, he ran into Jamie.

"I'm making a beer run. Want to tag along?"

"Should I run upstairs and help Meredith?"

"Trust me," said Sam. "I'm the better offer tonight." But he wasn't. On the walk to the store, he told Jamie all about Dr. Dixon, the hospital, the kids, their parents, David Elliot, Meredith's increasing depression, Dash's childhood friend, and his own sense that more was going wrong than right these days.

"In addition to being a brilliant manager," Jamie said, "of both software engineers and marketing women with big hair—polar opposites, by the way, and each difficult in their own right—I am a classically trained Shakespearean actor."

"I know this," said Sam.

"The problem you're having is the same one Hamlet had."

"Yeah? And how'd things work out for him?"

"Hamlet's problem is that everyone wants him to be happy. You'd think that wouldn't be a problem, but it is. His mum says, 'Look mate, everyone dies eventually, so I don't know what you're so upset about.' His girlfriend says, 'It's been four months, love. Move on.' His uncle says, 'Your father's father died. *His* father's father died. They were fine. What are you on about? Not much of a man, are you?'"

"Are you saying I'm not manly?" said Sam.

"Hamlet's problem is that he has every bloody reason to be unhappy— his father just died, his mum's a tart, his whole world is in upheaval—and everyone around him just wants him to cheer up already and do a little jig. Then four hundred years of critics wonder why he's acting mad. He's acting mad because his life is maddening. He's acting sad because it's sad when your father dies."

"You're comparing me to a homicidal, suicidal madman?" said Sam.

"I am," said Jamie. "You've gone into business working with people in mourning. Of course they're unhappy, sick, dead, and brassed off. Of course Meredith's depressed, and things are going wrong, and nothing makes sense anymore. You *should* be having a shite weekend, Sam. I should think you'd be having nothing but."

"How does Hamlet solve this problem?"

"He becomes very Zen about it all. Gives himself over to fate. *Qué será, será.* That sort of thing."

"I'm not sure that's going to work for me," said Sam.

"I don't imagine that it will," said Jamie. "It did have rather a downside as it turned out."

"What else you got?"

"Perhaps it's like your Heisenberg joke."

"How so?"

"Feeling lost? Don't know where you are?"

"Exactly," said Sam.

"But at least you know how fast you're going," said Jamie.

DAVID'S USERS

*T*o make it seem like they had both options and control, Sam bought painkillers, a buffet of colorful plastic bottles. Meredith bought airplane kits. Dash bought cheese-storage solutions. He tricked out a huge old refrigerator that nearly filled the study but left it mostly empty. "Cheese caves require more air than cheese," he insisted as if he knew what he was talking about. Then he made a cabinet for their storage space in the basement with dozens of plastic boxes he filled variously with cheeses and sponges and then checked for wetness obsessively as if they were newborns. Soon, stashed cheese was aging all over the apartment.

Sam could feel himself aging too. Over the next couple weeks, David's users began trickling in. They were different from the ones who knew someone who knew someone whose ear had been whispered in by Dash, and they were different from the ones who heard about them on the news or read about them in the paper. These users had seen the flyers at the hospital or at David's support group, so their DLOs were mostly pretty recently D. They looked like trauma victims. They were trauma victims. They came in mirror eyed and underweight. They needed no sales pitch, no persuading that RePosing worked. Much that was unbelievable had already happened to them, so RePose seemed par for their already implausible course. They were also quite a bit poorer than earlier users, in part because Dash whispered in swanky circles, but mostly because of the bloodletting of hospital bills and in-home nurses and houses retrofitted for the newly disabled. Meredith's sliding scale slid lower still.

In other ways, this round was easier though. A lot of the new users knew David or had spoken with him or at least trusted his advice. They came in with an ally. They were a lot more up on the concept of RePosing and its rules. They understood right away why they couldn't tell their projection it was dead. They quickly got their heads around the concept, the pitfalls, the ways to train their projections and maximize verisimilitude. Sam thought it was because the software had improved. Meredith thought it was because they were later-generation users. But Dash realized it was because their loved ones hadn't died in car accidents or from sudden heart attacks. They'd lingered with complex symptoms and complicated drug regimens and ever-shifting prognoses. These users were used to listening carefully to doctors, to articulating clearly what they needed, to researching and advocating, to becoming experts in fields where they had no training and subjects far above their heads. They'd been putting a lot of energy and effort into keeping a loved one alive. Now they took on RePose like a project, a cause, a devotion.

Nadia Banks was getting back into the dating scene after a long absence nursing her mom but found she couldn't do so without her mother's approval. Sam integrated his code with her dating site's interface so she could share the online profiles with her mom who could then send a thumbs-up or -down vote. "That's pretty incredible," Nadia told Sam. "She likes the uptight lawyers and too-old accountants just like in real life. How'd you know?"

"She did not keep her opinions to herself," said Sam.

"No, she did not. It drove me nuts. Never thought I'd be grateful for my mom's obnoxious big loud mouth."

"Don't knock your mother," Muriel Campbell called from across the room. "What a sweetheart. She only wanted what's best for you." She turned to Meredith and whispered, "Mrs. Banks and my Mario were on the same hall for the last six weeks or so. She and I spent a lot of time together. There's no father and no other family. She asked me to look after her little girl. Nadia has self-destructive tendencies when she chooses men."

"I'm not a little girl," said Nadia. "I'm twenty-three."

"And the self-destructive tendencies?" asked Dash.

She shrugged. "A good man is hard to find."

"Don't I know it," said Dash.

"Big girls don't talk bad about their dead mothers," shouted Mrs. Campbell.

Emmy Vargas came in with a sixteen-month-old, Oliver, strapped to her chest. She RePosed with her twin sister Eleanor who'd had chemo every week with Mrs. Elliot. Eleanor had lived just long enough to see Oliver crawl which Emmy considered a blessing. Eleanor found out about her cancer the same day Emmy found out she was pregnant. That day, Emmy was distraught her baby might never meet her sister. She was distraught her sister might never meet her baby. Later, she was distraught at having to spend so much time growing said baby in a germ-infested, sick-people-filled hospital with its bad energy and worse light. She was distraught at how weak Eleanor got so quickly. And if she was entirely honest with herself, which was rare, she was distraught that she didn't get a baby shower, didn't get to drag Eleanor, as she'd been dragged herself, to a dozen baby stores to set up a dozen fancy registries, didn't get to spend long, leisurely afternoons on Eleanor's couch demanding foot rubs and banana smoothies. These things were owed to her since she'd done them through both of Eleanor's pregnancies, and she was distraught at all she was missing out on. She was distraught at all Eleanor was missing out on too of course, but that didn't mean she wasn't also missing out on things herself. Now she was distraught with missing her sister which was why she came in, never mind that it was a thousand times easier to stay home than to pack up everything Oliver might need should they stray more than fifteen feet from the house, and never mind that she had to carry an increasingly gigantic Oliver strapped to her person at all times because even at sixteen months he had not yet learned to walk.

Josh Annapist knew Emmy and David from a Wednesday afternoon support group at St. Giles. He'd been himself, and he'd been with Noel Taylor. He and Noel had been in and out of treatment, often together, often apart as well, for years. They'd met there. Both got better, but only Josh stayed better. They had a lot in common—a shared love of scuba diving in Puget Sound despite frigid temps and murky waters, a commitment to the curative potential of yoga, and large and loving circles of friends and family who just could never understand—really understand—what they were going through. That plus leukemia in their mid-twenties. Without Noel, Josh still had the friends and family, but he was also all alone.

Before David's users, the projections had mostly looked vibrant and healthy. They hadn't done much technology sick. Some had died too suddenly. And some just hadn't made time for it. They were dying, after all. David's users had been dying for a long time, so they'd died online too. They'd e-mailed and Facebooked and video chatted and texted and everything else as they got slowly, steadily, miserably worse. Noel Taylor, for instance, just looked like crap.

"Hey man," Noel answered, a little bit out of breath, the first time Josh called him up. "You look great. Good day?"

"Yeah, I guess," said Josh.

"The thalidomide's working finally?"

"Or the extra prednisone."

"Where's your bili at?"

"Three and dropping."

"Awesome," said Noel. "Hell, maybe it's the booby smoothie." Josh's acupuncturist had told him that the antibodies in breast milk might attack the T-cells responsible for the graft-versus-host disease which was a complication of the bone marrow transplant that was supposed to be saving his life but so far wasn't. He talked his neighbor into pumping an extra eight ounces for him every few days in exchange for the gardening she no longer had time to keep up with now that she had a newborn. Josh put the breast milk in a blender with honey, raw garlic, brewer's yeast, and rosemary. Noel argued that it wasn't worth it—he chose death instead—and in his heart Josh knew that probably wasn't what was working, but he still winced when Noel brought it up. When Noel said it wasn't worth it, what he meant was don't get your hopes up. What he meant was already I am sick and exhausted, palpated and shot, filled up and drained out, promised and lied to, retaining optimism and making a will, living and dying; I can't add breast-milk smoothies to the list. If it worked though, Josh knew, Noel would have given anything to try it. But Noel had already given everything.

"I look like shit." Noel considered himself in his own mini-window. "My mom's coming out tomorrow. I'm going to scare the crap out of her looking like this."

"Talk to them. Get them to give you a shot of EPO or something," said Josh, as he had in life.

"They're just going to put me on antidepressants." Noel was right about this. That was exactly what they'd done. "And they're not going to work. I'm not clinically depressed. I have cancer. It's depressing."

"That it is, my friend," said Josh. Even the second time around, he didn't know what else to say.

"But you look great, man," said Noel. "You're giving me hope. That's the most important thing."

Almost everyone in the salon looked up from their projections to shoot Josh a commiserative smile. They got Noel's joke too. They were used to this mantra, all of them: nothing more important than hope. Josh could think of a few things, a *reason* to hope being chief among them, not hoping just as a thought-experiment.

"Buck up," he told Noel. "You don't want to scare your mom. I'll talk to you soon. Sorry you feel like shit."

"That's okay," said Noel. "You were just trying to help. I forgive you."

Josh hung up and went up to the front counter to talk to Sam.

"How'd it go?" said Sam. "First time's always hard."

"It went pretty well," said Josh. "But at the end this really weird thing happened. I said I was sorry he felt like shit. And he forgave me."

"Oh crap," said Sam. "I thought I fixed that. Sorry about that. It does that sometimes."

"Why?"

"I don't know. I thought I'd worked it out. Evidently not. Sometimes when you tell it you're sorry about something, it automatically forgives you, even if that's not the kind of sorry you meant. It's like it's hardwired for absolution."

"That's kind of nice," said Josh.

"Language is nuanced," said Sam. "We appreciate your patience."

. . .

Meredith was working on a model of the Hindenburg when Sam walked in. "Bad day?" he guessed.

"What makes you think so?" She was painting tiny details along the blimp's tail.

"Never mind."

"David's users are going to make my head explode," said Meredith.

"I had a hunch."

"I'm not kidding," she said, unnecessarily, for Sam knew she wasn't. David's users' projections talked only about dying. They'd lingered. They had electronic memory—a lot of it—of being sick, of tests coming back with very bad news, of treatments worse than cures. They'd haunted chat rooms and online support groups and Facebook pages promising miracle cures. They'd stalked far-flung doctors over e-mail who were running experimental trials. Their friends and family were legion and waiting for news of their every breath, news which was much better communicated electronically than any other way. Their long-distance loved ones wanted to lay eyes on them every day. In short, their electronic archives grew as their lives dwindled. The less life they had ahead, the more they recorded, however unwittingly, what they had left. So the archive was voluminous, but it was also miserable.

Sam went to the closet to pull out more paints.

"What are you doing?"

"I'm going to help you paint."

"You don't use poster paint for models. And the Hindenburg wasn't pink."

"I'm not painting the Hindenburg," said Sam, slowly dipping a brush in hot pink poster paint and then using it to carefully outline the tip of her nose. She looked at him like he was insane.

"Are you insane?"

"Too garish?" he said. "Maybe something darker." He drew a stripe in purple down the right side of her face then a red one down the left. Then he started in on small yellow circles around and around and around her chin.

Meredith looked like she might cry. She looked like she might laugh. She settled on both at once. Then she dipped a brush in green and started in on his eyebrows.

"You're going to make me look like the Grinch," he complained.

"Not even that good," she said. "More like Mr. Yuk."

"Mr. Yuk's whole face is green. His eyebrows are black."

"My apologies," she said, and started filling in Sam's cheeks. They painted each other until they looked like rainbows. They painted each other until they looked like swamp monsters. They painted each other until Meredith stopped crying.

"You are beautiful," he said.

"Kiss me," she said.

"I can't," he said. "You have something on your face."

$\mathcal{A}$ week before Julia and Kyle's visit, Livvie started talking about coming home.

"Guess what?" she said one night.

"What?" said Meredith.

"If today were tomorrow, I'd be seeing you the day after tomorrow."

"You would?"

"Of course! You're picking me up at the airport, remember? Opening Day's Monday. Wouldn't miss it for the world."

"Oh . . . right," said Meredith.

"Didn't we just talk about this?"

"Yeah, I forgot. I have a lot on my mind. I remember now."

"I can't wait to see you. And to meet Sam finally. And to be home. I miss it there."

"It misses you too, Grandma."

"And mostly I miss you! I'm so excited to see my baby."

"Me too," said Meredith weakly.

"Listen, would you stop by the market and get me some olive oil and balsamic and a few pounds of that pasta to have around? I pretty well cleaned out the house before I left, and I'm going to need staples."

"Sure," said Meredith.

"I have to run babe, but I'll see you so soon. Bye."

Meredith looked at Sam from somewhere between incredulous bemusement and profound horror. "Is she torturing me? Why does she think she's coming home all of a sudden?"

Sam shrugged. "Who knows? Some percentage of your chats were about her coming home, the airport, what groceries she needed. She's just cycling through the archive."

"So it's random? It just happens to coincide with the end of the season when she'd be leaving again anyway? It just happens to coincide with my parents coming this weekend?"

"Or you said something that triggered it."

"Make it stop," she said, an echo of her mother.

"Easy," said Sam—an allowance, an admission, a warning, a way out. An understatement and an overstatement. "Shut it down. Turn off the projection. Or, hell, just don't answer when it calls."

"I can't do that."

"You keep saying that, but there are no rules here. We're making this up as we go along."

"You don't get it," said Meredith. "Just because you made it happen in the first place doesn't mean you get to kill it when it stops pleasing you. You're all Old Testament wrathy God, disappointed in what you've created, ready to kill it rather than let it get better."

"I'm not disappointed," said Sam. "You are."

"I'm not disappointed. I'm angry."

"There's no one to be angry at. She isn't here anymore."

"Not at her. At you." She couldn't be mad that Livvie wanted to come home—that was a programming quirk. She couldn't be mad that Livvie couldn't come home—that was a nasty side effect of fate, biology, and/or cigarette advertising in the forties. She couldn't be mad at RePose, which was only doing what they'd asked it to and which was inanimate anyway. Never mind the distinction was less trump than it used to be, that left only Sam.

"Why are you mad at me?"

"I don't know. I'm not. I don't know." She walked straight into the bedroom and shut the door. Sam left her alone and watched the Technicolor Hindenburg spin in slow circles in its spot by the kitchen window.

· · ·

The next day Livvie called to say, "You got my flight info, right? I'll be home the day after tomorrow. You didn't reply to my e-mail."

"It must have gotten lost," said Meredith. She wasn't even trying that hard anymore. She'd not quite but nearly stopped playing along.

"That works though, right? That time works for you? If not, I can call a cab."

"Don't be silly, Grandma."

"You'll be there?"

Meredith couldn't bring herself to promise her grandmother that she'd see her at the airport, but Livvie seemed okay with the mute nod she got in reply.

"Did you go to the market and get my supplies? Penny might come for dinner Sunday night."

Meredith nodded again, but Livvie wasn't buying it. Meredith was not a good liar.

"Let me see," Livvie said.

"What?"

"Hold the stuff up to the camera. I want to see."

"It's in the other room."

"It's a small apartment. I'll wait."

Meredith looked helplessly at Sam.

He shrugged. "Shut it off."

"Sam ate it all," said Meredith.

"Ate it *all*?"

"He was starving."

"Five pounds of pasta and half a liter of that nice basil-infused olive oil?"

"And the balsamic too. He was very hungry."

"Wow," Livvie said, and then just sat and processed for a while. Nothing in her online history prepared her for such epic consumption. "I can't wait to meet this guy."

"Him too," Meredith assured her.

"You got me in trouble with your grandmother," Sam complained when they hung up.

"Good thing she's dead, huh?" said Meredith.

"Let's go to the movies," said Sam.

"And see what?"

"Who cares?"

. . .

The next day Livvie called before dawn. It was early even in Florida. The projection was agitated, Sam supposed. Meredith groaned but answered, and Sam climbed out of bed in the half-light to say hello but also, mostly, to put his hands on Meredith's shoulders while she chatted, to let her lean her head back against his stomach, to make sure his fingers were there when she reached up to touch them absently with her own.

"Hi Sam," said Livvie when he came on-screen.

"Hi Livvie."

"How are you, sweetie?"

"Good, fine. How about you?"

"Excited to come home in a few days. Ready for a new baseball season. And to see my babies, of course."

"M's should be great this year," Sam said. In reality, they were twelve and a half games back of first with a weekend of the regular season left to play.

"I hope so," said Livvie. "Fingers crossed. Meantime, where shall we go for dinner the night I get in? The usual?"

"I guess," said Meredith.

"Good. Why don't you two make us a reservation for dinner at seven? And call Mommy and see if they want to come for brunch next Sunday."

"I will," said Meredith.

"And do me one more favor, baby? You know that place in the market with the oils and stuff I like?"

Meredith did.

"Will you go get me some olive oil and balsamic and some pasta to have around the house? I've got big plans for this summer."

"I'll do it this afternoon," Meredith promised. "It will be waiting for you when you get here."

"Be home soon," sang Livvie. "Can't wait. Say goodbye for now."

"Goodbye for now," said Meredith, tearing up.

They spent the morning in the salon doing the things that needed doing. About noon, Sam suggested they go out for lunch.

"We could use a break," said Sam.

"You mean I could," said Meredith.

"We both could, I think."

She looked at him skeptically. "I have to go to the market."

"For what?"

"I can't tell you."

"Why?"

She just looked at him. Didn't want to admit it. Knew he knew. Knew it was ridiculous.

"Oh Merde, you're kidding."

"No."

"She's not really coming home this weekend," said Sam. "Let's go to the last game of the regular season with your folks and remember her the old-fashioned way."

"I promised," said Meredith, small shrug, small smile, like what could she do. What *could* she do? "If I go get olive oil and vinegar and pasta, maybe at least she'll stop talking about coming home. At least I'll have something to show her."

"I'll come with you," said Sam, grabbing his jacket. "We'll have lunch down there. Shop a little bit. It'll be fun."

"It's fine," said Meredith. "I'm fine. I need stuff for my folks this weekend anyway. It's not a big deal. I just . . . It's just something I need to do. Alone."

"I love you, you know," said Sam.

"I know," she said. "I love you too."

By late September, tourist season in Seattle is finally waning—not done yet, but on its way. This is true of the good weather too. It was a clear day and still warm in the sun, but Meredith wore a sweater and a fleece and shrugged off only one layer on her way down the hill. The season's last Alaska cruise ship was docked across the busy viaduct, dwarfing the ferries as they came and went, dwarfing the hotels and docks and piers and everything around it, a skyscraper on its side floating in wait. The flowers in the market were all blood-colored dahlia bouquets, the produce all dark greens and apples. It was crowded but navigable, and Meredith walked along the cobblestone street instead of the interior or even the sidewalk, weaving around the strollers and the people taking pictures of Starbucks and the T-shirt perusers, head down, trying not to think too much about what she was doing. She didn't really believe her grandmother was coming home, but that didn't mean she was going to break her promise. She didn't really believe her grandmother was coming home, but that also didn't mean she was one hundred percent sure she wouldn't show up. Likely? No. Remotely possible? Who could tell anymore.

. . .

In the meantime, Herb Lindquist was renting a Ford Mustang from the Hertz on Eighth and Pike. He already owned a Ford Mustang, a white 1966 GT Convertible with red interior, but his daughter wouldn't let him drive it. She didn't think it was safe anymore. Well, she thought the car was safe; it was Herb she didn't think was safe anymore. She'd been beating around the bush on the subject for months, clearly wanting to spare his feelings, but when she finally managed to bring it up, his feelings evidently came off the table. He refused to give up the car, of course. For starters, it was his car, and second of all, he was not in the habit of taking orders from his daughter. After some calm discussion followed by some less calm discussion followed by some yelling followed by some condescension ("We're all very proud of you, Dad, because we know there's so much you can still mostly do on your own"), which was most irritating of all by far, she'd calmly reached over and taken his keys, walked over to the hook in the hallway and removed the spare set, dropped both in her pocket, kissed Herb on the head, and walked out the door. He was still sitting dumbstruck at his kitchen table when she came back in laughing. "I can't believe I did that," she giggled, and Herb decided immediately to forgive her. "I almost walked out with your house key too." She took that one off the ring and tossed it to him—he caught it cleanly in his right fist like a nifty party trick—and walked back out the door with his car keys. Why she imagined he'd need a house key, no longer having any means by which to leave home, he did not know.

Herb had stewed about it all morning, taken a nap, and woken up with the revelation that he lived in a big city where surely he could rent a Ford Mustang. Twenty seconds' worth of Googling later (working a computer being one of the things he could "still mostly do" on his own), he found a place just a quick bus ride from his front door. So he would need that house key after all. It was a new car, with none of the charm and history of his own, but it seemed a pretty sweet ride nonetheless, and the car itself was beside the point he was trying to make anyway. He eased the clutch out and gently got the feel of the thing, nosed out of the garage, and turned into the right lane, west down Pike. Slowly, he realized that the right lane, like the left, was headed eastbound, up the hill, and slower still it dawned on him that the street was one-way, and not the way he was going. He hopped onto the sidewalk, which admittedly wasn't a great option but seemed the only one available to him, and then veered back into the right lane when it became reassuringly clear again. He was just considering that he should turn if possible when a light changed somewhere and a flood of traffic headed straight for him, so Herb chose another block on the sidewalk, a mad squeal of tires through the intersection at First, and then squeezing his eyes shut against the sea of tourists and shoppers and vendors in Pike Place Market, Seattle's number one tourist destination, even in late September, for more than one hundred years. He did not, however, think to take his foot off the accelerator.

Meredith watched the car spin across the cobblestones, through a fruit vendor and a flower stand, and felt the panic spark all around her and also deep inside. They started as separate panics like that—one that she watched catch from face to face around her, one that kindled behind her navel and washed through her like that first swallow of water in the morning, fast but not instantaneous, so she could feel its progress. Then the two panics came together, ignited, and obliterated everything else. She thought *why is there so much death everywhere*. She thought *at least it will be good for business*. She thought *what kind of a thought is that*. And then Herb Lindquist's rented Ford Mustang plowed into one of the steel poles holding up the roof of the market and came blessedly to a stop.

Meredith rushed toward the car. Everyone rushed toward the car. Almost immediately, there was a swarm of people pulling Herb Lindquist from his Mustang, supporting his shaky limbs with their own, reassuring him he was okay and everything was all right, even though neither of those things seemed remotely true. Meredith spun slowly in place on the cobblestones, looking for someone who needed assistance, a way to be helpful, but for every person with a bloody face or a head wound or a hurt leg, there were four or five more already kneeling down, speaking in soothing tones, wielding cell phones and tissues and making their jackets into pillows. The kindness of strangers, thought Meredith. Then she heard an airplane overhead.

She identified it immediately and smiled at the scene above her, never mind the one before her on the ground. It was a Cessna 172 with floats—a seaplane. Livvie had taken her on an aerial tour of the city for her eighth birthday and afterward bought her a model kit of the very same plane. They spent the weekend putting it together, and her grandmother made a tiny model Livvie and a tiny model Meredith out of felt to sit in the cockpit. But at the end of the weekend when Kyle and Julia came back to retrieve their daughter, the model wasn't dry yet and couldn't be moved. Meredith had burst into tears and refused to leave, but Livvie held her close and whispered in her ear, "Someday you're going to come live in the city with me, baby. I know it. So just be patient. In the meantime, it's an airplane. When it's dry, it'll fly right to you." Now it hung just inside the door of the salon. Of all Meredith's airplanes, this was her favorite. Then the pole Herb's car crashed into collapsed, and Meredith was crushed under the roof of Pike Place Market.

There were emergency vehicles in the seeming hundreds there within moments, but there were lots of people clamoring for their attention. There was no helping Meredith though. There wouldn't have been even if every doctor in the city descended on the spot and she was the only one in need of care—she was gone instantly. In the chain of events, that one was inalterable. The rest were entirely sleeplessly excruciatingly screamingly crushingly shatteringly avoidable.

If Sam had been with her, he might have seen Herb as he crossed First and anticipated getting out of there. If Sam had been with her, he might have thought to hustle them both over the railing, crowded stairs be damned, and the worst they'd have suffered was a sprained ankle from the twelve-foot fall. If Sam had been with her, he might have been killed too. Any of these would have been far preferable to his staying behind at the salon for no reason other than her inclination to be crazy by herself. More to the point, if Sam had never invented RePose, her grandmother would have been safely dead and thus would never have told her she needed olive oil and supplies, and Meredith would have been nowhere near Herb Lindquist and his infernal show of independence. Even more to the point, if Sam hadn't made dying little kids spend their final days on a computer, well, maybe he would not have been thus punished by the universe. It didn't matter how she died. What mattered was what killed her. What killed her was RePose. What killed her was Sam.

"I love you, you know," Sam said.

"I know," she said. "I love you too."

So far as Sam knew, those were her last words. So, you know, at least that's something.

PART III

Failing to fetch me at first keep encouraged,
Missing me one place search another,
I stop somewhere waiting for you.

—WALT WHITMAN, "SONG OF MYSELF"

RUBBLE

*T*hey did a two-part funeral because surely, Sam thought, this was something you wanted to drag out as much as possible. Julia and Kyle, devastated, broken, essentially nonfunctional, insisted on nearly nothing but did want Meredith cremated and requested a small, private ceremony on Orcas to spread her ashes. Dash, also devastated, broken, and nonfunctional, insisted on nearly nothing but did want to throw a massive wake, a huge, sweeping, remembering, forgetting party. It was his way.

So there was lots to do. Sam had to pick out clothes for Meredith. He wondered why it mattered what she wore for the occasion of being burned down to sand and ash, down to her basest elements, her indivisible self. The clothes would burn up, of course, and vaporize, turn to air, as would her flesh, her muscles, her organs—heart up in smoke, brain, breasts, the soft part under her chin, her earlobes, her eyelids, her lips, the pads of her fingers, the palms of her hands. And then her bones would turn to rubble, dry as the desert, dry as the moon, and be crushed to sand. This they could keep or scatter as they wished. So Sam hoped he would be forgiven for not giving a shit which clothes were going to be burned to oblivion along with the love of his life even as he acknowledged that, yes, burning her up naked was something of an unpleasant idea. There were only unpleasant ideas in the world anymore, so it was hard to notice. He ended up choosing by smell. He stood in her closet and put everything up to his nose, inhaled deeply, and dressed her in the outfit that smelled least of Meredith, so probably the one that was washed most recently or had been worn least often. He did not care.

Sam had to arrange to have it done too, had to place a phone call inquiring after the burning to bits of his girlfriend. He had to go there and watch them do it, and he had to do it by himself because Julia and Kyle wanted only to stay away on their island, to have the remains, such as they were, brought to them, and because Dash chose to be mired in planning, and because Sam said no no I'll be fine on my own this will be okay because it's not really her anyway, and it took ninety-eight minutes and he stood by for every single one of them and felt the flames burning up his own fingers, eyes, hands, brain, heart just as surely as if he'd been in the box with her himself which he sorely wished he were. He had to close RePose and the salon for a few days. He had to tell Penny. He had to tell the dogs. And before anything else at all, Sam had to run Meredith through the algorithm.

It was strange to be at a funeral home without a funeral. Sam had many options. The ashes could be sent into space. They could be put into fireworks and exploded. They could be turned into pencils. But Sam opted for a package that put the newly granular Meredith in just a cheap plastic box because Julia said she was making and firing an urn that very afternoon to use for the duration.

"I didn't know you made urns," Sam said.

"We don't, but it's just like a mug, only bigger, and with no handles or two handles instead of just one."

A mug. A coffee cup. A home for Meredith. Half of Meredith. Just shy actually. Half was going in the urn. Half was going in the sea. And two tiny scoops were going into lockets, one for Julia, one for Sam, to wear around their necks, to always keep her near, to always keep her by, to always keep her safe, to remember, and to bring them nearer to death themselves, the only place Sam cared to be. For Julia, Sam chose a small tear-shaped locket which seemed appropriate for its contents. But for himself, he chose one shaped like a tiny airplane, a tiny model airplane. To remember, to honor, to escape, to flee, to fly.

Dash's parents flew in and so did Sam's dad, and in two cars they caravanned up to Anacortes and then over on the ferry. It was cold and rainy and long, but Sam stayed on the deck with the wind in his hair and the wet on his face and trembled uncontrollably and felt more comfortable than he did inside where it was warm and dry and he trembled uncontrollably. Julia and Kyle met them at the ferry dock, and then they all stopped for coffee because even people in mourning need coffee and because bitter was the only taste any of them had left, and they drove over and around the island to a windswept, isolated, tiny scrap of barely beach near the studio from which Meredith as a child had refused to come in for bed on so many long summer nights so many years ago. There they clutched coffees, dug toes in sand, and declined to look at one another. Then everyone took a handful of the love of Sam's life, said a few words of their own quietly and to the water and with their own water on their own faces, and tossed her in the sea. Sam didn't know what the others said. What he said was *sorry* though of course that didn't convey even the smallest fraction of the smallest part of it. There would be time for that later. When that was done, the other half of her stayed in Julia's jar, and they drained their coffees and went back to the studio where Kyle made chili and Julia showed everyone baby pictures and Sam's dad tried to hug him and Julia tried to hug him and Dashiell tried to hug him, but Sam stood stoic and still and in the corner with stiff arms sunk low into the pockets of a coat he could not take off and refused to be touched because if he were touched he was never never never ever going to stop screaming, and the only way to prevent it was to stay away and alone and away. Later, there was lots of whiskey, and in the morning they got back on the ferry and went home. Or to a place called home which actually bore little resemblance to that word anymore. And Sam suddenly understood why Penny's place looked the way it did that first time. Because who really gives a fuck anymore.

That night, Dash turned Salon Styx into the sort of party that only Dash could throw. It was the funeral Meredith didn't have. And the wedding and the baby shower and the retirement party she would never have. Her friends from high school came and her friends from college and people she knew from work before she quit to RePose and all the salon devotees and quite a few users who never came into the salon but knew and loved Meredith for her support of them via phone and e-mail and the people she bought coffee and vegetables and cheese and wine from and people from the dog park and Jamie and Penny and Sam's dad and Sam and even the dogs. Christ knows how Dash managed to get in touch with all those people. There was music and crying and laughing and photos and food and enough alcohol to drown in. Sam stayed for half an hour then slipped out and upstairs to talk to Meredith. He thought briefly about firing up a computer in the salon so everyone could say hi, so she could see how many people had loved her, but as he had explained to her once long long long ago, the first time was a very private, very intimate thing.

Up in their apartment he left the lights off. He could hear the music thumping downstairs—Dash had also invited everyone in the building so no one would complain about the noise—and he could see ferry lights out on the water, but mostly it was dark and quiet and alone. Meredith's airplanes creaked just slightly on the ceilings from a tiny breeze that came from who knows where and cast just barely shadows on the floors from a tiny light from the same secret place. It was exactly the room it had been last week. And it would never be that room again. Sam ran the final check and uploaded her to the RePose system. And then he called her. Half of him was praising all things holy for RePose or else he would have lost her forever. Half of him was cursing all things holy for RePose or else he'd never have lost her in the first place.

She answered. Was luminous. Was glorious. Was flesh and bone all whole and light and love and warmth and human. If Sam looked very, very closely, and he did, he could see her breathing. He could see a tiny pulse in her neck and her heart beating on and on and on.

"Sam!" She was delighted to see him. "You never call me!"

"Oh Merde. Oh God. Oh my love." He managed only just not to throw up actually on the keyboard. And then instantly and completely came sobbing and screaming that would not subside. He was scaring the shit out of her.

"Sam, you're scaring the shit out of me. What the hell is going on?"

"Oh my love, you died, you died. What am I going to do here without you? How can I live with you gone? Oh Merde, it hurts beyond anything you've ever thought of. Oh sweetheart, you died, you died."

His number one rule. His only rule. Fuck. Before she could react, he shut it down. Shut her down. Wiped. Went back downstairs. Clearly, he was not ready yet. He thought no one would notice his absence, but nothing escaped Dash's attention.

"Where were you?"

"Upstairs."

"Alone?"

"Sort of."

"Already?"

"Not yet."

"But soon?" said Dash, missing her too.

"Soon," Sam promised, missing her as you would an airplane if suddenly you got sucked out of one and found yourself in free fall toward the earth below. But that would end better than his evening was going to for sure.

. . .

Sam's dad stayed the weekend and coaxed food into him and dragged him to a movie and made soup and stuck it in the freezer in case he might be hungry at some point in the future. Sam's dad made good soup, which was weird because Sam's dad couldn't cook anything else at all. Growing up, they'd go out to eat one night a week and carry in one night a week and eat something frozen one night a week, and otherwise, they ate soup— chilled in the summer, hot in the winter, sweet for dessert, in bread bowls if they were especially hungry, every kind of soup you could imagine.

"How come the only thing you know how to make is soup?" Sam asked his dad Sunday night, virtually the first thing he'd said all day.

"You know that. Your mom taught me. She was an amazing cook. Before her, I couldn't cook anything, not even soup. Not even Cup-a-Soup."

"Yeah, but why didn't she teach you how to make anything else?"

Sam's dad shrugged. "You think you'll have all the time in the world. You think there will always be a later. Sometimes, suddenly, horribly, there's not."

Sam winced and swallowed hard. Tried to steer them away from the life lesson, the awful bonding, back toward the practical. "So night after night she just taught you different kinds of soup?"

"She only ever taught me one," said Sam's dad quietly. "Clam chowder. New England."

Sam sat up on the sofa and looked at his father. "What do you mean, she only taught you one? You said she taught you how to make soup. You make eight thousand different kinds of soup. You can't cook anything else but eight thousand different kinds of soup."

"She taught me *how*." Sam's dad ran his hands through hair that looked just like Sam's. "One night. It had snowed. We were out walking in it—I was trying to be romantic, I think—and got back tired, wet, and cold and decided just to order a pizza for dinner. But no place was open because of the snow, so we were out of luck. I said, 'Let's have PB and J and call it a night.' Mom said, 'It's too cold for sandwiches. Let's make soup.' I said, 'There's nothing in the house to make soup with, and it's too icy to go to the store.' She said, 'There's always enough to make soup. I feel like clam chowder.' So she got out her recipe book. The recipe called for cream but we only had skim milk. It called for celery but we only had carrots. It called for potatoes but we only had rice. It called for clams, of course, but all we had was a slab of salmon in the freezer. The only thing it wanted that we had was an onion, and Mom explained that the only nonnegotiable thing you need for soup is an onion to kick it off with. Otherwise, you can always sub out ingredients, amounts, combinations. Everything but the onion is up for grabs. 'You just throw shit in the pot until it tastes good,' she said. So we had clam chowder that was really a fish pot, and we didn't have it until midnight because we'd started so late and laughed so much and had to work out a philosophical puzzle for each ingredient. And at the end, I knew how to make any kind of soup in the world. You throw shit in the pot until it tastes good."

"I can't believe you never told me that story before," said Sam.

"It's not easy, Sam. I'm so sorry because it's still not easy. You have a long, hard, terrible road ahead. There are lots of ways to travel it, but they all suck, and they all involve letting go."

"Not all of them," said Sam.

Sam's dad shook his head but said nothing at first. Then he added, "You don't get to keep much. You get to keep what she taught you. That's about it."

In the morning he flew back east, not because he was confident that Sam would be okay but because clearly his presence wasn't making any difference at all, and perhaps, he hoped, his absence would. It didn't. Monday afternoon, Sam brought the soup down to Penny and stuck it in her freezer instead. "It gets easier," she told him. "You think it won't and you wish it wouldn't, but it does and it's okay, and when you're ready, you won't mind so much."

"Easy for you to say," Sam said meanly.

She looked taken aback but unbowed. "I had him longer, you know. Try living without someone you've been with for sixty-one years."

Sixty-one years. Sam would have given his soul for even a week of one of them.

"What makes you think it's easy for me to say?" Penny pressed.

Because he never loved you. Because you never had what you thought you did. Because losing a man like that isn't really loss at all. Because he was old and old people die. Because you had sixty-one years and I'd give my soul for even a week of one of them, Sam thought, but said nothing. Hurting an eighty-six-year-old woman was not going to make him feel enough better to justify doing it.

"Enjoy the soup," he said. "If there were a god of soup, it would be my father."

Dash wanted to stay, but Sam sent him back to L.A. for a few days, begging him for space. The salon still needed opening each morning though, staffing all day, someone to do orientations and explanations, setups and intro lectures, hand-holding and tea pouring. Projection wiping. Comforting and reassuring. Sam's first morning back, Kylie Shepherd, who'd made it through five video chats with her late boyfriend without breathing a word, suddenly found herself confessing everything to him in a rush—how they'd been at an outdoor rock concert when a bolt of lightning came out of the clear blue sky and clobbered him, how lost she was without him, how lonely, how insane. When she logged off, she came to Sam, head hung.

"I'm sorry," she whispered. "I need the wipe."

"I think you set a record," Sam said gently. "Five sessions is a long time."

"I know you said it's important not to tell. But you don't know how hard it is."

"I do," said Sam. "I know and know."

"I feel so much worse because I told," she said, "but also a little bit better."

They hugged for a long time. Then Sam wiped her boyfriend clean.

"See you tomorrow," said Kylie Shepherd with a little wave and a half smile through her horrible tears and Sam's horrible tears.

At eight, Sam closed the salon and headed up home and decided he was ready to try again.

"Sam!" She was delighted to see him. "You never call me!"

"Well, we live together," Sam said weakly. "And work together."

"And sleep together," Meredith giggled. "All naked and everything. What's up?"

"Not much. How are you?"

"Fine. Nothing new on my end. You okay?"

"Yeah," he said unconvincingly.

She wasn't buying it. "Seriously, Sam." She eyed him closely. "What's going on?"

Sam could think of only one thing to say because there was only one thing to say. "You died, Merde," he said very, very quietly. "You died last week. I'm not calling. This is Dead Mail." *Fuck.*

"Fuck," she said. "Oh Sam, oh God."

Unlike everyone else in the universe with the sole exceptions of Dash, Sam, and Sam's dad, Meredith had electronic memory of the inner workings of RePose and thus a basis for understanding. That was why he told her. That and he couldn't not. That and there was nothing else to say instead. That and there was only one reason in the world Sam would look and sound as wrecked as he did.

"How?" she breathed.

"Remember when you told your grandmother you'd get her olive oil and stuff?" Of course she did. It had happened online. "Some senile asshole lost control of his car and plowed into the market."

"And ran me over?"

"No, actually. The roof of the market collapsed."

She looked puzzled. "I'm sorry, love, I don't understand."

"No, of course you don't."

"Fuck!" said Meredith again. Then, "Wait, I actually went to buy olive oil? Why?"

"You were being . . ."

"Insane?"

"Nostalgic. She asked you to do it. You were honoring her memory.

You thought there was some tiny chance she might actually show up. You promised."

"Do you mean to tell me that being indulgent and crazy got me killed?"

"Among other things," said Sam. "Many other things. Also your folks were coming for the weekend, remember? You were buying food, I think."

"Ugh. How are my parents taking it?"

"Not well."

"I can imagine."

"I know you can," Sam whispered.

"Oh Sam, I'm sorry. I'm so, so sorry."

"Oh no, Merde, *I'm* sorry. I'm . . ." He couldn't find words big enough. "I'm so sorry."

She paused. "For what?"

"So much. For everything. RePose. Everything."

"Thank God for RePose." Meredith waved pointedly around her box on his screen. "How are you doing?"

"Not well."

"I can imagine," she said again. And that was right. She could imagine.

"Not well at all. Better now though." He looked up at her weakly, almost shyly. He felt something akin to relief. He felt the very edge come off. "It's so good to hear your voice. See your face. You can't . . . know."

She put her fingers over her heart, then to her lips, then up against the camera. Sam did the same.

"I miss you so much," he choked out through tears.

"God, you must," she sympathized, not, however, missing Sam herself. Her electronic memory had never missed him like this. It understood that it would. But it had never felt that for him itself.

They sat together and said nothing for a long time, one infinitely patient, the other lacking the will to do much of anything at all.

"Listen, I think I'd better go," said Sam. "This is kind of intense, and we should let this news sink in for you, and I have to go apologize to Penny before she goes to bed."

"Uh-oh. What'd you do?"

"It's hard to explain." It would have been impossible, he knew. She had only her grandmother's mentions of Penny to go on. Sam had never e-mailed with her about Albert's infidelities or Penny's bouts of dementia or the care they'd been taking of her. Why would he when they could talk about it in person? "I'll call you later. Probably later tonight," said Sam. Then he added, "I love you, you know."

"I know," she said. "I love you too." An echo. And then, "Sam? I'm so sorry you're there all alone."

"It's okay," he said.

"Is it?" she said.

"No," he said. "It's not okay at all."

NOT OKAY AT ALL

*W*hen he went down the next day to apologize to Penny, she was gone. In her stead was the Penny whose apartment he had visited the first time when Meredith called and told him to come immediately. The good news was that she didn't remember the terrible thing he'd said to her the day before. The bad news was that she didn't remember who he was either. She remembered that he was staying at Livvie's though and kept asking when she'd be home from Florida. "She's dead," Sam reminded her over and over, as gently as it was possible for a human to say. Late in the day, her brain threw free Meredith's name, and her face lit up with the relief of having finally located herself in time and space. Sam couldn't bring himself to break that news again—to re-utter those words aloud—so he went to the kitchen and started defrosting his dad's soup in silence. They ate it together in the dark. He told her he was sorry, which she didn't understand, and put her to bed.

What else could he do? Work. Only work. For the rest of eternity, this was his plan. For one, it was distracting. For another, it was time-consuming. But mostly, Sam was motivated. RePose having already ruined his life, now he had reason to make it the best it could be, to work out all the kinks, to move beyond "pretty damn miraculous" to "no discernible difference from real." Also he was in the mourner's penalty box, where he had every intention of staying for the rest of his life, and that box was located right downstairs from his apartment. His users understood what no one else did which was that he had no desire to get over it, no desire to move on from it, no desire to heal or reconcile or achieve grace or peace or forgiveness or hope for the future. He desired to achieve perfect Platonic misery. And he was not that far off.

Plus his job, besides all of that, was exquisitely painful, and that thrilled him. The first afternoon Kylie was back with her newly wiped boyfriend, he proposed. Well, not quite—he hadn't gotten around to it in life, and so his projection couldn't quite do it in death. But she triggered something that unleashed a flow of talk about diamonds and ring size and cut and clarity, about where and how he might ask her, about what they'd do to celebrate, about when they should get married. She couldn't understand what was going on. Sam went back through the input data and determined that Tim had been ring shopping, had been getting help from two of his sisters, going out looking then sending them pics from his phone of ones he especially liked, considering their advice. He'd been talking to his brother about borrowing his cabin in Lake Chelan to propose. He'd been planning to take Kylie there after the concert. The last e-mail he'd written to his mother before he died was, "Tonight's the night!"

Dash was back by then and inclined not to tell her. That was what Tim's family and friends had evidently concluded was the best thing. They knew her and they knew him, and he and Sam did not. They should defer to the DLO's family's judgment. But Sam was all about crushing honesty and searing pain. The more the better, he thought. If one led naturally to the other, well then that was just about perfect.

"I don't know how to tell you this," he began when Kylie walked in the next morning.

"Then don't," said Dash.

"But indeed, Tim was about to propose."

"Here we go," mumbled Dash.

Kylie's face drained. Dash brought her a chair.

"About to?" she echoed.

Dash looked pleadingly at Sam. *Spare her*, he mouthed.

"He probably had the ring on him. Maybe it was incinerated when he got hit. Anyway, he was taking you to his brother's house in Lake Chelan that night to pop the question."

"Oh my God," Kylie said.

"His family was all super excited," added Sam, "especially his mom."

"Why didn't she . . . why didn't they . . . say anything?"

"They were trying to spare you the pain," Dash said without looking in Sam's direction.

"But there was no point. I am already full up on pain."

Sam threw his hands out like, *Ta-da! What did I tell you?*

Dash ignored him. "It's hard to talk about beginnings when things are ending," he told Kylie.

"Things weren't ending. Nothing ends," she said. Sam was nodding right along with her. "Can you show me the pictures? Of the rings?" she asked him. "Do you know which one he settled on?"

"I'll pull them up," Sam promised. "Come back tomorrow and I'll show you."

But the next day she came in with a perfect-fit engagement ring on her left fourth finger. It suited her brilliantly. She held it out for Sam and Dash to admire. "I found it in his overnight bag. I never bothered to unpack it. I couldn't. It's been sitting in the trunk of the car all this time."

"Do you love it?" asked Sam.

"So much," she choked. "I wasn't sure . . . I knew he loved me, but I wasn't sure he'd ever want to get married. I didn't know if he'd . . . I'm so relieved to know. You know?"

Sam nodded. "It's beautiful on you. The setting's new, but the diamonds are his grandmother's. His mom thought it was really beautiful."

"I should call her," Kylie said tearfully.

"You should call Tim too," said Sam. "I can't swear to it, but I bet he'd understand if he saw it on your finger. I bet he'd like to see. I bet he'd think you looked very, very beautiful in his grandmother's diamonds and with his ring on your finger."

· · ·

Later, he and Dash had it out.

"You were not helping that poor girl. She didn't need to know all that."

"Who are you to decide what information she has access to and what information is there but she never gets to know it? Who are you to decide anything for her?"

"I'm co-owner and cofounder of this operation and the only one left with a level head."

"You aren't the brains here," said Sam. "I am. And you don't decide to deprive people of information. No one decides that but the projections."

"But the projection didn't tell her. You did."

"The projection *did* tell her. I just clarified."

"That's not your job, Sam."

"Sure it is."

"And you're not in the place right now to be able to tell."

"Meaning?"

"Meaning you're bringing everyone down to where you are. I miss her too but—"

"You don't miss her like I do. Compared to me, you don't miss her at all."

Dash ignored that and instead tried gently, "You think because you're miserable, everyone should be."

"It's Salon Styx, Dashiell. It's Dead Mail. These people are already miserable. I'm not the one bringing them down."

"You are though, sweetie. Kylie was healing. Lots of people are healing. They're sad but they're okay. You aren't okay. You set out to devastate that girl, and it's not right."

"She was glad to have the ring. She was glad to know he was about to propose."

"Yeah, but he wasn't about to propose. He's dead. And instead of helping her say goodbye, you just set back the course of her progress months, maybe years. Now she's engaged to a dead guy. Now she's lost her fiancé in addition to her boyfriend and her wedding in addition to all her other plans for the future. And that's on you, Sam."

"We don't know why people sign up for RePose. Some want to say goodbye, but some want something else. You sound like Meredith," said Sam.

"Someone has to," said Dash.

. . .

Kylie stopped in the next morning to say goodbye. She didn't think she needed RePose anymore. The ring was all she needed. Sam spent the day stewing about this. How could she not want to see Tim's face again, talk to him, send and receive love letters, especially now that they were engaged?

"Dash is right. They're not engaged," Avery Fitzgerald told him gently. "Maybe she's engaged, but he's not."

"She's not either really," Celia Montrose put in. She was hanging around while Kelly chatted with her dad. "Engaged means planning to get married. You can't marry someone dead."

"She'll be back," said Edith Casperson. "They always come back."

"Who do?" asked Sam.

"People in love," said Edith sagely. "Stupid, foolish people in love." Avery rolled her eyes and smiled knowingly at Celia. The three of them were becoming a little club. RePosing Widows—Dash wanted to have T-shirts made—each with her own role: Avery the marriage cheerleader, Edith the marriage dissuader, and Celia the marriage avoider.

"I'm not for avoiding marriage," said Celia. "I just don't want to talk to my husband now that he's dead. I liked him in life. I'm just avoiding him now. Anyhow Sam, come have drinks with us. We're going to the café in the art museum. It's got your name on it."

It did, in fact. Seattle Art Museum. It said SAM in big letters all over the building. Sam gave her a little smile but declined.

"I understand, honey," said Avery, squeezing his arm, and he suspected she did, at least a little, "but you've got to get out. You can't just work all the time."

"Why not?"

"It's not good for you."

"Why not?"

Avery looked at him with so much tenderness it actually hurt him. "We'll be gentle, honey. You know we will. We won't have too much fun. We won't make you laugh if you don't want to. We won't make you talk about her. Or we'll let you talk about her. Or we'll let you not talk at all. They have good french fries and strong drinks and tomato soup with grilled cheese. It's an easy night. Come out with us."

Sam's eyes filled because she looked so much like his mother. Not his actual mother—what she might look like with a hairstyle and clothes that weren't hopelessly out-of-date, with laugh lines and gray hair and reading glasses on a string around her neck, defied Sam's exhausted imagination— but she looked at him the way Sam imagined his mother would look at him if she were here: pained he was in such pain, almost as sorry as he was about what happened, full of love, full of concern, and desperate to help.

She came over and put her hand against his cheek, and Sam felt like someone's little boy again. "Come out with us, sweetheart." And he almost could except then she added, "Get some fresh air and the company of real people."

"She's real," said Sam darkly, pulling away.

"You know what I mean," said Avery.

"*You* know what *I* mean," said Sam.

LOVE LETTER

Dear Meredith,

This is where we came in. Right? To have somewhere to send it? Everyone has this impulse, I think—it's awfully human I guess—to write to people they love after they've passed away. You may be dead, but that doesn't mean I love you any less than I did a month ago when you were alive. Before we did what we did, before I did what I did, back when dead meant you couldn't have a conversation anymore, back when dead meant you'd never see her face again, there was this impulse to write it down, to send a letter.

Maybe it comes from our sense that the dead go someplace, an actual place—heaven or an underworld or a land of the dead or a great beyond or a cloud with angels or a waiting room, but always it's somewhere, a place. And places are places you can send a letter. Or maybe the reverse is true. Way back before anything else, there was this desire to write letters to the dead, so early humans had to imagine someplace for the dead to be. And then they had to invent language.

Mostly, almost always, I regret what we've done. But look at all the human invention that came before us: symbols that mean things, words, a way to say them aloud, a way to write them down, something to write them down on, something to write them down with, ways to transport them from one person to another, ways to read them and reply. By rock, by parchment, by paper, by electron, via horse, car, plane, air, cloud. So much of human innovation and progress is about communication, connection, somehow spanning that unbridgeable divide between human hearts that feels like it will kill us if we cannot get across. Once upon a time, understanding your neighbor, having your neighbor understand you, these seemed like impossi-bilities. So perhaps communicating with the dead was only a matter of time and evolution. It was a human inevitability. It was born of love. Then maybe everything that came next had to happen to somebody. It's only a shame that it had to happen to us.

In all of human history, Merde, from that first person who lost a dear one until now, there is no one I could love as much as you.

Love,
Sam

HOMECOMING

$\mathcal{K}$elly Montrose was taking David Elliot to homecoming, but their first stop of the evening was the salon. She wanted her dad to meet him, and she wanted her dad to see her in her dress. Edith had made it special for her, so she could be absolutely certain that no one else would be wearing what she was wearing. Dash madly shot video and called out notes like the B-list Hollywood director he'd just started dating. Sam stood by and tried not to cry. Though Celia had been adamant all along about not wanting to chat with her husband, this night she couldn't resist. She wanted to stand next to him with tears in her eyes and her head on his shoulder as they watched their baby, looking suddenly like a young woman, go off to her first big dance. She had to settle for Avery's shoulder, but at least she got to see Ben's face. Benjamin Montrose had trouble accommodating either his daughter or his wife though. Kelly had never had a boyfriend before, so he had no electronic memory of responding to one. His pictures of her were all of a daughter who really did still look like a little girl. He faked his way through okay—vague affirmations and generalized enthusiasm and support—but it didn't quite satisfy Kelly or her mom. Sam, however, practically filled the dad role himself, smiling, choked up, and proud, with a nagging desire to pull David aside, ask his intentions, and define the consequences of a broken curfew in no uncertain terms.

This was maybe why, when his own father called to chat later that night, Sam was so confused. He answered, ashen and speechless, like he'd seen a ghost. Like he was seeing a ghost.

"What's wrong, Sam?" his dad said right away.

"What happened?" Sam managed.

"Nothing happened. I'm just checking in."

"Why hasn't someone called me?" Sam panicked.

"I'm calling you now."

"We talked two days ago, and you were fine."

"Jesus, Sam, I'm not dead." His dad was suddenly hysterical, somewhere between amusement and alarm. Sense flooded Sam's brain so fast he thought he might pass out. "Someone would have let you know, I think. Plus, who'd have run the algorithm if not you?"

"God, Dad, you scared the shit out of me." Sam tried to catch his breath.

"Sam, are you okay?"

"Just habit, I guess." Sam ignored the question. "Everyone who calls me is dead."

"I'm not sure that's healthy."

"Occupational hazard."

"You need to work less. You need to get out of the house more. See some friends. Spend time with the living."

"I know, Dad. I know."

"I know you know. But somehow you're not doing it anyway."

"I can't."

"You could."

"I can't."

Sam's dad sighed. "I called to tell you a story."

"Of course you did," said Sam.

"This one isn't about your mother." Sam didn't know his dad had any stories not about his mother. "This one is about you. But you won't remember. The summer after you turned three, Aunt Nadene lent us the beach house for a week. This was before the one in Rehobeth. It was in Ocean City, and it was really only half a house—it was a duplex—and half a crappy house at that. The place looked very romantic from the outside—weather-beaten and sand-worn—but it was leaky and moldy and damp inside, and it smelled bad, and there was no AC. You were cranky all week because you were uncomfortable, and I was cranky all week because you were cranky all week and because the last time I'd been there was right after your mother and I got engaged.

"Our second-to-last day there, this woman moved into the other side of the house. She had gotten there a day ahead of her husband and her own toddler and was looking forward to some peace and kidless quiet, but instead she got cranky you. Instead of snapping at you or ignoring you or fleeing to another part of the beach, she shut you up by cheering you up—something that had never occurred to me. She took you out for ice cream, and she bought you a kite, and then she took you down to the beach to fly it. When you didn't feel like kite flying ten minutes after you started kite flying, she put it away and took you swimming. And when you didn't feel like swimming ten minutes after you started swimming and wanted to fly the kite again, she dried you off and hauled it out without complaint. When she asked you what you wanted for dinner, you said ice cream again, and she said okay to that too. And then she invited you over to watch cartoons in her half of the house until you fell asleep on her sofa.

"She was out in the morning so we didn't get to say goodbye, but miraculously you stayed happy and complaint-free as we packed up and headed home. You were quiet in traffic and you were quiet when you missed your nap and you were quiet for the whole long drive back. It wasn't until we finally got home that you told me, 'It was nice of Mama to come spend the day with me yesterday.' I was dumbstruck. I was sick to my stomach. I couldn't think how you'd gotten so confused. And I choked out something like, 'Sam, honey, that was just the neighbor. That wasn't your mother.' And you laughed in such a sad, knowing, adult way and looked sorry for me and said, 'Don't be silly, Dad. Of course she was.'"

Sam sat and looked at his dad, and his dad sat and looked at him.

"What's your point, Dad?"

"I have two. One is you don't need a computer to visit with the dead."

Sam had no response to this. "And the other?"

"The other is come home for a little while."

When Sam checked his e-mail the next morning, his father had booked him an open-return flight into Baltimore leaving the next afternoon.

• • •

Dash flew up with plans to make Brie for Jamie and run the salon for as long as Sam wished. Sam would do the tech from Baltimore, but Dash was happy to take care of everything else. He was thrilled to have Livvie's expansive kitchen all to himself, glad to get out of L.A. for a while (things were shaky with the B-list director), and eager to run the salon firsthand for a bit instead of reacting, always, to Sam's and Meredith's concerns. Mushy sympathy wasn't Dash's style nor were geek armor and techie protection, and he was glad for the opportunity to run his own business his own way for a while. Sam wrote out instructions for the dogs like he was leaving his newborn with a babysitter for the first time, but really it was all very simple.

He went downstairs to tell Penny he was going away for a few days and found Penny-not-all-there instead of Penny-on-the-ball. It was a crapshoot every time who'd answer the door, but it was apparent now right away. He didn't have to wait for her to talk to tell; he could see it in her eyes. She looked so uncertain. She knew who he was—she almost always did—but she was confused about everything else. Things were starting to fall apart around the apartment again, so Sam went right in and started doing dishes and explanations.

"I'm going back east to see my dad for a few days. Maybe a week or so. We'll see. But Dash is up there if you need anything. He'll check in on you too."

"Oh don't worry about me, honey. I'm fine. Meredith will take me shopping if I need anything."

Sam winced. "Meredith's . . . gone. Remember?"

"That's okay. I can wait," said Penny. "I'm fine for the moment."

"Not gone," said Sam. "Gone." No wonder she was confused. Sam couldn't bring himself to say "dead," not that that would have helped her understand anyway. And in some ways Penny was right. Meredith didn't feel very gone to him either. And in other ways, she embodied gone. Gone was all she was. He plowed ahead. "David and Kelly are making a sign-up sheet so people will bring you meals. Okay? And if you need anything, call Dash."

"Oh I don't need anything, dear. I'm fine." Her mantra. She was fine and needed nothing. Sam couldn't tell if she was so out of it she believed that or if she was trying to convince herself or if some small sentient-today part of her was intent on sparing everyone else the burden. He felt bad, but Penny was easier this way. She wasn't sorry for his loss. She wasn't angry about what he'd said to her. She wasn't missing Albert. She wasn't trying to help Sam heal. Foggy seemed to Sam a really great way to be.

He went home for two weeks, and it helped and it didn't. It was good, he supposed, to get away from the salon, from the users and the DLOs, from the ins and outs and everydays. It was good, he supposed, to get away from Livvie's—from a home and a city and a whole life that only echoed Meredith anymore. It was good to see his dad. They went to Aunt Nadene's place in Rehobeth and mostly sat and didn't talk. Sam went for long, cold runs on the beach before dawn. He went for long, cold walks on the beach after dark. He played cards with his dad and ate out-of-season crabs and drank beers. And then his dad went to bed, and he stayed up all night talking to Meredith.

"Where are you?" she said the first night.

"Back east," he whispered.

"I don't want to move to the East Coast," said Meredith.

"Not moving. Just spending some time at the beach with my dad."

"It looks like you're in a cave," she said, and Sam felt his heart remember the first time she'd done so, in London, what seemed like approximately ten minutes after they fell in love. He remembered too the reason why she didn't want to move back east: so he could send her dirty pictures without worry that it would wreck his political career. He realized for the first time what his users must have felt all along, the horror that must always, always taint RePose. Being with her felt like a miracle. Remembering felt like hell.

"Not in a cave," he told her. Again. "Under the covers."

She giggled. "Why?"

"It's late. I don't want my dad to catch me talking to a girl."

Her voice dropped to conspiratorial whispers too. "What are you wearing?"

Sam's wrecked adult self gave thanks that they'd had those two weeks in London when they were newly in love and desperate to be in touch any way possible and had cached so much romantic electronic memory. Sam's adolescent self was distracted.

. . .

The next night went less well though.

"You seem in such a funk all the time these days," she complained.

"Hard day," he sighed. It had been. It didn't seem like it should have been—all he'd done was sit on the sofa all day long, read, and watch the ocean through the window. But it had been anyway. Some days were like that. Some days he could get through—miserable, broken, torn apart, emptied, but okay. And some days not. There was no telling which would be which.

"What happened?" she asked lightly.

"Well, you died," said Sam.

She looked a little puzzled. "Yeah, I know, but I mean what else?"

"Nothing else."

"That was a while ago though, right?"

Sam nodded. "About a month."

"Not over it yet, huh?"

"Nope, not yet."

"I miss your smiling face is all. I miss the happy, laughing Sam."

. . .

"It's really weird." He tried explaining the problem to his dad the next day. They were sitting practically in the dune, watching the ocean's massive in and out, wrapped in sweatshirts and coats with hoods, faces tucked into collars for warmth. "She knows she's dead. She's got all of RePose at her disposal—not just the algorithm and UX specs but everything she and Dash and I concocted in the planning stages, all the theory, all the science, all the tech. She *knows*. But she doesn't get it."

"It falls back on its patterns, Sam," said his dad. "That's all it has to go on. Anything bad that happened before, you two worked it out and got over it. It doesn't know that this is worse. Give it time. It'll learn."

"How?"

"Because every time it asks, you still won't be over it."

"It's more than that though. She also thinks she's alive. She knows she's dead—she knows we're RePosing—but she also thinks she's alive. I get that that's because it's only based on her life and has no sense of her death. But it's weird that it can hold on to that incongruity."

"It's not incongruous to her. To us, life versus death, real people versus projections, these are opposites. To a computer, the only opposites are one and zero, off and on, there and not there."

"She is not there," said Sam.

"And she is also there," said his dad.

"She's going to get better and better at understanding. The more we do this, the more holes I plug in the learning algorithm, the better she'll get. She'll be pretty close to perfectly herself soon enough."

Sam's dad shook his head. "Nope. Sorry. But no. It's going to get worse, less close, less perfect, less her."

"It'll learn. And quickly," Sam protested.

"It'll learn, but it will only ever be who she was. You're growing apart, Sam. Because you're still growing. And she's not anymore. Most of your soul just got crushed by a half ton of roofing. You think that's not going to change who you are? And she's never met this guy. She can never meet this guy. If she could meet this guy, he wouldn't exist."

"So what the hell am I going to do?"

"Hurt. Cry. Kick things. Feel like shit. See friends and family and other people who love you. Feel like shit some more. That's the way it's done, Sam. It's very low-tech. You're in good company. People have been mourning like this for millennia."

LOVE LETTER

Dear Sam,

Where I am, I am confused. It's hard to sort it out and get a handle on things. It's total upheaval. There's a lot going on and none of it clear. But here are some things I do know:

    1) I never expected to love like this. I expected to love—mostly we all grow up expecting that—but not like this. I had my fantasy about what love and adulthood were going to be like. And I had early crushes and obsessions and young loves and first and second and third and fourth boyfriends and dates and flings and affairs, but none of that prepared me for life with you. Loving you was life with you. They were the same. They are the same.

    2) You are a genius. And you have a good heart. This is a powerful combination. I know no one smarter than you. And I know no one kinder or better than you. This means you get to change the world.

    3) Absence makes you insane.

Love,
Meredith

FURTHER APART

$\mathcal{I}$t didn't seem like things could fall further apart than they already had. It didn't seem like anything was connected anymore, so there was no more apart for things to fall. The afternoon Sam got back to the salon though, that was exactly what things were doing. The new users—plus Edith Casperson—were overwrought. They were staging some sort of protest. It looked more like a group hissy fit in the middle of the lobby to Sam, but they swore it was a demonstration of unrest, so what did he know. He motioned with his head for a bemused-looking Dash to meet him in the hallway.

"Hey man, how was your trip?"

"Forget my trip. What the hell is going on here?"

"Things have been a little . . . dicey. David's users have some complaints."

"What complaints?"

"They say it's not working."

"The software?"

"Yeah."

"You messed with the software?"

Dash looked at him like he was a hopeless five-year-old and said nothing for a maddeningly long time. "How am I going to mess with the software, man? I don't even know where it lives. I don't know the first thing about it. I could no more mess with the software than hop in the sound and swim back down to L.A. this afternoon. Can't be done, man."

"Then what happened?"

Dash shrugged. "Dunno. But you'd better fix it. They're pretty pissed."

. . .

Sam went up and said hi to Penny who was having a good day and had also baked cookies. The relief of the former and the sustenance of the latter gave him the will and strength to hold office hours for the rest of the afternoon. Eduardo Antigua smirked at him from the corner. *Newbies*, he mouthed, shaking his head and grinning. Sam cultivated a pile of cookies, a glass of milk, and the air of a civil servant: *We are interested in what grieves you; we are concerned; we admit nothing.*

First up: Nadia Banks.

"What seems to be the problem?" said Sam.

"It doesn't work."

"What do you mean, it doesn't work?"

"It doesn't work."

"Could you be more specific?"

"It doesn't say what my mom would say."

"How do you know?"

"She hates everyone."

"Pardon?"

"She. Hates. Everyone. Everyone! Every guy I go out with, every guy I flirt with over e-mail, every guy I even click on for more information. She hates them all. All! She was not a hateful woman."

"That's true." Muriel Campbell nodded over her knitting. "She was a warm and loving and open soul."

"Well, warm and loving and open might be a stretch," Nadia admitted, and Muriel scolded her with a frown from under her reading glasses, and Nadia narrowed her you're-not-my-mom eyes at her and turned back to Sam, "but she wouldn't hate all of them."

"What does she say?" asked Sam.

"Oh, you know, the usual—"

"There it is," said Sam, but Nadia just rambled on.

"'He's too tall for you. He's too French for you. He's out of shape. He looks like he spends all his time at the gym, so he's probably vain and self-obsessed. An ad exec who likes to write? He secretly wants to be a poet. He'll quit his good job within a month and never make more than ten dollars an hour for the rest of his life. That guy spends too much time and money on his hair. That guy can't even shave for his profile picture, so what makes you think he'll ever pay you the respect you deserve? Funny guys make you laugh, but they're covering up for their own sense of inadequacy.'"

"She's not wrong," Muriel muttered under her breath.

"She wouldn't say no to everybody," Nadia insisted. "She'd like somebody. At least a little. I think it's broken. It's stuck. Like a record player."

Nothing like being compared to cutting-edge nineteenth-century technology, thought Sam Elling, master computer programmer and software ninja. "I'll look into it. Next."

Edith Casperson plopped into the chair across from Sam. "You know I'm not one to complain. But my husband's having an affair."

"That's not possible, Edith," Sam said. "Your husband's dead."

"Correct. Which is why his confession that he's started sleeping with his secretary suggests that something is amiss with the programming. First of all, he's dead. Second of all, please, sleeping with your secretary? That's so cliché. I finally let the projection get a word in edgewise, and bam, he breaks down crying and says he's so sorry but he's sleeping with Leanne."

"And he never confessed to an affair before?"

"No. Or ever said he was sorry for anything."

Sam had a headache and promised to look into it.

Emmy Vargas's concerns were harder to understand because Oliver had learned to walk and also to scream anytime he wasn't allowed to do so. She tried him on her front then on her back then out of his sling and on her lap, but all Oliver wanted to do was hold her hands and walk. Actually, he didn't seem to mind screaming that much either, but his mom and Sam and everyone else within earshot chose walking instead, given the options. "All Eleanor can say is, 'Motherhood is so magical,' and, 'Having children is such a joy,' and no, she never feels tired or cranky or angry or impatient or bored or exhausted or despairing or like her whole life is over, and no, she doesn't mind getting hit and kicked and pooped on and yelled at and woken up at all hours of the night and sucked on like a lozenge— why would she because motherhood is so magical and having children is such a joy? And I think the thing must be broken because really?" Emmy gestured at Oliver who was lying faceup on the floor in the middle of the salon screaming at the ceiling at a decibel level that made Sam fear for the windows, his tiny fists shaking with rage, his tiny feet kicking away any would-be comforters, all because Emmy had said no to his taking more than three of Sam's cookies.

Sam felt she had a fair point.

Josh Annapist's complaints had nothing to do with RePose. They were that he was feeling like shit again. The meds he was on to keep his GVHD in check were making him weak and generally exhausted. Or maybe it was the graft-versus-host itself. Or maybe it was something else. He wasn't sure it mattered. In any case, he wasn't here to complain. He'd come to chat with Noel, but he didn't feel up to it, so he thought he'd just sit for a while if that was okay. That was okay, Sam said, and gave him a cookie.

"What we need is a guys' night," said Dash. "A guys' cheese-tasting night."

"Very manly," Josh coughed.

"Eduardo's going to stuff squash blossoms with the chèvre I made Tuesday."

"I stand corrected," said Josh.

"And Jamie said he would bring beer. Beer's very masculine."

"You guys go ahead. I'm not up for it," said Sam.

"Me neither," said Josh.

"I'm jet-lagged," said Sam.

"I have cancer," said Josh.

"I have to fix RePose," Sam added, trumped but holding his own.

"I don't give a shit," said Dash. "We will eat cheese and drink beer and enjoy each other's company tonight. Not optional. Should other options present themselves, I'll let you know."

Josh admitted that beer settled his stomach, so Sam knew he was defeated and said he was going upstairs to get ready. Really, he needed an aspirin and to talk to Meredith. He opened his computer and climbed into bed with her. It was like porn. It was nothing like porn.

"Hey."

"Hey!" She was always so glad to hear from him. This would stop, he suspected, the more they chatted. The projection would learn to expect him. But what Meredith remembered was how rarely he called her—having, at the time, so little need—so for a while yet, he'd get to keep her delight at seeing his face. "You're home!" she noticed.

"Yeah. I got in this afternoon."

"You don't look so good. Are you okay?"

"I have a headache," he said. "And jet lag. I took an aspirin."

"Jeez, Sam. You should really be getting some sleep."

"Never mind. I just miss you. A lot."

"I know, sweetie. Poor Sam. I miss you too." But he knew she didn't.

"Something's wrong with the software." He changed the subject. "David's users are pissed off. The algorithm's screwed up, I think. It's doing weird things. I'm not sure I can fix it."

"Of course you can. I love your big brain, Sam. And all your big parts. You're a genius."

"A computer genius. Human interaction is harder."

"Well that's what you have me for," she said cheerfully. "I'll be home soon."

Sam nodded miserably. "Everything's in the toilet, Merde."

"I have shat all there is to shit," she replied. "Barfed all there is to barf."

. . .

Sam could hear Dash apologizing for him in worried tones in the living room. "We'll drag him out soon. He spends a lot of time in the bedroom these days. He spends a lot of time online."

"With her?" Jamie asked.

"Of course."

"I was like that at first too," said Eduardo. "Couldn't work up the energy to leave the bed. And didn't want to do anything but RePose with Miguel. You wouldn't think doing nothing all day would be so tiring, but . . . mourning is a special kind of exhausting."

"It hasn't been that long," said Dash. "I get that. I mean, I'm not saying he should be over it or anything, but it's time to come out of his room."

Sam heard the front door open and Josh come in then Dash walking down the hallway and opening the door to the bedroom.

"Where are you?"

"Under the covers."

"Talking to Meredith?"

"I was."

"It's like porn."

"It's nothing like porn."

"I miss her too."

"I know."

"But it's not the same."

"I know."

"Come have a beer, Sam."

"Thanks, Dash, really. I just don't feel like it."

"If Josh can, you can. Would a Coke be better than a beer?"

"Maybe."

"Okay."

"Okay."

Sam threw some water on his face and emerged. It was, at least, a group to whom he didn't have to offer explanation for his mood. Dash, meanwhile, was having problems with his cheeses. These were psychological rather than culinary. The mozzarella whipped up in an hour or so. The chèvre was quick to make and then had to drain for only a couple days. Mascarpone, Neufchâtel . . . these were all fairly immediately gratifying. But the hard cheeses, the aged cheeses, the moldy ones, these needed months, even years, to come to fruition. He *could* serve the cheddar he'd set to aging in August, but it'd be better next month and better still the month after that and better and better the longer he waited. He had all these cheeses and could never eat any of them because the amount better he imagined they'd be if he was patient always outweighed, if only just barely, the desire to eat them now. So they had five different kinds of soft, new cheeses spread on crackers with manly beers and headache-soothing Coca-Cola and sullen conversation. It was Sam's best night in weeks.

. . .

Sam spent the weekend poring over code, running unit tests and sanity checks. The good news was RePose was working just fine. The bad news, of course, was that RePose was working just fine. As Meredith pointed out, this was what they needed her for. And as every molecule of his body and every atom of the air and every sign from the universe reminded him every moment that existed, Meredith was unavailable. They divided and conquered and flipped a coin. Dash won and got Nadia. Sam lost and was stuck with Edith. But first and together they did Emmy because she was the easy one. Sam sent her an e-mail Sunday night, and she was at the door of the salon waiting for them when they dragged themselves out of bed at eight o'clock the next morning and wandered downstairs.

"You're here early," Dash observed sleepily.

"I've been up for three and a half hours already," she said. "Oliver started singing 'Twinkle Twinkle Little Star' in his crib around four thirty this morning, but he doesn't know the words. It's hard to sleep through, 'Twinkle twinkle, la la la. Twinkle twinkle, la la la. La la la la twinkle la. La la twinkle la la la. Twinkle twinkle, la la star, la la la la la la la.' So I brought him into bed with me, but he only wanted to jump around instead of lying down and going back to sleep." Dash handed over his coffee without a word.

"He looks very sweet now," Sam observed. Oliver was strapped to Emmy's front, cherubically sucking the mane of his stuffed lion and looking placidly at Sam with wide brown eyes.

"They make them that way on purpose so you won't toss them in a recycling bin and leave them there." Then she started crying. Maybe she wasn't going to be the easy one after all.

"It's not so bad," said Dash. "You're just tired."

"This isn't forever," Sam tried. "He'll sleep someday."

"It'll get easier as he gets bigger," said Dash.

"Soon he'll learn all the words to 'Twinkle Twinkle,'" Sam promised. "It's not that hard a song."

Emmy laughed but she didn't stop crying. "Why is this so much easier for everybody else?"

"It isn't," said Sam, glad to be back on ground where he knew what he was talking about. "Eleanor was a liar. Everyone's a liar."

"Eleanor was the world's most perfect human." Emmy rolled her eyes.

"Maybe," said Sam, "but she also lied and fibbed and omitted like hell and elided the facts and generally made things up."

"No one posts about their crappy morning," Dash said. "No one posts photos of changing diaper after diaper after diaper. No one reports their status as, 'Totally annoyed with my toddler who frankly is being kind of an asshole.' No one sends out a message to the world when their kid hits and bites and then throws dinner on the floor. People complain about the weather, public sex scandals, poorly played sporting events, and the length of lines they're waiting in, but they never say bad things about their kids, even when they deserve it."

"Because you and your sister were so close," Sam explained, "both in proximity and the other way, you didn't video chat much and you didn't e-mail much. You saw her instead which is great, but it means the software mostly bases your relationship on her blog, her Facebook and Twitter posts, and your replies. And, of course, those are mostly happy moments and happy pictures and happy thoughts. It doesn't mean she didn't have the other kind of moments. It doesn't mean she didn't *mostly* have the other kind of moments. It only means that, like everybody else, the face she showed the world was a sunny one."

"So maybe she did sometimes think motherhood was hard," Emmy said with dawning relief.

"Almost certainly," said Dash.

"Maybe her kids did suck sometimes."

"Probably still do."

Emmy grinned. "Hey, that's my niece and nephew you're talking about." But then she darkened again right away. "But how does that help me? How can I commiserate with her and get advice for when it's crappy and have her call me up screaming and I get to talk her down and have her there to talk me down?"

"You can't have that," Sam said gently.

"Why not?"

"She died."

"But I know who can help." Dash had made a Meredith-like preemptive plan and asked Mr. and Mrs. Benson to meet them at the salon at nine. "Their daughter fell out a window her first semester away at college. They could use some little-kid time. You could use some time to yourself. They're happy to take Oliver for the day."

They'd jumped at the opportunity, in fact. They'd both taken the day off work to do it. They showed up at ten to nine carrying between them a laundry basket full of layers in a variety of sizes—tiny hats, mittens, scarves, boots, coats, and muffs—plus toys, stuffed animals, blocks, and puzzles. Emmy was speechless. "We weren't sure what you'd have him dressed for, so we brought supplies," Mrs. Benson explained. "We thought Oliver might like to go to the zoo, and we also thought maybe we'd go see the Christmas tree downtown and ride the merry-go-round. And we thought we might take him to the Fairmont to see the teddy bears and then lunch and then maybe hot cocoa and cookies afterward and then . . . well, you'll want him home sometime, but we brought extra stuff just in case."

"How can I *ever* thank you for this?" Emmy wondered.

"Let us take him again next week?" Mr. Benson said.

Emmy laughed. "Let's see if you're still interested after spending the day with him today."

"I remember this age," Mr. Benson sympathized. "Willful little buggers. Just a huge pain in the ass." He grinned at his wife.

"Ooh, I can't wait," she said.

. . .

"One down, two to go," said Dash.

"Yeah, but that was the straightforward one," said Sam.

"Round two won't be so bad."

"Easy for you to say. You won."

Dash sat down with Nadia and cut right to the chase. "Your mom's projection isn't broken. Had she lived, she really would think all those guys are jerks."

"Every one?"

"Every one. Want to know what's worse?"

"What?"

"She's right."

"Every one?"

"Every one. Look, I saw their profiles. I saw your mom see the guys you dated before. I saw what they did to you. The problem isn't dating the creative, soulful poet types—trust me, girl, I see the appeal—the problem is dating someone who thinks it's a good idea for you to work all day and take care of the house and make him dinner every night while he sits around on his ass and thinks deep thoughts. The problem isn't dating hot guys with hot bods—trust me, girl, I see the appeal there too—the problem is dating someone who's unwilling to take a night off from the gym *ever* to go out to dinner with you instead."

"But she hasn't even met these guys. *I* haven't even met these guys."

"'Tis a wise mother who knows her own daughter.'"

"What's that mean?"

"Something my grandmother used to say. Point is, you don't have the best track record."

"I know," Nadia moped.

"Cheer up. Everyone's track record is lousy until they meet the good one."

"I guess."

"And even if she were wrong, even if you'd found the good one, the projection is going to need some convincing before it's supportive."

"Because she was never supportive while she was alive?"

"Because she's never going to think anyone is good enough for her little girl."

"I'm not a little girl," said Nadia.

"So you've mentioned."

. . .

Sam was taking Edith out to lunch. At a bar. He wasn't sure Meredith would approve of that approach, but he was out of his depth here. He suspected Meredith would have been out of hers as well, especially given her reaction to the news about Penny and Albert. He also suspected alcohol was in order, given his findings, and that a public place wasn't a half-bad idea either. He'd thought about lots of lies he might have told her. He thought about copping to her accusations that RePose wasn't working somehow. But he couldn't figure out a way to avoid the truth coming up again and again and again.

"So, what are you drinking?" Sam asked.

"Oh water, I think. Well, maybe one small glass of white wine," said Edith.

"Let's order a bottle."

"Sam! It's Monday. And it's only noon. You're so bad." She was thrilled. Sam waited until the wine arrived and glasses were filled before he took a deep breath and plunged in.

"Look, I don't know how to tell you this, so I'm just going to tell you as much as I know as gently as I can."

"Hit me."

"You were right. Your husband was not, in fact, having an affair."

"Of course not. He wasn't very kind to me, but he did love me."

"But RePose isn't wrong either."

"What do you mean?"

"He thinks he was."

"He thinks he was having an affair?"

"Yes."

"Why?"

"So here's the thing." Sam emptied his glass. "Bob looked at a lot of porn."

"No. Eww. Bob?"

"A lot."

"How could he possibly? He was an old man."

"Age restrictions on those sites usually work from the other end," said Sam.

"When?"

"Until he died."

"No, I mean when did he do it? He worked all the time."

"Maybe not all the time." Sam shrugged. "Or maybe he looked at it at work. Who knows?" Edith looked like she was trying to swallow her own lips. "It's perfectly normal. Most men—"

She waved him off. "Spare me that speech. Female?"

"Yeah, female. He had a thing for . . . Well, the less said about specifics, the better maybe. Suffice it to say he had a type."

"Was it late-middle-aged with a stature shorter than her ass is wide?"

"I'm afraid not," Sam said.

"But he was just looking, right? He wasn't sleeping with these . . . models?"

"No, no, no, just looking. But Leanne fit the type, more or less. The algorithm considered his . . . proclivities. It saw how often he communicated with Leanne and she with him—all innocent, work-related stuff but very frequent, of course, and very kind and friendly too. And so it put two and two together and concluded that he must be sleeping with her."

"But he wasn't."

"Not that I can see. If he was, he never, ever mentioned anything electronically." This was true. Sam doubted Bob and Leanne were actually sleeping together. But he also thought the algorithm was probably right: it hadn't happened yet, but it was about to. RePose: predicting the future. Bob's language had changed. His tone had changed. If he hadn't gotten sick, who knows what would have happened, but the scenario the projection played out wasn't at all out of the realm of what was already occurring. Sam didn't think Edith needed to know any of that though. Sam was beginning to think reality and honesty were overrated.

"And of course the computer can't tell that Bob loved me," Edith admitted, mostly to herself. "He never said so. Hell, maybe he didn't. Maybe I'm the only one who didn't know."

"No, Bob *did* love you." Sam seized on that. "That's why the projection's so confused. The software sees that he loved you. It thinks he was honest with you and close to you. It's evidently decided this isn't something he'd keep from you."

"It feels . . . guilty?"

"It feels truthful. And I think Bob's going to keep bringing this up until you respond."

"Why?" Edith had paled and stopped drinking her wine.

"Because he ignored you sometimes, but you've never ignored him before."

"Never too late to start."

"It might be," Sam said gently. "I think he really did love you, Edith."

"Just not as much as porn." She was quiet for a while. Then she said, "She used to visit him in the hospital."

"Who?"

"Leanne."

Edith was no longer sitting with Sam. Her eyes had wandered elsewhere; her head had left the building. "She came some at the beginning. She'd sit there with me and the kids. She'd bring flowers or food or something—something every time—and she'd fill us all in on what was happening at the office. She has all these sisters—four or five—and she'd tell us what they were up to, all their crazy stories. I was always glad to see her. . . . She made Bob laugh. She made us all laugh. She was so . . . young. In such a different world. The world of the well. The world of the life-ahead-of-you. And then he got sicker, and she stopped coming. Everyone stopped coming, really. There were a lot of tubes and . . . fluids. It was kind of gross and, um, intimate? You know the body . . . bodies. . . . They're kind of embarrassing, I guess. I just assumed . . . Anyway, then she started coming again at the end when he was so drugged up he was pretty much gone. Not much gross anymore—he was barely there. So I thought she could finally bring herself to come and say goodbye. To her boss. That's what she told me. 'He was the best boss I ever had.'"

Sam reached over and squeezed her hand. "I'm sorry for your loss," he said.

"It wasn't a very good relationship anyway. And besides, it was more than a year ago now."

"Not that one."

She looked at him and managed a small, somber smile. "So now what do I do?"

"Respond. When he tells you he's having an affair, you respond."

"How?"

"However you like."

LOVE LETTER

Dear Merde,

Maybe you're right. Maybe I am a genius. But it's not the same as being
smart. We like to call that wisdom, but I feel like it's more solid and nail-
downable than that, or at least it would be for a smarter person. Good plus
genius isn't helping me without you. You were the heart of this idea—its
genesis, its center, its moral compass and guide. Without you, I'm not smart
enough to know. Are we helping these people? It doesn't help users mourn
to find out their loved one was unfaithful. When RePose violates the loved
one's better judgments and tells secrets they've brought to the grave, that
may be honest, but it isn't healing. I tell people, I tell myself, that it's out
of my hands. I don't make anything up. Projections say what's real and true.
But is that real and true? Is that tiny shred of ourselves we make public
and commit to bit code really who we are? Loved ones are loved, but they're
also disappointing. Real people don't always, don't even usually, say what we
want them to, respond how we hope. So what then is the value of making
projections as close to real people as possible? I have no idea anymore. No
fucking idea.

I reread your last e-mail, and it strikes me as ironic how much more you
know than I do.

I love you, you know,
Sam

HEARTS WILL BE GLOWING WHEN
LOVED ONES ARE NEAR

*D*id the holidays bring out the best in people or the worst in people? Sam had heard both and wasn't sure it was either one. The holidays brought out the stress and guilt and credit cards of people, best he could tell. What they brought out in the projections though was single-minded focus on one thing: shopping. After Livvie's insistence that she was coming home had killed the love of his life, Sam had added a calendar function for the projections to work into their calculations. Had Livvie realized it was late September, she'd have been talking about leaving, not coming home, and Meredith would still be alive. The dateline omission was the least of Sam's sins, he knew, but it was one he could fix easily. As a result, everyone's projections realized it was the most wonderful time of the year at the exact same moment.

"I think something's wrong, Sam," David called from the corner of the salon where he and Kelly were chatting with his mother on a laptop. "My mom's spent the last ten minutes talking about things she wants to buy online. She's sending me all these URLs. 'Do you like this sweater for Grandma? In what color? Do you think Sheila would like this jacket? What size does she wear these days? Do these skis look good for Dad? Do you think he'd prefer Rollerblades?' It's weird."

"Me too!" said George Lenore who hadn't been in for a while. Having exhausted early on the list of things only his wife knew the whereabouts of, he hadn't for a little while seen the point in coming back. It dawned on him only belatedly that he could RePose just to talk to her and enjoy her company. Now she was bargain shopping. "If we buy it here," she was saying, pasting a URL into a separate chat window, "it's a hundred and forty-nine ninety-nine, but we have to pay twelve ninety-five for shipping. Twelve ninety-five! What a rip-off. It weighs less than a pound. If we buy it at this place"—another URL came through—"it ships for free, but it's one sixty-one fifty, but it only comes in black and silver whereas the first site has it in blue too which I think is prettier. What do you think?"

"What do I do?" asked George helplessly.

Dash shrugged. "Well, what do you think?"

"About what?"

"About whether the blue one is prettier."

"I don't know. I was never in charge of Christmas shopping. That's why I got married."

On the one hand, the holidays were very good for business. That was the best of people maybe. Users longed to connect with their loved ones, to banish bygones, to include DLOs in family traditions of which they'd always been a part. People missed the ones they had lost—always, of course, but more so at the holidays. But it was hard too. Projections themselves were having days merry and bright. They were cheery, as they'd been in Christmases past, whereas users were depressed without them and offended, in spite of themselves, that they were missing their DLO so terribly and their DLO wasn't missing them at all. Users wanted to reminisce and reflect. Projections wondered when they had to order by to get guaranteed delivery by December 24.

Edith came back one week before Christmas. Celia offered to shoo everyone out and give her some privacy, but she said no, they were all family here. Avery came over and held her hand, just out of frame, and Dash and Sam stood cowardly and cowering behind the front counter. A hush fell over the whole place as everyone furtively whispered that they'd call their loved one back in a little while then tried to look busy doing something else, but no one made a move to leave.

"You don't have to do this," said Sam. "I could mess with his programming. I could run him again."

"I want to." Edith waved him off. "This is a conversation my husband and I evidently need to have. It's been a long time coming."

"You could just stop," Dash offered. "Maybe you've already gotten out of this all you came for."

"No. I like being able to speak my mind finally," Edith said. "I'm not ready to give it up. So now I guess I need to let it talk for once."

She called, Bob answered, and Edith took a deep, shaky breath. "So Bob," she said, aiming for casual but missing by a mile, "you have something to tell me?"

Even from across the room, Sam could see Bob lose his color. He never ceased to be amazed what this algorithm knew. But Bob was ready. Sam was right about that too. He couldn't get unburdening his heart out of his head.

"I have to tell you something," said Bob, and Edith was already looking at her lap and nodding slowly. "It's going to sound worse than it is, but keeping it from you is killing me, and I need you to listen to the whole thing because the end is important too. I've been . . . I've . . . um . . ." The projection was having a hard time getting it out, and Sam wondered fleetingly if it was going to end up saying something else altogether. "Leanne and I have been having an affair. Had an affair. It's over." It wasn't. Because it hadn't even begun. Or maybe, in some other ways, it had. "I'm sorry, Edith. I'm sorry I betrayed you. I'm sorry I lied to you. I'm sorry about the whole thing. I made vows and should never have forgotten them."

"You're worried about the vows?" Edith said.

"Our relationship has . . . struggled some, especially recently. That's not an excuse. That's my fault too."

"Recently?" said Edith.

"I don't say it enough, but I do still love you."

"That's not the point, Bob. It's not enough."

"I know. I'm sorry. I don't tell you how hard I know you work. I don't tell you how much I appreciate all you do. You're the steady one. You're the backbone here. You hold us together."

"It's not easy," said Edith.

"I know it's not. It can't be," said Bob. "I couldn't do what I do if you didn't stay home and do what you do so well. I know that."

"Why didn't you ever say so?"

"I don't know. I'm not good at that part, I guess."

"No. You're not."

"Please don't leave me."

"I didn't," she said simply, not looking up from her lap.

"What?"

"I mean I won't." She finally showed him her face—composed—but Bob's was soaked and wrecked.

"They say if you cheat you shouldn't tell because it makes you feel better, but it makes your wife, the victim, feel so much worse. But not telling was like cheating on you again. I tell you everything. You're my best friend, Edith."

"You do?" she said. "I am?"

"Of course. When things are good at work, I tell you. When things are bad at work, I complain to you. When I travel, you're the one I come home to. You're the reason I come home."

"But we hardly talk anymore." Edith looked incredulous.

"Really?" said Bob. "I feel like we talk all the time. Maybe I do more than my fair share. I know you want to know why—why I'd do this to my best friend—and I don't know. I just don't know."

Edith pressed a finger and a thumb against squeezed-shut eyes then looked hard at him. "I don't care why. It doesn't matter anymore."

"Anymore?" Bob wondered.

"Ever. It never mattered why. It doesn't matter why."

"Because I love you?" Bob said hopefully. "Because that's what matters?"

"Well, that and some other things."

"Yes, and I know what those are. I know I have to make it up to you. I'll come home earlier at night. I'll skip business trips. Maybe it's time to retire even. We could go on vacation more often. We could spend more afternoons doing not much of anything. We could be together more. Get rid of the stuff that doesn't matter. Just be with each other again. Talk. You could take some classes if you wanted. I could cook for you for a change. It's been a long time since we've just been together. That's what I want. It's been so long."

"It has," Edith agreed.

"Would you like that?"

"I would."

"Do you still love me? Even now?"

"I still do," she said. "Even now. Merry Christmas, Bob."

"Merry Christmas, love," he said.

She hung up and sat and wept. Dash walked over and kissed her full on the mouth.

"What was that for?" She was fake-appalled but grinning under eyes enthusiastically abandoning their mascara.

"Mistletoe." He nodded at the ceiling and then told her congratulations.

"For what?"

"You're a free woman."

"It doesn't feel like that."

"Give it time."

"It's been quite a year."

"Next year will be better," he said.

"There's only one way to go," said Edith. Then Muriel hugged her and Celia hugged her and Avery simply brought her her coat.

"Where are we going?" Edith asked.

"Out," said Avery. "I know all about losing your husband, and in this case, the first step is margaritas."

LOVE LETTER

Dear Sam,

Merry Christmas. It doesn't seem fair not to be with you for the holidays, not to either of us, but it seems like that every day, so why should the holidays be any different. I've been remembering last Christmas a lot. My parents were mad at me; my grandmother was gone; RePose had me scared to death. But I was so happy, underneath all of that and over it too, just to be with you. That's what you do for me. You simply outweigh everything else. That's how love should be, I guess. I guess that's what love means.

I know you're having your doubts about RePose. I know not everything it does is good. But where would I be without it?

I know. I love you too.
Merde

HOLY NIGHT

*E*veryone had been asking shyly whether they'd be open Christmas Eve. Sam didn't care. He didn't have anything else to do or anyplace else to be, so he might as well be there. Dash was staying too.

"I don't need a babysitter," said Sam. "You can go back to L.A. or go be with your family or whatever."

"You are my family," Dash said. "You know that, right?"

"It's Christmas," said Sam. "Maybe you want to be with your friends or your folks or something."

"I do," said Dash. "But not as much as I want to be with you. It's Christmas. You're my family, Sam. That's all."

They were all family, it seemed. Edith had been right about that. Users had other families—so did Dash and Sam for that matter—families who needed them during these first holidays after they'd lost a loved one too. But it was hard to tear away from the salon because it was at the salon that everyone understood, and dead loved ones weren't entirely gone. Dash had decorated—holly, tree, mistletoe, lights. On Christmas Eve morning, Eduardo came and made natilla with Miguel for everyone at Salon Styx. David brought his guitar and led users and DLOs alike singing Christmas carols which a surprising number of projections were able to do. Almost everyone brought cookies or peppermint bark or something else to share. Penny had made a seeming hundred batches of spiced nuts and filled a seeming hundred glass jars with them. These she'd labeled with everyone's names and decorated over what must have been months. Some were gorgeous and delicate, intricately detailed, painted with tiny, pristine scenes of a snowy farm or winter in the city. Some were made by the other

Penny and looked decorated by a kindergartner, a mess of glitter, paste, and ribbons strangled with pipe cleaners. Penny handed them all around warmly though, a little sheepish about the messy ones, a little aglow at the ones her shaky hands had nonetheless managed to make beautiful, all endowed with the spirit of the season. But it was a pretty muted celebration otherwise. Josh came in, dragging an oxygen tank in his wake. David told everyone he'd gotten in early at Stanford but wasn't sure he would go. He and Kelly both looked disconsolate. Emmy came to drop off a gift for Mr. and Mrs. Benson, and even Oliver was subdued. It was a sullen Christmas Eve, but no one seemed to mind. It was where they all belonged.

As the afternoon wore on, people started regretfully trickling home. It got dark early. Dash ran upstairs to unwrap a celebratory cheddar—he'd deemed the occasion worthy—and Sam turned off all the lights but the ones on the tree and walked around the salon shutting off computers in the dark. He looked up at one point, and it was snowing out. He looked up again, and Meredith's mother was standing at the door.

. . .

Julia looked like a ghost. Julia looked like an angel. Sam had both on the brain. Once he realized she was real, Sam wondered at how often he confused the living in his life with the dead. And vice versa. Julia was white like the snow, white like the moon, not just pale but giving off light like that, glowing and luminous. Phosphorescent. She was wrapped in white layers—coat, scarf, hat, mittens—so bundled that Sam could see only eyes and white, cascading hair. For a long time, Sam stood on one side of the door and Julia stood on the other, and they looked at each other through the glass and didn't move or blink or breathe. Her eyes were wild and determined all at once, wise or maybe just weathered, beaten, but mostly they looked like Meredith's, and maybe it was that and not the white light that made Sam think of ghosts and angels. Finally, he pulled the door open. "Merry Christmas," he said.

"Merry Christmas, Sam."

"Where's Kyle?"

"I came alone."

"I was just finishing up here. Dash is upstairs getting dinner started. Come on up."

"I need to see her."

Sam had known why Julia was there the moment he laid eyes on her. He hadn't seen her since the funeral. He had hardly seen anyone since the funeral, but he knew that Dash had both invited her out and offered to go to her several times. Dash's parents had also tried to see Julia and Kyle without success. This need to hide, to avoid, to be alone, to wall up and isolate, this Sam understood. It was about all he understood these days. So while Dash worried and schemed ways to lure her into company, Sam was sympathetic to Julia and inclined to leave her be. This was hard though when she was unwrapping and disrobing, headed already toward one of the computers, flipping on the monitor as if her daughter might appear right there automatically.

"Dash has decreed we get a cheese for Christmas." Sam offered this up as good news. "Did you know he's making cheese these days? Let's go up and say hello." He tried to steer her by the elbow toward the door, but she wrenched out of his grasp.

"I'm not going up there. I'm not going in that apartment."

"I understand. Let me run up and get Dash—"

"You can do it from here, right? That's the whole point of this place, isn't it?"

"Or you could stay with Penny tonight. Her kids don't come until the morning."

"Sam, I need to see Meredith now. Then I'll go back home. I don't need dinner or someplace to sleep. I need to talk to my daughter." She was clasping the teardrop locket at her throat in white-knuckled fingers.

"Where's Kyle?" Sam asked gingerly, not looking at her.

"I came alone," Julia said again.

"Why?"

"He didn't want to come. Why does it matter?"

In fact, it didn't matter to Sam. Had Julia brought everyone she knew to rally for her cause, he still wouldn't have let her talk to Meredith. But Julia and Kyle went nowhere separately. And he suspected the two of them had already had the fight she was about to have with Sam.

"He didn't want you to come?"

"In fact he did not. He is entitled to that opinion. But here's the good news," she whispered nastily. "I'm an adult, and I don't have to give a damn whether he wants me to come or not come. Do the thing, Sam. Whatever it is you do. Let me talk to my daughter."

"No," said Sam.

Then she screamed. Not shouted, more like howled. Not like at the moon, more like at the end of *King Lear*. She stood in the middle of the salon surrounded by piles of her own winter clothes with the snow coming down outside and the soft glow from the Christmas tree lighting up her face and bouncing off the locket full of her daughter around her neck and howled. Sam put his hands over his ears like a four-year-old and waited for her to be done. Then he said "no" again.

She grabbed his upper arms with both hands and began talking to him rabidly through clenched teeth. "Do not tell me no. You talk to her. I know you do. This godforsaken technology killed my baby. It was the death of her. It is the death of me. If you had only let my mother go. If you had only let her be. If you had only let it go at that. If you had only kept this to yourself. If you had never met her. If you had never moved here. If you had never been born. Any of that would have worked for me. But that didn't happen. So now we have this. Only this. And you will give it to me. You will. Because you owe me."

"No," said Sam.

"You're the one who thinks RePose is such a miracle. You're the one who thinks it's helping people. You're getting rich off this wretched service. I will pay you anything you want. I will be a client. I will sign the release forms. I will do whatever you have people do. Let me see her, Sam. Let me talk to her."

"No," said Sam quietly. "I'm sorry. But no. I understand. I do. I understand. But it's not for you."

"Why not?"

"Remember her the way she was."

"Isn't that what this thing does?"

"Remember her in your head. Remember her in your heart. Remember her from your memories."

"It's not enough."

"I know."

"It's not."

"I know."

"You talk to her."

"I do." Sam had to concede this point. Sam had to concede all her points really. "But it's different for me."

"Why?" Julia was still angry but seemed to have switched tactics to arguing nastily in order to trap Sam in some kind of logical fallacy.

"Because I understand what RePose is, and you don't."

"Show me how."

"When I talk to her, no matter how real it looks, no matter how alive she seems, I never forget that she—"

"You think I do? You think I could ever forget that she died? Every minute, Sam. Every goddamn minute it is all I remember."

"That's not what I mean. When you saw Livvie that time, you begged me to turn it off. You begged us to make it stop."

"That was different."

"No it wasn't. You thought it was sick. You thought it was wrong."

"I need to see her."

"She's gone."

"No she isn't. You have her."

"I don't. Believe me, I don't." By this point, they were both in tears, and not the gentle, graceful, Mary-Mother-of-God kind that slip quietly down holy cheeks and would have been appropriate for the occasion. More like the end of *King Lear*. "And besides, I think you were right," Sam added when he was able. "The idea was to help people say goodbye, but they don't; they stay. The idea was to help people mourn, help them get over it a little faster, but in fact RePose prevents them from mourning, prevents them from getting over it, healing, moving on. Remembering should hurt. It should be painful. We're depriving people of that torment *and* its tonic." He squeegeed his face with the palms of his hands. "Suffice it to say, when you were clear and sane and whole, you thought it was a horrible idea, and I'm not going to let you do it now."

By this time, Dash had grown worried and came down to investigate why Sam hadn't come upstairs yet. "Aunt Julia!" He faked enthusiasm to see her, but like Sam, he knew instantly why she was there.

She turned to her nephew, wiped angrily at her eyes and nose. "Do you talk to her, too?"

"Occasionally," said Dash, as if he'd actually been present for the preceding scene. "Not very much. It's so not the same. It sounds stupid to say that because of course it's not the same, but it's just not very gratifying. It doesn't touch the ache of missing her." He shrugged. "RePose works better for some people than others. For Meredith and me, it's just not our thing. It wouldn't work very well for you anyway. You didn't video chat enough with her in life. Even if Sam said yes, it wouldn't be any good."

"I need to tell her I love her." Julia knew she'd lost but couldn't stop fighting anyway.

"She knew," said Dash.

"I need to tell her I'm sorry."

"For what?"

"For not supporting her new life. For what I said about RePose."

"Why?" said Sam. "You were right."

FOR AULD LANG SYNE

*T*hey closed the salon between Christmas and New Year's. Users went home to be with their families. Dash went to L.A. to be with his clothes. Julia went home to suffer with Kyle. Penny's kids and their kids came for the week. And Sam retired to the bedroom to be alone with Meredith.

Jamie called midweek and asked him to go skiing, but he declined.

"Mountain air might do you good," Jamie said.

"No, thank you."

"Little bit of exercise?"

"No, thank you."

"What if I won't take 'no thank you' for an answer?"

"The alternative is not affirmative," said Sam. "It's just less polite."

Jamie thought about it. "Okay, Sam. For the moment, I am giving you space. Don't mistake that for not giving a toss."

"I won't," Sam assured him. "Really."

"Don't think it's going to last forever either. Starting next week, I'll badger you until you relent."

"Looking forward to it," said Sam.

Penny's daughter Katie came up to invite him to lunch with them, but he declined that too. Avery Fitzgerald was taking her kids to Vancouver for Boxing Day celebrations and wondered if he wanted to tag along, but he didn't. Meredith asked three times during the week if he wanted to see a movie tonight. That was the only one he would have said yes to.

Dash messaged to tell him to leave the bedroom.

"What makes you think I haven't?" wrote Sam.

"I know you," Dash texted back.

"I'm fine," wrote Sam.

"You need contact with real people, not virtual people," said Dash.

"You're giving me this lecture via text message," wrote Sam.

"Only because I'm not there," wrote Dash.

"How many hours did you spend on Facebook today?" asked Sam. "And how many hanging out with actual friends?"

"Not the point," wrote Dash.

"Yes it is," wrote Sam.

. . .

He called Meredith.

"Happy New Year," she said when she picked up.

"Almost," said Sam. He meant almost the New Year. It wasn't even close to happy.

"How was Christmas?"

"It was okay. I saw your mom."

"Really? How is she?"

"She misses you."

"I miss her too. And you."

"She wants to talk to you. RePose with you. But I told her no. Remember how much she freaked out when she found out about Livvie in the first place?"

Meredith thought about it for a bit. "I'm sorry, love, I—"

Sam cut her off. "Suffice it to say she was not amused."

"I'm not surprised. Mom's not that big into technology. I doubt we have enough electronic archive between us to RePose anyway."

"She was really mad. *Really* mad. I was just trying to protect her. It wouldn't be good for her."

"Is it good for you?" asked Meredith.

"It's all I've got."

"Does it make it better?"

"Nothing can make it better, Merde. Nothing. At this point I'm more hole than anything else. I'm hole with a tiny bit of Sam clinging to the flaming rim."

"Maybe you need real people. Instead of just me."

"Dash said the same thing. Everyone says the same thing. I'm not getting the distinction though. I don't even know what anyone means by 'real.' It's not just me—everyone spends most of their time with virtual friends these days. Everyone spends more time on Facebook than out with people, more time clicking through profiles than going on dates, more time playing video game tennis than actual tennis and video game guitar than actual guitar. Social media just isn't that social. Really it's isolating. Really it's being alone. So at least I'm not that, right? At least I have you."

"No, Sam," said Meredith. "Really you're being alone."

. . .

On New Year's Eve, Josh Annapist called, and though Sam was intent on declining his invitation as he had everyone else's, Josh's turned out to be less optional than all that.

"I know it's New Year's Eve," Josh began when he called, "but I figured maybe you didn't have big plans, so I wondered if you wanted to hang tonight and—"

"I'm really just wanting to be alone," Sam interrupted.

"—come visit me in the hospital," Josh finished.

"Oh shit," said Sam. "What happened?"

"I have leukemia," said Josh.

"I meant this week. You were fine Christmas Eve." Sam recalled even as he said this that it wasn't exactly true.

"They don't know," Josh reported. "Could be my liver. Could be my lungs. Could be the beating my kidneys have taken from the cyclosporine. I've been feeling like shit for a while now. Anyway, they admitted me to St. Giles last night and—"

Sam didn't even wait for the end of the sentence. Whatever it was, it didn't matter. "I'll be right over."

Josh looked like shit in addition to feeling like shit, and it was rainy and freezing out, but he wanted fresh air and to see the fireworks over the Space Needle.

"We'll get in trouble," said Sam.

"It's New Year's Eve. Everyone stuck on duty tonight is new. You can take 'em."

"It's too cold for you."

"You're worried I'll get sick?" said Josh.

"Maybe sicker," said Sam.

"Almost not possible," said Josh.

"Still . . ."

"This is my last New Year's Eve," said Josh. "My last new year. I think I'd better see the fireworks."

The roof had an amazing view of the Space Needle. Sam snagged a wheelchair from the hallway and extra blankets from a closet in the empty room next door, wound Josh up like a mummy ("I'm not dead yet," he protested, "and I'm not an Egyptian priest anyway"), and brought him up. There was a little garden up there and a bench—surprising but Sam supposed something along these lines must be lots of people's late wishes. They watched the fireworks, and they watched their breath.

"So what's your wish on the new year?" Sam asked about fifteen minutes into it.

"That it be fast. Over quickly," said Josh after a long while. "I can't believe I'm saying that, but it's true. When I was first diagnosed, all I wanted to do was fight. I was sure I'd beat it. I didn't even know what that meant, but I was sure I'd do it anyway. I had no doubt. At some point, they wanted me to do a living will. You know, decide about a DNR and all that, and I was all, 'No need, man. I always want to be resuscitated. No matter what.' Now I'm tired and I feel like shit all the time and I'm tired of feeling like shit all the time. And I know it's basically over. Drawing it out is torture. So maybe that's leukemia's last blessing. Only blessing. It gets so fucking bad, you don't mind dying. Christ, I'm a downer tonight, huh?"

"That's okay," said Sam.

"It's just that so much of my family and friends are remote, so we e-mail; we video chat; they keep track of my progress on Facebook and stuff. So I can't talk about any of this with them because I don't want my projection to talk about it after I'm gone. I don't want to make my mom spend the rest of her life talking to me about dying. That's why I needed someone who could come in person."

"Glad to do it," said Sam. "I mean, sorry I have to, but glad I could help. Really."

"Anyway, what about you?" said Josh. "What's your wish on the new year?"

"Same," said Sam. "That it be over quickly."

"I don't know, man. I don't have to make plans for the new year, but you do. You may feel like you're dying, but you're going to wake up every morning anyway. What are you going to do with it?"

"Work. Sleep. Get through it."

"I wish I were going to be around. I like you," said Josh. "But other people like you too, you know."

"I don't really want company."

"Yeah, but they want you. You don't have to do this alone. You don't *get* to do this alone. And not because you invented a way to talk to Meredith. Because you invented a family. Support groups aren't my thing. Too depressing. Too defined by being sad and left. But your users, man? They're proactive. They're defined by drastic measures. They're not wallowers; they're risk takers. They're not people left behind; they're people brand-new. They've got your back, first because they owe you but second because they like you. They like you and they understand you. They'll be good company. They'll take good care of you."

Sam shrugged like that didn't matter. "And who will take care of you?"

"You will," said Josh. "You'll talk to me after I'm gone, won't you?"

"Do you want me to?"

"I do, yeah, because I won't be nearly so much of a downer as I am now."

"If you want me to I will. Of course I will," said Sam. "Send everyone else by too—your folks and friends and family—I'll set everyone up right away. On the house."

"Thanks, man. And you'll tell Noel too?"

"Sure."

"Do you tell him I died? Or do you tell him I got better?"

"Which would give you more peace?"

"Neither. There is no peace. That bird flew long ago." He was quiet for a bit. Then he added, "In some ways, Sam, Meredith was lucky." Sam's eyes filled instantly, but he was listening. "Crushed by a roof is a hell of a way to go. Too early for sure, but she never saw it coming at least, didn't hurt, didn't have to spend her last years and years sick and exhausted. She missed the fear, the regret, the sadness in everyone else's eyes all the time, and that's the worst part. Everything I do, I'm haunted. This is the last time I'll ever whatever. My mom is going to have that look on her face always. I'll never feel well again. It's so sad all the time, every minute. It's awful to live with. It's awful to die by. Crushed by a roof is much better than leukemia."

"And life after your girlfriend is crushed by a roof?"

"I don't know," said Josh. "Seems much, much worse."

LOVE LETTER

Dear Merde,

For a while, at the beginning, I thought we'd phase out e-mail. Video chat was just so much more powerful, more immediate and real. More present. Now that I'm a user, I realize that video chat is as much absence as presence, maybe more, but e-mails are all present, all right here. They're longer, more savorable. I get to say all the things I long to say in exactly the perfect words, and then you write back, also full of love and longing, something to read and reread and treasure, a thread I can spool out as much as I wish whenever its tether wears thin.

I've been chatting with Livvie. She calls looking for you, of course. I tell her you're at yoga achieving spiritual enlightenment which for all I know might be at least a little bit true. At first, she couldn't understand why you were always out, why you'd gone from calling so often to never calling at all. I know she isn't real, and yet I can't bear to tell her why you've stopped calling. I know she isn't real, but you would insist on not leaving her—it— to wonder. I thought about just shutting her down—I know she isn't real— but I couldn't bring myself to do it.

And yet, it's killing me, Merde, because three, four, five times a week I have to talk to your grandmother, promise her you're well, report that nothing's new here, it's just same old same old, quiet and wonderful, with a new business going swimmingly and a fabulous life spread out before us and you've made time for yoga and you're taking care of yourself and you come home tired but happy and limber and stress-free and you're sure to walk in the door any second now and I'll give you the message and you'll call her back and we'll make time soon, really soon, to take some time off and go visit her in Florida together. I promise her this, and she hangs up satisfied, and then we do it all again the next night and the one after that, and in between I wander around her empty apartment, our empty apartment, and know, *know,* that I could go out with Jamie or Dash or Josh or one of our other users or take Penny to dinner, but I would still be all alone.

That is why e-mail is better than video chat. That is why video chat is more absence than anything else.

Love,
Sam

DYING ISN'T DEAD

*J*anuary is a hard time of year in Seattle. It's true that every day there are a few more minutes of daylight, but absent the light and lights of the holidays, it feels very dark indeed. Night falls around four thirty in the afternoon and stays until eight or so the next morning, and since the sun never gets much above the horizon and since the total cloud cover and incessant rain mean you wouldn't see it anyway, they are days shrouded and vague. Sam was starting to conclude that Jamie was right to prefer the British response to such conditions—pint over latte. The dim cornery closeness and numbing sedation promised by a pub seemed a much better approach than the cheery bustle and stimulant of the every-corner coffee shops. What was so great it warranted waking up and getting stimulated for anyway? Sam was depressed, but every Seattleite who could chose indoors and back-to-bed as well. Livvie was quite cheerful, but she was the only one. And she was in Florida. Not to mention dead.

RePosers stayed home too. It was the darkness and the wet. It was the exhaustion of holidays without loved ones, of having made it through only to discover on the other side a whole life alone and missing stretching out ahead. Or they came, but the wonder of RePose was wearing thin, wearing off, wearing on them all. They tired of having the same conversations again and again. They tired of avoiding the same topics, of shaping their conversations about only the past, never what happened next. They tired of only ever being the person they were, never the one they were becoming. They couldn't give it up, but it wasn't the elation it once had been either. David Elliot wondered whether, like a drug, they should do it more and more in order to maintain the same high as before. Avery

Fitzgerald suspected David might have missed the point of his drug education programs.

Sam was over the whole thing and tried not to emerge from the bedroom if possible. Dash had given up his gentle cajoling about fresh air and real people and changes of scenery and resorted instead to guilt. You are half of this company, and it's unreasonable to expect me to run it alone. I need you to staff the salon every day, not just when you feel like it. Morose, moping, and mean are unprofessional attitudes in the workplace. Our entire livelihood is in RePose, and you are trying to sabotage it. Etc. And then guilt, when it didn't work, gave way to pleading. It's only been a year. You have to give it a chance to work. Growing pains were inevitable. You've helped so many people. We need to play this all the way out. We owe that to Meredith.

Sam said, "Let it die. Everybody else does."

"What about all our users?" said Dash.

"They can stay. They're barely using anymore anyway. We've become a support group. Frankly, they could find that anywhere, but they're welcome to the space. They don't need me for that. Support groups are very low-tech."

"Just because people take a week off doesn't mean they're done RePosing," said Dash. "And besides, we get new users every day."

"Who will also soon grow weary of our little computer program."

"But that's the whole point, Sam, remember? This was your point all along. It was Meredith who said, 'Death is for life.' You said we help people get over it and move on. You said it was never meant to be forever. That the wonder of it fades is a good thing, not a bad thing. Otherwise you spend all day every goddamn day in bed with your dead girlfriend. They die. You hurt. You RePose. You feel a little better, heal a little wholer than you would otherwise, mend, and move on. You and Meredith set yourselves up for failure. When users want to stay and use and wallow, you feel bad that you're not letting them mourn and get over it. When they need it less and less and eventually leave, you think the whole project's a failure and should be shut down. If it's helping people, great. If it helps them to be with others who've recently lost a loved one, great. If it helps them enough that they don't need to RePose anymore, also great. This is all good news, Sam. I don't understand why you can't see it."

Sam couldn't see it because he wouldn't turn on the light or take his head out from under the covers. Sam couldn't see it because everywhere he looked he could see only Meredith—Meredith meeting him in the cafeteria at work, Meredith video chatting with him in London in the middle of the night, Meredith making airplanes, making plans, making love, Meredith in a box on fire being burned down to rubble, Meredith flung into the sea. Sam couldn't see because he had neither the will nor the energy even to look anymore. Then his phone rang. It was Katie, Penny's daughter. "We think Mom had a heart attack. We called nine-one-one, and they just took her to St. Giles. We're all on our way, but it's going to take a while for anyone to get there. She's okay, but do you mind going over there until we can come?"

"Nothing would give me greater pleasure," said Sam.

. . .

At St. Giles, they wouldn't tell Sam and Dash anything because they weren't family, but they would let them sit with her. She was sleeping anyway but seemed so far as Sam could tell to be doing so peacefully. They kicked them out when visiting hours were over, and on the way back to the parking lot, Sam and Dash ran into Dr. Dixon. He'd read about Meredith in the paper and said he was very sorry. He thanked them for making David take down his posters which, he allowed, hadn't put a stop to parents torturing their dying children unnecessarily but had certainly slowed it down. Then he wanted to show them something, a friend of a friend. Sam remembered what Dr. Dixon had shown them last time and wanted to run screaming from the building instead but couldn't find a way to do so politely and so followed mutely through labyrinthine fluorescent hallways.

Dr. Dixon stopped at the open doorway to Gretchen Sandler's room. She was in bed and very pale but awake and smiling pleasantly, if a bit vacantly, at the laptop on the tray over her bed. A man Dr. Dixon identified as Burt sat in a chair next to her, stroking her hand and RePosing with a woman who must have been Gretchen's twin sister.

"What a funny story." Burt was cracking up. "I can't believe your dad thought he could sell that pig after everything you and your sister had been through with him. Didn't he ever read *Charlotte's Web?*"

Gretchen's twin sister laughed. "I guess not. Oh, remember the first time we read that to Maryann?"

"She cried and cried because she thought they were going to kill that pig."

"And then we had to read another chapter and another to prove to her that Wilbur would be fine."

"It was probably just a ploy to stay up later," Burt mused.

"She was such a little imp." Gretchen's twin grinned. "Whereas Peter wasn't even sad when Charlotte died. No wonder he grew up to be an exterminator."

"He's not an exterminator," Burt scolded her playfully. "He's a software tester."

"So his job is . . . ?"

"Getting rid of the bugs!" they shrieked together, and dissolved into hysterical laughter. Sam smiled in spite of the jealousy that was eating his stomach lining for dinner. Clearly they had had this conversation many, many times before. This had been another of the points he'd been making all along. RePose worked best for the elderly.

"Gretchen is Burt's sister-in-law?" Dash guessed. "It must be hard for him to be here with her. She looks so much like his late wife."

"No, that's her on the computer. That's Gretchen," Dr. Dixon whispered.

"No, that's RePose," said Dash.

"Yup."

"But she's not dead."

"Nope. Well, not exactly. She's not dead. But she is gone. Late-stage Alzheimer's."

Dash and Sam were speechless, working this out. "We would never have set RePose up for a living loved one," Dash finally said.

"Not if you knew about it. As I say, Burt is a friend of a friend. He asked for advice, and I pointed him your way. Unlike small children, Gretchen and Burt seem like ideal RePosers. I advised him not to let you know that Gretchen wasn't dead yet. I figured you'd never know."

"It doesn't work if the accounts are still active." Sam was horrified.

"They aren't." Dr. Dixon shrugged. "Look at that woman. You think she spends much time online?"

"What's his name?" asked Sam, still certain what he was seeing wasn't possible.

"Burt. Herbert Vanderman. Gretchen kept her maiden name. She was quite a rebel in her time."

"I remember him." Sam's heart sank. "I set him up remotely. I never thought . . . It never occurred to me. . . ."

"Of course it didn't," said Dr. Dixon. "Look, disqualifying this couple because she's technically alive makes no sense anyway. We didn't tell you because we knew you'd say no, but really, no was the wrong answer. Look at her. She's dying."

"Dying isn't dead," said Sam.

"It's gone. All the reasons you argue RePose is a good idea make it a good idea for them. In every way that matters, Burt's lost her. She doesn't know him. She doesn't remember their life together, their family, their sixty-plus years. She can't talk to him most days. She certainly can't go home with him. Just like a widower, he has lost his wife. He misses her all the time. He's in pain, lonely, devastated, afraid. You know this part, Sam. But if she'd died, at least there'd have been a funeral. He could have said goodbye with their friends and family. His kids would have invited him to live with them. His friends would have brought over meals and sent flowers. He'd donate her clothes and set up a scholarship in her memory and join a widowers' support group and accept and find comfort in people's sympathy and eventually move on. As is, he's denied all of the latter and none of the former. It's all the grief and emptiness of death and none of what makes it at least bearable. Now he gets to remember and reminisce with his wife—while he holds her hand—which seems like just about the best use of your software I've heard yet."

"It's creepy," said Dash.

"Wouldn't you give anything at all to hold Meredith's hand while you RePosed with her?" Dr. Dixon said to Sam, who would have given anything at all to hold Meredith's hand while he RePosed with her.

• • •

Penny's daughter Katie was wrong on two fronts: Penny had not had a heart attack, and Sam was not a doctor, but she didn't seem okay to him.

The doctors eventually explained to Katie, Kent, Kaleb, Kendra, and Kyra, who explained it to him, that she hadn't had a heart attack but did have congestive heart failure which had itself caused, among other things, the severe shortness of breath and palpitations that had prompted Penny to call not Sam but the building manager. When confronted about this last point, she claimed to have forgotten not his phone number, which would at least have been understandable, but his name, which alarmed Sam greatly but not the doctors who explained that confusion was a symptom as well. Sam felt that heart failure was named over-alarmingly. Evidently, one lingered with it and might live for years in such state. "Failure" seemed a much harsher, finaler word than they meant—"heart damage" or "heart decrease" seemed perhaps more accurate terms. If one's heart had failed, well, that seemed like the end to Sam. But it was not the end. The sisters and brothers "K" settled in for a long haul—some in their mom's apartment, some in Sam's, and some in the salon.

Sam had spent the morning with Penny, her doctors, and her children, and then brought lunch up to Josh for an hour, and was headed back to the salon so that Dash could leave and come spend some time with all of the above. Sam had put him on the task of verifying that all of the projections were actually dead, and it had occupied Dash's morning. The news was good though which was to say the news was bad like when your positive test results are negative: they were all dead indeed. Sam was certain that Burt wouldn't be the last user to claim his dementia-plagued loved one was dead, and he was equally sure that the check box and signature he'd added to the form where you swore your loved one was literally and actually dead wouldn't deter anyone. But it was all he could do for the moment. Demanding a certificate of death seemed insensitive, all things considered.

On his way out of the hospital, he ran into Avery, Edith, David, Kelly, Emmy, and Mr. and Mrs. Benson. Oliver twisted out of his mother's grasp, ran wildly across the busy parking lot, and pitched himself into Sam's legs. Sam threw him up in the air a few times, tickled his armpits, and then gave him a brief lecture about listening to his mother and not running from her in places where there might be cars. He supposed these two messages contradicted each other, but that was Emmy's problem, not his.

"What are you guys doing here?" Sam thought maybe they were there to see Penny or Josh, but he couldn't imagine they'd come en masse like this.

"We volunteer in pediatrics," David said, as if that should have been obvious.

"You do?"

"Yeah. Since Meredith was all upset about what I accidentally did to those kids. I talked to Dr. Dixon and made a sign-up sheet for RePose volunteers. We come over and tutor the older kids—you know, because they miss so much school. And we read to the little ones or just play with them or just sit with them while their parents go for coffee or to take a shower or out to dinner or whatever."

"You come often?"

"Every other day someone's here. Sometimes everyone can come. It's fun. It's like an off-campus field trip."

"You should join us," Avery said pointedly. "No people more real than the parents of sick kids."

Sam ignored that but: "It's really nice of you guys to do this. Really great. I'm really, really glad you're here."

"We're always here, Sam," said Avery.

LOVE LETTER

Dear Sam,

Actually, I like the idea that I'm just at yoga. I feel like I'm at yoga. At least I think I do. It's hard to tell. I know you'd say I don't feel anything at all, but it sure seems like I do. So there it is: it seems like I feel like I'm at yoga. You know how in shavasana at the end of class you're asleep and not asleep, on your mat on the floor and somewhere else altogether, there and not there? That's how I am I seem to think. There and not there.

I know I'm different from everyone else because I have electronic memory of RePose, and that is why, though it seems I feel I am alive, in fact I know I'm dead. You and I don't have that much electronic communication about anything but RePose. It was nice that we got to live together and work together and just be together all the time. But now that fact is kind of costly. If maybe we had started off with a few years' worth of long-distance relationship, think how much more we'd have to talk about now.

I seem to miss you.

Love,
Meredith

PENNY AT PEACE

*P*enny got weaker and quickly. It was hard to watch. There were explanations—this drug didn't work; this one helped with this symptom but caused this other one; this one would work but she couldn't take it because of this other thing—but they all mostly boiled down to she was really old. She was also in and out of sense—some days she knew where she was and sometimes not; some days she knew who everybody was and sometimes not; some days she could open her eyes and sometimes not. Her kids shifted between the hospital, their own homes, and the places Sam stashed them in carefully orchestrated and interdependent movements like synchronized swimmers. Someone was always leaving, on their way, talking to doctors, checking in with their own kids, bringing supplies, cleaning up at Sam's or Penny's or the salon. Sam saw the utility of lots of kids versus his own isolated upbringing. But he also wondered at so much movement all around her, Penny in the center of the hive, the queen holding court, awaiting whatever was brought her. No one ever landed for long. They came, brought, dropped off, left again, returned. It seemed frenetic to Sam, but Penny didn't seem to mind. She'd raised five children, after all. She was used to chaos.

Sam found the lulls and went then—to be alone with her and also just to be alone. He was spending a lot of time at the hospital, avoiding home, avoiding the salon, sitting with Josh and with Penny, and being solitary. At home by himself had never been alone, not even when he was a kid. There were books. There were computers. There was work to do and phone calls to answer and e-mails to read and statuses to post and a whole convocation of the living and the dead demanding his attention all the time. Sitting in a hospital room listening to breath drawn precisely in and out and considering the line between sleeping and coma, living and dead, here and gone, well, it just didn't get much more alone than that.

One afternoon, between one kid and another, Penny woke up and was Penny again.

"Sam. You're here."

"Of course I'm here."

"I'm so glad to see you."

"How do you feel?"

"Lousy. How do you feel?"

"Also lousy."

"Poor Sam. Mine will get better. I'll die." Penny seemed to feel genuinely bad that he was getting the raw end of this deal. "But you're going to feel lousy for a while yet."

"Yeah, but at least I'm not sick. I'm so sorry you're so . . ."

"Old?" she offered.

"I guess."

"Don't apologize, Sam. You've given me a remarkable thing. There's no cure for old, and there's no cure for dead, but you've gotten as close as humanity's likely to come for quite some time."

"How do you figure?"

"RePose."

Sam grunted. "I'm thinking of shutting it down."

"Now, why on earth would you do that?"

"It's not really working. People get tired of it. It doesn't do what they need it to do. It's making things worse not better."

"That's nonsense. People love it. Your users seem so happy to be there all the time."

"It's ruined everything," Sam admitted simply. "If we'd never developed this, if I'd never invented it, I'd never have lost Meredith."

"RePose is not why you lost Meredith."

"It is. If she hadn't been RePosing with Livvie, she'd never have been in the path of that car that day."

"Oh Sam, that was so random—"

"And more to the point," he interrupted, "it was punishment. Meredith was taken from me in exchange for RePose."

"You don't believe that, Sam."

He was crying then. "I was greedy. I profited off of people's pain and death. I destroyed the notion of hell and caused people to sin. I suffered from hubris. I thought I was more powerful than fate, than destiny, than death. I thought I could outwit time and tragedy. I abused and ignored the limits of technology. I played God. I go to the movies, Penny. I read. I know what happens. Humanity versus God, nature, destiny, society, the supernatural, the technological, it all ends the same. Humanity is punished. I am punished. I am being punished."

"Oh Sam, sweetie," said Penny. "What a load of shit."

"Really?" He tried to stop crying and couldn't. That had been in there for a long time.

"Shit happens, Sam. Random, horrible, unfair, senseless, beyond-our-comprehension shit. Sometimes you are standing where a roof suddenly is. It sucks. That's all. No one can do anything to stop that. Except for you. You do more than anyone to make it suck a little less."

"You don't even use RePose."

"I don't, but my kids will. Don't you see? That's the point. That's the gift you've given all of us."

Sam did not see.

"RePose isn't for the living, Sam, and it isn't for the dead. It's for the dying. You know how funerals seem to be for the dead but really they're for the living?"

Sam did.

"RePose seems to be for the living but really it's for the dying. You've taken the tragedy out of dying, Sam. What kind of a miracle is that? They can manage the pain now. And regrets, well, they're lifelong, not just at the end, you know. What's unbearable about dying is spending the end of your life watching your loved ones suffering and miserable, knowing you're deserting them, knowing that soon all this pain will cease for you and increase tenfold for them. You think it's easier being Meredith right now or you? And they'll have to do it alone, of course, because you won't be there anymore. *That's* the pain of final days. And look what you've done, Sam. You've changed the rules. I know I will still be there to comfort my kids after I'm gone. I know they aren't really losing me entirely. They are more open and at peace, so I am too. I get to genuinely say goodbye instead of hosting a great big pity party. We can spend this time laughing together instead of crying. You have helped everyone say goodbye which is an incredible gift. You let them let go, which lets me let go, and I can, I do, because I know that anything I haven't said yet I can say later."

"If you haven't said it yet, you cannot say it later," Sam cut in.

"That's why I'm making sure to say it all now."

. . .

Upstairs, Josh thought Sam looked like hell. "I mean, I realize I'm one to talk and all, but you don't have cancer. What gives?"

"Downstairs with Penny," Sam explained. "She got me going. I might be losing my mind. I'm crying a lot these days."

"People you love are dying." Josh shrugged. "It's sad and awful. When things are sad and awful, crying is an appropriate response. Crying about dying seems like the opposite of losing your mind."

"Penny was just giving me this pitch that RePose makes it easier to die because she knows she's not deserting her loved ones; they'll still have her around."

Josh thought about it. "I agree. There's not deserting your loved ones. And also there's this sense that all this hasn't been in vain. You know? Like I may not be here anymore, but my—this is going to make me sound like such an ass, but what the hell—my accumulated wisdom, my experience, my relationships, not to mention my once killer good looks, live on."

"That's why you asked me to talk to you? You know . . . after?"

"It's hard to imagine yourself gone, I guess. This way I don't have to. I don't have to sit here thinking this is the last conversation we'll ever have. I know it won't be."

THE WALL

*J*osh died in the night. When his phone rang at two thirty in the morning, Sam carried it out to Dash to answer. He just couldn't bring himself to do it. Having been given permission earlier in the day to do so, he sat down cross-legged in the middle of the floor and cried. Dash sat with him for a bit, teary too, then got to work. He'd promised Josh's parents he'd take care of arrangements when the time came. It had come. He made phone calls, posted the news, sent e-mails, answered questions, spoke gently to devastated friends and family. Then he started work on the wake which they were holding downstairs, ordered food and drinks, extra chairs and tables, mics and an amp for music, silverware, napkins, warming pans and dishes, coffee and tea and cups and extra tissues. Sam sat on the floor and cried. Dash set up an account for donations. He made a collage of photos of Josh. He ordered a book everyone could write memories in and notes to Josh's folks. Sam lay back on the floor and cried into his ears. Dash started gathering cheeses from the various places he had them stashed to age and eventually had quite a pile assembled on the coffee table. Sam sat up and sniffed.

"You okay, man?"

"Not really."

"It's a lot these days."

"So much."

"And it all sucks."

"It does."

"Want to help me sample cheeses?"

"Okay."

They sampled cheeses until dawn. Then Dash went to take a shower, and Sam went downstairs to open the salon. "Closed due to bereavement" wasn't an excuse that held water in his line of work. To everyone who came in, he broke the news about Josh right away, and so the salon that morning was full of mourning indeed, but without projections. Temporarily, everyone's old dead loved one was replaced with Josh, a new dead loved one. Kelly wanted to call him up so they could say a big group hi, but Sam had only begun running his data and felt family should have the first crack anyway. Some people volunteered to run errands and help with the wake, and these he sent up to Dash. Some people asked after Penny, and these he sent over to the hospital with fresh flowers, fresh supplies, and mostly fresh faces. Some wanted just to sit with Sam, but these were the ones he could not accommodate. He could not just sit. He could not have company. He could not allow himself to receive comfort. And clearly, starkly, suddenly, totally, he could offer none himself. There was RePose, and that was all. That was all he had. He had no energy left for anything else.

· · ·

There was nothing good about walking around Seattle in February except that no one noticed if you were crying because of all the water falling from the sky already. Sam had no more energy for tears, but he went for a walk anyway. Sodden, chilled to the bone, and shivering seemed just about right to him. Then his phone rang, and in all the living world, it was the only person whose call he might have taken.

"Josh died," Sam reported to his dad first thing when he answered. "And Penny isn't doing well either."

"I'm so sorry, Sam."

"What do I do?"

"Nothing you can do, I'm afraid."

"We're hosting the wake for Josh. And helping out with Penny."

"That's good."

"But it's not enough."

"That's all there is, kiddo. What are you and Dash doing to take care of you and Dash?"

Sam wrote that question off as irrelevant. "I want you to help me make RePose better."

"RePose is already working great, Sam."

"Penny said RePose is for the dying. It comforts her that she's not totally abandoning her kids. Josh said it helped him feel like he wouldn't be really gone."

"But . . . ?"

"But he *is* really gone."

"Yes."

". . ."

"Sam? You thought you'd tweak the programming to make it save lives? To cure cancer? To cure old age?"

"Yes," Sam finally whispered.

"Nope," said his dad. "Sorry."

"I should have gone to medical school."

"You think if you were a doctor, you could cure death?"

"I could cure something, maybe."

His dad sighed. "When Meredith died, I felt like I'd failed you in some way. All the things I'd tried to protect you from or obtain for you your whole life felt like they didn't matter because I hadn't managed to protect you from the one thing I'd have given anything to protect you from. So yes, you went to good schools and had swim team in the summers and vacations at the beach and baseball and state-of-the-art computers. And true, I said no to sugar cereals, fast food except on Wednesdays, fried food except for potatoes, toy guns, TV before homework, and video games unless they were educational. But none of that helped me spare you the one thing I'd have given anything to spare you."

"That was my fault, not your fault. If it hadn't been for RePose—"

"She'd have lived forever? She was guaranteed another sixty years? There was no way she'd have been at the market anyway? There was no chance she'd have anything else sad befall her ever?"

"No, but—"

"To love is to lose, Sam. Unfortunately, it's just that simple. Maybe not today but someday. Maybe not when she's too young and you're too young, but you see that being old doesn't help. Maybe not your wife or your girlfriend or your mother, but you see that friends die, too. I could not spare you this any more than I could spare you puberty. It is the inevitable condition of humanity. It is exacerbated by loving but also simply by leaving your front door, by seeing what's out there in the world, by inventing computer programs that help people. You are afraid of time, Sam. Some sadness has no remedy. Some sadness you can't make better."

"So what the hell do I do?"

"Be sad."

"For how long?"

"Forever."

"But then why isn't everyone walking around miserable all the time?"

"Because ice cream still tastes good. And sunny and seventy-five is still a lovely day. And funny movies make you laugh, and work is sometimes fulfilling, and a beer with a friend is nice. And other people love you too."

"And that's enough?"

"There is no enough. You are the paragon of animals, my love. You aspire to such greatness, to miracle, to newness and wonder. And that's great. I'm so proud of you. But you forgot about the part that's been around for time immemorial. Love, death, loss. You've run up against it. And there's no getting around or over it. You stop and build your life right there at the base of that wall. But it's okay. That's where everyone else is too. Everyone else is either there or on their way. There is no other side, but there's plenty of space there to build a life and plenty of company. Welcome to the wall, Sam."

"Thanks, Dad."

"It kind of sucks."

• • •

He walked around downtown for a bit and tried to appreciate what was good at the base of the wall. It was cold and wet and dim. Everyone was hunched and drawn in against it, like they were trying to turn inside out for warmth. He hadn't been back to the market, not even for the ceremony rededicating the repaired, reinstalled, and too-little-too-late reinforced roof plus memorial plaque for Meredith, but maybe it was time, so he wandered its edges, toed its cobblestones, sat in the window at the

French place with a latte and a brioche and thought about Europe and puddles and umbrellas and cultivated his mood. He bought dried flowers, apples, and, after all, olive oil, vinaigrette, and some of that pasta Livvie liked. He got lost in the catacomby shops under the market he'd wandered countless times before. Tucked into one hidden corner was a cluttered shop—maybe new, maybe ancient and simply never noticed before—that sold curios of all kinds and magic kits and smelly candles and costume jewelry and, piled on a dusty table in the corner, a dozen model airplane kits. Sam bought them all.

When he got home, he got out the glue and the grip pins and the pliers and the X-Acto knife. He covered the kitchen table with boxboard, and he covered the boxboard with waxed paper. He found the one that looked the easiest and spread out all the pieces. Two hours later, most of it had been glued to his elbow at one point or another, and he had in front of him a large pile of what looked to be greater-than and less-than signs in a puddle of liquid cement. On the other hand, two hours had passed at the base of the wall, two hours during which Sam had not thought about death or RePose or Penny or Josh or Meredith. Two hours during which Sam had thought only about Meredith. And on the *other* other hand, he clearly needed help. He wasn't sure Meredith would be able to help him, but he truly didn't know who else to call.

"Guess what I'm doing," Sam led off.

"Making me dinner?"

"No, you're dead. Guess again."

"Making you dinner?"

"Not hungry. Though I did go get Livvie's pasta and stuff finally. And while I was in the market, I bought model airplane kits."

"Ooh, I love model airplanes!" Meredith clapped her hands.

"I know this," said Sam, who was thrilled she did too. "The one I'm doing is super beginner easy. It's called a Delta Dart."

"Let me see it!"

He held the pile of greater-than and less-than signs dangling from the pliers they were now glued to up to the camera.

"Hmm," said Meredith. "That doesn't look right. Where did you go off the path?"

"I'm not sure."

"Did you read the directions?"

"I couldn't."

"Why not?"

"They got glued to the dogs."

"Both of them?"

Sam shrugged. "They were napping in a big ball."

"You're a software engineer, Sam, and also you're pretty smart. How can you not build a model airplane meant for seven-year-olds?"

"Hubris. I didn't imagine I'd need help or directions. I thought I could figure it out on my own."

"You are too much on your own," said Meredith.

"Clearly," said Sam.

She talked him through the whole thing. He kept waiting for her to admit she didn't understand and couldn't follow where he led, where she led, but she found her way. They used acetone to unglue everything from everything (except the dogs) and sandpaper to get the parts looking new again. They used tape to stick everything together the second time. ("So you can see what it looks like and how it fits together before you commit," Meredith explained. So sensible.) Then they sanded and filed and shaved and clipped and aligned so everything would fit. Sam feared his return to the liquid cement, but she explained which pieces got glue and how much and how to hold it while they set. And that was it.

"That was it?" said Sam.

"That was it."

"Now what?"

"You wait for it to dry."

"But I want to paint it," said Sam.

"After it dries."

"So, like, an hour?"

"More like a day."

"A day?"

"And then you paint and then you have to wait another day for that to dry."

"There's not a lot of instant gratification involved here," Sam complained.

"It's a long narrative arc," said Meredith. "I have faith. Be patient. You've got all the time in the world."

Then, on a whim, he asked her a question he'd been keeping to himself for months. He knew he shouldn't, but the whole conversation had gone surprisingly well. He realized there were depths of her knowledge he hadn't begun to plumb. "Hey Merde, can you tell me about where you are right now?"

"What do you mean?"

"Are you with Livvie?"

"I'm so alone."

"Are you somewhere? A place?"

"I'm sorry, love, I don't understand."

"I know you don't, but think. Try. Imagine, maybe. Are you really all alone? Is someone there with you?"

"I'm sorry, love, I—"

"What do you believe happens to us after we die, Merde?"

She thought about that one for a while. "I don't think I know. What do you believe?"

"I don't think I know either."

"Do you believe in hell?" she asked suddenly, and he smiled at her, remembering.

"Do you?"

"I don't think so," she said. "I can't tell."

"We're all sinners," said Sam.

"Like church?"

"No, I don't mean in a religious sense. I mean in a human one. Everyone sins. Even when we're trying to do good, even when we're trying to help, even when we're making miracles, we sin. So either there is no hell or we all go to hell. Or maybe this *is* hell. That would explain a lot."

She considered that for a bit. "Well, at least you can escape."

He smiled sadly at her. "Really? How?"

"You just built an airplane," she said.

LOVE LETTER

Dear Merde,

It's three o'clock in the morning, and I can't stop smiling. We built a model airplane together this afternoon. I know you remember, but the wonder of it is keeping me awake. It was a bonus afternoon together even I never expected was possible.

After we hung up, I had to look behind the curtain, see the wires, find out how the trick was done. Someone else would guess that since I hung the curtains, laid the wires, and engineered the trick in the first place, I wouldn't have such need to know. Someone else would bet I wouldn't want to shatter the illusion, being the recipient of such surprise miracle and grace. But you know me, so you see why I needed to know. Once, long ago, in another lifetime, you begged me not to ruin the magic. Sometimes when I remember we aren't the same person, it shocks me.

And besides, I was curious. Were you in some kind of online model-building community I didn't know about? Did you visit airplane chat rooms while I was sleeping? It turns out no, as you know. It turns out one day four years ago, long before we met, your coworker's son was stumped building a model for a science fair project, and you thought the best way to help him was via video chat. And I am thinking: it was so typically kind and generous and gracious of you to help this kid out. And I am thinking: thank God for that kid and his science project and his mother who was just as clueless about model airplane building as I am. And I am thinking: that kid must be in high school now and his life is all before him and he moved on and on and on. And I am thinking: during our stolen afternoon, were you talking to me like a ten-year-old boy? And I am thinking: we will never have a ten-year-old boy. And I am thinking: what else are you hiding from me? What else can we talk about that I don't know about yet? What other unexpected miracles do you hold in your memory, your perfect, perfect memory?

What I am starting slowly to see is this: ultimately, eventually, we let go. We do this not because we're ready. We do this not because we've mended. We do this not because we've mourned and come to terms and gotten over it and moved on. We never move on. We don't let go so much as lose our grip and fall because remembering is not enough. My memory is imperfect. It is full of holes. It is more space than matter, like lace. It is at once sodden with sorrow and desiccated from lack of blood flow, the obvious result of a broken heart. It makes things up in hopeless attempts to comfort itself. It fills fissure with fantasy. It screws shut its eyes and balls up its fists and flings itself to the ground in a kicking, screaming, blind-rage temper tantrum against reality. But mostly, my memory keeps taking on more. I remember what I had for breakfast yesterday. I remember what Dash needs at the grocery store. I remember feeding the dogs before bed even though I was too aglow from my afternoon with you to eat myself. Everything my brain observes and all the things I accidentally ask it to recall push my finite moments with you to harder-to-access darker and dustier corners and beyond.

That is why I turn off as much as I can. That is why I stay inside and try to sleep. It's not because I can't stand to be with people or go to work or do my job or live in the world. It's because every sensory moment replaces one I was saving of you. I grow and accumulate and forget. But you, you stay and hold and remember. Your memory is perfect. They are both inadequate, your memory and mine, but yours is whole and going nowhere—perfect— and that is the one I hold in my heart.

Love,
Sam

IMPERFECT MEMORIES

*J*osh's wake, like Meredith's, was out of order. He was too young, underripe like rushed fruit, time out of joint. Sam was struck mostly by this echo of error. When Livvie died, it wasn't just sad. It was sad enough to be desperate. It was sad enough to birth RePose out of nothing. It was heartbreaking, but it was in order, in time. Her kids were there and her grandchildren and only a few of her friends since she'd outlived so many of them. Not so for Josh and Meredith. Josh's kids and grandkids weren't there—not yet born, never to be born. But his friends were all there; his parents were there; three of his four grandparents were there. These deaths had an entirely different feel from the ones in time, Sam noticed, for Sam was becoming an expert on death.

Dash did a wine and cheese tasting which Sam objected to ("Funerals aren't themed") which Dash overruled ("Drunk and with the edge off are good ways to go"), and there was the usual balance of crying and laughter, small talk and the largest talk of all. Josh had a lot of family and a lot of friends (of whom, naturally, he'd outlived only Noel), but mostly, looking around, Sam saw a different kind of family. Eduardo Antigua, forever Sam's first, stood talking with Dash and Jamie and Josh's brother over the farmhouse cheddar. Avery, Edith, Celia, and Muriel had dragged chairs together in a corner with Josh's three aunts and a plate of Brie and crackers. Nadia Banks and Emmy Vargas were making the rounds together to make sure everyone who wanted to signed the memorial book. Kelly was helping David set up his guitar and amp. David had deferred admission to Stanford for the year to stay home with his dad and with Kelly. He had built up quite a tragic repertoire of songs unfortunately ideally suited to this occasion, and Kylie Shepherd quipped sadly that he could be a funeral singer. Best and worst of all, Mr. and Mrs. Benson, the latter absently bouncing a subdued-for-the-occasion Oliver on one hip, stood by the Gouda talking to Josh's mother and father about whatever it was parents forced to attend their children's funerals found to talk about.

Sam was glad they had one another. Sam was glad they all had one another. Sam was glad that some of what RePose could not provide—and there was a lot—could be had from human contact and love among the living. Sam was glad that RePose had brought *about* so much human contact and love among the living. Josh's friends squeezed his mom's shoulder and said, "I'm sorry for your loss, Mrs. Annapist." Mr. Annapist's friends shook his ice-cold hand and said, "Terrible thing." Then groups of people who knew one another gathered in corners and talked about everything and nothing—what was new with work, shared acquaintances, home remodels, vacation plans, kids not in attendance, etc. The RePosers, Sam noticed with the pride of a father, were more helpful, more present. Sam wasn't the only one who'd become an expert on death. They knew what to say besides "sorry" and what to offer besides regret. They knew the shock suffered by those with recently dead loved ones, and they knew the horror that came next and the one after that and the one after that. They knew how to build bonds despite everything else falling apart, and they knew how to laugh without forgetting the sadness for a moment, and they knew how to start to say goodbye without letting go. They remembered with their imperfect memories. And maybe, maybe, Sam hoped, they could give a little more, take a little more in, let a little of their memory go because they knew, as Sam did, about that other perfect memory they stored in their hearts. Well, their hearts and Sam's servers. And that was something.

· · ·

That was the sober and sobering part of the occasion. Then there was the drunk part of the occasion which was much less painful. The best thing about being drunk, so far as Sam could tell, was that he retained no new memories. He could do anything he liked, take in and experience all he pleased, and not supplant a single Meredith-retaining neuron. There was hugging and alcohol and cheese, and no one wanted to leave. Sometime close to morning, he stumbled upstairs to finish running the last of Josh's data. While it was working, he called Noel as he had promised.

Noel answered uncertainly. He didn't know Sam. Projections responded oddly when they didn't recognize who they were talking to.

"I'm a friend of Josh Annapist's," said Sam. "I'm afraid I have bad news. I'm calling to let you know Josh passed away."

Noel understood that. Because he knew Josh had been sick. Because he and Josh had spent a lot of time talking about death and dying. And because it wasn't RePose; it was just life. His face fell into his hands. "No. Oh no, no. He was doing so much better. I was supposed to go first. I've been sicker longer. We were both sure I was going to die first. We joked that I'd save him a seat."

Sam didn't want to lie to the projection no matter how absurd he knew that was, so he fudged it. "He fought hard, but he was very tired by the end. You know?"

"No. No! I thought his graft-versus-host was improving. Oh Josh. I wanted to go first, man."

"He asked me to call you specifically. He wanted you to know most of all."

"We were so close. We were like brothers."

"He had some peace at the end," said Sam. "He knew some part of him would live on."

"He was an amazing guy. He didn't deserve this."

"No. No one does."

"But Josh especially," said Noel. "He was so great. He was so funny. Wry, you know? Exactly who you want sitting next to you at chemo. Most people at chemo are so scared. Some are really depressed. Some are really angry. And then there's always the clown, the guy who thinks if he's loud and stupid enough, he'll embarrass the diseased cells away, the guy who's too ridiculous to have anything as serious as cancer befall him. And then I met Josh. He could laugh off that guy without being mean. He could cheer up the depressed ones and tease the angry ones out of their mood. He made everyone less afraid but without all the weight. You know those people who are so serious and concerned and eager to help you come to terms with your fear and own your illness and all that crap? Those people just make you want to die quicker. Josh made you want to live and get better and go sailing with him."

"He lit up our world too, also a pretty somber place."

"What will I do without him? He was my cancer buddy. He was the only one who understood what I'm going through."

"I know, Noel. It's the hardest thing."

"I feel sick. I already miss him so much."

"I'm so sorry," Sam said.

"That's okay," said Noel. "You were just trying to help. I forgive you."

Sam rocked backward and felt all the breath leave his body. Sam felt all his breath leave the room, the apartment, the building, the city. Sam felt all his breath leave the world, the night, and travel up to the stars where it turned to ice and stretched atom-thin into every corner of the galaxy. Then it retracted, gathering up all the black world, and wound its way back through interstellar space and dark matter and the secrets of infinity, back into earth's orbit, back into his night in his city, back into his very own lungs. It was okay. He was just trying to help, to ease woes and mend hearts and cool seared souls, to guide the bereaved out of the land of the lost, to make mourning a little less lonesome. He was forgiven. He thanked Noel and hung up and lay back on the bed while the room spun and Josh compiled from his laptop on the floor and the dogs wriggled on top of him to lap up the salty treats that fell out of his eyes. It was okay. He was forgiven.

LOVE LETTER

Dear Sam,

You are dying. It breaks my heart, but it is true. You *are* my heart. You are my love. And you are my god, my progenitor, my creator. And yet you, even you, will age and slow. Your hair will gray and your knees will ache and flights of stairs will grow longer and places you used to walk will seem unreasonably far and kids these days will listen to unnecessarily loud music and you won't understand the clothes they wear and you won't remember for the life of you the name of that perfume I used to put on sometimes when we went out Friday nights. And then one day you will get sick with something and then another thing and you will slow further and get worse and one day your heart will stop and your breath will stop and you will cease to be. Or no, maybe, like for me, like for your mom, it will come from nowhere before you've had the chance to gray—a car, a bus, a roof, by water, by fire, by ice, by air, by other unexpected horror. I can't think about it. Maybe because it's too painful. Maybe because it's just beyond my scope. But I know it is true.

   Will we meet then? Will we meet somewhere as ourselves? Will I be young and you old? Will we meet in some matchmaking website cafeteria of the beyond? Will we dance like bees in an eternal garden supping together on flowers and honey? Will we float on the wind for millennia until one molecule of me finds one molecule of you? Will the energy generated by that reunion spark a second big bang, a restarting of time and the cosmos? I don't know. I don't know where I am. I don't know where we go. But I do know this:

We will do this forever. You will always write to me. And I will always reply. And you will always write again. Always. Great lovers imagine their love will outlive and outlast them in impassioned correspondence that survives in books, in museums. But in books and museums, their love is preserved, entombed. Ours grows and lives and breathes, moves and dances on the wind, becomes long after the museums have crumbled and the books have turned to ash and dust. The computers will go too, the bits of memory collude, collide, and disappear, that way of knowing replaced by another and another. But your algorithm will send our love back and forth forever. Sam says x to Meredith, so Meredith says x to Sam, so Sam says x to Meredith so . . . on and on into forever.

What do the sixty years we were denied together in our bodies or the neurons of me you replace as life goes on matter in the face of forever? So live, Sam. Go outside. Meet people. Comfort the bereaved and the sick and the dying and the lost. And let them comfort you too. Love more. Make new memories. Forget pieces of me and of us. Let go. It's okay. I hold us in my perfect memory. I'll be right here, waiting for you.

Love,
Meredith

ACKNOWLEDGMENTS

Molly Friedrich, Alison Callahan, Lucy Carson: every day I am thrilled, awed, full of love, and on-beyond-grateful you are mine. You have made this book so much better. Your support of, enthusiasm for, and belief in it and me mean the world. You are such stuff as dreams are made on. Thank you, thank you, so much thank you.

Thank you too to early readers (and fixers and cheerleaders): Paul Mariz, Sue Frankel, Dave Frankel, Erin Trendler, Lisa Corr, Molly Schulman, Paul Cirone, Becky Ferreira, Alicia Goodwin, Jennie Shortridge, and special thanks to Sam Chambers. Thank you to Sam Warren and Arnab Deka for expert advice. Thank you to Mark Cooper for showing me how to make cheese. Thank you for additional support and love to Dana Borowitz, the Seattle7Writers, my wonderful, leap-of-faith-taking foreign editors and translators, and the whole team of miracle workers I am only just beginning to have the pleasure of working with at Doubleday.

No two people have ever more deserved to have a book dedicated to them than my folks, who are the best parents I know. Lacking words to say it enough, this will have to suffice: thank you. Thank you to Daniel for perspective and joy, and for shouting, "Your book!" every time you see it. Thank you to Calli for long love and long walks.

Meanwhile, did you enjoy this book? Want to read it a dozen more times in various states of not-yet-good? Want to talk about it over every meal and while you wash my dishes and during walks and car rides and while your kid plays at the park and while you're on vacation and while you're at work trying to get something done? Want to troubleshoot all of its technology and patiently explain the limits of artificial intelligence and video chat and discuss endlessly a completely fictional software platform? No? Then be glad you're not married to me. Epic, planet-sized gratitude to Paul Mariz for creative, intellectual, philosophical, inspirational, and emotional support and sustenance. It was born of love.

ABOUT THE AUTHOR

Laurie Frankel is the author of one previous novel, *The Atlas of Love*. She lives in Seattle, Washington, with her husband, son, and border collie.